LEGENDS OF ANGRIA

ALEXANDER PERCY
EARL OF NORTHANGERLAND

LEGENDS OF
ANGRIA

—

COMPILED FROM
THE EARLY WRITINGS OF
CHARLOTTE BRONTË
BY FANNIE E. RATCHFORD
WITH THE COLLABORATION OF
WILLIAM CLYDE DeVANE

NEW HAVEN
YALE UNIVERSITY PRESS
LONDON · HUMPHREY MILFORD · OXFORD UNIVERSITY PRESS
1933

To

MR. C. W. HATFIELD
GREATEST OF BRONTE SCHOLARS
IN APPRECIATION OF HIS KINDNESS

Editorial Note

In a volume of this sort, the product of a collaboration, it is proper to state the share of labor borne by each of the collaborators. All the collecting of materials relating to the Brontës—and the manuscripts are so widely scattered through Europe and America as to make a study of them very difficult indeed—has occupied Miss Fannie E. Ratchford for several years. The study of these manuscripts—many of them in minute handwriting—and the critical approach to the Brontës as it may be seen in the Introduction and elsewhere in the book, is Miss Ratchford's work. The present form of the book is the contribution of Professor William Clyde DeVane, who suggested the chronological sequence of the stories to illustrate the growth of the Angrian legend, who aided in the selection of the material and the preparation of the link pieces, and who generally settled and supervised the plan of the book as a whole.

Preface

THOUGH the existence of voluminous Brontë *juvenilia* has long been known to collectors and bibliographers, it has received but scant attention from biographers and critics. Mrs. Gaskell had almost finished her *Life of Charlotte Brontë* when a mass of the very early manuscripts came to her attention, necessitating the rewriting of about forty pages included in Chapter V. Her examination of the material was superficial, and she missed its significance. Forty years later the same group of manuscripts, augmented by the stories of the Angrian cycle from the hands of Charlotte and Branwell, came into the possession of Clement Shorter. But Mr. Shorter no more than Mrs. Gaskell realized the value of the material before him, and passed it by with the brief statement that it was worthless. He did, however, give us in Appendix V of his great work, *The Brontës, Life and Letters* (1918), a useful though incomplete list of the early Brontë manuscripts.

In 1925 Mr. C. W. Hatfield initiated the proper appreciation of Charlotte Brontë's early work by publishing with Mr. Shorter a volume of excerpts from the *juvenilia,* which was called, after one of Charlotte's titles, *The Twelve Adventurers*. This was a great step forward, though it may be said that the excerpts are too brief to give the reader a coherent picture of Charlotte's creations. In 1931 a different experiment was made, when Mr. George Edwin MacLean published, with an Introduction, a single novel, *The Spell,* from Charlotte Brontë's early work. The weakness of this book lies in the assumption that the single novel, plucked from the Angrian cycle, would be self-sustaining.

The present volume is the first to present a panoramic view of Charlotte Brontë's early work, and in that larger view, with its implications, lies its excuse for being. Four novels have been selected, all concerned with the imaginary kingdom of Angria, and all supplementing each other. These stories have been chosen with the double purpose of illustrating the growth of Charlotte Brontë's powers as a writer and of tracing the development of the Angrian legend. It is not too much to say that if the novels are read as a series they become the most informing and illuminating of Brontë documents, far more significant of the character and genius of this remarkable family than the letters upon which previous studies have been based.

Although this book offers fresh material and suggests a new thesis, it has of necessity been built in many particulars upon the work of those before me who have devoted themselves to the study of the Brontës. Besides the work of Mrs. Gaskell, Mr. Shorter, Mr. Hatfield, and Mr. MacLean, I have drawn freely upon such Brontë studies as Mr. T. J. Wise's *Bibliography of the Writings of the Brontë Family,* Miss May Sinclair's *The Three Brontës,* and the latest Brontë biography, Mr. E. F. Benson's *Charlotte Brontë.* To all these I make grateful acknowledgment of indebtedness. I should especially like to express here my gratitude to Mr. MacLean, who kindly supplied me with his own transcripts of the Brontë manuscripts in the British Museum. Here, too, my thanks are due to the editors of *The Yale Review* for permission to incorporate in my Introduction material which I first published in an article for its pages.

In particular I wish to express my warm thanks to those who have helped me in a more personal way: first, to those who have contributed to the contents of the volume—to Mrs. Miriam Lutcher Stark for the use of her manuscript of "The Green Dwarf," to Mrs. H. H. Bonnell for the use of the manuscripts of "Zamorna's Exile" and the "Farewell to Angria," to Mr. C. W. Hatfield for the transcript of "Mina Laury," to the Harry Elkins Widener Collection at Harvard University for permission to publish "Caroline Vernon," and to Mrs. Flora Livingston for her transcript of it, to Mr. T. J. Wise for the use of Branwell Brontë's map of the Glass Town Country, and to Mrs. H. H. Bonnell and the Brontë Society for the use of the portraits by Branwell Brontë and for Charlotte Brontë's water-color of the death scene of Mary Percy; and, second, to those who have given generous help in the preparation of the material—Miss Sarah Clapp, Miss Lois Trice, and Mrs. Daisy Barrett Tanner in the tedious task of transcribing the manuscripts, and to my nieces, Shirley Ratchford and Myrtle Ratchford Agee, for their untiring patience in reading proof and checking, and to Dr. R. H. Griffith for his help and advice at every stage of the work.

From the Brontë Society Council I have received the most cordial coöperation at all times. They have made the rich resources of the Brontë Museum and Library freely available to me, and they have generously supplied such photostats as I desired from their collection. My gratitude is due the Council as a whole, and, in a very personal sense, to their officers who have so courteously represented them—Dr. J. Hambley Rowe, Chairman; Dr. C. Mable Edgerley, Secretary; and Mr. Rosse Butterfield, Curator of the Brontë Museum and Library.

I take particular pleasure in expressing my deepest gratitude to the John Simon Guggenheim Memorial Foundation for the opportunity to carry out this investigation, and to Mr. Henry Allen Moe, its kind and understanding Secretary.

FANNIE E. RATCHFORD

The University of Texas,
December 10, 1932.

Illustrations

The History of Angria

ON July 29, 1835, Charlotte Brontë exchanged the freedom of Haworth parsonage and moors for the drudgery of a teacher's life in Miss Wooler's school, Roe Head, Mirfield, which she had left as an honor student three years before. She was then nineteen. With her, as a pupil, went her sister Emily, two years younger. Emily's stay was of short duration. She fell ill of homesickness and was allowed, through Charlotte's intervention, to return home, thus establishing a tradition for devotion to her native environs that has overshadowed all her other characteristics. More enduring Charlotte remained with Miss Wooler for almost three years and gave her biographers, from Mrs. Gaskell to the latest psychoanalyst, excuse for innumerable chapters on her "ill health," "despondency," and "nervous terrors" of these months. No one seems to have suspected that she, too, might have been homesick, or that behind the nostalgia of the girls lay something far more deeply interfused with their spirits than home and moors.

Charlotte's account of Emily's homesickness is almost as familiar as the Brontë name, but the story of her own sufferings has been known to fewer, perhaps, than half a dozen persons. It has remained hidden for almost a century under the microscopic script of her youthful "books" and manuscripts, now scattered among the libraries of England and America, valued as literary curiosities but deemed worthless in content. These juvenile writings from the formative period between Charlotte's fourteenth and twenty-fourth years —more than fifty in number and aggregating more pages than her printed works—tell, when read in chronological order, an astonishing story.

This story has its beginning on the night of June 5, 1826,

when the Reverend Patrick Brontë returned from Leeds with a box of wooden soldiers for Branwell and a set of ninepins and perhaps other toys for the girls. The children were asleep for the night, and the soldiers were placed where Branwell's eyes lighted upon them when he awoke in the morning. Catching them up, he ran to his sisters' room, calling them to come to see his treasures. Out of bed they sprang, Charlotte in the lead. Snatching up the best looking of the lot, she claimed it for her own, calling it the Duke of Wellington. Emily likewise took up one and said it should be hers; and Anne, following their example, made her choice. Emily's soldier was a grave-looking fellow, whom the children dubbed Gravey, and Anne's "was a queer little thing, much like herself"; it received the name Waiting-Boy. Branwell, like a polite little gentleman, made his choice last, calling his soldier Buonaparte. He was careful that his sisters should understand that he was merely lending the toys to them, though he later gave each her particular soldier for her own.

The wooden soldiers became the heroes of countless games. Their names varied amusingly with the adventure in hand. Sometimes they were drawn from the children's reading of politics and history—Arthur Wellesley, Ferdinand Cortez, Francis Stewart, and Frederick Brunswick; sometimes they indicated the moral characteristics of their bearers—Goody, Bady, Naughty, Bravey, Sneaky, and Rogue; and sometimes they suggested the ligneous nature of their toys—Captain Tree, Sergeant Bud, General Leaf, Major Arbor, and Corporal Branch. Collectively the toys were "The Young Men," or "The Twelves," to distinguish them from fragments of sets that remained from former days.

The children, taking a suggestion from the *Arabian Nights,* constituted themselves the guardian genii of "The Young Men." Chief Genius Talli, Chief Genius Branni,

Chief Genius Emmi, and Chief Genius Anni they called themselves. As one of their adventures the twelve heroes were sent on a voyage in the ship *Invincible* and were wrecked upon the Guinea coast. Their guardian genii, having saved them from the hostile blacks who inhabited the land, erected for them at the mouth of the Niger River a magic city, known at first as Glass Town, later as Verdopolis, fortunate for commerce, beautiful in its situation, and magnificent in its public buildings such as the Hall of Justice, Tower of All Nations, the Genii's Inn, the Great Bridge.

In the course of time reports of the magnificence of the city and the valor of its "mighty Twelves" reached Europe, then "under the iron heel of the tyrant Napoleon"; an embassy was straightway dispatched, headed by General Leaf, to implore one of the "Young Men" to undertake the deliverance of Europe. The lot, cast according to the directions of the genii, fell upon Arthur Wellesley, then a "common trumpeter," and right well he justified the wisdom of the great beings who directed the choice. After "defeating the tyrant and freeing Europe," this hero, now the Duke of Wellington, returned to Glass Town, bringing with him fifteen thousand of his veterans. The increase of population in the city necessitated the election of a king, and again the choice fell upon Charlotte's hero, "the most noble Field Marshal Arthur Duke of Wellington," as a "fit and proper person to sit on the throne of these realms."

Thus far, with many amusing details, the play had progressed when it was interrupted by Charlotte's departure for school at Roe Head, in January, 1831. It was not forgotten in her absence of eighteen months, and on her return it was revived with renewed interest by herself and her brother, though the toys that were its original inspiration, to quote Branwell, "had departed and left not a wreck behind." There is no indication that the younger girls took any further part in the game, and it is probable that they had already launched their separate play, "The Gondals," which absorbed them in later years.

The survival of the Glass Town game through Charlotte's absence is attributable to the fact that it had, two years before her departure, attained the dignity of a written literature. As books and periodicals occupied a place of dominant importance in the Brontë household, it is but natural that the children should have projected them into their play. As early as January, 1829, the two older children in the persons of the wooden soldiers were recording the adventures of these heroes in tiny books and magazines proportionate in size to their supposed authors, Charlotte writing as Captain Tree and the two sons of the Duke of Wellington, the Marquis of Douro and Lord Charles Wellesley; Branwell, as Young Soult and Sergeant or Captain Bud. The average size of these miniature volumes was about 1½ by 1¼ inches. They were executed in minute hand printing, with elaborate title-pages, and their leaves were carefully sewed into covers of wrapping paper. Their subject matter—histories, stories, poems, dramas, and book reviews—was for the most part drawn from the world of imagination. On August 3, 1830, six months before she went away to school, Charlotte had made a catalogue of her books, listing twenty-two volumes, all published by Captain Tree, Biblio Street, Verdopolis, and sold by all booksellers in town and country. Branwell, by this same date, had written at least three rather long volumes and a number of shorter ones, and had initiated a magazine which he edited alone for several months.

On Charlotte's return this writing and publishing was revived with renewed enthusiasm, and in the course of her three uninterrupted years at home became the dominating passion of her life.

Regarding their absorbing pastime the little Brontës

were consistently silent to the outside world, even to their father and aunt. Only one time, so far as the records tell, was their secret in danger. Then, fortunately, the significance of Charlotte's impulsive confidence was not understood by her auditors, or by her biographer Mrs. Gaskell, to whom it was repeated many years later. In answer to Mrs. Gaskell's request for information concerning Charlotte Brontë's school days, Mary Taylor, who shared with Ellen Nussey the honor of being her closest friend, wrote:

She had a habit of writing in italics (printing characters), and said she had learnt it by writing in their magazine. They brought out a "magazine" once a month, and wished it to look as like print as possible. She told us a tale out of it. No one wrote in it, and no one read it, but herself, her brother, and two sisters. She promised to show me some of these magazines, but retracted it afterwards, and would never be persuaded to do so.

Not once in all her apparently confidential letters to Ellen Nussey following her return from school did Charlotte give the slightest hint of the play which colored all her thoughts. Rather she tacitly denied it at the time that it most absorbed her:

An account of one day is an account of all. In the morning, from 9 o'clock to half past 12, I instruct my sisters, and draw; then we walk out till dinner-time. After dinner I sew till tea-time, and after tea I either write, read, do a little fancy work, or draw, as I please. Thus in one delightful, though somewhat monotonous course, my life is passed.

Years later, Charlotte told Mrs. Gaskell that at the period in question, drawing and walking out with her sisters formed the two great pleasures and relaxations of the day. Not one word to anybody of "that divine, silent, unseen land of thought," whose landscape she knew "in every variety of shade and light" as she knew her own moors!

Never a mention of its people, whom to herself she called "my friends and my intimate acquaintances . . . who people my thoughts by day and not seldom steal strangely into my dreams at night"! Not one hint of "that bright, darling dream," whose magic transported her to strange lands to walk as an equal with other "transcendently high and inaccessibly sacred beings whose fates are interwoven with the highest of the high"!

Notwithstanding her implied denial, Charlotte, during the three years between her school days and teaching days at Roe Head, was living a life of golden romance, walking with kings, guiding the destinies of a mighty empire, and receiving the plaudits due genius from an admiring world. As a visible evidence of this unseen life, she produced with astonishing facility and rapidity innumerable novels and poems of the so-called "Angrian" society and politics. Her earlier hero, the Duke of Wellington, had receded into the background, and in the center of the stage was now his elder son, Arthur Augustus Adrian Wellesley, Marquis of Douro, an unrestrained Byronic hero, possessing in a highly exaggerated degree the characteristics of Rochester of *Jane Eyre*. She herself, in the person of his younger brother, Lord Charles Albert Florian Wellesley, was the omnipresent, all-observing recorder of his doings and misdoings. Branwell, under the pseudonym, first, of Captain John Flower, later, of Lord John Flower, Viscount Richton, introduced revolutionary changes with a suddenness and rapidity that would have bewildered a collaborator less adaptable than Charlotte.

Early in the game she had married her arch-hero to Florence Marian Hume, a gentle green-and-white maiden of snowdrop purity and sweetness. Their union had been violently opposed by the mad jealousy of Lady Zenobia Ellrington, the most brilliant and learned lady of all Verdopolis, whose strong mind had been temporarily upset by her hopeless but enduring passion for the Marquis. While Charlotte was picturing Marian as an adored and adoring wife and happy mother, Branwell was preparing her death-blow. He brought forward from wooden-soldier days a Luciferian pirate called Rogue, who appears as one of the principal characters in the stories of this volume. This dubious hero, with the more aristocratic name Alexander Percy now added, he married, after an astonishing courtship, to Lady Zenobia. He then introduced Mary Henrietta, Percy's daughter by an earlier marriage, to court, where she instantly won the interest and admiration of the Marquis of Douro. Charlotte, delightfully adaptable as always, accepted this new situation and obligingly allowed Marian to die the romantic death of a broken-hearted and devoted wife so that the Marquis might marry the more regal Mary Percy.

The Marquis and Percy now entered into a political coalition for their mutual aggrandizement. Douro, having saved his country from an invasion of allied French and Negroes, demanded of the Verdopolitan parliament, through his father-in-law, the cession of a large and fertile but unpopulated province to the east, called Angria, which he received, after a bitter fight, in full sovereignty, though it was to remain, like Wellingtonsland and the other original kingdoms, "part and parcel of the Glasstown Confederacy." This new kingdom he populated with his own devoted followers from Verdopolis, who comprised the greater part of "the young and rising generation of the city." Despite the opposition of the other kings of the Union, with the exception of Wellington and Sneaky, and the Ministry of Verdopolis headed by the Marquis of Ardrah, Secretary of the Navy, and the bloody threats of the native blacks led by the notorious African, Prince Quashia, the organization of the new government was pushed rapidly forward. The country was divided into provinces, officers were appointed, and a magnificent capital was laid out on the banks of the Cala-

bar, energy and consummate ambition taking the place of
the magic that had reared Verdopolis. In keeping with his
elevation in rank, the Marquis assumed in rapid succession
the titles Duke of Zamorna, King of Angria, and Emperor
Adrian, showing with each a corresponding change in character which made him in the end a compound in about
equal parts of an Oriental despot, Napoleon, and Byron.
The first and last were, apparently, Charlotte's conceptions,
the second Branwell's patchwork.

From each new complication Charlotte drew themes for
her "books." While her brother was fixing the boundaries
of the new nation, laying out its cities, and rearing its buildings, she was peopling them with human beings, breathing
the breath of genius into his crude absurdities. Not content
with merely writing the history of her characters, she continually went back in their lives to repeat great scenes and
events and to imagine new ones. There are in the present
volume, for example, one "tale of the perfect tense," and
another tale dealing with the death of a favorite heroine
whom Charlotte, not content to give her up irrevocably,
was later to resuscitate to play an important part in other
stories.

Percy, with the title of Earl of Northangerland, by Branwell's dispensation, was prime minister of the new nation,
Zamorna's ablest lieutenant. But Percy could not long support a subordinate part in any affair, or keep faith with any
friend. Nor could Branwell long endure the monotony of
peace. The play which had its beginning in a set of wooden
soldiers remained to its end, in his mind, a game of war.

Percy joined with Zamorna's enemies in criticism of his
private life and public acts; the newspapers of Angria and
Verdopolis were full of the threatened break. Zamorna
hurled down the gauntlet in his melodramatic "Address to
the Angrians," and Percy defiantly took it up in "Northangerland's Famous Letter." Zamorna, despite the protest

of other kings, dragged his quarrel into the general parliament. On the opening night of the new session, he publicly
charged his father-in-law with disloyalty to himself and
declared he would have his revenge, even if he must take it
through his own wife, the only person in the world whom
Percy loved. He threatened that unless Percy broke immediately and finally with his, Zamorna's, enemies and returned to his former attitude of unquestioning loyalty, he
would put away his wife, Percy's daughter; this, all knew,
would mean her death. To the further events of the story—
the long struggle between the two men, Zamorna's execution of his threat to send Mary away, and the desolation of
Angria by war—there are many references in two of the
stories included here, "Zamorna's Exile" and "Mina Laury."

Such was the exciting and eventful life that Charlotte
was living during the months designated by Mrs. Gaskell as
"A Dreary Season at Haworth," and such was the uncertain
and threatening state of Angrian politics when Charlotte set
out to teach at Roe Head. To the pain of leaving her family
was added intense anxiety for Angria as Branwell launched
simultaneously civil war and foreign invasion, wasting the
land, desolating the magnificent capital, Adrianopolis, killing the Duchess by breaking her heart, and sending the
mighty Duke of Zamorna into Napoleonic captivity. Something of what she suffered may be read in her secret out-
pourings of the next three years, in which she voiced her
heartbreaking grief at her exile and her poignant longing
for Angria. Haworth and the parsonage signified little more
to her than the portals of her lost paradise. It was the land
of her imagination for which she pined because that was
the only outlet she had ever known for her creative impulse,
strong in her as life itself. Thus she wrote:

Once more on a dull Saturday afternoon I sit down to try to
summon around me the dim shadows . . . of incidents long de-

parted, of feelings, of pleasures whose exquisite relish I sometimes fear it will never be my lot again to taste. How few
would believe that from sources purely imaginary such happiness could be derived! Pen cannot portray the deep interest of
the scenes, of the continued train of events, I have witnessed in
that little room with the low, narrow bed and bare, white-
washed walls twenty miles away. . . . There have I sat on the
low bedstead, my eye fixed on the window, through which appeared no other landscape than a monotonous stretch of moorland, a gray church tower rising from the center of a church-
yard so filled with graves that the rank weeds and coarse grass
scarce had room to shoot up between the monuments. . . .
Such was the picture that threw its reflections upon my eye but
communicated no impression to my heart. . . . A long tale
was perhaps then evolving itself in my mind, the history of an
ancient and aristocratic family . . . young lords and ladies
. . . dazzled with the brilliancy of courts, happy with the ambition of senates.

As I saw them stately and handsome, gliding through these
salons, where many well known forms crossed my sight, where
there were faces looking up, eyes smiling and lips moving in
audible speech, that I knew better almost than my brother and
sisters, yet whose voices had never woke an echo in this world,
. . . what glorious associations crowded upon me! Far from
home I cannot write of them; . . . except in total solitude I
scarce dare think of them.*

Again she confides her secrets to her journals—

Haworth and home wakes sensations which lie dormant elsewhere. Last night I did indeed lean upon the thunder-waken-
ing wings of such a stormy blast as I have seldom heard blow,

* These fragmentary journals kept by Charlotte—now in the Bonnell
Collection at the Brontë Museum and Library at Haworth, England—
have been wholly unused by biographers and critics, although a few excerpts from them were printed in the *Brontë Society Publications,* XXXIII
and XXXIV (1923 and 1924), from texts prepared by Mr. C. W. Hatfield. Yet with "We Wove a Web in Childhood"—hitherto unpublished
except for the opening stanzas—and Emily Brontë's poem "Plead for
Me," they are the most revealing Brontë documents in existence.

and it whirled me away like heath in the wilderness for five seconds of ecstasy; and as I sat by myself in the dining room, while all the rest were at tea, the trance seemed to descend on a sudden. Verily this foot trod the war-shaken shores of the Calabar, and these eyes saw the defiled and violated Adrianopolis shedding its lights on the river from lattices whence the invader looked out.

Roe Head and her duties there she hated because they held her spirit in bondage. She writes:

All this day I have been in a dream, half-miserable; half-ecstatic,—miserable because I could not follow it out uninterruptedly, ecstatic because it showed almost in the vivid light of reality the ongoings of the infernal world.

And at another time:

I now resume my own thoughts; my mind relaxes from the stretch on which it has been for the last twelve hours, and falls back on to the rest which nobody in this house knows of but myself. . . . I fulfil my duties strictly and well. . . . As God was not in the fire nor the wind nor the earthquake, so neither is my heart in the task, the theme, or the exercise. It is the still small voice always that comes to me at eventide, that—like a breeze with a voice in it over the deeply blue hills and out of the now leafless forests and from cities on distant river banks— of a far and bright continent; it is that which takes up my spirit and engrosses all my living feelings, all my energies which are not merely mechanical.

The howl of winter wind reminded her of Haworth, but Haworth was but a link with Angria. The sound of Huddersfield Parish Church wafted her away to Verdopolis:

That wind, pouring in impetuous currents through the air, sounding wildly, unremittingly from hour to hour, deepening its tone as the night advances, coming not in gusts, but with a rapid gathering storm swell—that wind, I know, is heard at this moment far away on the moors of Haworth. Branwell and

Emily hear it, and, as it sweeps over our house down the
churchyard and round the old church, they think, perhaps, of
me and Anne. Glorious! That blast was mighty; it reminded
me of Northangerland; there was something so merciless in
the heavier rush that made the very house groan, as if it could
scarce bear this acceleration of impulse. . . .

I listened—the sound sailed full and liquid down the descent: it was the bells of Huddersfield Parish Church. I shut
the window and went back to my seat. Then came on me,
rushing impetuously, all the mighty phantasm that this had
conjured from nothing,—from nothing to a system strange as
some religious creed. I felt as if I could have written gloriously.
The spirit of all Verdopolis—of all the mountainous North—of
all of the woodland West—of all the river-watered East, came
crowding into my mind. If I had had time to indulge it I felt
that the vague suggestions of that moment would have settled
down into some narrative better at least than anything I ever
produced before. But just then a dolt came up with a lesson.

Even her letters from home were prized chiefly because
they brought her news of war-torn Angria and the exiled
and dying Duchess of Zamorna:

About a week since I got a letter from Branwell containing a
most exquisitely characteristic epistle from Northangerland to
his daughter. . . . I lived on its contents for days. In every
pause of employment it came chiming in like some sweet bar
of music, bringing with it agreeable thoughts such as I had for
many weeks been a stranger to. . . . A curtain seemed to rise
and discover to me the Duchess as she might appear when
newly risen and lightly dressed for the morning, discovering
her father's letter in the mail which lies on her breakfast table.

Again:

I wonder if Branwell has really killed the Duchess. Is she
dead? Is she buried? Is she alone in the cold earth on this
dreary night? . . . I hope she's alive still, partly because I
can't abide to think how hopelessly and cheerlessly she must

have died, and partly because her removal, if it has taken place, must have been to Northangerland like the quenching of the last spark that averted utter darkness.

Not once in the many pages of microscopic script that have survived from her Roe Head days does she voice any direct homesickness for Haworth; all her longing was for Angria, the land of her spirit's freedom. Even her Christmas and summer vacations, as the dates of numerous manuscripts attest, were spent in the palaces of Angria and Verdopolis rather than in the parsonage and on the moors of Haworth.

Her "otherworldliness" and her tendency to withdraw herself from companionship were noted by those about her and discussed as "ill health," "despondency," and "irritability," terms which Charlotte admitted herself in her letters to Ellen Nussey. But to her diary she poured out a different story.

Mary Taylor, the most understanding and discerning of Charlotte's friends, visited her at Roe Head, and wrote Mrs. Gaskell, more than ten years later, of her visit:

She seemed to have no interest or pleasure beyond the feeling of duty, and, when she could get the opportunity, used to sit alone and "make out." She told me . . . that one evening she had sat in the dressing-room until it was quite dark, and then observing it all at once, she had taken sudden fright. . . . She told me that one night, sitting alone, about this time, she heard a voice repeat these lines:

> Come thou high and holy feeling,
> Shine o'er mountain, flit o'er wave,
> Gleam like light o'er dome and shieling.

There were eight or ten lines which I forget. She insisted that she had not made them, that she had heard a voice repeat them.

Yet even Mary Taylor had no intimation that Charlotte's "making out" was the calling up of realistic spirits from her imagination, or that the lines which she quoted were the cry of genius in travail. In one of her diary-like fragments of this period, Charlotte recounts this incident, or one similar to it:

Miss Wooler tried to make me talk at tea-time and was exceedingly kind to me, but I could not have roused if she had offered me worlds. After tea we took a long weary walk. I came back [fatigued] to the last degree. . . . The ladies went into the schoolroom to do their exercises, and I crept up to the bed-room to be alone for the first time that day. Delicious, to be sure, was the sensation I experienced as I lay down on the spare bed and resigned myself to the luxury of twilight and solitude. The stream of thought, checked all day, came flowing free and calm along the channel. My ideas were too shattered to form any defined picture, as they would have done in such circumstances at home, but detached thoughts soothingly flitted round me and unconnected scenes occurred, then vanished, producing an effect certainly strange but to me very pleasing. The toil of the day, succeeded by this moment of divine leisure, had acted on me like opium and was coiling about me a disturbed but fascinating spell such as I had never felt before. What I imagined grew morbidly vivid. I remember I quite seemed to see with my bodily eyes a lady standing in the hall of a gentleman's house as if waiting for someone. It was dusk, and there was the dim outline of antlers, with a hat and a rough greatcoat upon them. She had a flat candlestick in her hand and seemed coming from the kitchen or some such place. . . .

I grew frightened at the vivid glow of the candle, at the reality of the lady's erect and symmetrical figure, of her spirited and handsome face, of her anxious eye. . . . I felt confounded and annoyed I scarcely knew by what. . . . A horrid apprehension quickened every pulse I had. I must get up, I thought, and did so on a start. I had had enough of morbidly vivid realizations. Every advantage has its corresponding disadvantage. Tea's real. Miss Wooler is impatient.

The picture that had frightened her was an Angrian scene strongly foreshadowing one in *Villette*.

A more connected story of what the Angrian dream meant to Charlotte as an escape from her schoolroom surroundings is found in a long narrative poem written at Haworth, in the course of her Christmas vacation, in 1836. The first three stanzas are familiar, but separated from the rest of the poem, they lose their significance. They were copied out from the original manuscript, now in the Huntington Library, by Clement Shorter, who included them in *Complete Poems of Charlotte Brontë* (1925). The "web of sunny air," the "spring in infancy," the "mustard seed," and the "almond rod" are fitting figures for the childish play which had spread and swelled and towered to transcendent proportions.

> We wove a web in childhood,
>   A web of sunny air;
> We dug a spring in infancy
>   Of water pure and fair.
>
> We sowed in youth a mustard seed;
>   We cut an almond rod.
> We now are grown up to riper age:
>   Are they withered in the sod?
>
> Are they blighted, failed, and faded?
>   Are they mouldered back to clay?
> For life is darkly shaded,
>   And its joys fleet fast away.
>
> Faded! the web is still of air,
>   But how its folds are spread!
> And from its tints of crimson clear,
>   How deep a glow is shed!
> The light of an Italian sky,
> Where clouds of sunset lingering lie,
>   Is not more ruby red.

But the spring was under a mossy stone,
   Its jet may gush no more.
Hark, skeptic, bid thy doubts be gone;
   Is that a feeble roar?
Rushing around thee, lo! the tide
Of waves where armed fleets may ride,
Sinking and swelling, frowns and smiles,
An ocean with a thousand isles
   And scarce a glimpse of shore.

The mustard seed in distant land
   Bends down a mighty tree;
The dry, unbudding almond wand
   Has touched eternity.

The poem, in another meter, goes on to tell how when the writer "sat 'neath a strange roof-tree," in the black hour of twilight, "longing for her own dear home and the sight of old familiar faces," the dream by its magic bore her away to scenes of joy and excitement:

Where was I ere an hour had passed?
Still listening to that dreary blast?
Still in that mirthless, lifeless room,
Cramped, chilled, and deadened by its gloom?

No! thanks to that bright, darling dream!
Its power had shot one kindling gleam,
Its voice had sent one wakening cry
And bade me lay my sorrows by,
And called me earnestly to come,
And borne me to my moorland home.
I heard no more the senseless sound
Of task and chat that hummed around;
I saw no more that grisly night
Closing the day's sepulchral light.
The vision's spell had deepened o'er me,
Its lands, its scenes were spread before me.

In one short hour a hundred homes
Had roofed me with their lordly domes,
And I had sat by fires whose light
Flashed wide o'er halls of regal height,
And I had seen those come and go
Whose forms gave radiance to the glow,
And I had heard the matted floor
Of ante-room and corridor
Shake to some half-remembered tread,
Whose haughty firmness woke even dread,
As through the curtained portal strode
Some spurred and fur-wrapped demi-god,
Whose ride through that tempestuous night
Had added somewhat of a frown
To brows that shadowed eyes of light
Fit to flash fire from Scythian crown,
Till sweet salute from lady gay
Chased that unconscious scowl away.

After painting a detailed picture of the Duke of Zamorna
in his drawing-room, the poem shifts the scene to a heath
on a moonlit summer's night, as the Duke and a companion have come to sound a requiem for a kinsman who has
fallen in battle:

It was Camalia's ancient field.
I knew the desert well,
For traced around a sculptured shield
These words the summer moon revealed,
"Here brave Macarthy fell!
The men of Keswick leading on,
Their first, their best, their noblest one.
He did his duty well."

Never shall I, Charlotte Brontë, forget what a voice of wild
and wailing music now came thrillingly to my mind's, almost
to my body's, ear, nor how distinctly I, sitting in the schoolroom at Roe Head, saw the Duke of Zamorna leaning against
that obelisk with the mute marble Victory above him, the fern

waving at his feet, his black horse turned loose grazing among the heather, the moonlight so mild, so exquisitely tranquil, sleeping upon the vast and vacant road, and the African sky quivering and shaking with stars, expanded above all. I was quite gone. I had really utterly forgot where I was and all the gloom and cheerlessness of my situation. I felt myself breathing quick and short, as I beheld the Duke lifting up his sable crest which undulated as the plume of a hearse waves to the wind, and I knew that that music which sprung as mournfully triumphant as the scriptural verse,

O Grave, where is thy sting? O Death, where is thy victory?

was exciting him and quickening his ever rapid pulse. "Miss Brontë, what are you thinking about?" said a voice that dissipated all the charm, and Miss Lister thrust her little, rough black head into my face. *Sic transit &c*

Of the other Brontë children only Emily shared Charlotte's power of losing herself in her own imagination. To Branwell, Angria was never more than a childish game. Had he developed normally, he would have forgotten it before he was grown. His innovations, always overbold and literal, never carried conviction, and cumbered with detail though his narratives were, they never succeeded in giving the impression of actuality. Stories that from a lad of twelve or fifteen were delightfully amusing became boring from a youth of nineteen, and intolerably disgusting from a man of twenty-five or twenty-eight, for Branwell never varied his theme and never developed his powers of presenting it. His last effusions were the same old plots that he had introduced fifteen years before, with added details of the grossest profanity and dissipation.

Though Anne collaborated with Emily in "The Gondal Play" and its attendant literature as closely as Branwell with Charlotte in the Angrian cycle, it never took root in her spirit. It is evident from her journal fragments of 1841

and 1845 that in her grown-up years she grew heartily tired
of its pretensions, just at the time when Emily, a year and a
half older than she, was finding it most absorbing. And
when Anne came to write her novels for publication, she
drew not upon her dream world, as did both Charlotte and
Emily, but upon her actual experience in the world of
reality.

Despite Mr. E. F. Benson's elaborated argument for an
estrangement between Emily and Charlotte in the last years
of Emily's life, the fact remains clear that there existed between the two a closer tie of understanding than between
any other two members of the parsonage group. Charlotte
alone of all the world understood Emily's suffering at Roe
Head and obtained her release. Her confession to her Roe
Head diary gives a new meaning to her explanation of her
sister's early return to Haworth:

Every morning when she woke, the vision of home and the
moors rushed on her and darkened and saddened the day that
lay before her. Nobody knew what ailed her but me. . . . I
felt in my heart that she would die, if she did not go home,
and with this conviction obtained her recall. . . .
My sister Emily loved the moors. Flowers brighter than the
rose bloomed in the blackest of the heath for her;—out of a
sullen hollow in a livid hill-side, her mind could make an
Eden. She found in the bleak solitude many dear delights; not
the least and best-loved was—liberty. Liberty was the breath of
Emily's nostrils; without it she perished.

Charlotte knew that the flowers that bloomed on the heath
for Emily were the halls of Gondal; that the Eden which
she conjured from the bleak hillside was the land of King
Julius, and that the liberty which was as the breath of life
to her was freedom to worship without interruption her
"God of Visions."

Analogy need not be strained; the facts, few as they are,

are suggestive enough. Of the great mass of prose written by Emily and Anne in their girlhood and early womanhood, there remain but five short fragments, four of these being notes exchanged between the two on Emily's birthday, to be opened four years from that date. All of these five bits speak of Gondal as an inherent part of their lives. On November 24, 1834, Emily chronicled along with other events of family importance, "The Gondals are exploring the interior of Gaaldine." Anne's pencilled notes in the family geography explain that Gondal was a large island in the North Pacific, and that Gaaldine was an island newly discovered in the South Pacific. In her birthday note of July 30, 1841, Emily says, "The Gondals are at present in a threatening state, but there is no open rupture as yet," and Anne, on the same day, looking forward four years, wonders "whether the Gondalians will still be flourishing."

On July 30, 1845, Emily answers:

The Gondals still flourish as bright as ever. I am at present writing a work on the First Wars. Anne has been writing some articles on this and a book by Henry Sophona. We intend sticking firm by the rascals as long as they delight us, which I am glad to say they do at the present.

Anne's companion note gives more details:

Emily is engaged in writing the Emperor Julius's life. She has read some of it, and I want very much to hear the rest. . . . We have not yet finished our Gondal Chronicles that we began three years and a half ago. . . . The Gondals are at present in a sad state. The Republicans are uppermost, but the Royalists are not quite overcome. The young sovereigns, with their brothers and sisters, are still at the Palace of Instruction. The Unique Society, about a year and a half ago, was wrecked on a desert island as they were returning from Gaul. They are still there, but we have not played at them much yet. The Gondals in general are not in firstrate playing condition. Will they improve?

But it is in her Gondal poems that Emily voices the depth
and intensity of her devotion to "her own, her spirit's
home!" In them the childish tone of the birthday journals
falls away before elemental passions rising to sublime
heights of joy and tragedy. It may be that these, like Charlotte's Angrian poems, were originally incorporated in prose
tales as songs and emotional outbursts of her favorite characters, or it may be that they are but fragments of a long
epic. However they were composed, she had copied them
out in the volume "accidentally lighted upon" by Charlotte
in the autumn of 1845, when their vigor and sincerity and
their "peculiar music, wild, melancholy, and elevating" so
pleased the discoverer that she persuaded their author to
join in the famous publication of 1846.

The qualities which impressed Charlotte have been felt
by all who have read Emily's poems, but the obscurity of
their background has denied them the popularity that their
merits deserve. Only from other sources, such as Anne's
notes in the family geography, could one learn that Alex-
andria, Almedore, Zelona, and Elseraden—names that occur
frequently in Emily's poems—were kingdoms of Gaaldine,
together with "Ula, . . . governed by four sovereigns," and
"Zedora, . . . governed by a viceroy." And without careful
and repeated reading one would never guess that the
greater number of Emily's poems recount the fortunes of
King Julius (who for the love of his proud and ambitious
wife, Rosina, usurped the throne of Gondal in violation of
his oath, and for his perfidy fell by an avenger's dagger)
and the fate of Gondal under his successors, with many
ramifications inspired always by the elemental passions of
love, hate, and revenge.

To inherent obscurity has been added the misconception
spread abroad by biographers who have persisted in inter-
preting autobiographically poems reflecting experiences and
feelings of purely imaginary characters in a purely imagi-

nary world. The tradition of a mysterious lover who died in Emily's early youth is based on the magnificent poem of intense and lofty passion which begins,

> Cold in the earth—and the deep snow piled above thee,

which Emily's own manuscript tells us is the lament of Rosina for her murdered husband.

Yet Emily has spoken with startling plainness to those who have ears to hear. Her poem "Plead for Me" is hardly less explicit that Charlotte's "We Wove a Web in Childhood." She is calling her dream to defend her before the "scornful brow" of "Stern Judgment":

> . . . Radiant angel, speak and say
> Why I did cast the world away,—
> Why I have persevered to shun
> The common paths that others run;
> And on a strange road journey on. . . .

As earnestly and devoutly as Charlotte invoked her "high and holy feeling" to lighten her days at Roe Head, Emily, at Haworth, worshipped her "God of Visions":

> Am I wrong to worship where
> Faith cannot doubt, nor hope despair,
> Since my own soul can grant my prayer?
> Speak, God of Visions, plead for me,
> And tell why I have chosen thee.

Yet there was one important difference between these sisters who were so closely akin in spirit and in genius. While to both of them the glory of the world was in that world created by their imaginations, Emily gave up her spirit to that world. Imagination dominates her whole nature, and her poems tell only of the rivalry between the perceptions of her senses and the emotions of her unseen world. Nature spoke to her in the forms and voices of her native moors; she listened and gathered into her great heart all these sights and sounds and wisdoms, and with these furnished her spirit's home. She knew nothing of the hard conflict, nothing of the tearing and rending of warring personalities, which Charlotte suffered. For the way was not so easy for Charlotte—not for her the retreat from reality.

In 1837 Charlotte, ambitious and anxious about her prospects of literary success, submitted to Southey, then poet laureate, a specimen of her verse, asking his opinion. Two years later she asked Wordsworth's good office as critic of one of her prose narratives. Both answers were discouraging, and both, by implication at least, warned her against her tendency to romanticism. One or two sentences in the long and kindly letter which she received from Southey deserve our attention here:

There is a danger of which I would, with all kindness and in all earnestness, warn you. The day dreams in which you habitually indulge are likely to induce a distempered state of mind; and in proportion as all the ordinary uses of the world seem to you flat and unprofitable, you will be unfitted for them without becoming fitted for anything else. . . . But do not suppose that I disparage the gift which you possess; nor that I would discourage you from exercising it. I only exhort you so to think of it, and so to use it, as to render it conducive to your own permanent good.

This advice made a great impression on Charlotte, as her reply to Southey shows. She explains, after thanking him for his kindness, that she is not entirely an "idle dreaming being," but that she is doing work that is of some use in the world.

I find enough to occupy my thoughts all day long, and my head and hands too, without having a moment's time for one dream of the imagination. In the evenings, I confess, I do think, but I never trouble any one else with my thoughts. I

carefully avoid any appearance of pre-occupation and eccen-
tricity, which might lead those I live amongst to suspect the
nature of my pursuits.

But after this defense and a fresh burst of gratitude, she
adds an illuminating postscript:

Pray, sir, excuse me for writing to you a second time; I could
not help writing, partly to tell you how thankful I am for
your kindness, and partly to let you know that your advice
shall not be wasted; however sorrowfully and reluctantly it may
at first be followed.

Probably in consequence of her recognition of the wisdom of Southey's advice, Charlotte, two years later, took a
formal farewell of her dream world and its people in such
loving, almost caressing, terms as to give it a place next to
"We Wove a Web in Childhood" in her confession of faith.
Her sorrow and reluctance were natural, for she had begun writing novels of Angria in her seventeenth year, and
had continued well into 1839, after she had passed her
twenty-third birthday. This "Farewell to Angria" may mark
the end of her literary work of this period; yet her dream
world did not perish utterly with her leave taking. As late
as 1843 she wrote Branwell from Brussels that in the evenings, when she was alone in the great dormitory of the
Héger *Pensionnat* she recurred as "fanatically as ever to the
old ideas, the old faces, and the old scenes." But for the rest
of her life, her literary efforts were spent in an attempt to
Europeanize her Africans. Her success is attested by the
certainty with which Mr. Yorke, Paul Emanuel, Shirley,
and others have been identified as portraits of real persons.
The outward Charlotte, once alive to the danger of living
too much in her dream world, was strong enough and determined enough to wage cruel war upon her inner self,
persecuting it and threatening its very life, until at last per-

secutor and persecuted found lasting peace in the perfect fusion of actual experience with pure imagination.

IT is in the hope of helping readers to a better interpretation of the personality and literary development of Charlotte Brontë that the present volume has been prepared. It is not intended as a complete or exhaustive presentation of her early work, but as a selective introduction to it. The object throughout the preparation of the text has been to give the reader as nearly as possible a *verbally* accurate transcript of the text as Charlotte intended it. She wrote fluently, and, as if the fluency of her thought were not to be interrupted, omitted almost all marks of punctuation. What she wrote was written only for herself and her collaborators—a fact which explains the lack of punctuation, errors and inconsistencies in spelling, inconsistencies in the spelling of proper names, the omission of an occasional word, etc. It has seemed best to the editors to correct obvious misspellings, to supply obvious omissions (though indicating where this has been done), and to supplement the punctuation, in order that the reader may find no fortuitous stumbling-blocks between him and the sense of the text as Charlotte Brontë would have written it if she had herself been preparing it for publication.

Exigencies of space have not permitted a full transcription of all the manuscripts chosen for presentation. In "The Green Dwarf" there has been omitted an episode told by one of the Frenchmen at the Inn, already published by Mr. Hatfield in *The Twelve Adventurers* under the title "Napoleon and the Spectre." The only other omissions of any length are in "Caroline Vernon," which, being the last story in the cycle, seemed the one which could with least unfairness to the reader be cut. These omissions are of two sorts: some, digressions which contribute items to the Angrian story in general but nothing to this story in particular;

and others, repetitions of scenes where Charlotte, evidently practising her art, decided to try another version of the same situation. All the omissions, however, are clearly indicated in the text.

Of the five pieces here printed, the four long ones have been chosen as best representing the development of Charlotte Brontë's literary genius along with the growth and expansion of her dream world. The first, "The Green Dwarf," written in 1833 when she was seventeen, partakes somewhat of the character of "The Young Men's Play," with its wooden toys and its frolicsome exaggeration, and yet foreshadows, in the personality of Percy, the great themes of friendship, love, hate, and revenge which inspired "Zamorna's Exile." In a literary sense it is Charlotte at her gawkiest age, all loose joints, angles, and awkward movements—interesting to watch but neither fulfilling the earlier promise of such pieces as "The Twelve Adventurers" and "Albion and Marina," nor giving evidence of power to come. "Zamorna's Exile," the second piece, written in 1836–37, to a greater degree than any other of the entire cycle is the spirit of Angria, summarizing its history and exemplifying the newly awakened emotionalism of Charlotte, dominated and directed by Byron. It has the further merit that it demonstrates her ability to tell a story in verse. The third piece, written in 1838, here given the tentative title of "Mina Laury," represents the post-war reconstruction period of Angrian history, when Charlotte was rebuilding her dream world, shattered and almost destroyed by Branwell, and rebuilding it on a plane which he was never able to reach. In it one may see the signposts pointing to *Jane Eyre*. "Caroline Vernon," the next piece, written probably in 1839, is something of a new departure in its attempt to weave the usual series of vignettes into a closely unified novel devoted to the fortunes of one individual. Probably the last of the Angrian stories, it suggests at the same time the new era of her published novels. Between the stories, and between the two cantos of "Zamorna's Exile," link pieces have been supplied in order to refresh the reader's memory, or to give in more detail than in the Introduction the facts necessary to a proper understanding of the text itself. The volume closes with the "Farewell," as a fitting conclusion to these legends of Angria.

MAP OF THE GLASS TOWN COUNTRY

Redrawn by Lois North

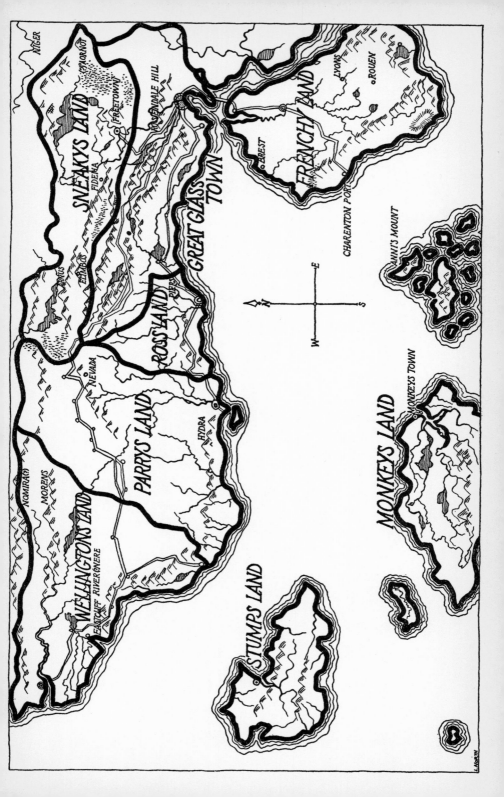

Introduction to "The Green Dwarf"

"THE GREEN DWARF" was written in 1833, when Charlotte Brontë was seventeen years old, more than a year after her return to the Haworth parsonage from her school days at Roe Head. This year was the most productive of her life. Under the pseudonyms of Captain Tree and Lord Charles Albert Florian Wellesley—in the play world of the Brontës the second son of the Duke of Wellington—she wrote ten novels, according to her own lists, though only four are known to be extant; and as the Marquis of Douro, the elder son of the Duke, she produced a proportionate amount of verse. The influence of Scott and Byron is evident in all.

"The Green Dwarf," as the title-page indicates and as the setting of the story within a story demands, is a reminiscent novel, "a tale of the perfect tense." "The Young Men's Play" had begun in 1826, and Charlotte was now old enough to be a bit ashamed of it. Yet her hungry pen had nothing else to feed upon, and she seems to have fallen eagerly upon the suggestion found in Sir Walter Scott, of casting her tales in past times and other days. The Verdopolis we see in "The Green Dwarf" is in its early pioneer days, and hardly gives an indication of the great metropolis it is to become. This novel, also, has the distinction of being the last of Charlotte's stories in which the Duke of Wellington, the founder of the Glass Town Confederacy, takes a leading part. From this time forward his greatness is usurped by his Byronic son, the Duke of Zamorna.

The plot of "The Green Dwarf" is, in the main, an adaptation from *Ivanhoe*, with all its romantic paraphernalia—the hero returned in disguise, the tournament, the abduction of the heroine, and the ancient hag to guard the fair prisoner. The immaturity of the imitation is in amusing contrast to the maturity of Charlotte's appreciation of Scott's genius, expressed in a letter to Ellen Nussey in the same year:

I am glad you like *Kenilworth;* it is certainly a splendid production, more resembling a Romance than a Novel, and in my opinion one of the most interesting works that ever emanated from the great Sir Walter's pen. . . . He [Varney] is certainly the personification of consummate villainy, and in the delineation of his dark and profoundly artful mind, Scott exhibits a wonderful knowledge of human nature, as well as surprising skill in embodying his perceptions so as to enable others to become participators in that knowledge.

Varney's "consummate villainy" and his "dark and profoundly artful mind" are curiously grafted on to the wooden soldier Rogue, or Percy, by Charlotte in "The Green Dwarf." Four years earlier, in a manuscript entitled "Characters of the Celebrated Men of the Present Time," she had thus described Percy, who was to be the villain of her Angrian stories: "His manner is rather polished and gentlemanly, but his mind is deceitful, bloody, and cruel. . . . He dances well and plays cards admirably, being skilled in all the sleight-of-hand blackleg tricks of the gaming table." At the end of the sixteen years of exile meted out to him in the *dénouement* of "The Green Dwarf" he reappears in Verdopolis as a reformed pirate and becomes, after many vicissitudes, the great Earl of Northangerland and father-in-law to Zamorna, who is to be the arch-hero of Charlotte's imaginary world.

THE GREEN DWARF

A TALE
OF THE PERFECT TENSE

BY

LORD CHARLES ALBERT FLORIAN WELLESLEY

PUBLISHED BY
SERGEANT TREE BIBLIO STREET VERDOPOLIS
AND SOLD BY ALL OTHER BOOK SELLERS
IN TOWN AND COUNTRY

CHARLOTTE BRONTË

SEPTEMBER 2ND 1833

Preface

I AM informed that the world is beginning to express in low, discontented grumblings its surprise at my long, profound, and (I must say) very ominous silence.

"What," says the reading public, as she stands in the market place, with gray cap and ragged petticoat, the exact image of a modern blue, "what is the matter with Lord Charles? Is he exspiflicated by the literary captain's lash? Have his good genius and his scribbling mania forsaken him both at once? Rides he now on man-back through the Mountains of the Moon,[1] or—mournful thought!—lies he helpless on a sick bed of pain?"

The last conjecture, I am sorry to say, is, or rather was, true. I have been sick, most sick. I have suffered dreadful, indescribable tortures, arising chiefly from the terrible remedies which were made use of to effect my restoration. One of these was boiling alive in what was called a hot-bath; another, roasting before a slow fire; and a third, a most rigid system of starvation. For proof of these assertions apply to Mrs. Cook back of Waterloo Palace situated in the suburbs of Verdopolis. How I managed to survive such a mode of treatment, or what the strength of my victorious constitution must be, wiser men than I would fail of explaining. Certain it is, however, that I did at length get better, or, to speak more elegantly, become convalescent; but long after my cadaverous cheek had begun to reassume a little of its wonted freshness, I was kept penned up in a corner of the housekeeper's parlour, forbid the use of pen, ink, and paper, prohibited setting foot into the open air, and dieted on rice gruel, sago, snail soup, panad, stewed cockchafers, milk-broth, and roasted mice. I will not say what was my delight when first Mrs. Cook deigned to inform me about two o'clock one fine summer afternoon that, as it was a mild, warm day, I might take a short walk out if I pleased. Ten minutes sufficed for arraying my person in a new suit of very handsome clothes, and washing the accumulated dirt of several diurnal revolutions of the earth from my face and hands.

As soon as these necessary operations were performed, I sallied out in plumed hat and cavalier mantle. Never before had I been fully sensible of the delights of liberty. The suffocating atmosphere which filled the hot, flinty street was to me as delicious as the dew-cooled balm-breathing air of the freshest twilight in the wildest solitude. There was not a single tree to throw its sheltering branches between me and the fiery sun. But I felt no want of such a screen, as with slow but not faltering steps I crept along in the shadow of shops and houses. At a sudden turn, the flowing, ever-cool sea burst unexpectedly on me. I felt like those poor wretches do who are victims to the disease called a calenture. The green waves looked like widespread plains covered with foam, white flowers and tender spring grass and the thickly clustered masts of vessels my excited fancy transformed into groves of tall, graceful trees, while the smaller craft took the form of cattle reposing in their shade.

I passed on with something of that springing step which is natural to me, but soon my feeble knees began to totter under the form which they should have supported. Unable to go farther without rest, I looked round for some place where I might sit down till my strength should be *un peu rétablis*. I was in that ancient and dilapidated court, called pompously enough Quaxmina Square, where Bud Gifford, Love-dust, and about twenty other cracked old antiquarians reside. I determined to take refuge in the house of the first mentioned, as well because he is my most intimate friend as because it is in the best condition.

Bud's mansion is indeed far from being either incommodious or unseemly. The outside is venerable and has been very judiciously repaired by modern masons (a step by-the-bye which brought down the censure of almost all his neighbours), and the inside is well and comfortably furnished. I knocked at the door; it was opened by an old footman with a reverend gray head. On my asking if his master were at home, he showed me upstairs into a small but handsome room where I found Bud seated at a table surrounded by torn parchments and rubbish and descanting copiously on some rusty knee-buckles which he held in his hand, to the Marquis of Douro, and another puppy, who very politely were standing before him with their backs to the fire.

"What's been to do with my darling?" said the kind old gentleman as I entered. "What's made it look so pale and sickly? I hope not chagrin at Tree's super-annuated drivel."

"Bless us," said Arthur before I could speak a word; "What a little chalky spoon he looks! The whipping I bestowed on him has stuck to his small body right well. Hey Charley, any soreness yet?"

"Fratricide," said I, "how dare you speak thus lightly to your half-murdered brother? How dare you demand whether the tortures you have inflicted continue to writhe his agonized frame?"

He answered this appeal with a laugh intended, I have no doubt, to display his white teeth, and a sneer designed to set off his keen wit, and at the same instant he gently touched his riding wand.

"Nay, my lord," said Bud, who noticed this significant manoeuvre, "let us have no more of such rough play. You'll kill the lad in earnest if you don't mind."

"I am not going to meddle with him yet," said he. "He's not at present in a condition to show game. But let him offend me again as he has done, and I'll hardly leave a strip of skin on his carcass."

What brutal threat he would have uttered besides, I know not; but at this moment he was interrupted by the entrance of dinner.

"My lord and Colonel Morton," said Bud, "I hope you'll stay and take a bit of dinner with me if you do not think my plain fare too coarse for your dainty palates."

"On my honour, Captain," replied Arthur, "your bachelor's meal looks very nice, and I should really feel tempted to partake of it, had it been more than two hours since I breakfasted. Last night, or rather this morning, I went to bed at six o'clock; it was twelve before I rose. Therefore dinner, you know, is out of the question till seven or eight o'clock in the evening."

Morton excused himself on some similar pretext; and shortly after, both of the gentlemen, much to my satisfaction, took their leave.

"Now, Charley," said my friend when they were gone, "you'll give me your company, I know. So sit down on that easy chair opposite to me, and let's have a regular two-handed crack."

I gladly accepted his kind invitation, because I knew that if I returned home Mrs. Cook would allow me nothing for dinner but a basin-full of some filthy vermined slop. During our meal few words were spoken, for Bud hates chatter at feeding time. And I was too busily engaged in discussing the most savory plateful of food I had eaten for the last month and more to bestow a thought on anything of less importance. However, when the table was cleared and the dessert brought in, Bud wheeled the round table nearer the open window, poured out a glass of sack, seated himself in his cushioned arm-chair, and then said in that quiet satisfactory tone which men use when they are perfectly comfortable, "What shall we talk about, Charley?"

"Anything you like," I replied.

"Anything?" said he; "why that means just nothing. But what would you like?"

"Dear Bud," was my answer, "since you have been kind enough to leave the choice of a topic to me, there is nothing I should enjoy so much as one of your delightful tales. If you would but favour me this once, I shall consider myself eternally obliged to you."

Of course Bud, according to the universal fashion of all story-tellers, refused at first; but after a world of flattery, coaxing, and entreaty, he at length complied with my request and related the following incidents, which I now present to the reader, not exactly in the original form of words in which I heard it, but strictly preserving the sense and facts.

C. Wellesley.

Chapter the First

TWENTY years since, or thereabouts, there stood in what is now the middle of Verdopolis, but which was then the extremity, a huge irregular building called the Genii's Inn. It contained more than five hundred apartments, all comfortably and some splendidly fitted up for the accommodation of travellers, who were entertained in this vast hostelry free of expense. It became, in consequence of this generous regulation, the almost exclusive resort of wayfarers of every nation, who in spite of the equivocal character of the host and hostesses, being the four Chief Genii, Talli, Brani, Emi, and Anni, and the despicable villainy of the waiters and other attendants, which noble offices were filled by subordinate spirits of the same species, continually flocked thither in prodigious multitudes.

The sound of their hurrying footsteps, the voice of rude revel, and the hum of business have ceased now among the ruined arches, the damp, mouldy vaults, the dark halls and desolate chambers of this once mighty edifice, which was destroyed in the great rebellion, and now stands silent and lonely in the heart of great Verdopolis. But our business is with the past, not the present, day; therefore let us leave moping to the owls, and look on the bright side of matters.

On the evening of the Fourth of June, 1814, it offered rather a different appearance. There had been during that day a greater influx of guests than usual, which circumstance was owing to a grand fête to be held on the morrow. The great hall looked like a motley masquerade. In one part was seated cross-legged on the pavement a group of Turkish merchants, who in those days used to trade largely with the shop-keepers and citizens of Verdopolis in spices, shawls, silks, muslins, jewelry, perfumes, and other articles of Oriental luxury. These

sat composedly smoking their long pipes and drinking choice
sherbet and reclining against cushions which had been provided for their accommodation. Near them, a few dark, sun-
burnt Spaniards strutted, with the grave, proud air of a pea-
cock, which bird, according to the received opinion, dares not
look downward, lest his feet should break the self-complacent
spell which enchants him. Not far from these lords of creation
sat a company of round rosy-faced, curly-pated, straight-legged,
one-shoed beings from Stump's Island,[2] where that now nearly
obsolete race of existences then flourished like the green bay
tree. More than a dozen genii were employed in furnishing
them with melons and rice pudding for which they roared out
incessantly.

At the opposite extremity of the hall five or six sallow, bilious
Englishmen were conversing over a cup of green tea. Behind
them a band of withered monsieurs sat presenting each other
with fine white bread, peculiarly rich, elegant Prussian butter,
perfumed snuff, brown sugar, and calico. At no great distance from these half-withered apes and within the great carved
screen that surrounded a huge blazing fire, two gentlemen had
established themselves before a table on which smoked a tempting dish of beefsteaks with the due accompaniments of onions,
ketchup, and cayenne, flanked by a large silver vessel of prime
old Canary and a corresponding tankard of spiced ale.

One of the personages whose good fortune it was to be the
devourer of such choice cheer was a middle-aged man who
might perhaps have numbered his fifty-fifth year. His rusty
black habiliments, powdered wig, and furrowed brow spoke at
once the scholar and the despiser of external decorations. The
other presented a remarkable contrast to his companion. He
was in the prime of life, being apparently not more than six
or seven and twenty years of age. A head of light brown hair
arranged in careless yet tasteful curls well became the pleasing,
though not strictly regular, features of his very handsome countenance, to which a bright and bold blue eye added all the

charms of expression, and his form, evincing both strength and symmetry, was set off to the best advantage by a military costume, while his erect bearing and graceful address gave additional testimony to the nature of his profession.

"This young soldier," said Bud, with a kindling eye, "was myself. You may laugh, Charley," for I could not forbear a smile on contrasting the dignified corporation of my now somewhat elderly fat friend with the description he had just given of his former appearance; "you may laugh, but I was once as gallant a youth as ever wore a soldier's sword. Alackaday! Time, trouble, good liquor and good living change a man sorely."

"But," the reader will ask, "who was the other gentleman mentioned above?" He was John Gifford, then the bosom friend of Ensign Bud as he is now of Captain Bud.

There was a profound silence so long as their savory meal continued. But when the last mouthful of beef, the last shred of onion, the last grain of cayenne, the last drop of ketchup had disappeared, Gifford laid down his knife and fork, and uttered a deep sigh, and opening his oracular jaws, said, "Well, Bud, I suppose the fools whom we see here gathered together from all the winds of heaven are come to our Babylonian city for the worthy purpose of beholding the gauds and vanities of tomorrow."

"Doubtless," replied the other, "and I sincerely hope that you, sir, also will not disdain to honour their exhibition with your presence."

"I," almost yelled the senior gentleman, "I go and see the running of chariots, the racing and prancing of horses, the goring of wild beasts, the silly craft of archery, and the brutal sport of the wrestlers! Art thou mad? Or are thy brains troubled with the good wine and the nutmeg ale?" Here the speaker filled his glass with the latter generous liquid.

"I am neither one nor t'other, Gifford," answered Bud, "but I'll venture to say that forasmuch as you despise those gauds and vanities as you call them, many a better man than you is longing for tomorrow on their account."

"Ah! I suppose thou art among the number of those arrant fools."

"I've truly said I see no shame in the avowal."

"Don't you indeed? Oh, Bud, Bud! I sometimes hope that you are beginning to be sensible of the folly of these pursuits. I sometimes dare to imagine that you will one day be found a member of that chosen band who, despising the weak frivolities of this our degenerate age, turn studiously to the contemplation of the past, who value, as some men do gold and jewels, every remnant, however small, however apparently trivial, which offers a memento of vanished generations."

"Goodness, Gifford! How you talk! I like well enough to see Melchisedec's cup for the sacramental wine, the tethers by which Abraham's camels were fastened in their pasture-grounds, or even the thigh-bone and the shoulder-blade of one of our own worthy old giants,[3] even when these latter articles turn out to be the remains of a dead elephant. (Ah, Giff, touched ye there, I see!) But as to making such matters the serious business of my life, why hang me, if I think I shall turn to that trade before a round dozen of years have trotted merrily over my head."

"You speak like one of the foolish people," replied Giff solemnly; "but still I glean a handful of comfort from your last words. At some future period you will give serious attention to the grand purpose for which we were all brought into the world."

"Maybe aye, and maybe nay. But whether I do or not, my cherub there, Stingo, seems as if he would have no objection to turn both antiquarian and lawyer already."

"Ha! What! Is it that same sweet boy whom I saw yesterday at your house, whose young features express a promising solemnity far beyond his tender years?"

"The same, and a sour, squalling, ill-tempered brat he is."

"My dear friend," said Gifford with great earnestness, "take care that you do not check the unfolding of that hopeful flower. Mind my words, he will [be] an honour to his country. And here, give him these toys," (taking a number of roundish stones from his pocket) "and tell him I have no doubt they were used as marbles by the children of the ancient Britons. Doubtless he will know how to value them accordingly."

"To be sure he will. But my dear friend, the next time you make Stingo a present, let it be some slight treatise on the law. He is continually hunting in my library for books of that nature, and complains that he can scarcely find one of the sort he wants."

"The angel!" exclaimed Gifford in ecstasy; "the moment I get home I will send him a complete edition of my compendium of the laws. He shall not long pine in the agonies of inanition."

"You are very kind," said Bud. "But now let us change the subject. I understand that Bravey is to occupy the president's throne tomorrow. I wonder who will be the rewarder of the victors."

"It is not often that I remember the idle chat which passes in my presence, but I heard this morning that Lady Emily Charlesworth is to be honoured with that dignity."

"Is she? That's well. They could not possibly have made a better choice. Her beauty alone would give *éclat* to the whole routine of tomorrow's proceedings. Now tell me honestly, Giff, do you not think Lady Emily the most beautiful of earthly creatures?"

"She's well enough favoured," replied Gifford. "That is, garments ever become her person, but for her mind, I fear it is a waste, uncultivated field, which, where it is not wholly barren, presents a rank crop of the weeds of frivolity."

"Prejudiced old prig!" said I angrily. "Would you have a

spiritual essence of divinity like that to wither her roses by studying rotten scrolls and bending over grub-devoured law books?"

"Not precisely so, but I would have her cultivate the faculties with which nature has endowed her by a diligent perusal of abridged treatises on the subjects you mention, carefully digested by some able and judicious men. I myself, when her uncle appointed me her tutor in the more solid and useful branches of a polite education, mentioned a small work of ten quarto volumes on the antiquities of England, interspersed with explanatory notes, and having an appendix of one thick volume quarto.[4] If I could have got her to read this little work carefully and attentively through, it might have given her some insight into the noble science of which I am an unworthy eulogist. But while by strange perversion of intellects she listened to openly, and even followed attentively, the instructions of those trivial beings who taught her the empty accomplishments of music, dancing, drawing, modern languages, &c., &c., while she even gave some occasional odd moments to the formation of flowers and other cunning devices on the borders of silken or fine linen raiment, I alone vainly attempted to lure her on in the honourable paths of wisdom, sometimes by honied words of enticement, sometimes by thorny threats of correction. At one time she laughed, at another wept; and occasionally, to my shame be it spoken, bribed me by delusive blandishments to criminal acquiescence in her shameful neglect of all that is profitable to be understood by either man or womankind."

"Bravo, Giff!" said Bud laughing, "I wish she had boxed your ears whenever you bothered her on such subjects. By-the-bye, have you heard that your fair quondam pupil is about to be married to Colonel Percy?"

"I have not. But I do not doubt the rumour. That's the way of all women. They think of nothing but being married, while learning is as dust in the balance."

"Who and what is Colonel Percy?" said a voice close behind.

Bud turned hastily around to see who the strange interrogator might be. He started as his eyes met the apparition of a tall slender form dimly seen by the decaying embers which now shone fitfully on the hearth.

"Friend," said he, stirring up the fire to obtain a more perfect view of the stranger, "tell me first who and what you are who ask such abrupt questions about other people."

"I," replied he, "am a volunteer in the cause of good government and suppression of rebels; and erelong I hope to be able to call myself a brother in arms with you, it being my intention shortly to enlist under the Duke's standard."

As the unknown gave this explanation, a bundle of brushwood which had been thrown on the half-extinguished fire, kindling to a bright blaze, revealed his person more clearly than the darkening twilight had hitherto permitted it to be seen. He appeared to be full six feet high. His figure, naturally formed on a model of the most perfect elegance, derived additional grace from the picturesque but rather singular costume in which he was attired, consisting of a green vest and tunic reaching a little below the knee, laced buskins, a large dark robe or mantle which hung over one shoulder in ample folds and was partially confined by the broad belt which encircled his waist, and a green bonnet surmounted by a high plume of black feathers. A bow and quiver hung on his back, two knives whose hafts sparkled with jewels were stuck in his girdle, and a tall spear of glittering steel which he held in one hand, served him for a kind of support as he stood. The martial majesty of this imposing stranger's form and dress harmonized with the manly, though youthful, beauty of his countenance, whose finely chiseled features and full bright eyes shaded by clusters of short brown curls shone with an expression of mingled pride and frankness, which awed the spectator while it won his unqualified admiration.

"Upon my word, friend," said I, struck with the young soldier's handsome exterior, "if I were the duke, I should be well pleased with such a recruit as you promise to be. Pray, may I enquire of what country you are a native? For both your garb and accent are somewhat foreign."

"You forget," replied the stranger smiling, "that you are my debtor for a reply. My first question remains yet unanswered."

"Ah, true," said Bud, "you asked me, I think, who Colonel Percy might be?"

"I did; and it would gratify me much to receive some information respecting him."

"He is the nephew and apparent heir of the rich old Duke of Beaufort."

"Indeed! How long has he paid his addresses to Lady Emily Charlesworth?"

"For nearly a year."

"When are they to be married?"

"Shortly, I believe."

"Is he handsome?"

"Yes, nearly as much so as you; and into the bargain his manners are those of an accomplished soldier and gentleman, but in spite of all this he is a finished scoundrel, a haughty, gambling, drinking, unconscionable blackguard."

"Why do you speak so warmly against him?"

"Because I know him well. I am his inferior officer, and have daily opportunity of observing his vices."

"Is Lady Emily acquainted with his real character?"

"Perhaps not altogether; but if she were, I do not think she would love him less. Ladies look more to external than internal qualifications in their husbands elect."

"Do they often appear in public together?"

"I believe not. Lady Emily confines herself very much to private life. She is said not to like display."

"Do you know anything of her disposition or her temper? Is it good or bad? close or candid?"

"I am sure I can't tell you: but there is a gentleman here

who will satisfy your curiosity on that point. He was her tutor, and should know all about it. Pray, Gifford, favour us with your opinion."

Gifford, hearing himself thus appealed to, emerged from the dark corner, which had hitherto nearly concealed him from view. The stranger started on seeing him, and attempted to muffle his face with one end of the large mantle in which he was enveloped, as if for the purpose of avoiding a recognition. But the worthy antiquary, at no time sharp-sighted, and whose brain, at this particular juncture, happened to be somewhat muddled by the draughts of spiced ale which he had just been administering to himself with no sparing hand, regarded him with a vacant stare of wonder, as he drawled out,

"What's your business with me, Bud?"

"I merely wished to know if you could inform this gentleman what sort of temper Lady Charlesworth had."

"What sort of temper? Why, I don't know. Much the same as other girls of her age have, and that's a very bad one."

The stranger smiled, gave a significant shrug of his shoulders, which seemed to say, "There's not much to be had from this quarter," and bowing politely to the corner, walked away to a distant part of the hall. . . .*

* The digression here omitted—a story related by one of the Frenchmen in the Inn—was published by Mr. Hatfield in *The Twelve Adventurers* under the title, "Napoleon and the Spectre."

Chapter the Second

A BRIGHT and balmy summer's morning ushered in the first celebration of the African Olympic Games.[5] At an early hour (as the newspapers say), the amphitheatre was crowded almost to suffocation in every part, except the open area, a square mile in magnitude, alloted to the combatants, and those private seats which were reserved for the accommodation of the nobility and other persons of distinction.

The scene of the games was not exactly then what it is now. The houses which surrounded it on three sides were at that time but newly built. Some, indeed, were but half finished, and a few had only the foundations dug. The lofty hill called Frederick's crag,[6] which completes the circle on the fourth side, and whose summit above the seats is at the present day covered with gardens and splendid private dwellings, was then a sombre forest, whose ancient echoes were as yet unviolated by the sound of the woodcutter's axe. The stumps of a few recently felled trees likewise appeared in the midst of the newly cleared arena, but it is a question in my opinion whether by the vast improvements which have since taken place in the neighbourhood of the amphitheatre, the scene has not lost in picturesque variety what it has gained in grandeur and perfect finish.

On that memorable morning, the tall magnificent trees, waving their still dewy arms, now towards the blue sky which seemed not far above them, and now over the heads of as many peoples, nations, tongues, and kindreds as Nebuchadnezzar's decree called together on the plains of Dura, flung into the prospect a woodland wildness and sylvan sublimity, which in my opinion would be a more potent and higher charm than any of the artificial forms of beauty our great city has created in their stead are capable of infusing.

After an hour of anxious expectation the distant sound of

musical instruments announced the approach of the principal
personages. Bravey advanced slowly and majestically, followed
by a brilliant train of nobles. His tall and imposing person was
set off to the best advantage by an ample robe of purple splendidly wrought with gold. He took his seat on the president's
throne amidst bursts of universal applause. After him came
Lady Emily Charlesworth, his niece. The flutes and softer instruments of the musicians breathed a dulcet welcome as the
fair rewarder of victors with a graceful rather than stately
tread moved towards her decorated seat. Her form was exquisitely elegant, though not above the middle size. And as she
lifted her long white veil to acknowledge the thunderous applause of the multitude, a countenance was revealed such as
painters and poets love to imagine, but which is seldom seen
in actual life. The features were soft and delicate, the general
complexion transparently fair, but tinged on the cheeks and
lips with a clear, healthy, crimson hue which gave an idea of
vigour and healthy freshness. Her eyes, dark, bright, and full
of animation, flashed from under their long lashes and finely
penciled brows an arch, laughing, playful light, which though
it might not have suited well in a heroine of romance, yet
added to her countenance a most fascinating though indescribable charm. At first as she removed her veil and met the gaze
of more than a million admiring eyes, a blush mantled on her
beautiful cheeks, and she bowed timidly though gracefully, and
her white hand trembled with agitation as she waved it in
reply to their greetings. But she soon regained her composure.
The scene before her awoke feelings of a higher nature in her
susceptible mind.

The blue and silent sky, the wild, dark forest, and the broad
glimpse of a mountainous country opening far beyond, tinged
by the violet hues of distance, contrasted with the mighty
assemblage of living and moving beings, the great city and the
boundless sea beyond. These circumstances, together with the
solemn sound of the music which now in subdued and solemn

but most inspiring tones accompanied the heralds as they summoned the charioteers who were to contest the first prize to approach, could not but kindle in every bosom admiration for the simple sublimity of nature and the commanding magnificence of art. Three chariots now drew up around the starting-posts. In the first sat a little man with a head of fiery red hair and a pair of keen, malicious black eyes, which kept squinting around the arena and regarding everyone on whom their distorted glances chanced to fall with a kind of low blackguard expression, which accorded well with the rest of his appearance and equipments. His chariot was rather out of character when compared with the gorgeousness of all surrounding objects, being neither more nor less than a common spring cart drawn by four of those long-eared and proverbially obstinate animals called asses, whom he alternately held in check by means of a rough straw rope bridle or goaded forward with the assistance of a black-thorn staff pointed at one end.

The occupier of the second chariot was a fashionable, dandified gentleman in pink silk jacket, and white pantaloons, whose whole attention seemed absorbed by the management of his four handsome bay chargers. His name was Major Hawkins, at that time a celebrated hero of the turf and ring.

But it was the third and the last charioteer who excited the most general attention. He was a tall and very handsome young man whose symmetrical form appeared to the utmost advantage as he stood upright on his small, light car, gallantly reining in the proud, prancing steeds that seemed by their loud snorting and the haughty elevation of their stately arched necks to be conscious of their master's superiority over the other combatants. The countenance of this gentleman was, as I have said, handsome. His features were regularly formed. His forehead was lofty, though not very open. But there was in the expression of his blue, sparkling, but sinister, eyes and of the smile that ever played round his deceitful looking mouth, a spirit of deep, restless villainy which warned the penetrating

observer that all was not as fair within as without, while his
pallid cheek and somewhat haggard air bespoke at once the
profligate, the gambler, and perhaps the drunkard. Such is the
description, as well as my poor pen can express it, of Colonel
the Honourable Alexander Augustus Percy.

All being now ready, the signal for starting broke from a
silver trumpet stationed near the president's throne. The three
chariots shot off bravely with the swiftness of arrows, running
nearly abreast of each other till near the middle of the course,
when, to the surprise of all, the little red-headed gentleman
with the asses got ahead of the other two, and by dint of a
most vigorous system of pricking reached the goal two minutes
before them.

No pen or pencil can give an adequate picture of the deep,
subdued rage which glowed in Colonel Percy's eye, and covered his pale cheek and forehead with a dark, red flush of
anger. He threw one glance of concentrated malignity on the
fortunate winner, and then throwing the reins to a groom who
stood near in attendance, leapt from his chariot, and mingled
with the crowd.

It is not my intention to give a full and detailed account of
all that took place on this memorable day. I shall merely
glance at the transactions that followed and then proceed to
topics more nearly connected with my tale.

The sports of horse-racing, wrestling, and bull-fighting followed, in all of which Colonel Percy was engaged. In the first,
his favorite horse Tornado carried away the gold chaplet from
ten of the most renowned steeds in Verdopolis. In the second,
he himself successively overcame five powerful antagonists, and
in the third, when everyone else turned in dismay from a
mighty red bull of the Byson breed, after it had ripped up ten
horses, and gored their riders to death, he mounted Tornado,
and with a red crest waving from his Hussar's cap and a scarlet
cloak depending from his shoulders, rode courageously into the
middle of the amphitheatre. The combat for a long time was

dubious; but at length by a well-timed stroke his lance drank the huge monster's heart's blood, and it fell bellowing to the earth, which was crimson with its gore.

The last prize now remained to be tried for. It was that of archery. Here, too, Colonel Percy presented himself as a competitor. The mark was a tall white wand set at a distance of sixty feet. Twenty noble members of the Archer's Association, all accounted marksmen of the first order, contended for this prize. But the arrows of all fell either more or less wide of the mark. It now became Colonel Percy's turn. He advanced, and discharged a carefully directed arrow, which, though it came much nearer than any of the rest, failed also in hitting the appointed mark. The heralds, now, according to an established form, demanded if there were anyone amongst the spectators who would undertake to shame the unsuccessful archers. A dead silence followed this demand, for none thought themselves qualified to attempt an enterprise apparently so impracticable, and the President proceeded to adjudge the prize to him whose arrow had come nearest, in default of a better.

He had scarcely uttered the words, when a young man of a form as noble and majestic as that which the ancients attributed to Apollo, advanced from the crowd. His dress and appearance I have described before, for it was the identical stranger who on the previous night had arrived at the Genii's Inn. But now instead of the green bonnet and plume which he then wore, a helmet covered his head, and the visor being closed, entirely concealed his features.

"My lord," said he, approaching the president's throne, "will you permit me the honour of discharging a single arrow before you and the fair rewarder of victory? I delayed my request till now that I might not deprive Colonel Percy of the prize which justly falls to his lot."

Bravey readily gave his consent, and the stranger, stationing himself twenty feet further off than the appointed distance, unslung his bow and quiver which hung at his shoulder, chose

an arrow, tightened his string, and ere another second had
elapsed, the splintering of the white wand proclaimed his triumph and skill. A loud thundering cheer rose from the thousands gazing round, and when it had subsided, Bravey, rising
from his seat, declared that he rescinded his former decision regarding the prize, and awarded it to the successful stranger.
All eyes now turned to Colonel Percy. But no symptom of
mortification or anger appeared either in his countenance or
behaviour. On the contrary, he turned immediately to the unknown, and with the most friendly cordiality of manner, con-
gratulated him on his good fortune. His civilities were received,
however, with a cold and haughty courtesy which told that they
were unwelcome as effectually as the most prompt and decided
rejection of them could have done.

Still the Colonel did not seem piqued, but continued to converse with his unsocial conqueror in the free and unembar-
rassed strain which was natural to him as a man of the world.

"Upon my word," observed Ensign Bud, who with his friend
Gifford (for he had persuaded the old gentleman to accompany him to see the games) was seated in the front row of
seats, "upon my word, I believe the Colonel has some fiendish
scheme of revenge in his mind or he would never put on that
smooth quiet face."

"Doubtless," returned Gifford. "But who is that fantastically
arrayed foreigner? Methinks I have heard a voice like his before, though where or when I cannot for my life call to mind."

Bud was about to reply, but he was prevented by the loud
summons of the herald and the sudden rich swell of music
which burst grandly forth as the victors advanced to the foot
of the throne and one by one knelt before Lady Emily Charlesworth from whose hands they were to receive their recompense.

First came the carroty-locked hero of the cart and asses.

"Sir," said the lady as she strove vainly to suppress the smile
which his odd appearance excited, "you have this day gained a
miraculous victory over one of the most gallant and high-born

gentlemen of Verdopolis and are well worthy of the golden wreath which I thus twine around your illustrious temples."

"Thank you, madam," replied he, bowing low. "The Colonel's certainly a Roman, but I've matched him well today, and if you knew all, you'd say so too."

"I do not doubt your ability to match any man," she replied laughing, "and the Colonel, in my opinion, has no reason to be ashamed of his defeat, since it was effected by such a consummate master in the art of overreaching as you appear to be."

He thanked her again, and with another low bow gave place to Colonel Percy. As he, the claimer of three crowns, knelt gracefully at her feet, and whispered some flattering compliment in an undertone, Lady Emily seemed visibly embarrassed. She did not blush, but her forehead, before so open and smiling, grew dark and sad. For a moment she sat silent as if scarcely knowing how to address him, but almost immediately regaining her self-possession, said in a soft yet firm voice while with her slender and bejeweled fingers she bound the garland among his thickly clustered light brown curls, "It gives me pleasure to be the instrument of rewarding one who has not found his equal in three ardent contests. I trust our city will have as able a champion in every succeeding anniversary of the African Olympic Games."

"Fair lady," replied the Colonel, "your approbation would be worth more to me than the transitory applause of ten thousand times the number that have shouted at my trivial exploits today."

"Strive to deserve it," said she, in a low, quick voice, "and it shall not be withheld."

The herald now summoned the nameless stranger to draw near. Slowly and half reluctantly he advanced.

"Shall I bid the attendants to remove your helmet?" asked Lady Emily, smiling.

The unknown shook his head, but made no reply.

"Well," returned she playfully, "you are an uncourteous though a gallant archer. But notwithstanding your refusal to comply with my request, I will acknowledge that I think you worthy of the bright garland which I thus twine amongst the eagle's feathers which form your crest." He rose, and with a stately inclination of the head withdrew.

All was now concluded. The first celebration of the African Olympic Games was past, and amidst a loud and triumphant peal of warlike music, the mighty assembly of a million souls broke up and, with a crush and tumult that might have annihilated worlds, left the amphitheatre.

This dispersion I need not describe. No lives that I am aware of were lost, but hundreds of bags, pockets, fobs, and reticules yielded up their contents in the *mêlée,* while thousands of sides were bruised almost to mummies by an equal proportion of elbows. Amongst the principal sufferers, I am sorry to inform the reader our worthy friend, Mr. Gifford, must be reckoned. At the first crush, in spite of Ensign Bud's supporting arm, which was tenderly passed round the excellent antiquary's waist, he fell prone to the ground, and in attempting to rise, got entangled among the extended legs of half a score of French messieurs, who, greatly to their own edification, were pursuing their way through the huge press, not on their heels like sensible people, but on their heads. When these gentlemen felt the not very slight pressure of Mr. Gifford's falling carcass, they testified their sense of its inconvenience by that disagreeable agitation of the limbs called kicking. With the utmost difficulty, and with the loss of his best hat and wig, the lawyer was at length rescued.

But he had hardly gone twelve paces, when his shoes were trodden from his feet and five minutes later his Sunday coat, a rich black plush, was torn violently from his back and borne off by some audacious thief. Groaning and sighing, he still, with the assistance of Bud, continued gradually and painfully to push his way, and had almost cleared the thickest part of the crowd when a hand was unceremoniously introduced into his breeches pockets and all the contents most dexterously extracted. But I need not trouble the reader with more of the unhappy man's misfortunes. Suffice it to say that he did at length get home, and was put to bed with unbroken bones. Hot gruel and brandy administered in large doses induced a comfortable night's rest; and next morning when he awoke, he was able to curse all games, whether Greek, Roman, or African, in unmeasured terms, and to denounce instant vengeance on all who should hereafter propose attendance on their vanities to him.

Chapter the Third

THE sun which had risen so brightly and cheerfully sank to repose with a magnificence worthy of its glorious advent. A short twilight followed. The sea billows for a time rolled in a dimly lustrous light to the fading shore. Then came the moon. The evening stars began to look out singly from the soft, pure sky. The night wind rose, and before it a few pearly clouds, which had been resting motionless on the horizon, glided away beyond the skirting hills. At this tranquil hour the unknown archer, emerging from a grove on the Niger's shady banks, where he had been walking since he left the arena, turned his back to Verdopolis, and striking into a bye-path which led up the, at that period, wild valley in which our city lies, (for there were then no gardens or palaces and but few cultivated fields to variegate its natural beauties), soon forgot in the calm evening hush which surrounded him all remembrance of the scene which he had quitted an hour before.

Slowly he entered a little sequestered glen formed by the juncture of two lofty hills, whose summits were covered with wood, but whose bases, excepting here and there a tall, spreading tree, exhibited a green slope of unencumbered pasture land. He stopped, and leaning on the tall spear which, as I have before mentioned, he carried in one hand, stood a few minutes gazing at the lovely moonlight landscape which surrounded him on every side. Then drawing a bugle from his belt, he blew a clear but not loud blast, which awoke many faint echoes in the wooded hills above. After a brief interval of expectation, steps were heard approaching, and a figure wrapped in a mantle entered from the opposite end of the valley.

"Andrew," said the archer, "is that you, my lad?"

"Yes," replied a voice, whose shrill, childish tones, and the speaker's diminutive size announced the tender age of the new comer.

"Come hither then and show me where you have hid the baggage. I am half dead with hunger, for it is full twelve hours since I have either eaten or drunk."

Andrew immediately scampered off, and in a few minutes returned with a large portmanteau on his shoulders. He now threw aside his mask; and the bright moonshine revealed the person of a boy who might be about thirteen years of age, though from his countenance he seemed upwards of twenty, the sharp, keen features lighted by a pair of little, quick, cunning eyes, retaining no traces of that juvenile rotundity which is considered the principal characteristic of a child. His dress was as singular as that of his master, being a short plaided petti-coat or kilt, and a round cap of the same stuff, and laced leather buskins. He speedily unlocked the trunk, and took from it a kind of basket, the contents of which when spread on the clean and smooth sward under the shadow of a mag-nificent elm tree, formed a supper which no hungry man would have passed by with contempt. There was a couple of cold fowls, a loaf of white bread, some cheese, a bottle of palm wine, a vessel of the purest water, which Andrew had procured from a small rivulet which half-hidden by wild flowers washed the roots of the ancient elm tree as it wandered slowly through the valley. While the archer satisfied the cravings of his own appe-tite, he did not forget his follower who sat at a little distance ravenously devouring one of the fowls and a large portion of bread and cheese. When their meal was concluded and the fragments were cleared away, Andrew produced from the trunk a large plaided cloak in which his master wrapped him-self; and, lying down on the clean dewy grass with a moss-grown stone for his pillow, he, as well as the boy who lay at his feet, were soon lulled by the low wind rustling in their leafy canopy and drowsy murmur of the monotonous stream to a deep and dreamless slumber. An hour elapsed, and they still continued in a state of the most profound repose. The moon now high in heaven shone with a silvery clearness that almost transformed night into a fairer noon. In Arthur's words, or something like them, "all felt the influence of moonlight's milder day," when a human step suddenly broke the delicious calm reigning around, and (unromantic incident) the apparition not of

> "A lady fair and bright
> With a crown of flowers and a robe of light,"

but of a smart footman in a blue coat with silver epaulettes appeared stealing down from the brow of one of the nearest hills. Softly, almost noiselessly, he advanced to the unsuspecting Andrew and, clapping a gag into his mouth which happened to be wide open, bore him off, kicking and struggling in his arms. Andrew's abduction, however, did not last long. An hour had scarcely passed before he returned alone, and without awakening his master to inform him what had occurred, he lay down in his former place, and in a few minutes was as fast asleep as ever.

The bursting sunshine and singing birds aroused the archer just as the first beams broke forth in summer splendour. Springing lightly from his hard couch, he stirred with his foot the still slumbering page.

"Get up, Andrew," said he, "and roll out the contents of that trunk onto the grass. I must change this outlandish gear before I venture again into the city, so stir yourself, boy. And, here, help me first to unbuckle this belt. Why," continued he as the lad rose up reluctantly, rubbing his eyes and yawning like one overcome with sleep, "now what ails you, child? Have you been disturbed by fairies tonight that you are so sluggish and drowsy in the morning?"

"No, not I," said Andrew, laughing rather hollowly, fixing his keen eyes on his master's face as if he would have penetrated to his inmost thoughts. "No, but I have been troubled with some ugly dreams."

"Ugly dreams; you little idiot! What were they about?"

"About selling my soul to the Old Gentleman."

"Well, did you complete the bargain?"

"Yes, and sealed it with a written oath."

"Come, that was managing the affair in a businesslike way, but now a truce to your nonsense, sir, and help me on with this strait waistcoat."

In a few minutes the archer had stripped off his becoming, though peculiar, dress, and assumed in its stead a fashionable suit of clothes, consisting of a blue frock coat that had something of a military air, and white waistcoat and pantaloons.

"Now," said he, when he had completed his toilette, "do you stay here, Andrew. I am going to the city, and shall most probably be back before evening. Keep close in the wood till I return, and speak to no mortal creature."

Andrew loudly promised implicit obedience, and his master took his departure.

The archer in his new costume displayed none of that awkwardness which people usually feel when attired in a novel garment for the first time. On the contrary, it was evident from the perfect ease and grace of his movements, which all partook of the lofty and martial character, that he was not unaccustomed to such a mode of dress. With a slow, melancholy step he retraced the winding bye-path by which he had ascended the valley on the previous evening. The passengers he met were few and far between for in those days it was a road but little frequented. Two or three milkmaids singing on their way and a few illegal, rare lads who were returning from poaching overnight among the hills, together with five or six straightish-legged gentlemen, "wahking out befahr braukfast to get an auppetite to de [malons?] and brahd and bautter," were the only persons with whom he exchanged a morning's salutation; and these did not make their appearance till the latter end of the walk.

At about eight o'clock he reached Verdopolis. Entering at the North Gate, he proceeded through a series of streets, squares, rows, and alleys, along which, even at this early hour,

the living stream of population had begun to flow rapidly, till
he reached a quiet street leading from Monmouth Square,
formed by two rows of respectable-looking houses whose white
window curtains and green Venetian blinds proclaimed the
comfortable circumstances of those who inhabited them. Halting at the twelfth mansion, he gave a rousing alarm by means
of the well-scoured, bright, brass knocker. In about two minutes, the door was opened by a clean-looking elderly dame,
who, the moment she caught a glimpse of our hero's person,
uttered a loud exclamation of surprise.

"Bless us, Mr. Leslie!" cried she, "is that you? Lord! My
poor eyes never thought to see your handsome face again."

"It is me indeed, Alice, but how is your master? Is he at
home?"

"At home? Yes indeed, where else should he be, I wonder,
when you are standing at his door? But come in, and I'll run
to tell him the good news this minute."

Here the good woman led the way forward and, showing
Mr. Leslie to an apartment, ran off to do her errand.

The room into which she had ushered him was a middle-
sized parlour comfortably and even elegantly furnished. A
bright fire was burning in the polished steel bars of a handsome grate, and all the paraphernalia of a good breakfast appeared on a snow-white damask cloth which covered a round
table in the centre of the room. But what principally attracted
the eyes was a number of very beautiful oil-paintings, principally portraits arranged with judgement on the wall. All betrayed the hand of a genuine master in the art, and some were
executed with surprising grace and delicacy.

The visitor's countenance expressed something like astonishment as he looked carefully round. But his attention was soon
attracted by the unclosing of the door. He started up and
stepped eagerly forward as a young man rather above the middle size with a pale but interesting countenance and large, intelligent black eyes entered.

"Well, my dear Frederick," said he, "I need not inquire how you are. Your appearance and that of the house tells me; and I suppose I have now only to congratulate you on fortune's altered disposition."

"My Noble Benefactor!" began Frederick De Lisle, while a flush of joy suffused his colourless cheek. "How I rejoice to see you once again! Are you still Mr. Leslie, the artist, or may I now be permitted to address you as—"

"No, no," interrupted his guest, "let Leslie be my name for the present. But Frederick, you must have made good use of the small sum I gave you, if it has entitled you to reside in such a comfortable house as this."

"Yes," replied the young man, "I think I may fairly claim the praise of having employed it to the best advantage. Yet it was not that alone that has obtained the affluence I now enjoy. Your Lordship must know that about three years since I fell in love (to use the common phrase) with a young and very lovely girl who soon appreciated the sincerity of my affection, and returned it. Obstacles, however, apparently insurmountable, opposed our union. Her parents were rich, and they disdained to unite their daughter to a man whose whole wealth lay in a brush and palette.

"For a long time Matilda wept and entreated in vain, but at length her altered looks, her pallid cheek, and her attenuated form so far moved their compassion that they promised to sanction our marriage on the condition that I should previously free myself from the pecuniary embarrassment in which I was then entangled. This, however, was impossible. I had scarcely sufficient employment to secure bread, and as to laying by anything, that was not to be thought of. At this wretched period your lordship consented to become my pupil. The liberal salary which you paid me enabled me to discharge my debts in part, and by the aid of your further munificent gift when you left Verdopolis, I ultimately cleared the whole. My dear Matilda's parents kept their word, and about six months since,

I was made the happiest of men. Employment has since poured in rapidly upon me, and I trust that fame, the meed for which I have striven so long and perseveringly under distresses and difficulties that might have daunted the spirit of a saint, will at length reward my unwearied endeavours."

Here the door again opened, and Mrs. De Lisle entered. She was a young and elegant woman with a pretty face and very genteel manners. Her husband introduced our hero to her as "Mr. Leslie, the gentleman of whom you have often heard me speak." She curtsied and replied with a significant smile, "I have indeed. And the pleasure of seeing him in my house is as great as it is unexpected."

All three now sat down to a substantial breakfast of coffee, eggs, ham, and bread and butter. The conversation during this meal was animated and interesting, Mrs. De Lisle joining in it with a propriety and good taste which did honour to Frederick's choice of a wife. When it was over, she left the room, pleading as an excuse for her absence the necessity of attending to household concerns. The two gentlemen being thus left alone recommended the conversation in which they had been engaged before breakfast. Presently, however, they were again interrupted by the arrival of a carriage and the entrance of Alice to announce Colonel Percy and Lady Emily Charlesworth.

"Ah!" said De Lisle, "this is fortunate. Your Lordship, I think, will recollect Lady Emily. She used to come often when you painted at my house, and would sit for hours conversing with you about the fine arts. My lord, what is the matter? Are you ill?"

"No, Frederick," replied Leslie, though the deadly paleness which overspread his countenance seemed to contradict the truth of what he said. "Merely a sudden pain in the head, to which I am subject. It will soon pass off. But in the meanwhile, I should not like to be seen by the strangers. Will they come into this apartment?"

"No, I have ordered them to be shown into my study. Lady E. is come to sit for her portrait, which I am painting for Colonel Percy, to whom it is said she is shortly about to be united. They will make a fine couple. Pity the Colonel is not as good as he is handsome."

"De Lisle," said Leslie, quickly, "I think it would amuse me if I could watch you paint this morning, but at the same time I should like to remain concealed myself. Can you not contrive some means of effecting this?"

"Easily, my lord. The library window looks into my studio. You may sit there and amuse yourself if you like."

"Come, then," returned Leslie. And both left the room together.

The library into which De Lisle conducted his guest was a small apartment furnished with a few well chosen books, principally of the *belles lettres* class. One window looked into the little garden at the back of the house, and the other, partly shaded by a green curtain, formed a post of observation by which the studio might be easily reconnoitred. Here Leslie placed himself. The blood returned in full force to his pale cheeks as he beheld Lady Emily, more beautiful than he had seen her at the games, reclining gracefully on a sofa. A large velvet carriage mantle trimmed in costly fur fell in rich folds from her shoulders. Her hat which was ornamented with a splendid plume of ostrich feathers she had laid aside; and her hair, turned up behind and fastened with a gold comb, fell down on each side of her face in a luxurious profusion of glossy brown ringlets. She was quietly arranging the collar of a small silken-haired spaniel which lay on her lap, and appeared to take little notice of the passionate protestations of the Colonel, who was kneeling devotedly beside her. This circumstance, however, was unnoticed by Leslie. He marked only the attitude of both, and an indignant frown darkened his lofty brow. Their love conference, however, (if such it was) was soon interrupted by the entrance of De Lisle.

"Good morning," said he bowing low.

"Good morning," replied Colonel Percy. "Now, sir, call up all your skill; summon inspiration to your aid, for the beauty you have to depict is not earthly but heavenly."

"I have," replied the artist, as he seated himself at his easel and began to touch the lovely though still unfinished resemblance which was placed there. "I hope you do not consider the attempt I have already made quite a failure."

"No, not quite. But Mr. Painter, surely you have not the vanity to imagine that an imitation in oil and earths, however skillfully managed, can equal the bright reality of such a form and face as that you have now before you."

"Do you mean yourself, Colonel, or me?" inquired the fair sitter, shyly.

"You, to be sure. Why do you ask the question?"

"Because you gave so many furtive glances into that mirror that I thought your glowing panegyric must have been designed for the figure therein reflected."

"Hum! I was merely admiring the countenance of a tolerably good-looking monkey which I saw peering through that window at you, and which, by the bye, I have seen before in your company, De Lisle."

Lady Emily turned to the point indicated. But nothing was now visible. She continued to sit for about two hours. Then, becoming weary of a compulsory state of inactivity, she ordered the carriage to be called, and together with her escort, Colonel Percy, departed.

Chapter the Fourth

CLYDESDALE CASTLE, the seat of the Marquis of Charlesworth, was one of the few mansions which at that period adorned the Glass Town Valley. It was a large and magnificent structure erected during the time of the Second Twelves.[7] The architecture was not of the light Grecian cast in which our modern villas are built, but grand and substantial. Tall arched windows lighted the lofty turrets, and pillared Norman gateways gave entrance to the numerous vast halls which were contained under its embattled roofs. The noble proprietor of this feudal residence was uncle and guardian to the beautiful Lady Emily Charlesworth, whose parents dying when she was yet a child committed her with their last breath to the protection of her only surviving relative.

This trust the Marquis discharged faithfully, as the reader may perceive from the circumstances of his having appointed John Gifford, Esquire, tutor to his niece. And she in her turn regarded him with that affection which an amiable mind will always cherish towards those from whom it receives any benefit.

About a week after the time mentioned in my last chapter, Lady Emily was sitting one afternoon in her solitary chamber in the west turret. She was alone. Her elbow rested on the little work table beside her, and her full, dark eyes fixed with an expression of deep melancholy on the blue and far-distant mountain boundary which appeared through the open lattice. I cannot tell what she was thinking of, for I never heard. But soon a few tears trickling down her soft cheek betrayed that her meditations belonged rather to *Il Penseroso* than *L'Allegro*. These mute monitors seemed to rouse her from a sad revery. With a deep sigh she turned away from the window and, drawing a harp toward her which stood near, began to sing in a sweet, low voice the following *petit chanson:*

The night fell down all calm and still,
The moon shone out o'er vale and hill,
  Stars trembled in the sky;
Then forth into that sad pale light
There came a gentle lady bright,
With veil and cymar spotless white,
  Fair brow and dark blue eye.

Her lover sailed on the mighty deep,
  The ocean wild and stern;
And now she walks to pray and weep
  For his swift and safe return.

Full oft she pauses as the breeze
Moans wildly through those giant trees,
  As startled at the tone;
The sounds it waked were like the sigh
Of spirit's voice through midnight sky,
So soft, so sad, so dreamily
  That wandering wind swept on.

And ever as she listened
  Unbidden thoughts would rise,
Till the pearly teardrops glistened
  All in her starlike eyes.

She saw her love's proud battleship
Tossed wildly on the storm-dark deep,
By the roused wind's destroying sweep,
  A wrecked and shattered hull;
And as the red bolt burst its shroud
And glanced in fire o'er sea and cloud,
She heard a peal break deep and loud,
  Then sink to echoes dull.

And as that thunder died away,
She saw amid the rushing spray
  Her Edward's eagle plume.
While thus that deathly scene she wrought
And viewed in the deep realms of thought
  His soul-appalling doom,

A voice through all the forest rang:
Up like a deer the lady sprang—
  " 'Tis he! 'tis he!" she cried,
And ere another moment's space
In time's unresting course found place,
By Heaven, and by Our Lady's grace!
  Lord Edward clasped his bride.

The song was ended but her fingers yet lingered among the harp strings from which they drew long wailing notes whose plaintive sound seemed all unsuited to the happy termination of the romance she had just been warbling. The tears she had before checked were now suffered to flow freely, and faint sobs were beginning to reveal the secret grief which oppressed her, when suddenly the door opened and a servant entered with the intelligence that a gentleman had arrived who wished to see her ladyship.

"A gentleman!" exclaimed Lady Emily, wiping her eyes and trying to assume some degree of composure. "What is he like? Have you never seen him before?"

"Never, my lady; he is a personable young man with a very piercing look."

"Did he not tell you his name?"

"No, I asked him what it was but he gave me no answer."

"That is strange. Is he alone or accompanied by servants?"

"He has one little page with him, but that is all."

"Well, show him into my drawing room and say that I will be down directly."

The servant bowed and withdrew. Lady Emily now hastened to remove the traces of recent tears. She bathed her face in water, carefully arranged her dress, and smoothed her dishevelled ringlets. Having thus discharged the duties of the toilette, she proceeded to attend the unknown visitor.

With a light tread, she glided from her apartment down the staircase and through a portion of the corridor till she reached the drawing room. Its rose-wood folding doors rolled back noiselessly at her touch on their well-polished hinges, and she entered unobserved by the stranger whose tall and kingly form stood before her opposite the great arched window through which he was gazing with folded arms.

For an instant she paused to admire the statue-like dignity of his attitude. Her heart, she could not tell why, beat wildly as she looked at him. But fearing that he might turn suddenly and take her unawares, she proclaimed her presence by a gentle cough. He started and turned round. Their eyes met. The pensive expression which had dwelt in Lady Emily's vanished like magic, and a brilliant ray of animation sparkled in its stead.

"Leslie! dear Leslie!" cried she, springing joyfully toward him. "Is it you? How long have you been in Verdopolis? Why did you not return long since? Oh, how often I have thought and cried about you since you went away!"

She was going on, but observing that a cold and haughty bow was the only return her cordial welcome met with, stopped in embarrassment. A mutual silence of some moments followed, which at length was broken by Leslie, who stood with his arms still folded gazing earnestly at her.

"Beautiful hypocrite," said he, and paused again, while his finely cut lip quivered with the strongest emotion.

"What is the matter?" asked Lady Emily faintly. "Have I been too forward, too ardent in my expressions of pleasure at seeing you again after so long an absence?"

"Cease this unworthy acting," said her lover sternly, "and do not think so meanly of me as to imagine I can be deceived by pretensions so flimsy. You have been too well employed during my absence to think much of me. Another, and doubtless in your opinion a higher prize, has been ensnared by your false though incomparable loveliness, and now I come to cast you from me as a perjured woman, though my heartstrings should burst in agony with the effort. But," he continued in a voice of thunder, while all the lightnings of jealousy gleamed in his fierce dark eyes, "I will not tamely give you up to the scoundrel who has dared to supplant me. No! He shall have an even struggle. He shall wade through blood to obtain his stolen reward."

"Leslie, Leslie," replied Lady Emily in a soft soothing tone, "you have indeed been deceived but not by me. Sit down now calmly and tell me all you have heard to my disadvantage. You see I am not angry, notwithstanding this is a far different reception to what I had ever expected to meet with from you."

"Siren!" said her yet unappeased lover. "Who would imagine that so sweet a voice could be employed in the utterance of falsehoods, or that such a lovely countenance should be a mere mask to conceal the hollow insincerity of a coquette's heart?"

Lady Emily, whose fortitude was unequal to sustain this continued severity, now burst into tears. Leslie, deeply moved by her distress, whether real or apparent, began to reflect what right he had to upbraid her in such haughty terms, and to ask himself whether the reports which had awakened his suspicions might not be in themselves destitute of foundation.

Under the influence of these thoughts he approached the sofa on which she had thrown herself when unable to stand from excess of agitation, and sitting down beside her, took her hand. But she withdrew it with becoming pride.

"Mr. Leslie," said she starting up, "your words show the regard you once pretended to entertain for me is no more. You desire that we should part. And be assured that whatever pain I may experience in renouncing one whom I have hitherto looked upon as my dearest friend, yet I shall not hesitate a moment to take this necessary though painful step. Farewell then, I trust that the bitterness of remorse for wrongs inflicted upon others will never be added to your portion of this world's evils."

As she spoke the blood rushed back to her terror-blanched cheek. Her tearful eye shone like a meteor, and her slender form seemed dilated with the swell of justly aroused pride. Leslie sat silent till she turned to depart. Then springing from his seat, he hastily placed himself between her and the door.

"You shall not go," said he, "I am convinced that I was mistaken. The man who could hear your words and look on your countenance would be more or less than human if he could still doubt that you were innocent."

Lady Emily continued to advance with an irresolute step, but a smile now began to dimple her fair cheek.

"Well, Leslie," she said, "you are like a true artist, one of the most capricious of men. But this moment you were so angry with me, that I was almost afraid to remain in the room, and now you will not let me leave you. But," she continued, while the arch smile more fully lit up her face, "perhaps I shall not choose to remain now. I really am very angry and feel a great mind to tell Colonel Percy next time he comes (for I suppose he is the person you are jealous of) that I have cut his rival, and shall marry him forthwith."

"Hush, Emily," replied Leslie, leaving his post near the door, "I cannot bear to hear you speak thus, even in jest. But come, let us sit down, and tell me seriously who and what is the wretch whose name has just passed your lips."

"He is a very handsome and accomplished man," she replied provokingly, "and, my uncle says, one of the bravest soldiers in the army."

Leslie's eye flashed, and his brow darkened again. "Am I still to think," he asked, "that you entertain a partiality for the infamous villain?"

"Goodness," exclaimed the lady, "can't I like two people at once? How monopolizing you are!"

The convulsive grasp with which her lover seized her hand and the flush which rose suddenly to his cheek warned her that she had trifled long enough. She proceeded in an altered tone, "But, though the Colonel is all I have described him, yet I assure you you have nothing to fear, for I detest him most thoroughly, and nothing on earth should either tempt or compel me to change my name from Emily Charlesworth to Emily Percy."

"Bless you!" exclaimed the enthusiastic Leslie, "for that assurance. It has relieved me of a mighty load. But tell me, dearest, how these vile reports by which I have been misled arose. Colonel Percy I presume visited you."

"He did, and made proposals to me, but I remembered the absent, and peremptorily rejected him. He then applied to my uncle, who, as ill luck would have it, behaved like all guardians and commanded me forthwith to receive him as my husband elect. I demurred, my uncle insisted, the Colonel implored. Hints of compulsion were thrown out. This only served to render me more restive. The chaplain was sent for. I then had recourse to tears. The Colonel, seeing me so far softened, became a little insolent. He said that instead of crying and pouting, I might think myself very highly honoured by the preference of one whom all the ladies in Verdopolis would be glad of. This effectually awoke my spirit. I got up, for I had been kneeling to both the oppressors, and told him that he was the object of my scorn and hatred, and that he never need hope to obtain any interest in a heart that was entirely devoted to another. When he heard this, he stormed and frowned just as you did just now. My uncle asked who the favoured suitor was. I said instantly that he was neither lord nor knight, but a young and gifted artist. If you had seen the fit of astonishment that seized them both! They stood with mouths gaping, and eyes staring like two images of surprise. The effect was perfectly ludicrous, and despite of fears which filled me, I laughed outright. This only irritated them still more. The Colonel swore that he would compel me to marry him or die, and my uncle took oath on belt and brand that no man from king to beggar, from duke to artist, should be my husband except Colonel Percy. I smiled, but said nothing. Well, for a while after this, I was confined to my room, and not suffered to cross the threshold, lest I might run away. This rigour injured my health. I grew pale and thin. My uncle (who I know loves me notwithstanding his harshness) perceived the change, and commanded that I should be set at liberty on condition of my consenting to accompany the Colonel for the purpose of having my portrait taken. The first time I went to De Lisle's in order to sit, Colonel Percy told me that he had discovered who my lover was, and had even seen him several times. This frightened me a little, but I consoled myself with the knowledge that you were at present absent from Verdopolis, and therefore out of his reach; but now you are returned, I fear greatly that he will never rest until he has accomplished your destruction by some means."

"Emily," said Leslie, as she concluded her brief narrative, "you have acted generously and truly. You have been faithful to a poor and friendless artist, or one whom you thought such, and have rejected a man whose birth, expectations, and personal accomplishments render him an object of the highest admiration to every other individual of your own sex. I now know with a degree of certainty which admits no shadow of doubt that you love me for myself, and that nothing of a selfish nature mingles with your regard. I owe it therefore to your disinterested affection to reveal my real rank and station in life. I am not what I seem, a servile minion of fortune, a low-born son of drudgery. No, the Head of Clan Albyn, the Earl of St. Clair, the Chieftain of the wild children of the mist, descends from a line of ancestors as illustrious as any whose brows were ever encircled by the coronet of nobility. Alliance with me will not bring you to want and beggary, but pure blood will be mingled, broad lands joined, and loving hearts united in bonds dissoluble only by death. Come with me then, Emily; shake off at once the shackles which restrain you, free yourself from the importunities of a villain. I will take you to my mountainous lands in the north, and you shall be at once Countess of Saint Clair and Lady of seven thousand of the bravest warriors that ever gathered round a chieftain's banner. My castle on Elimbos is larger than your uncle's here. And my brave clan will pay their lovely and gentle mistress the adoration due to a divinity."

As Leslie, or, as we must now call him, Roland Lord St.

Clair, revealed his rank and power, the proud blood mounted
to his forehead; his eye flashed like that of one of his own wild
eagles, and the majesty of his step and bearing as he slowly
paced the apartment, proclaimed the descendant of a hundred
earls. Lady Emily caught the lofty enthusiasm which infused a
higher beauty into his noble countenance, and, rising from her
seat, she frankly extended her hand towards him and said,
"Accept the pledge of my inviolable faith. Though the whole
earth should unite against me, I will never love another. 'True
till death' shall be my chosen motto. I cannot love you more
than I did, but I rejoice for your own sake that you can vie in
rank with the proudest nobles of Africa."

"Do you consent to go with me?" asked he.

"I do. At what time must I depart?"

"This night, at twelve o'clock, meet me in the chestnut
avenue."

"I will be punctual," said the lady, "and now, my lord, tell
me what your reason was for playing the incognito in Verdopolis."

"Why, Emily, you must know that I was educated in England. After leaving Oxford, I resided some time in London.
There I was, of course, admitted into the highest circles of society. Being young and rich, great attention was paid me. The
ladies, in particular, treated me very graciously. But I suspected that much of this especial favor was owing rather to
my rank and fortune than to my personal qualities. This idea
having once entered my head, I could not by any means drive
it out, so I determined to take a voyage to Africa and try
what luck would befall an unknown and apparently friendless
stranger.

"In Verdopolis I met with De Lisle. His manners and address pleased me, while his merits and poverty excited my
warmest sympathy. Enjoining the strictest secrecy, I told him
who I was and my motives for wishing to remain unknown.
Having some knowledge of painting, I determined to assume

the character of an artist and accordingly placed myself under De Lisle's tuition. At his house I met with you, for you used to come there occasionally under the protection of your worthy tutor, Mr. Gifford, to purchase copies and drawing materials. The consequence of these interviews I need not relate. In a short time we became firmly attached to each other. And when I was about to declare my rank, and formally to solicit your hand of Lord Charlesworth, I was suddenly called away to my northern estates among the Branni Mountains. Legal affairs and business connected with the clan unavoidably detained me for nearly twelve months, and now I have returned to Verdopolis for the double purpose of claiming you as my bride and, when that is accomplished, joining the Duke of Wellington's standard against the rebellious Ashantees."

"I have but one more question to ask," said Lady Emily, "how did the Colonel become acquainted with your person?"

"I know not, except it be by having seen me at De Lisle's house. I remember a gentleman strongly resembling him entering the studio one day while you were conversing with me, and regarding us with an eye of the strictest scrutiny. But the circumstance had slipped my memory till your question recalled it."

"There still remains a single point on which I wish to be satisfied," said Lady Emily, smiling as if a sudden thought had struck her. "Were you present at the Olympic Games in disguise?"

"I was."

"What dress did you wear?"

"The costume of my clan."

"Then you were the gallant archer whose arrow shivered the white wand when every other failed."

"You have guessed cleverly, Emily. It is as you say."

"Then depend upon it, my lord," said she seriously, "Colonel Percy recognized you. His eye is keener than a hawk's; and I saw him glance sharply at you when you half lifted your visor to speak. Could I have heard your voice, I should have remembered it, I am certain, and doubtless he did so. Oh, I fear his revengeful spirit will never rest till it has accomplished your destruction."

"Fear nothing for me, Emily. My sword is as good as his, and my arm also. If he causes a tear to spring from that bright eye, his heart's blood shall pay for it. And now, my dearest, farewell. We must part for the present. But before another sun rises, the conjoined powers of earth and hell will be insufficient to divide us. Only remember the appointed time. Be punctual, and trust to me for the rest."

Lady Emily repeated the promise she had before given, and the lovers separated, each to make the necessary preparations.

As Lord St. Clair left the drawing room, he saw a shadowy form hastily glide down the dark corridor. Fearful of their conversation having been overheard, he pursued the retreating figure. At first he appeared to be gaining some advantage, but suddenly it turned down a side passage, and he lost sight of it. Chagrined at this failure and somewhat apprehensive of what this nimble-footed personage's design might be in lurking so suspiciously about, he thought of returning back and acquainting Lady Emily with what he had seen. But just then the Marquis of Charlesworth's gruff, stern voice was heard in the hall; so our hero thought it best to take his departure instantly, lest his presence might be discovered by that dignitary and the whole plan of elopement blown up. He proceeded therefore to the stables, where he found both page and horse in readiness. Mounting his beautiful Arabian charger, with one glance at the western turret, and one sigh for his lady-love, he dashed out of the yard, and in a few minutes was half way on the road to Verdopolis.

Chapter the Fifth

FOR the present I must leave Lord St. Clair and Lady Charlesworth to see what Colonel Percy was about while they were preparing to cheat him so cleverly. The Colonel occupied a large and splendid mansion in Dimdim Square, then a fashionable quarter of the city, though now the favourite abode of briefless lawyers, non-commissioned officers, unpatronized authors, and others of the tag-rag and bob-tail species. This residence, together with the expensive establishment of servants, carriages, and so forth appertaining to it, was kept up partly by the owner's pay, partly by his gains at the billiard and card table, and partly by liberal borrowings from usurers on the strength of his great expectations. There, in a magnificent saloon furnished with all the elegance that luxury or taste could devise, Colonel Percy sat alone on the afternoon spoken of in my last chapter. His fine form was stretched in very unmilitary ease on a silken sofa. His languid eyes and pale cheek revealed the dissipation of the previous night, while the empty decanter and glass which stood on a table near him showed that the stimulus of wine had been employed to remove this lassitude, though without effect. While he was lying thus with his hands pressed to his lofty and aristocratic forehead, a window of the saloon was suddenly opened, and a man with a red head and ragged inexpressibles sprang in from without.

"Beast!" said Percy, starting up with a loud oath, "how dare you enter my house in such a brazenly impudent manner? How dare you come near me, in fact, after the manner in which you have lately treated me?"

This reception did not in the least seem to daunt the unabashed *entré* whom no doubt our readers will have already recognized as the hero of the ass-drawn chariot. On the contrary, he advanced with a smiling countenance, and seizing the Colonel's hand with his horny paw, replied, "How is all with you, my sweet Rogue? I am afraid you are not quite as your best friends could wish. That pale face and this feverish hand tell tales."

"Curse you for the heartiest scoundrel that ever deserved a hempen neckcloth," replied the Colonel, at the same time dashing the other hand into his face with a violence that would have felled any other man, but which only drew a horselaugh from the sturdy charioteer. "Curse you ten thousand times, I say. How in the name of body and soul dare you face me alone and without arms after our last transaction?"

"Why, what have I done to thee, my Emperor of Rogues?"

"What have you done to me, brute? Did I not bribe you with two hundred guineas to cut out Captain Wheeler from running his chariot at the games by becoming a competitor yourself with your vile cart and asses? Did I not give you fifty guineas more in advance to let me win? And after swearing a hundred oaths of fidelity, did you not break them all; and by so doing swindle me out of twenty thousand pounds, for I had laid a wager to that amount on my success?"

"Well, and if I did all this," replied the carroty-haired gentleman, "was it not just what you would have done in my situation? I had your two hundred and fifty pounds safe in my breeches pocket when by ill or good luck, which you please, as soon as it was publicly known that I was to run, upward of forty bets were laid against me. I accepted them all and so in self-defence was obliged to do my best. But come," he continued, "this is not what I intended to talk about. My purpose for coming here was to beg the loan of a few pounds. I have spent every farthing of what I got last week in drink and other matters."

This demand was made in a quiet, self-complacent tone, as if the request had been one of the most reasonable in the world. Colonel Percy could bear it no longer. Quivering all over and deadly pale with rage, he snatched a loaded pistol from his pocket and discharged it full at him. This attack, like the former, produced no other effect than a fiendish laugh. The shot flew from his head and in the rebound one of them struck the Colonel so smartly as to produce blood. Baffled in this manner a second time, he threw down the weapon and began to pace the apartment with furious strides. "Fool that I am," cried he. "Why do I waste my strength in vain? The demon, as I might have known before now, is impervious to fire or shot.[8] My fruitless attempts only expose me to his derision."

"Ha, ha, ha," shouted his tormentor. "That's true, Rogue, so now sit down, and let's have a little sensible conversation."

Percy, exhausted with the efforts he had made, threw himself mechanically into a chair. "S'death," said he in a calmer tone, "you are not a man. As sure as I live, you are an evil spirit in the flesh, a true fiend incarnate. No human being could have lived after a shower of such hailstones as those."

S'death (for such was the unblushing swindler's name) made no answer, but rising from his seat went to a sort of buffet, or side-board, on which stood several bottles of wine, &c., and taking a case of liqueurs, first helped himself to a brimming bumper and then pouring out another, advanced with it to Rogue, Percy, I mean.

"Here, Charmer," said he, lifting it to his lips, "here, taste this cordial. You look faintish, I think, and should have something to comfort your poor heart."

The Colonel, who at that time was no drunkard, whatever he may have become since, just sipped of the offered beverage, and returned it to Mr. S'death by whom it was annihilated at a draught.

The conversation was now carried on in a more animated and less violent strain than before. Percy's anger seemed to have been in some measure appeased when he found that it was useless to exert it against one whom he could not possibly injure. Still, however, half at least of every sentence they addressed to each other was composed of oaths and execrations. S'death continued to demand a loan of twenty pounds which Percy for some time refused, declaring that he had not that sum in the world. S'death then tried to intimidate him, and threatened to inform against him for certain highly criminal transactions in which he had been concerned. This had the desired effect. The Colonel immediately unfastened a diamond clasp from his stock, and throwing it on the floor, commanded him with an oath to take that and be off.

The hardened villain picked it up with a chuckle, and, going again to the side-board, helped himself to another tumbler of liqueur. He then made his exit through the open window, saying as he went away, "Good-bye, Rogue! At this moment I have bank-bills for two thousand pounds in each waistcoat pocket."

With these words he scampered off, followed by the discharge of a second pistol.

"Infernal scoundrel," said the Colonel, as he closed the sash with violence, "I wish the earth would yawn and swallow him up, or the skies rend and strike him dead with a flash of his native element."

As he uttered this pious aspiration, he flung himself again on the sofa, from which he had been roused by his unwelcome visitor.

Two hours elapsed before he was again disturbed, but at the end of that time a low tap was heard at the door.

"Come in, beast, whoever you are!" shouted he in a loud voice.

The door softly unclosed, and a footman in livery entered.

"What do you want now, scoundrel?" asked his master furiously.

"Merely to tell your honour that the Green Dwarf has just arrived quite out of breath and says he has important information to communicate."

"The Green Dwarf? Show him into my library, and say I'll come directly."

The servant bowed and left the room. Colonel Percy followed him almost immediately, and proceeded to the library. There we shall now leave him to revisit Clydesdale Castle.

Lord St. Clair had hardly left Lady Emily's private drawing room before her uncle, the Marquis of Charlesworth, entered it. He was a tall and stately old gentleman between sixty and seventy years of age. His gray locks, curled and powdered with the most scrupulous nicety, surrounded a countenance whose fresh weather-beaten skin, stern aquiline features, and peculiar expression would have at once marked him out to the attentive observer as a veteran soldier, even if his military jack boots and enormous sword had not done so more decidedly.

"Well, Emily!" said he, saluting his niece, who had run forward to meet him. "How are you this evening, love? I'm afraid you've had a dull day of it sitting here alone."

"O, no, uncle," said she, "I never in the least feel the want of company. My books and music and drawing give me sufficient employment without it."

"That's well. But I think you have not been quite alone this evening. Has not the Colonel been with you?"

"No," replied Lady Emily. "Why do you ask me, uncle?"

"Because I saw a very handsome horse standing in the yard, which I concluded to be his. But since it was not, pray what other visitor have you had?"

This was an unexpected question. Lady Emily, however, was not thrown off her guard by it. She instantly did what perhaps will not be thought very becoming in the heroine of a novel, viz: coined a little lie.

"Oh," said she carelessly, "I suppose the horse must have belonged to Mr. Lustring, the linen-draper's apprentice. He has been here this afternoon with some articles which I bought at his master's shop the other day. And now uncle," she continued, willing to change the conversation to some less ticklish subject, "tell me what you have been doing in the city today."

"Why," said he, "in the first place, I went to Waterloo Palace for the purpose of soliciting an audience of the Duke. Our interview lasted two hours, and when it was over, his Grace requested my company to dinner. There I saw the Duchess, who was as affable and agreeable as ever. She asked kindly after you, and desired me to say that she should be happy to have the pleasure of your society for a few weeks at Verdopolis."

"Sweet creature," exclaimed Lady Emily, "I love her more than anybody else in the world except you, uncle, and perhaps one or two besides. But did you see the little baby?"

"Yes."

"Is it a pretty child?"

"Remarkably so, but I fear it will be spoiled. The Duke seems disposed to indulge it in everything, and the Duchess's whole existence is evidently wrapped up in it."

"And no wonder! Pray, what is it called?"

"Arthur, I believe."

"Does it seem well-dispositioned?"

"I really don't know. It will be tolerably headstrong, I think. There was a regular battle between it and the nurse when she attempted to convey it out of the room after dinner. Now, have you any more questions to ask concerning the little imp?"

"Not at present. What did you do when you left the palace?"

"I stepped into the Genii's Inn and had a bottle of wine with Major Sterling. After that I proceeded to our barracks, where I had some business to transact with the officers of my regiment. When this was finished, I went to Mr. Trefoil's and purchased something for my niece to wear on her wedding day, which I intend shall soon arrive."

Here the Marquis took from his pocket a small casket, in which, when it was opened, appeared a superb diamond necklace with ear-rings, finger rings, and brooches to correspond. He threw them into Lady Emily's lap. A tear started into her eye as she thanked him for this costly present, and at the same time thought what an act of disobedience to her kind uncle's will she was about to commit.

He observed it and said, "Now my love, let us have no piping! The Colonel is an admirable fellow, a little wild, perhaps, but marriage will soon cure him of that."

A long silence followed. Both uncle and niece, judging by their pensive countenances, seemed to be engaged in sorrowful reflections. At length the former resumed the conversation by saying, "In a few days, Emily, we shall have to be separated for some time."

"How?" exclaimed Lady Emily, starting and turning pale, for her thoughts instantly reverted to Colonel Percy.

"Why, my love," replied the Marquis, "news has lately arrived that the Ashantees are mustering strong. The Duke therefore considers an addition to the army requisite. Several regiments have been ordered out as reinforcements, among which number is the Ninety-sixth, and I being commander must of course accompany it. It is on this account that the Duchess of Wellington has invited you to pay her a visit, for she very kindly considers that you will feel Clydesdale Castle a very dull and lonely residence in my absence. I hope you will accept the invitation, my love."

"Certainly," replied Lady Emily in a faint voice, for her heart misgave her when she thought of the deceitful part she was acting towards the careful and affectionate guardian from whom she was about to be separated, perhaps forever.

Supper was now announced, and when this meal was concluded, Lady Emily, pleading a slight headache as an excuse for retiring early, bade her uncle goodnight, and with a heavy heart proceeded to her little chamber in the western turret. When she reached and secured the door, she sat down to consider a little of the decisive step she was about to take. After a long and deep meditation she arrived at the conclusion that there were but two practicable modes of acting, namely: either to obey her uncle, prove false to her lover, and sacrifice her own happiness for life, or to disobey the Marquis, be faithful to St. Clair, and run away with him according to her promise.

Driven to such a dilemma, who can blame her if she made a choice of the latter course, and determined to run the hazard of an elopement rather than to await the evils which delay might produce? Just as her resolution was fixed, the castle bell began in deep and solemn tones to announce the eventful hour of midnight. Each stroke of the resounding hammer seemed in her excited imagination a warning voice enjoining her instant departure. As the last hollow echo died away to the profoundest silence, she started from the chair, where she had hitherto sat motionless as a statue, and proceeded to wrap herself in a large hooded mantle such as was then frequently worn by the ladies of Verdopolis and which served the treble purpose of a veil, hat, and cloak.

Thus attired, she stole noiselessly from her chamber, and instead of proceeding toward the grand stair-case, directed her steps to the winding turret stair which led to an unoccupied hall in which was an arched gate opening directly into the park. As she softly entered this hall, she perceived by the moonlight which was streaming brilliantly through the tall latticed windows a dark figure standing near the gate through which she was to pass. Lady Emily was not much of a philosopher, and this appearance startled her not a little, for she instantly remembered a traditionary story of a wicked fairy, who was said to haunt this apartment. Her fears on this head, however, were soon relieved by hearing the rattling of a bunch of keys accompanied by the gruff, murmuring tones of a man's voice.

"I wonder," said the supposed apparition in soliloquy, "I wonder what that beast of a light chose to go out for. It's a rare thing, to be sure, for me to be in this dog-hole at midnight without a candle. That last pint made my hand rather unsteady, and I can't see to find the key-hole."

Lady Emily recognized in the speaker a man-servant whose office it was to secure all the castle gates before retiring to rest. The urgency of her situation immediately suggested an expedient, which, considering the muddled state of the man's brain, could hardly fail of success. She wrapped herself closely in the mantle and, advancing into the middle of the hall, said in a voice as commanding as she could muster, "Mortal, I command thee to depart from the great fairy Ashurah's abode."

The effect of this ruse was instantaneous. He flung down the keys with a shout of terror and scampered off as fast as his heels could carry him. Lady Emily had now no difficulty in unbarring the portal and making her premeditated escape. With the lightness and swiftness of a liberated deer, she bounded across the moonlit lawn towards the appointed place of rendezvous. A chill and dreary wind was sweeping among the lofty chestnut trees as she wandered under their huge boughs, impatiently awaiting her lover's arrival. The uncertain light, now streaming through a wide opening as the swelling breeze suddenly bowed all the branches in one direction, and now, when it died away and they sprang back to their former station, flinging a thousand silvery chequers on the leaf-strewn path-way, produced shadows equally uncertain. Sometimes it seemed as if a hundred ghosts were gliding among the mighty trunks, beckoning with their dim hands and vanishing as she approached them. Occasionally, too, a cloud would suddenly obscure the moon; and then, in the dense darkness which followed, the creaking of branches, the rustling of leaves, and the wild howling of wind, formed a combination of doleful sounds which might have impressed the stoutest heart with terror.

For half an hour she continued to walk slowly about, shivering in the cold night air, and at intervals pausing to listen for some advancing step. At length she heard a rumbling noise like the wheels of some vehicle. It drew near. The tramp of horses' feet became distinctly audible, when suddenly it ceased altogether. Five anxious minutes passed. Nothing was heard. Lady Emily listened and listened. She began to doubt whether her ears had not deceived her, but now the rustling of dead leaves foretold an approaching footstep. She knew the tread: none but St. Clair had such a stately and martial stride. Forward she darted like an arrow from a bow, and in another instant was clasped to Lord Ronald's bosom.

After the first mute greetings were over, he said in a low smothered tone, "Come, dearest, let us not lose a moment. Silence and dispatch are necessary for our safety." They accordingly proceeded down the avenue, at the end of which a carriage was awaiting their approach. Into it Lady Emily was handed by her lover, who, as he warmly pressed the hand which had been put into his as she entered the chaise, whispered in the same suppressed voice as before, that he would follow her on horseback.

"Very well, my Lord," said Emily, gently returning his grasp.

He closed the door, mounted a horse which stood near, gave the word of departure, and soon by the aid of four wheels and six steeds, the fair runaway left her guardian's castle far behind. In less than a hour, they had rolled over the four miles of road which intervened between them and Verdopolis, passed through the wide streets of that city, now all still and desolate, and entered a great road which ran northward through an extensive forest.

After two hours of travelling through the dense gloom of woodland shade, the carriage turned aside from the main path into a bye-way. They now struck still deeper into the brown obscurity of oak and palm, elm and cedar. Darkly and dimly branch rose above branch, each uplifting a thicker canopy of night-like foliage till not a single ray of light could find an opening by which to direct the belated travellers passing underneath. At last to Lady Emily's great satisfaction, the trees began to grow thinner. Gradually they assumed a scattered appearance, and ere long, the carriage entered an open glade where, standing in the full brilliancy of moonlight, there appeared a lofty and ruinous tower. Wall-flowers were waving from its mouldering battlements, and ivy-tendrils twined gracefully round the stone mullions of windows from which the glass had long disappeared. Lady Emily shuddered as the carriage stopped before the iron gate of this dreary edifice.

"This will be a dismal hole to sleep in," said she to herself, "but why should I be afraid? St. Clair is certainly the best judge of the places we ought to halt at."

The door was now unfastened by a footman, who, as the Earl had not yet come up, offered to assist her in getting out of the carriage. When she had descended, the man proceeded to demand entrance. The loud, clamourous din which was produced by the agitation of the rusty knocker strangely interrupted the profound and solemn silence which reigned through the primeval forest, while it awoke a hollow echo within the gray, desolate ruin. After a long pause, the withdrawal of bolts and bars was heard. The portal slowly unfolded and revealed a figure whose appearance was in the most perfect keeping with everything around. It was that of an old woman bent double with the weight of years. Her countenance, all wrinkled and shrivelled, wore a settled expression of discontent, while her small red eyes gleamed with fiend-like malignity. In one shaking hand she held a huge bunch of rusty keys, and in the other a dimly glimmering torch.

"Well, Bertha," said the footman, "I have brought you a visitor. You must show her up to the highest chamber, for I suppose there is no other in a habitable condition."

"No. How should there, I wonder," replied the hag in an angry mumbling tone, "when nobody's slept in them for more than sixty long years. But what have you brought such a painted toy as this here for? There is no good in the wind, I think."

"Silence, you old witch," said the man, "or I'll cut your tongue out." Then addressing Lady Emily, he continued, "I hope, madam, you'll excuse such an attendant as she is for the present. Had there been time to procure a better, my master would not have failed to do so."

Lady Emily replied that she could make every allowance for old age, and was proceeding to speak a few kind words to the miserable being, when she turned abruptly away, and muttering, "Follow me, my fine madam, an you want to see your sleeping place," hobbled out of the apartment.

Our heroine immediately complied with her request, or rather command, and, leaving the roofless hall in which she then stood, followed the hideous crone through a suite of damp, empty rooms through which the wind was sighing in tones too wildly mournful not to communicate a feeling of sympathetic melancholy to the heart of every listener. At length they reached a room smaller than the others, to which a canopy couch with faded velvet curtains, a few chairs, a table, and an old-fashioned carved ward-robe gave a habitable, if not a comfortable, appearance. Here the old woman stopped, and placing the candle on the table said, "Now, here you may be till tomorrow if spirits don't run away with you."

"Oh, I have no fear of that," replied Lady Emily, forcing a laugh. "But my good Bertha, can you not light a fire in that grate, for it's very cold?"

"No, not I," replied the hag. "I've something else to do, indeed." And with these ungracious words she walked or rather crept out of the room.

When she was gone, Lady Emily very naturally fell into a fit of rather sorrowful musing. The clandestine and secret nature of the past, the dreariness of the present, the uncertainty of the future, all contributed to impress her mind with the deepest gloom. Erelong, however, the image of St. Clair, rising like the sun above a threatening horizon, dispelled the sadness which hung over her mind. "Soon," thought she, "he will be here. And then this decayed tower will to me wear the aspect of a king's palace."

Scarcely had this consoling reflection been uttered in a half-whispered soliloquy, when a stately stride and jingling spurs sounded from the antechamber. The door, which stood ajar, was gently pushed open, and the Earl's tall form, wrapped in a travelling cloak, and with a plumed bonnet darkly shading his noble features, appeared at the entrance.

"You have come at last," said Lady Emily. "How long you have been! I was almost beginning to fear that you had lost your way in that dismal wood."

"Beautiful creature," replied he in a tone which thrilled through her like an electric shock, "I would give everything I possess on earth to be in reality an object of such tender interest in your eyes. But alas, I fear that your sweet sympathy is directed to one who while I live shall nevermore hear it expressed by that silvery voice. Behold me, fair lady, and know into whose power you have fallen!"

So saying he flung off at once the enshrouding cloak and hat, and there stood before the horror-stricken lady, not the form of her lover St. Clair, but that of his rival Colonel Percy. The ghastly paleness which instantly overspread her face and the sudden clasping of her hands alone proclaimed what feelings passed through her mind as she beheld this unexpected apparition.

"Come, cheer up!" continued the Colonel, with a scornful smile. "It's as well to settle your mind now, for I swear by everything earthly or heavenly, sacred or profane, that this painter-lover of yours, this romancing, arrow-shooting artist, has seen your face for the last time."

"Wretch," exclaimed Lady Emily, her eyes sparkling with scorn and hatred, "know that he whom you call my painter-lover has higher and purer blood in his veins than you. He is

Earl St. Clair of Clan Albyn, and you are but the dependent hanger-on of a noble relative."

"So he has told you!" returned Percy. "But damsel, be he lord or limner, I have fairly outwitted him this time. His chariot wheels tarried somewhere too long. Methinks mine were better oiled; they ran smoother. I won the race, and have borne off the prize triumphant. He may now cry 'St. Clair to the rescue!' but none of his plaided minions can reach the length of this dark and unknown retreat."

"Unprincipled villain!" said Lady Emily, whose high spirit was now fully roused. "You have acted treacherously; you have adopted means totally unbecoming the honour of a gentleman, or never should I have been thus ensnared by your toils."

"Humph," replied the Colonel, "I am not one of those punctilious fools who consider honour as the god of their idolatry. Eavesdroppers, spies, or false-witnesses are all equally acceptable to me when there is a great end in view which can be more easily attained by their assistance."

"Colonel Percy," said Lady Emily, "for I can call you by no name so detestable as your own, do you intend to keep me in this tower or send me back to Clydesdale Castle?"

"I shall keep you here, most assuredly, till you promise to become my wife, and then you shall reappear in Verdopolis with a magnificence suitable to the future Duchess of Beaufort."

"Then here I remain till death or some happier chance relieves me, for not all the torture that man's ingenuity could devise should ever induce me to marry one whose vices have sunk him so low in the ranks of humanity as yours have, one who openly renounces the dominion of honour and declares that he has given himself up to the blind guidance of his own depraved inclinations."

"Excellently well preached!" remarked the Colonel with a sneer. "But fair worshipper of honour, this resolution will not prevent the proposed incarceration, which shall be inflicted on you as a sort of punishment for having flagrantly violated the decrees of that deity whose cause you so eloquently advocate. Pray, my lady, was it quite consistent with the dictates of honour to deceive your old, doting uncle, and elope at midnight with an unknown adventurer?"

This taunt was too much for Lady Emily. The remembrance of her uncle and of what his sufferings would be when her disappearance should be known, instantly destroyed that semblance of dignity which pride had taught her to assume in order to overawe her suitor's familiar insolence. She leant her head on her hand, and burst into a flood of bitter tears.

"Those crystal drops," said the Colonel, totally unmoved by her distress, "tell me that it would be no very difficult matter to soften your apparently stubborn heart. Could I but remain here one day longer, I am certain that the powers of persuasion I possess would succeed in bringing my Queen of Beauty to reason. But unfortunately, dire necessity commands my immediate departure. Before sunrise I ought to be in Verdopolis, and day is already breaking over those eastern hills. Farewell," he continued in a more serious tone, "farewell, Lady Emily, I am going where there is likely to be hot work, and perhaps some black rebel's sabre may before long rid you of a sincere though rejected lover, and the world of what most men call a villain."

"Farewell, Colonel," replied his weeping captive, "and remember that if such should be your fate, the recollection of what you have this night done will not tend to alleviate the agonies of death."

"Pshaw!" said he with a reckless laugh. "Do you think I have any fears on that score? No! My conscience, if I ever had any, has been long seared. Immortality finds no place in my creed, and death is with me but an abbreviated term for lasting sleep. Once more farewell."

With these words he snatched her hand, kissed it fervently, and departed. The twilight glimmer of dawn was now stealing through the narrow casement of Lady Emily's prison and, falling on her face and person as she lay stretched on the tattered velvet couch, where overcome with fatigue she had now thrown herself, revealed a touching picture of beauty in distress. Her hair hung in loose and neglected curls on her snowy neck and shoulders; her eyes were closed; her long dark lashes, wet with tears, rested motionless on her cheek, except when a fresh drop trembled on their silken fringes. Her face, usually blooming, was now pale as alabaster from the misery of the sleepless night she had passed. One white hand and arm supported her head on the pillow, and the other confined the folds of the dark mantle in which she was partially enveloped.

After some time, in spite of the wretchedness of her situation, separated, it might be forever, from all she held dear on earth, and confined in a solitary ruin with no other attendant than the withered hag, Bertha, she fell into a deep slumber and while she enjoys this temporary respite from affliction, we will revert to other matters.

Chapter the Sixth

IT is well known that the great war between the Ashantees and Twelves[9] ended, after many bloody and obstinate battles, in the complete subjugation of the former, their Prince[10] being slain, their nation nearly annihilated, their metropolis[11] destroyed, and the circumjacent country reduced to a condition of the wildest and most appalling desolation which the imagination of man can conceive. Quashia, the king's only son, then at the tender age of four or five years, was taken prisoner. At the general partition of booty, he with other captives fell to the share of His Grace the Duke of Wellington, from whom he experienced as much care and tenderness as if he had been that monarch's son instead of his slave.

In these gilded fetters the young prince grew up. His literary education was duly cared for, but he declined to profit by the instructions bestowed on him further than as it regarded the acquisition of the English and Ashantee languages and the capability of expressing himself in both by pen as well as tongue. In bodily exercises and military affairs, however, the case was different. Everything relating to these he learnt with an avidity which showed how fully he inherited his father's warlike spirit.

At the age of seventeen, he was a tall handsome youth, black as jet, and with an eye full of expression and fire. His disposition was bold, irritable, active, daring, and at the same time deeply treacherous. It now began to appear that notwithstanding the care with which he had been treated by his conquerors, he retained against them, as if by instinct, the most deeply rooted and inveterate hatred. Since his fifteenth year he had been accustomed to take long excursions by himself among the mountains and forests of Ashantee for the purpose, as he said,

of hunting the wild animals that abound there. But subsequent
events showed that his real employment during these expedi-
tions was discovering and prompting to rebellion the hidden
tribes of Africans, who, after the destruction of Coomassie
and the slaughter of king Quamina, had concealed themselves
in fastnesses inaccessible to any but a native of the country.
When he had sufficiently kindled in these wild savages the
spirit of slumbering discontent and roused them to make an
effort for regaining that independence as a nation which they
had lost, he in conjunction with the celebrated brothers Eredi
and Benini, formerly his father's favourite counsellors, un-
furled the royal standard of Ashantee and summoned the scattered remnant of that once mighty empire to join him without delay at the foot of Mount Pindus.

It seemed as if this invocation had called from their graves
a portion at least of the vast army which fourteen years since
had reddened with their blood the lofty heights of Rosendale-
Hill.[12] Multitudes flocked to his banner from the mountain
glens and caverns of Jibbel Kumri, from the unexplored regions of inner Africa, and from the almost boundless desert of
Sahara, so that in a few weeks no less than fifteen thousand
armed natives of a kingdom which was supposed to have been
extirpated, declared themselves ready to shed the last drop of
their blood in vindication of Quashia the Second's claim to
his ancestral throne.

With this determination they marched toward Verdopolis,
and had arrived within four hundred miles of that city before
intelligence of what had taken place reached the Twelves.

When the fact of this rebellion was known, however, the
Duke of Wellington immediately desired that the punishment
of the rebels might be left to him, as the young viper who
commanded them had been nourished on his own hearth and
brought up by him with almost parental tenderness. His request was immediately granted, and the Duke dispatched ten
thousand troops under the command of General Leaf, a de-

scendant, by the way, of the famous Captain Leaf, to stop the
progress of the insurgents.

When Quashia heard of the formidable force which was
advancing against him, he sent an ambassador to Gondar, re-
questing assistance from the Abyssinian king, and in the meantime commenced a very orderly retreat. Ras Michael, who
detested the British, readily permitted an army of eight thousand soldiers to assist Quashia in his bold enterprise against
them. With this reinforcement, that young warrior ventured
to give the enemy battle. An engagement accordingly ensued
near Fateconda on the Senegal, which, after a very obstinate
contest, ended rather in favour of the Verdopolitans, though
the victory they gained was of that nature that another similar
one would have been total destruction.

A fresh addition now arrived from Abyssinia, so that the
army of the rebels was very little the worse for their defeat,
while Leaf's force amounted barely to six thousand men. The
Duke being informed of this state of things, immediately ordered out sixteen regiments and, placing himself at their head,
marched without delay to the scene of action. On his arrival he
found that the enemy had been joined by a large body of
Moors from the North, so that he was still far inferior in number, but, trusting to the superior discipline of his troops, he
determined to stand his ground without further reinforcement.

Having given the reader this necessary information, I will
now proceed with my narrative in a more detailed and less
historical style.

It was a glorious evening in the end of summer when the
hostile armies lay in camp on opposite banks of the River
Senegal. The sun was slowly approaching the horizon of a
speckless sky and threw his parting rays with softened brilliancy over a scene of unsurpassed loveliness. Between the two
hosts lay the beautiful valley where groves of delicate-leaved
tamarind trees and the tall palmyras sweetly shadowed the
blue, bright waters of the wandering stream. A cluster of de-

serted huts, whose inhabitants had fled at the approach of soldiers, crowned the gently sloped acclivity which embosomed the glen. On one side, in the largest of these, the Duke of Wellington had taken up his quarters, and here he now sat surrounded by four of his principal officers. Two of these are already known to our readers, being the Marquis of Charlesworth and Colonel Percy. Of the remaining two, the first was a middle-sized man with broad shoulders and spindle shanks. His forehead was rather high, his nose large and projecting, his mouth wide, and his chin remarkably long. He was dressed in uniform, with a star on his breast, and large cambrick ruffles at each wrist. The other was a little personage with jointless limbs, a chubby face, and a pale pink wig of frizzled silk surmounted by a tall black hat on which was an ornament of carved wood.

These officers were conversing with each other in undertones, not to disturb the Duke's meditations, who sat with his eyes fixed on the wide prospect which opened before him and which was bounded by a dim, sweeping, milk-white line indicating the commencement of the great sandy desert.

"Bobadil," said he, suddenly addressing himself to the former of the two gentlemen I have just described, "do you not perceive something moving in the direction of the enemy's camp? It is under the shadow of that lofty hill to the north, and appears like a dark and compact body of men. Surely it is not some new ally."

Bobadil came forward, and began to poke out his neck, strain and wink his eyes, look through his fingers, but finally declared he could perceive nothing. The Marquis of Charlesworth and General Leaf, the wearer of the pink wig, were equally unsuccessful.

"You are a set of moles," said the Duke. "I see them most distinctly. They have rounded the hill, and their arms glisten brightly in the sunshine. Come hither, Percy, can't you see that flashing hedge of spears with a banner displayed in the rear?"

"Certainly, my lord," replied Percy, whose younger eyes

could easily discern what was quite lost to the dimmed optics of the old generals. "They are now turned from the rebels, and seem advancing toward us."

A silence of a quarter of an hour here ensued during which the duke continued to gaze intently at the approaching army, for such it was now distinctly seen to be. They slowly wound away from the Ashantee camp and, entering a deep valley, were for the present lost to sight. But ere long a burst of wild music heralded their reappearance. Gradually they emerged from the sinuous windings of the glen which had concealed them, and in martial array advanced to the sound of shrill pipes and the deep-toned kettle drums along the right bank of the Senegal.

"These are not foes but friends!" exclaimed the Duke starting up. "Upon my word, St. Clair has kept his promise well! I did not think his northern hills could send forth such a fine body of troops."

"Who are they, my lord?" exclaimed all the officers at once, with the exception of Percy, whose brow had suddenly grown dark at the mention of St. Clair.

"The men of Elimbos, the lads of the mist," replied his grace. "Here, Percy, order my horse and your own, and attend me whilst I go to meet them."

Percy left the hut, and in a few minutes the Duke and himself were galloping down the valley. As they drew near that Highland host, my father frequently expressed his admiration at the perfect order in which the ranks moved, the athletic appearance and uncommon stature of the men who formed them, and the clean, well-burnished appearance of their arms and equipments. Just as they reached the advance guard, a general halt was called. Both rode through the unfolding columns till, on gaining the centre of the little army, they perceived the Earl surrounded by his choicest vassals, all dressed in the green tartan of their clan, and bearing spears, bows, quivers, and small triangular shields. Near him stood a gigantic warrior, whose snow-white hair and beard proclaimed advanced age, while from his erect bearing, herculean frame, and sinewy limbs, it was easy to perceive that he retained unimpaired all the vigorous powers of youth. He bore in one hand a huge spear proportionate to his own titanic size, from which floated the broad folds of a green banner bearing as a device a golden eagle with expanded wings and the motto, "I dwell on the rock." This person was the celebrated Donald of the Standard, called in common parlance the Ape of the Hills. He is now one hundred and ten years of age, and consequently was at that period ninety. After a cordial greeting on each side, the Duke proceeded to direct St. Clair how to encamp his men and to give him other instructions which it is unnecessary here to recapitulate. Their conference being ended, he took leave for the night and returned with Colonel Percy to his own quarters.

It may now be as well to connect the broken thread of my rambling narrative before I proceed further.

When St. Clair reached Verdopolis after his interview with Lady Charlesworth at Clydesdale Castle, he ordered his page to go to the nearest place where carriages were let out to hire and order one to be in readiness by eleven o'clock that night. From some unexplained cause of delay, it was not prepared till past twelve, and, consequently, the bird was flown before he arrived at the appointed place of rendezvous. In a state of impatience amounting almost to madness, he continued to pace the chestnut avenue watching the setting of the moon, the slow vanishing of the stars, and gradual approach of daylight, listening to every breath of wind, and transforming the rustle of each falling leaf into the steps of his expected fair one. Morning broke, however; the sun rose; the deer awoke from their light slumbers, and still Lady Emily came not.

Stung to the heart at her apparent infidelity, he determined to learn the cause of it from her own mouth, and if a satisfactory excuse were not assigned, to bid her an eternal farewell. With this resolution, he hastened to the castle. On his arrival he found all in confusion, the servants hurrying to and fro with countenances of doubt and dismay. On inquiring the reason of this unusual movement, he was informed that Lady Emily had disappeared that night, and no one knew where she was gone. Terror-struck at this intelligence, he immediately returned to Verdopolis, where he remained for some days, during which time the most diligent research was made after the unfortunate lady by her afflicted uncle, but all to no purpose. Finding this to be the case, St. Clair, who had now lost all motive for desiring a continuance of life, and whose bitter and heart-gnawing anguish rendered a quiescent state of existence the most terrible of all others, determined immediately to offer his own services and those of the clan whose chieftain he was, to the Duke of Wellington in his intended expedition against the Ashantees. This proposal, of course, was gratefully accepted; and St. Clair soon after departed to gather his warriors and lead them from their native mountains. With his opportune arrival the reader is already acquainted. And, having cleaned scores, I may trot on unencumbered.

On the evening of the day which followed that event, the Earl sat in his tent with no other company than that little page Andrew, who, squatting like a Turk in one corner, was employed in burnishing his master's spear and silver quiver. Colonel Percy rode up on his gallant warhorse and informed St. Clair that the Duke was about to hold a council of war in which his presence would be required. It was with difficulty that our hero managed to return a civil answer to the unwelcome envoy. With a haughtiness of gesture and a sternness of tone that ill-suited the courteous nature of the words, he replied that he felt highly flattered by the Duke's request and would attend him without delay.

Whether Percy experienced any reciprocation of animosity, I know not, but his countenance expressed none, as with a bland smile, and low inclination of the head, he touched his horse's sides, and caracoled gaily away.

The council was held in a large tent covered with scarlet cloth, richly ornamented with gold embroidery; and from the summit waved a crimson flag bearing the arms of England. When St. Clair entered this superb pavilion, he found the Duke surrounded by about twenty officers. At his left hand sat the Marquis of Charlesworth, whose pale countenance and abstract air told a melancholy tale of recent affliction. The Earl was invited by His Grace to take the seat at his right hand which was vacant. At this flattering mark of distinction, Colonel Percy, who sat near the entrance of the tent amongst the junior officers, was observed to smile with a peculiar expression.

"Now, gentlemen," said the Duke when all were assembled, "I do not intend to detain you long. My motive for assembling you together was merely to obtain your approbation of a proposal for settling our black friends on the other side of the river in a few hours, without, I trust, incurring much risk to our own army."

His Grace then proceeded to unfold a scheme for attacking the enemy's camp at night when they would be wholly unable to make any adequate defence, it having been ascertained by means of spies that their watch was not one of the most diligent in the world. The advantage of their plan being obvious, the council gave a unanimous opinion in its favour, and the next night was assigned as the period for putting it into execution.

Business being thus summarily disposed of, the Duke proceeded to say, "Since, gentlemen, I have called you together for an affair of such brevity, some reparation is due, I hope. Therefore, you will not refuse to partake with me of a soldier's supper. It is prepared and now only awaits your approach."

As he spoke, the curtain at the upper end of the tent was withdrawn, and revealed an inner pavillion brilliantly lighted, in which was a long table covered with the material for an excellent and substantial, though not, perhaps, a luxurious supper. All willingly accepted the invitation except the Marquis of

Charlesworth, who pleaded an inability to enjoy festivities as an excuse for declining.

"I will not press you, my lord," said the Duke kindly, taking his hand, "but remember that solitude nourishes grief."

The old man's only reply was a mournful shake of the head.

"That poor fellow has had a heavy stroke in his old age," observed Colonel Percy, who happened to be seated next to St. Clair at supper. "He has lost a very pretty and accomplished niece in a most unaccountable manner."

"Has he?" said the Earl, eyeing his neighbour with a glance that might have struck terror to the heart of a lion.

"Yes," pursued the Colonel in a tone of the most provoking calmness. "Ah! she was a sweet girl, rather capricious, though, as most women are. One of her fancies was particularly absurd."

"What might that be?" asked St. Clair.

"Why, you'll hardly believe it when I tell you. She took it into her head to fall in love with a poor, silly, sneaking puppy of a painter, and for some time declared she would marry him in preference to the nephew and heir of a duke. But at length the latter lover prevailed, and then the little witch confessed she had only been playing the coquette to try her suitor's fidelity, and that in reality she despised the man of canvas as much as she did the meanest of his sign-post daubs."

The flush which crimsoned St. Clair's cheek and brow and the light which sparkled in his fierce eyes would have quelled the insolence of any ordinary man. But they only increased that of the demi-fiend who sat by, rejoicing in his agony.

"You are not subject to apoplectic fits, are you, sir?" said he, gazing on him with affected wonder.

"No," replied the Earl, suppressing his wrath by a strong effort. "But, sir, how will the successful lover bear the loss of his intended bride?"

"Oh, they say he displays a laudable degree of resignation under the affliction."

"Then his affection for her was a pretense?"

"No, I don't say that. But you know, my lord, he is perhaps better acquainted with her whereabouts than other people. Hum, don't you understand me?"

"Indeed, I do not."

"Why then, to speak more plainly, some folks don't hesitate to say that she has eloped."

"Sir," said the Earl in a low, deep voice, "let me tell you I am in some degree acquainted with the parties we have been conversing about. And let me tell you further that if I were her uncle and entertained the least suspicion of the kind you hint at, I would cause the infernal scoundrel her lover to be torn limb from limb by wild horses, or force him to tell me where the unhappy creature is concealed."

"Ha! would you?" said the Colonel, while a cloud at once fell on his brow, and he instinctively grasped the weapon at his side. But almost directly after, he muttered, "The hour is not yet arrived." And his countenance resumed its former state of deceitful composure.

The dishes were now removed, and wine was introduced. After the first few rounds the Duke of Wellington, rising from his seat at the head of the table, begged to be excused from a longer stay at the festive board. He then drank to the health of all of his guests and, bidding them good-night, withdrew.

St. Clair, who was in no mood for joining in the riotous mirth that now became the principal characteristic of the military meal, took the first opportunity of following his example. The night was still and calm. Its dewy coolness and the mild moonlight which poured down upon him at intervals as he wandered among the silent tents and through the dark groves, which waved with scarce visible motion along the river's shelving bank, served in a great measure to soothe his roused and exaggerated passions. But not all the deep tranquillity which fell like balm from the blue, starry sky, not all the images of rest and serenity which a sweet summer's night ever creates, could bring corresponding peace to his love-tortured heart, or expel the worm of jealousy which now gnawed his very vitals. To be despised by her for whom he could have given his life's blood, to be the object of her derision and scorn, to have all his suspicion of her good faith so fearfully verified, was worse than death to his proud, haughty spirit.

As he stood on the river's brink and looked down on the deep clear water, which flowed so gently and wooingly at his feet, he longed to cool the delirium of his brain by a spring into their liquid freshness. Putting aside, however, this suggestion of the tempter, and half despising himself for being so moved by the falseheartedness of a fickle woman, he turned from the stream and proceeded towards his own tent. Just as he was about to enter it, a voice whispered in his ear, "Beware of Percy. It is a friend who warns you."

The Earl looked hastily round. He saw a dark figure gliding away, which was soon lost in the shadow of a lofty cluster of palm trees.

For a long time after he had laid himself on his deer-skin couch that night, slumber refused to visit his aching eyelids. The warning of his unknown friend, joined to the other subjects of deep and intense thought which filled his distracted mind for some hours, effectually banished sleep from his pillow. But at last wearied nature, being quite worn out, was compelled to seek refuge in temporary repose. Scarcely had kindly oblivion fallen over the sorrows which oppressed him, when a slow and peculiarly shrill whistle sounded without the tent. Andrew, who till this moment had been apparently fast asleep in a corner, now softly and cautiously left his couch and, taking up a small lamp, stepped on tiptoe to his master's bedside. Having ascertained that he was really slumbering, by holding the light to his closed eyes, &c., the page wrapped himself in a green plaid and without noise left the tent. At the outside a man was standing whose blue coat and liveried hat showed him to be the same person that had abducted Andrew about a

month since. Without a word spoken, both walked or rather
stole away towards a neighbouring grove, the footman leading
the way and beckoning Andrew to follow. Here they were
joined by another figure in a cloak. All three then proceeded
down the river; and in a few minutes the intervening trees
entirely concealed them from view.

Chapter the Seventh

WELL, my lord, the day is ours at last, but we've had a hard tug for the victory. Upon my word, those black rascals fought like devils!"

"They did indeed. And I think their overthrow, considering all the circumstances of the case, may be accounted almost a miracle."

"Truly it may. By the bye, St. Clair, I shall hold a second council of war this evening. Those circumstances you allude to require explanation. They must be carefully looked into. You will attend of course?"

"Certainly, my lord."

Such was the brief dialogue between St. Clair and the Duke of Wellington as the latter rode by with his staff. A bloody but decisive victory had just been gained over the Ashantees, though in a manner different from what had been at first intended.

At eleven o'clock of the night appointed for the secret attack, the Duke of Wellington crossed the Senegal at the head of his whole army. As they drew near the hostile camp, not a voice whispered, not a light glimmered among the long silent rows of snow-white tents. Unopposed they held on their course to Quashia's own pavillion. They entered. It was empty. A short space of time sufficed to ascertain that not a living thing, save themselves, remained in all the deserted camp. Those who were near the Duke when this discovery was made said that for a few moments his countenance expressed a depth of disappointment akin to despair. He recovered himself, however, almost directly, and ordered scouts to disperse instantly in every direction and to find out in which direction the enemy was gone. Ere long some of them returned with the information that they had marched northward and were now halting about ten miles off. The army immediately received orders to take the route indicated, which led up the valley.

About day break they arrived at a wild mountain pass, through which might be seen a vast plain where the allied forces of the Moors, Ashantees, and Abyssinians were all drawn up in battle array. It was a gorgeous but terrific spectacle, as the first sunbeams flashed on that dusky host and lighted up to fiercer radiance their bright weapons and all the barbarous magnificence of gold and gems in which most of the warriors were attired.

As the Duke's Army with himself at their head filed slowly through the narrow gorge, a young horseman sped suddenly to the front of the African array, and waving his long lance in the air, exclaimed, "Freedom would this night have received her death-stab from the hand of the White Tyrant had not a traitor arisen in the camp of oppression."

With these words he plunged again into the ranks and disappeared, but not before the golden diadem glittering on his forehead had revealed the arch-rebel, Quashia.

The contest which then ensued and which dyed the plains of Camalia with blood, I need not describe; it is matter of history. Suffice it to say that of the twenty-five thousand gallant rebels whom the sun's rising rays had that morning lighted to the contest, high in hope and strong in valor, the bodies of seventeen thousand eight hundred, ere evening, lay cold and still on a lost field of battle, waiting till the vultures of Gibbel-Kumri should scent the banquet from afar and grant them a living sepulchre in their devouring maws.

Our hero, St. Clair, had played one of the most conspicuous parts in the day's tragedy. Reckless of life, which was now hateful to him, he sought glory at the head of his brave Highlanders wherever the fight raged thickest, and almost wished that the renown his dauntless courage was certain to earn might ring through the world whilst he himself lay in the voiceless

tomb, shrouded in his last garments, and hushed to repose in
the slumber from which none can awake.

Fate, however, had decreed otherwise. The scimitar of the
turbaned Moor, the war spear of the savage Ashantee, and even
the renowned arrows of the quivered Abyssinian seemed all to
have lost their powers of destruction when turned against him;
and when the battle was past, and he with his little army
slowly retraced their steps over the gory plain, it was with feelings approaching to envy that he viewed the ghastly corpses,
which, pale and mangled, lay scattered around. On arriving at
his own tent, he called Andrew to assist him in changing his
soiled and bloody dress. The page, however, did not obey his
summons, and after waiting some time in expectation of his
appearance, he was obliged to manage as well as he could
without any aid. Having completed his toilette, and partaken
of some refreshment, he hastened, as it was now late, to attend
the council.

A profound silence pervaded the pavillion as he entered,
broken only by an occasional whisper. The Duke was sitting at
the head of the table in an unusually pensive and meditative
posture, his head resting on his hand, his brows contracted, and
an expression of deep solemnity diffused over his whole countenance. When St. Clair was seated, he looked up and glanced
quickly round as if to ascertain that all the members were assembled; and then, rising, he proceeded to address them briefly
thus:

"Gentlemen, the cause for which you are convened this night
is of the last importance. It is to make an inquiry which will
involve the life and honour of some individual or individuals
amongst you. Two days ago a plan was broached in this place
for attacking our enemies by night. They obtained intelligence
of it, and it was frustrated. Our business is now to discover
how that intelligence reached them. I grieve to say that the
words which you all heard the rebel leader utter this day in the

face of both armies have raised a horrible suspicion in my mind that it was by treachery. The traitor must be in this apartment. And if he will now confess his guilt, I solemnly promise to spare his life, but if he leaves it to be found out by another, then a death of the most painful and dishonourable shall be his."

The Duke ceased. His stern and keen eye scrutinized the countenances of all who surrounded him one by one, as if he would by that means have read the thoughts passing in each heart.

For some minutes not a word was spoken. Each regarded his neighbour with a visage in which awe, curiosity, and aimless suspicion were strangely mingled. The dim torchlight of the pavillion, however, showed one person whose calm and noble features displayed none of these emotions; but on the contrary, something like a lurking smile played round the corners of his mouth. It was Colonel Percy.

In a short time he rose and, advancing to the table where the Duke sat, said in a low voice, "Will your Grace permit me to speak?"

"Certainly," was the reply.

"Then," continued the Colonel, drawing his tall form up to the fullness of its majestic height and coolly folding his arms, "I have it in my power to reveal the wretch who betrayed his general and his comrades. But before I mention the craven's name, he shall have one more opportunity of saving his worthless life. Conscience-stricken Traitor, step forward and avail yourself of that mercy which is even now passing away never to return!"

A breathless pause followed this awful appeal. Not a whisper sounded. Not a foot or hand moved.

"You will not accept the offered boon?" said Percy in deep thrilling tones. "Then your blood be upon your own head. My Lord," he went on, turning to the Duke, while a supernatural light rose in his triumphant glance, "know that the base traitor sits at your right hand. Yes, the most noble Roland, Lord of St. Clair, and chieftain of Clan Albyn, has been bribed by the negro's wealth to blot with treachery a scutcheon owned by a hundred earls."

One universal exclamation of "Impossible!" broke forth at the strange accusation. Each member of the council started from his seat, and an expression of astonishment amounting almost to horror appeared in every countenance. The Duke and St. Clair alone sat unmoved.

"Sir," said the former calmly but somewhat sternly, "the most ample proof of this bold charge must be furnished, or that punishment intended for the accused will recoil upon the accuser."

"I accept your Grace's alternative," replied the Colonel, bowing low. "The testimony is not wanting. But first let me ask his lordship if he denies the charge."

"No," replied the Earl in a tone of startling vehemence, while he sprang from his seat, as if actuated by some overmastering impulse. "No. I scorn to deny the hellish falsehood. But I will prove its baseness on that tool of Satan, with my sword."

As he spoke, he snatched the weapon from its scabbard.

"Gentlemen," said Percy, wholly undisturbed by this action, "that sword condemns him. Mark it well and tell me if such a one ought to be in the hands of a British soldier."

All eyes turned on the glittering blade. It was a curved Moorish scimitar, the handle richly decorated with gems of the highest value.

"That certainly has not been purchased in Verdopolis, my lord," said the Duke after examining it.

"How did you obtain it?"

"I know not," replied St. Clair, regarding the weapon with evident surprise. "It is not my own. I never saw it till this moment."

"Recollect yourself," continued his friendly judge; "did you take it by mistake on the field of battle?"

The Earl shook his head.

"Perhaps," observed Colonel Percy with a sneer, "I could inform his lordship how it came into his possession, if your Grace will allow me to produce my witness."

The duke signified his assent, and Percy, advancing toward the first door, called out, "Travers, bring me in the prisoner."

This summons was answered by the appearance of a footman leading a boy whose keen eyes and shriveled, ill-favoured features instantly proclaimed him to be no other than our friend Andrew.

"How is this?" exclaimed St. Clair, stepping back in amazement. "Why is that boy in your custody? I claim him as my vassal, and, as his liege lord, have a right to know of what he is accused."

"He shall inform you himself, my lord," said the Colonel significantly.

"No," interposed the Duke, "I should like to hear it from you, sir, in the first place."

"I found him, my lord," returned Percy, "beyond the prescribed boundaries of the camp early yesterday morning, when I was going my rounds as officer of the watch. On questioning him where he had been, he appeared much agitated, and returned no answers but such as were insufficient and evidently false. I then threatened to punish him severely if he did not speak the truth. This had the desired effect. He immediately confessed that he had been in the African tents. Further questions evoked from him the information on which I have grounded my charge against his master and which he is now ready to communicate to your Grace."

"Andrew," said the Duke, "come here. Will you promise to answer me truly such questions as I shall now ask?"

"I will," said the boy, laying his hand on his heart with great apparent sincerity.

"By whom, then, were you sent to the Ashantee camp?"

"By my lord, the Chief."

"What for?"

"To deliver a paper which was sealed and directed to Quashia II, King of the Liberated Africans."

"Had you ever been there before?"

"Yes, once."

"When?"

"That same night."

"And why did you go then?"

"I was sent to ask for a certain reward which Quashia had promised my master some time before, in case he would tell him of all that passed in such councils as he should attend."

"Did you hear that promise made?"

"Yes."

"At what time?"

"The first night after we arrived here; a black man came to my lord's tent, and offered him twelve ackies (I think he called it) of rock gold if he would do as he wanted him."

"And your master consented?"

"Yes."

"Did you see Quashia when you went to his camp?"

"Yes."

"What was he like?"

"He was a young man, and very tall. His nose and lips were not flat and thick like the other blacks, and he spoke English."

"The description you have given is very correct. Now tell me what the reward was you carried to your master."

"There was a black box filled with something very heavy, a large mantle made of different coloured silk, and a sword which Quashia took from his own belt."

"Describe the sword."

"It was crooked, almost like a sickle, and had a great many precious stones about the handle."

Here a general murmur of surprise broke from the bystanders. The Duke, however, sternly rebuked them and went on, "Do you know where the black box and silk mantle were put?"

"Yes; my master commanded me to dig a hole in the center of the tent, and bury them there."

"Bobadil," said his Grace, "take one or two men with you to the Earl's tent and see if you can find these articles."

Bobadil made a deep and silent reverence and departed to execute his commission. General Leaf now advanced to the table.

"May I ausk," said he, addressing the page in a tone which retained something of the ancient long-drawn twang, "whether you were by yourself when you went to the Raubels?"

"My master went part of the way with me the first time," replied Andrew.

"I thought so, for the night before last when I was returning from de counshel saupper, I saw a tall man and a little boy going towards the camp boundaries, and the man was dressed in a green plaid, such as Laurd St. Clair wears."

"That is conclusive evidence," observed Colonel Percy.

"It's corroborative," said the Duke, "but I do not allow it to be quite conclusive."

Steps were now heard approaching the door of the pavillion, and in another moment General Bobadil entered, bearing a black box in one hand and a folded silk garment in the other. He silently deposited both on the table. The Duke first examined the latter article. It was one of those splendid Ashantee cloths which exhibit in their ever-varying hues all the vivid colours of the rainbow.

He then opened the casket and took out its contents, which consisted of five double gold chains, each two yards long, a collar, and a pair of bracelets of the same costly metal, several ornaments in aggry beads, and an amulet in a gold case blazing with the finest diamonds.

"Good God!" said he, when he had completed the survey, "I could not have thought that these paltry trinkets would have purchased a British soldier's faith. St. Clair, rise, let me hear your defense. I wish with my whole heart that you may be able to disprove all we have heard this night."

"My Lord," said the Earl, who had hitherto been sitting motionless with his head muffled in his plaid, "I have no defense to make. Heaven knows my innocence, but how can I prove to man that all the seemingly fair and consistent evidence which has just been delivered is in reality a most Satanic compound of the deepest and blackest falsehoods. My destiny is at present dark and gloomy. I will wait with patience till a better prospect rises."

So saying, he folded his arms and resumed his former attitude. The Duke then proceeded to say that he should not yet pronounce sentence, but should give the accused six weeks to collect witnesses and prepare for a formal trial. He informed him likewise that he should be instantly conveyed to Verdopolis and intimated his intention of repairing thither himself as soon as the rebellion should be finally quelled. The council now broke up; and St. Clair was removed by a band of soldiers to the tent usually appropriated to prisoners.

I must beg the reader to imagine that a space of six weeks has elapsed before he again beholds my hero, during which time he has been removed to Verdopolis and placed in one of those state dungeons that lie under the Tower of All Nations.

It was a gloomy place a thousand feet below the upper world. The thick walls and the low roof elevated on short, broad arches as massive as the rock whence they were hewn, admitted no sound, however faint, transient, and far away, by which the tenant of this living tomb might be reminded that near three millions of his fellow men were living and moving in the free light of heaven above him. The dead, the dreary silence which hung in the grave-like atmosphere was, however, broken at intervals by a noise which low, indeed, and seemingly as distant as the earth's central abyss, yet shook the dungeon's walls, and as it reverberated among the other subterranean caverns which were excavated above, below, and around, rung on the ear with a deep hollow boom that chilled the heart and brought the sweat-drops of terror to the brow. This was the clam-clam sounding through under-ground passages a thousand miles in length, from the haunted hills of Jibbel Kumri.

Here on the evening of that day preceding the one appointed for his final trial, St. Clair lay stretched on a bed of straw. A glimmering lamp was placed on the damp ground beside him; its feeble, rays inadequate to dissipate the almost palpable darkness which shrouded the remote recesses of this fearful prison, yet shed a faint, dying light on the unfortunate nobleman's wasted person and features. Not a trace remained of that bright bloom which health and youthful vigour had once communicated to his now wan and sunken cheek. The light of his eye, however, yet remained unquenched. The princely beauty of his countenance, though faded, was not destroyed.

Suddenly, as a harsh grating sound like a key turning in a rusty lock proclaimed the jailer's approach, he started from his recumbent posture and sat upright. It was full ten minutes before all the fastenings which secured the dungeon door were removed. But at length the last bolt was withdrawn, and the heavy iron portals being unfolded gave admittance, not to the jailer, but to a tall man whose form and face were wholly concealed by the foldings of his ample mantle. With a slow and cautious step he advanced towards the Earl's straw couch, and placing himself on that side which was most dimly illuminated by the lamp, addressed him thus,

"Earl of St. Clair, if I mistake not, you lie here on the charge of treachery."

"And if I do," replied the prisoner, whose high spirits confinement had not in the least subdued, "does that circumstance give strangers a right to insult me by the mention of it?"

"Certainly not," returned the unknown visitor, unmoved by the indirect reproach which his words conveyed. "Nor did I intend to insult you by the question I have just asked. My firm conviction is that you are innocent of the crime laid to your charge. Do I err in the belief?"

"Do you err in the belief of your own existence?"

"I should think not."

"Be as certain, then, of the one fact as you are of the other, and you will be right."

"That is decisive," replied the stranger in a tone which revealed that a smile was curling his lips. And after a pause he added, "My lord, does not your trial for this false offence come on tomorrow?"

"It does."

"And are you prepared with evidence to dispute it?"

"No; and I doubt not that before forty-eight hours go by, I shall have fallen a victim to the hate of a malignant enemy. Yes; the last son of the lords of Roslyn will go to his grave branded with the name of traitor."

"Not if I can help it," said the unknown. "And I will do my utmost."

"Stranger, you are kind. But what, alas! is it in your power to effect? The evidence against me is strong, the web of deceit has been woven with impenetrable art."

"Oh, but fear nothing. Truth shall prevail at last. Tell me only who your concealed enemy is."

"Colonel Percy, my accuser."

"I thought as much. And now I come to the object of my visit to you in this loathsome dungeon. Why does he hate you?"

"Before I answer that question, I must know who it is that asks me."

"That cannot be," replied the stranger, drawing his ample cloak more firmly round him. "Thus far, however, I may say— I am the person who sometime since warned you to beware of Colonel Percy. I was present when the charge was brought against you, and I know something of the accuser's character and disposition. I was led to suspect the truth of what he said, knowing that nothing but a motive of the most powerful kind could induce him to be so active in an affair of that nature. I ask you to inform me what that motive is. If you will be candid with me, the young vulture shall miss his prey this time."

"Sir," replied the Earl, "there is something in your voice which tells me I ought to trust you. Know, then, that I loved a woman who, as I thought, was the most beautiful and excellent of her sex. The Colonel was my rival and—"

"You have said enough," interrupted the stranger. "I need no more to convince me fully of your perfect innocence. In such a case I know Colonel Percy would never rest till he had wreaked on his rival the deepest and deadliest revenge, were that rival his own brother. The whole black conspiracy is now revealed. He is the traitor. And heaven willing, he shall die the traitor's death. Tomorrow, when you are called upon to produce evidence of your innocence, do not hesitate to say that there is one in the court who, if he will, can prove you guiltless of the crime. Leave the rest to me. And now farewell. I hope tomorrow night you will lay your head on a different pillow."

"Farewell!" said St. Clair, warmly grasping the stranger's hand. "And doubt not, my unknown friend, that Roslyn will know how to recompense those who have saved his honour."

With these words the Earl fell back on his lowly pallet, while the stranger hastened to regain the upper earth, which he had quitted to fulfill his benevolent errand.

Chapter the Eighth

THE old Hall of Military Justice (it has lately been pulled down and a new one erected in its stead) was a vast and gloomy building, surrounded by galleries and surmounted by a huge, dark dome upheld by massive columns, the shadow of whose ponderous shafts united with the louring roof diffused round an air of profound and appropriate solemnity.

Here on the twenty-fifth of September 1814, upward of ten thousand people were assembled to view the trial of the Earl of St. Clair for high treason. The Duke of Wellington occupied the principal seat among the judges, who were twelve in number. A degree of intense interest contracted every brow as the noble prisoner, loaded with irons and attired in the striking costume of his clan, was led by a guard of soldiers into the centre of the hall. None could behold his lofty bearing, his majestic form, his youthful and handsome features, and the stately gait with which he moved in spite of his heavy fetters, without experiencing an involuntary conviction that he who stood before them was no traitor.

The first step taken by the court was to demand a recapitulation of the evidence which had been already adduced. This was accordingly gone into. The jewels, the amulet, the cloth, and the sword were all sedulously displayed, and it appeared that nothing was wanting to prove the prisoner's guilt in a most satisfactory manner.

"He is lost beyond redemption," was the general feeling which pervaded the bosom of every spectator. The Earl was now called upon for his defence. Slowly he rose and with a calm dignity of manner proceeded to assert his innocence and deprecated the clemency of his judges.

"My lord," said he, rising in energy as he went on, "I do not implore an acquittal. That would be the part of a man who, conscious of his guilt, seeks mercy as a boon. No. I claim it: it is my right. I am innocent, and I demand to be treated as such. I conjure you to do your duty, believe the word of a nobleman, whose honour till now was never doubted, and reject that of a—what shall I call him?—of a man, who, to speak in mild terms, is well known utterly to disregard both truth and honour when injuries, real or supposed, awake in his bosom the blood-thirsty passion of revenge. And my lord, for the other witness" (here he turned his full dark eyes on the perjured page, who shrunk as if blighted by his glance) "I know not what demon has possessed my vassal's breast, what hell-born eloquence has persuaded the orphan, who, since his birth, has existed only on my bounty, to aid in the destruction of his lord and benefactor. But this I know, they who shall condemn me for such cursed testimony, will sin both in the eyes of men and angels. My lords, avoid the sin for the sake of that Justice whose servants you profess to be, and whose image stands there the Guardian of your hall" (every eye turned as he spoke to the colossal statute of Justice which stood conspicuous in the light of the lofty window).

Meantime the Earl continued: "My lords, avoid it for your own sake, for I warn you the last St. Clair will not die unavenged. There are on the heights of my own Elimbos ten thousand unconquered warriors. Seven times that number, fierce as lions and free as the eagles that furnish their crests, dwell in the bosoms of those hundred glens that, ruled by no sovereign, controlled by no laws, lie among the wild Branni Hills. And when the news that I am dead, that the house of their chief is fallen, that his name and fame are blasted, shall reach these wild sons of the mist, let my murderers who cut me off with the sword and under the mask of justice tremble in their high places. My lords, I will say no more. Do as you list, and gather the fruits of your deed."

The question was now put whether he had any witnesses to call. For a moment he was silent, and seemed lost in deep thought, but almost immediately, raising his head, he said in a firm tone, "I believe there is one in this hall, who, if he will, can do me that service."

There was a pause. The judges (except the Duke, who throughout the trial had preserved his usual imperturbable calmness of demeanour) regarded each other with looks of astonishment. The exulting smile which had begun to dawn on Colonel Percy's cheek vanished. The page turned pale, and St. Clair's own countenance assumed an expression of anxious expectation. At length a slight bustle was heard in one part of the hall. A movement became perceivable among the dense and hitherto almost motionless mass of spectators. Their close ranks slowly opened, and a young man of handsome and genteel appearance, attired in a chieftain's undress uniform, advanced to the judges' seats.

"Are you come to bear testimony in favour of the prisoner?" asked the Duke of Wellington.

"I am," replied the young officer, bowing respectfully to his interrogator.

"What is your name and profession?"

"My name is John Bud, and I hold the rank of Ensign in the Sixty-fifth regiment of horse commanded by Colonel Percy."

"Repeat what you know concerning this affair. But first let the oath be administered to him."

This formula being complied with, Ensign Bud proceeded to give evidence to the following effect; that on the night preceding that on which the army received orders to attack the enemies' camp, he was returning to his own tent after passing the evening with a friend, when just as he passed the outskirts of a thick grove of trees beside the river, the words "Thou shalt obey me this instant, dwarf, or I'll stab thee to the heart," caught his ear; that on looking through the branches he beheld Colonel Percy and a man dressed in livery holding between them a little boy, whom he believed to be the same now present in their lordships' court; that the child fell on his knees and promised to obey them in everything; that the Colonel then told him to go to the African camp and claim a reward in the name of his master the Earl of St. Clair for intelligence of an important nature concerning certain plans which had just been resolved on in a council of war; that on the boy's declaring he did not know the way, the Colonel said he would go with him as far as the boundaries; that then, after wrapping himself in a green plaid which he took from the child, all three left the place and were soon out of sight. As the witness concluded this singular piece of evidence, Colonel Percy started from his seat and sprang rather than stepped to the bar.

"My lord," he exclaimed in a loud and agitated voice, which, while his flushed cheek, fierce eye, and the veins swelled almost to bursting on his forehead, proclaimed the violence of the emotions that were contending within him, "my lord, I implore you not to believe a word which has been uttered by that forsworn, that perjured minion. Mean revenge has dictated—."

He was going on with increasing vehemence when the Duke of Wellington demanded silence. A short conference carried on in such low tones as scarcely to be audible then succeeded among the judges, the result of which was that they declared that Ensign Bud's testimony was not sufficiently clear and decisive to warrant an immediate acquittal, but that they should remand the prisoner for the present in order that he might have an opportunity of procuring additional evidence. The court was now about to dissolve, when a movement became again visible among the crowd. It opened a second time and our friend Mr. S'death appeared, followed by six men bearing a litter on which lay a man dressed in the blue silver-laced coat of a footman. His countenance was ghastly pale, and his clothes were covered with recent stains of blood.

"Set him down here at the foot of his master, as in duty bound," said Mr. S'death, coming forward with an air of bustling assiduity, and carefully assisting the men to deposit their doleful burden just beside Colonel Percy.

"What do you mean by this, you villain?" asked he, turning as pale as the dying man before him.

S'death answered this question by a quiet, inward chuckle and a significant nod of intelligence. Then turning to the Duke, he said, "You see, my lord, I was daunering out this morning up the valley to get a breath of country air, when just as I got to a very lonely and quiet spot, I heard a long rattling groan, like as it might be of a man that's either drunk or discontented; so I turned to the place it seemed to come from. And what should I see but this here carrion lying writhing on the ground like a trodden snake.

" 'What's to do with you?' says I. 'And who's brought you to this smart pass, my beauty?'

" 'Colonel Percy,' he squeaks out. 'Oh carry me to Verdopolis! Carry me to the Hall of Justice! Let me be revenged on the wretch before I die!'

"There was no resisting this pathetic appeal. Besides, I have a great affection for the Colonel, and knowing him to be a wildish young man (Youth, alas! has its follies as well as old age!) I thought the sight of his poor servant in the dead thraws might do him good: so I ran, hired a litter, and brought him here according to his wish."

"What is the meaning of all this?" asked the Duke. "Who is the wounded man?"

"I am a miserable and deluded being," replied Travers in a hollow, tremulous tone. "But if it please heaven to grant me time and strength for confession, I will relieve my conscience of a part at least of that fiery burden which presses on it. Let it be known to all in this place that the Earl of St. Clair is totally innocent of the crime laid to his charge. My master is the traitor. Yes—but—but I cannot get on."

Here he paused from exhaustion. His eyes closed. His breath

came thick. And to all present it appeared as if he were dying. On a glass of wine being administered to him, however, he revived in some degree. Raising himself on his litter, he requested to speak with St. Clair in private. Orders were immediately given for the crowd to be cleared out. The subordinate judges likewise removed to a distant part of the hall. None remained within hearing of his confession except the Duke of Wellington, Ensign Bud, and the Earl himself. This being done, the poor wretch proceeded thus:

"My lord, Colonel Percy hates you, for what reasons, you yourself best know. He recognized you for an old enemy at the Olympic Games, and ordered me after the prizes were distributed to watch your motions and inform him where you should take up quarters for the night. I dogged you as far as the Zephyr Valley and then returned to tell my master. When we returned, you were fast asleep, and that boy, whom, from his dress, short stature, and withered, unnatural features, my master always called the Green Dwarf, was laid at your feet.

"The Colonel then bade me go and fetch the boy to him. I did so, and when he was brought, Percy drew his sword and threatened to kill him on the spot if he would not instantly swear to obey him in everything he should command. The lad called out that if he did obey him, it should be for the promise of a reward rather than for a threat of punishment. My master told him to name his own reward. He said he would do so when he knew what his business was to be. Colonel Percy told him that in the first place it was to tell him who his master was. He said he would do that for five pounds, and then confessed directly that you were the Earl of St. Clair. Afterwards the Colonel told him that he was to be a spy on all your actions, to note particularly whether you went to Charlesworth Castle, to follow you thither, if possible to listen at the door of the apartment to which you might be shown, and to report everything that was said to him. The little mercenary wretch swore to do all this for a hundred pounds. He was then informed in what part of the city his employer resided and dismissed to commence his villainous system of espial. About a week afterwards he arrived at our house panting and quite out of breath and desired to see the Colonel instantly. He had brought information that you and Lady Emily Charlesworth had concerted a plan of elopement together which was to be put in practice at twelve o'clock that night. My master commanded him to delay you as much beyond the time as he could, and then dismissed him. At eleven o'clock he and myself set off in a carriage and six for the castle. We reached the place of rendezvous, a chestnut avenue, shortly after twelve. At the entrance my master got out and went a little way up the walk. He soon returned with the lady and handed her into the carriage."

"Did she go with him willingly?" asked St. Clair, in a tone of the deepest agitation.

"Yes. But it was because he had passed himself for you; and as he had on a travelling cloak, and the trees threw a very dark shade, it was impossible for her to discover the cheat."

"But she might have recognized his voice. He spoke to her, did he not?"

"Very seldom; and when he did, it was scarcely above his breath."

"Well, proceed. Where did you carry her?"

"That I cannot, dare not, tell. I am bound by a solemn oath never to reveal it, and surely you would not have me add fresh agonies to my dying hour by committing the crime of perjury!"

In this determination the man seemed fixed. St. Clair tried in vain arguments, entreaties, and commands; and, seeing it was impossible to prevail with him and that the sands of life were running very low, he at length permitted him to continue his confession.

"When she was secured," said he, "we returned to Verdopolis, and the next day accompanied the rest of the army on their march against the rebels. You arrived at the camp shortly after us. And as soon as he saw you, my master resolved to rid himself of an abhorred rival in your person, and was confirmed in this resolution by seeing the distinction with which His Grace the Duke of Wellington treated you. Accordingly one night he ordered me to fetch him the Green Dwarf. I proceeded to your tent for this purpose and, by means of a peculiar signal with which he was acquainted, called him out. Subsequently, by means of threats and promises, the Dwarf was induced to lend his aid in executing the scheme which my master had devised for your disgrace and death. He went to the camp, betrayed the secrets of the council in your name, and brought back as a recompense the articles which are now lying on that table. These he afterwards buried in your tent. He removed the sword which was fastened to your belt, and put that scimitar in its place; and, finally, he completed his treachery by delivering that false evidence which has so nearly been the means of causing you to incur an undeserved, a shameful death."

Here Travers paused again to wipe off the death-sweats which were starting in large drops from his pallid forehead.

"You have nobly cleared St. Clair's character," said the Duke of Wellington. "Now inform us by whom and how the wound of which you are dying has been inflicted."

"By my master," replied the unhappy man. "I informed him this morning as we were returning from his Uncle's country seat in the valley that I intended to reform and lead a better life, for that the sins I had already committed lay like a leaden weight at my heart. At first he laughed at me, and pretended to think that I was in jest, but on my assuring him that I was never more serious in my life, he grew gloomy. We walked together for some time in silence; but at length, just as we came to a very lonely part of the road, he drew his sword and stabbed me suddenly in the side, saying as I fell, with a loud laugh,

'Now go and reform in Hell!' I can speak no longer, and you know the rest."

The last part of Travers' communication was uttered in a very faint and broken voice. When the excitement of talking was past, he fell into a sort of lethargy which continued about ten minutes, and then with a single, gasping groan and convulsive shudder of the whole frame, his soul and body parted forever asunder.

The crowd were now again admitted into the hall. The judges returned to their station, and the Duke of Wellington, after publicly declaring that St. Clair's honour was unblemished and that the charge brought against him had risen entirely from the machinations of a malignant enemy, ordered his fetters to be taken off, and commanded them to be fastened on the limbs of Colonel Percy and the Green Dwarf instead. Subsequently he condemned the former of these worthy personages to death and the latter to ten years labour at the galleys.

Matters being thus settled, the Duke rose from his seat, and taking St. Clair by the hand, he said, "My lord, I claim you as my guest whilst you remain in Verdopolis. You must comply with my request were it only to show that you bear no malice against me for the six weeks imprisonment to which you have been subjected."

Of course St. Clair could not resist an invitation thus courteously urged, and accordingly, he accompanied the Duke to Waterloo Palace. On his way thither he informed his noble conductor of the mysterious incognito who had visited him in his dungeon and expressed a strong desire to discover who he was, that he might recompense him according to the signal service he had received at his hands.

"Was it Ensign Bud, do you think?" said the Duke.

"No," replied St. Clair. "He was taller and the tones of his voice were very different. Indeed, if I may be permitted to form so presumptuous a conjecture on such slight grounds, I should say that I am at this moment conversing with my un-known friend."

The Duke smiled, but returned no answer.

"I am not mistaken then," continued St. Clair eagerly, "and it is to your Grace that I owe a continuance both of life and honour."

As he spoke, the silent gratitude which beamed forth from his fine eyes expressed his thanks more clearly than any words could have done.

"Well," said the Duke, "I will confess that you have made a true guess. And now I suppose you would like to know the reasons which led me to give you that warning on the banks of the Senegal. It was simply this: I had witnessed the sort of quarrel between you and Colonel Percy which took place dur-ing supper in my pavillion. I saw him lay his hand on his sword and then relinquish it with a look and a muttered ex-clamation which told me plainly that the gratification of pres-ent revenge was postponed only for some more delicious future prospect, and as the life of the chieftain of Clan-Albyn was of some value in my estimation, I determined at least to set him on his guard against the attempt of an insidious enemy. Then for my visit in the prison, that was prompted by the informa-tion Ensign Bud had communicated to me. And I thought that that method of summoning him to give evidence which I pointed out would make a deeper impression on the minds of the other judges than if the ordinary way of calling a witness were followed."

As the Duke concluded this explanation, they reached Water-loo Palace. They immediately proceeded to the dining room, where dinner was already prepared. During this meal, St. Clair spoke little and ate less. His spirits, which had been in some degree excited by the unexpected events of the morning, now began to flag. The thought of Lady Emily and of the forlorn and wretched condition to which she was probably reduced, communicated a mournful gloom to his mind. The Duke perceived this, and after a few vain attempts to dispel it he said, "I see what you are thinking of, my lord, so come. I'll carry you to my wife. Perhaps her sympathy will be some consolation to your distress."

St. Clair followed almost mechanically as his host led the way to the drawing room. On entering they found the Duchess seated on the sofa engaged in some ornamental labour of the needle. Beside her was a little Indian stand supporting her work-box and a few books. Near this and with her back turned to the door was seated another elegant female form over whose rich brown tresses was thrown a transparent veil of white gauze according to the graceful fashion of the times. Her head was resting on her hand with a pensive gesture and, when the Duke and his guest were announced, she did not rise or give any other symptom of being conscious of their presence except a sudden and convulsive start. The Duchess, however, left her seat, and advanced to meet St. Clair with a benignant smile.

"I was sure," said she, "that justice would be done, and that your fame would come out of the fiery ordeal seven times purified. Now, my lord, will you permit me to introduce you to a friend of mine? Here, Love," (addressing the silent lady) "is one whom fortune has severely tried, and who now expects from her and you a recompense for all he has suffered."

The lady rose, and threw back her veil. There was a momentary pause, a joyful exclamation, and St. Clair clasped to his bosom his dear and long-lost Emily.

It now only remains for me to explain how this happy catastrophe was brought about, which duty I shall discharge as briefly as possible.

During a period of four weeks Lady Emily had pined in her lonely prison under the surveillance of the wretched Bertha, who regularly visited her three times a day to supply her with food, but at all other times remained in a distant part of the castle. At the usual hour on the first day of the fifth week, she did not make her appearance. Lady Emily, whose appetite was much impaired by grief and confinement, at first was rather pleased than otherwise with the omission. But when night came, she began to feel some symptoms of hunger. The next day likewise elapsed and neither food nor drink passed her now parched and quivering lips. On the morning of the third day she was reduced to such a state of weakness from inanition that she felt totally unable to leave her bed.

While she lay there expecting death and almost wishing for it, the tramp of a heavy step in the ante-chamber, and the sound of a gruff voice calling, "Is there any living body besides owls and bats in this here old ancient heap of a ruin?" roused her from the lethargic stupor into which she had fallen. Collecting her remaining strength with a strong effort, she answered that there was an unhappy woman imprisoned that would give much for deliverance and restoration to her friends. Apparently the querist heard her voice, faint as it was, for he immediately broke open the door of her chamber, and appeared in the shape of a tall and athletic man, dressed in the usual garb of rare lads and armed with a long fowling piece.

"What's to do with you, poor heart, that you look so pale and thin?" said he advancing towards her.

She shortly informed him that she had eaten nothing for three days, and begged a little food for the love of heaven. He directly took from his pouch, which was slung over his shoulders, a little bread and cheese. While she was eating these coarse, though acceptable viands, he told her that his name was Dick Crack-Skull, and that while poaching a bit in the forest, he had lit upon this old tower, which, from motives of idle curiosity, he had entered through one of the unglazed windows; that in his perambulations through the desolate halls he had, to his horror, stumbled upon the corpse of an old hideous woman, who, to his mind, looked for all the world like a witch; that he then supposed that there must be some other inhabitants, and so he had gone on, bawling as he went, till he reached the ante-chamber of Lady Emily's apartment, whose life he had thus been the providential means of saving.

Next day, after covering Bertha's dead body with a heap of stones, Dick set out with his charge for Verdopolis. On arriving there, he accompanied the lady at her own desire to Waterloo Palace. Here she put herself under the Duchess's protection, who after bestowing on Dick a reward that made his heart leap for joy, dismissed him with all honour.

From my mother the unfortunate damsel received the most tender and assiduous kindness, in so much that she won her entire confidence, and all the tale of Lady Emily's mournful loves was poured into her beloved patroness's sympathizing ear.

When the news of Lord St. Clair's incarceration for high treason arrived, her grief may be better imagined than described. But now the pleasure of this happy meeting, when she received her lover with life untouched and honour unsullied, more than counterbalanced all her past fears and agonies. The good old Marquis of Charlesworth was now easily brought to consent to their union, and, according to all accounts, never was felicity so lasting and unbroken as that which crowned the future lives of the noble Earl of St. Clair and the beautiful Lady Emily Charlesworth.

Having thus wound up the dénouement of my brief and jejune narrative, I will conclude by a glance at the future fortunes of Colonel Percy and his accomplice.

The Sentence of Death which had been passed on the former was afterwards commuted to exile for sixteen years. During this period he wandered through the world, sometimes a pirate, sometimes a leader of banditti, and ever the companion of the most dissolute and profligate of mankind.

At the expiration of the term of banishment, he returned to Verdopolis, broken both in health and fortune, to claim the inheritance of his uncle, the Duke of Beaufort, who had been for some time dead. On inquiry, however, he found that that nobleman had married shortly after his disgrace became known, and had become the father of two sons, on whom, consequently, his estates and title devolved. Thus baffled, the Colonel turned his attention to political affairs, and, finding himself disowned by all his relations, discarded his real name and assumed a feigned one. Few now can recognize in that seditious demagogue, that worn-out and faded debauchee Alexander Rogue, Viscount Ellrington, the once brilliant and handsome young soldier Colonel Augustus Percy.

As for Andrew, when he was released from his service in the galleys, he became a printer's devil; from this he rose to the office of compositor; and being of a saving and pilfering disposition, he at length by some means acquired money enough to purchase a commission in the army. He then took to the trade of author, published drivelling rhymes which he called Poetry, and snivelling tales, which went under the denomination of novels.

I need say no more. Many are yet living who can discover a passage in the early life of Captain Tree[13] in this my Tale of The Green Dwarf.

CHARLOTTE BRONTË. Septbr 2nd. 1833.

FINIS.

PERCY AS A PIRATE

Introduction to "Zamorna's Exile"

THE reader is to imagine that much time has elapsed in the Brontës' African empire since the conclusion of "The Green Dwarf." Early in 1833, eight months before Charlotte "published" that novel, Branwell Brontë wrote a story called "The Pirate," showing Percy, or Rogue, in the midst of the piratical activities hinted at in the *dénouement* of "The Green Dwarf," and recounting his astonishing marriage to Lady Zenobia Ellrington. This marriage brought about revolutionary changes in the cycle. Percy, now rehabilitated, introduced Mary Henrietta, his daughter by an earlier marriage, to Verdopolitan society. Arthur Wellesley, the elder son of the Duke of Wellington, who is now to take his father's place as hero of the cycle, and whose name is gradually to be expanded into Arthur Augustus Adrian Wellesley, Marquis of Douro, the Duke of Zamorna, and Emperor Adrian, fell in love—notwithstanding his obligations to his wife Marian and his child—with Mary Percy; and she, forgetting her engagement to Sir Robert Pelham, eagerly returned his passion. Marian meekly agreed to step aside for Mary, but she died of consumption before the decree could be put into effect, and left her infant son to the care of Mina Laury, Zamorna's earliest and most faithful mistress.

Zamorna's marriage to Mary ended for a time the political enmity between himself and her powerful father. A coalition was arranged by which Zamorna received from the Verdopolitan parliament the cession, in full sovereignty, of a vast stretch of fertile though sparsely settled country to the east. His kingdom, making the seventh in the Verdopolitan Union, was called Angria. The new monarch built upon the Calabar a capital which rivalled in magnificence and splendor the magic glories of Verdopolis, from which it drew most of its population. Zamorna, who was now Emperor Adrian, called the new city Adrianopolis. The prime minister of the new kingdom was his father-in-law, Rogue, or Percy, now bearing the titles of Lord Ellrington and Earl of Northangerland.

The history of Angria, with its endless details of boundaries, population, and governmental machinery, was apparently Branwell's care; but it was Charlotte who made literature of these bare events. Where he gives a census list, she shows the actual flight of the swarm from the mother hive, in the opening passages of a "volume" which she called "My Angria and the Angrians." Since this piece purports to be written by Zamorna's disapproving younger brother, Lord Charles Albert Florian Wellesley, we should not be surprised at the tone of contempt and ridicule which the author adopts toward the Emperor and his mushroom nation. Lord Charles writes:

With that love of ostentatious pomp and flashy display which circulates through the veins of every Angrian as unceasingly as his blood, the grand migration was so contrived that at one day, almost at one hour, the carriage of each oriental noble stood at the door of his Verdopolitan residence, and in splendid cortège the gathered host of vehicles with their attendant outriders went pouring from sunrise to sunset in a tide of thunder along the eastern highway. Previously had been the farewell visits and the last interviews, the solemn prognostications, the significant shakes of the head of the old regime, the insolent bantering and triumphant hilarity of the juvenile upstarts. . . .

It was hard for a steady, sober Glass-towner (to say nothing of an irritable old aristocrat) to endure the swaggering effrontery of those latter days; to see the throngs of high-born scoundrels, the hordes of low-born rapscallions, jostling about from house to house and from street to street, talking loudly and incessantly of their preparations for the "great move," which preparations in the majority of cases must have been limited to the packing up of the second shirt, neckcloth, and pair of stockings, together with the careful securing of the sow's ear containing the only half-sovereign in shillings and half-pence, which treasure must of necessity be placed in the adventurer's fob, unencumbered by watch, lest some of his travelling companions, in the ardour of their enterprising dispositions, might have proved their dexterity on his person, lightening him of that "filthy lucre" while he sat unsuspiciously reposing himself on the ale-bench of the "Rising Sun," or the "Scarlet Banner," or the "Northangerland Arms."

Lord Charles had great and just scorn for those who preferred "the marble toy-shop of Adrianopolis" to "the old city where they dwelt so long, the home of their fathers, the Queen of the Earth, who looks down on her majestic face mirrored in the noble Niger." Yet there were some who found Verdopolis dark and dismal after the exodus. The Honorable Julia, Lady Sidney, was sick at heart for Angria now that her friends were gone, and in a letter to her bosom friend, Lady Maria Percy, she expressed the feeling of emptiness and desolation which had settled on Verdopolis. She had been to the Theatre Royal. There she had seen many ancient countesses, venerable viscounts, and the like, but for her the splendor had departed:

But when I looked for Castlereagh, the noble, dashing dandy; for Arundel, the brilliant, courteous chevalier; for Edward Percy, the haughty and handsome, who at intervals grave and gay between used formerly to appear like a star in his box under the chandelier; for Northangerland with his countenance of such strange and interesting melancholy; for honest Thornton who always came to see the play and not to look about him; for Dudley; for Seymour; for Abercorn; for Lennox—I protest, Maria, that when I looked for all these, and saw nothing but old Trojans and their dowager-dames, I had much ado to keep tears from running down my cheeks.

Of course, Lady Julia was a poor thing and her end was divorce, but even the scornful Lord Charles finally felt the lure of Adrianopolis and through sheer curiosity went afoot to visit that mushroom on the Calabar. Once there, he succumbed to the natural scenery of the place, and again was fascinated by the career of his profligate brother:

I see Zamorna sometimes when twilight closes, glide down Saldanha Park to the beach where a small barge with two rowers, generally William Ireton, one of the palace sentinels, and Sergeant Edward Laury, is moored in waiting. He steps on board, and the white-winged vessel skims off as swiftly and silently as a bird. When the moon is shining I can, by the aid of a small glass, track its course on over the deep and foaming stream to a landing place on the opposite side, surrounded, as I well knew, by sedges and shadowed by a giant willow. Behind rises a long low wooded brae, crowned with the twinkling lights, the black roof, and the high turret-like chimneys of Fort Adrian.
Often at this moment as I sit in moonlight on the marble terrace of Zamorna Palace, the evening gun is fired from the city batteries, and then, like a deep echo, a cannon answers from the Fort, five miles across the water. In still evenings the effect is indescribably solemn, especially, when I know who is visiting his hid treasure in the stern domicile that looms from the opposite shore.

Meanwhile, the building of the kingdom of Angria went on with unabated enthusiasm. Adrianopolis rose, the frontiers of the new country were pushed toward the boundaries of Abyssinia, and the Duke held court in Wellington House. We may see Zamorna in a characteristic mood as he addresses his wife:

"Mary, Mary," said the Duke, drawing himself quickly to the height of his stately stature and passing his hand over his brow, "Adrianopolis is rising, soaring (not so, either, or it may soar away!) but the buildings spring like magic, and I and

Warner see that they are solidly put together. Men gather in my kingdom as if they gather at beat of drum. There have been new inroads on the frontier, fresh raids on the borders, some of Ham's blood has been shed. Naughty spitted a horde of sable rascals by means of ten bayonets and sent them to heave and lift in—Hades, I'll say for the sake of euphony."

But Charlotte is always happy to turn away from public affairs to intimate scenes in Zamorna's domestic life. Across the Calabar from the city stands Fort Adrian, and there Zamorna has established Mina Laury, the first and most constant of his many mistresses. She was a peasant girl, the daughter of Ned Laury, a forester on the Duke of Wellington's estate. The friendship between her and Zamorna dates almost from their childhood, and she has played an important part in every crisis of his life. She is beautiful, strong-minded, and loyal unto death, and Zamorna often shakes the cares of state and of his household from his shoulders and escapes across the Calabar to visit Mina Laury.

So sure of her loyalty was Zamorna that he confided two of his sons to her keeping. On the death of Marian Hume, his first wife, his infant son was sent to Mina, but her devotion proved powerless to save the lad from the disease which had killed his mother. The other child, Ernest Edward Gordon Wellesley, was the Emperor's oldest son, by his mistress Helen Victorina, "the young and beautiful lily of Lake Sunart"; and he plays a part in "Zamorna's Exile." The boy resembles his "splendid, dark-souled, vicious, magnificent father," and this perhaps accounts in part for the Duke's great affection for him. The keen observer might notice on occasion the sinister shadow which distinguished all of Zamorna's line, upon his brow. The boy is often a visitor to his father's palace in Adrianopolis, and there he charms many by his grace and imagination; but on occasion he shows violent fits of rage and jealousy against Mary Percy's children. On one occasion he inflicts a wound upon a servant who has come to take him home. Not for nothing was it said that "Zamorna is his father, and the Gordons, the dark, malignant, scowling Gordons, are his blood relatives. He is a true descendant of both." Charlotte Brontë knew that where a Gordon was, a Byron was not far away.

Angria did not long enjoy the peace and progress which its fair beginning promised. Branwell, in the rôle of fate, had grown weary of a calm world, and from September, 1834, until March, 1835, both he and Charlotte were busily engaged in recording the gathering storm between Zamorna and his treacherous, intriguing prime minister. The matter came to a crisis when the Emperor dismissed Percy from office before the general parliament of the Confederacy, and threatened that unless Percy changed his course immediately he would take the most certain and dreadful revenge he could think of—to divorce Percy's daughter, the only creature in the world that Percy loved. This act, cruel as it was to Mary, who would die if she were sent away from her husband, Zamorna was prepared to carry out in order to have vengeance.

At this critical juncture in the affairs of Angria, in the summer of 1835, Charlotte began teaching in Miss Wooler's school. We have seen in the introductory chapter with what torturing anxiety she there awaited news of Angria. The inevitable happened, and Branwell loosed upon the fair land both foreign invasion and civil war.

From the beginning the war went against Zamorna. Overwhelmed by numbers and outmaneuvered by the conspiracy of Northangerland, he was forced back into his capital, and, when his position proved untenable, Adrianopolis was burned to prevent its falling into the hands of the enemy. For a time Zamorna maintained his shattered army in the mountains; then, risking all in a mad dash for Verdopolis, he was defeated, his army broken, and he himself taken prisoner. True to his threat, he had sent Mary away to her father's castle at Alnwick, where she lay dying of grief. Though the other conspirators clamored for Zamorna's death, Northangerland caused the Emperor to be secretly taken on board his old pirate ship *The Rover,* under the command of S'death, and taken into exile on Ascension Isle. Meantime, as soon as Adrianopolis had been threatened, Mina Laury and the child under her care had been removed to a place of safety; but in the struggle they fell into the hands of the enemy, and Ernest was torn from the arms of Mina and fiendishly tortured and murdered. After this tragedy Mina managed to escape, and followed her master into exile. Curiously enough, Marseilles was a port of call on the journey from Verdopolis to Ascension Isle, and there Mina Laury boarded *The Rover* in the disguise of a flower girl, and was carried away with Zamorna.

All these events were reported by Branwell in letters to Charlotte, herself in heartbreaking exile at Roe Head. In the course of her summer vacation she wove them into a long narrative poem, reminiscent of Byron's *Childe Harold* (Canto III) and *Don Juan;* it imitates the stanzaic form of the latter. The poem begins as Zamorna, aboard *The Rover,* is being carried into exile.

"Zamorna's Exile"

Canto I

AND when you left me, what thoughts had I then?
    Percy, I would not tell you to your face,
    But out of sight and thought of living men
I, wandering away on the lone ocean's face—
I may say what I think, and how and when
    The mood comes on me, I may give it space,
Confessing like a dying man to heaven,
Anxious alone to have his sins forgiven,

Not caring what the world he leaves may say,
    Heedless of its forgotten hate and scorn,
But giving full and free and fearless way
    To secrets that the fear of death has torn
From his concealing bosom where they lay,
    Scorching the soul in which their sparks were born.
Aye, Alexander, just as recklessly
I give my dreams to the wild wind and sea.

You are a fiend! I've told you that before;
    I've told it half in earnest, half in jest.
I've sworn it when the very furnace-roar
    Of Hell was rising fiercely in my breast,
And calmly I confirm the oath once more,
    Adding, however, as becomes me best,
That I'm no better, and we two united,
Each other's happiness have fiend-like blighted.

Let us consider, let us just look back
    And trace the pleasant path we've trod together.
The retrospect is dreary, cold, and black,
    And threatens rain—our own grim Angrian weather.[1]

There are some slips of greensward on the track
 Glorious with sunshine; but dark slopes of heather,
Copses of night-shade, thickets void of flowers—
These are the chief types of those by-past hours.

How oft we wrung each other's callous hearts,
 Conscious none else could so effectively
Waken the pain, or venom the keen darts
 We shot so thickly, so unsparingly,
Into those sensitive and tender parts
 That, veiled from all besides, ourselves could see
Like eating cankers, pains that heaven had dealt
On devotees to crime, sworn slaves of guilt.

And still our mutual doom accomplishing,
 Blind as the damned, our anti-types, if one
Had in his treasures some all-priceless thing,
 Some jewel that he deeply doted on,
Dearer to him than life, the fool would fling
 That rich gem to his friend. He could not shun
The influence of his star, though well he knew
His friend that treasure to the winds would strew.

Percy, your daughter was a lovely being.
 Truly you must have loved her! Her sweet eyes
Showed in their varied lustre, changing, fleeing,
 Such warm and intense passion! That which lies
In your own breast, and, save to the All-seeing,
 Not fully known to any, could not rise
To stronger inspiration than their ray
Revealed when I had waked her nature's wildest play.

When Mary was grown up, an open rose,
 A Western girl,[2] just ripe for womanhood,
With those Milesian eyes whose lids disclose
 Spirits that only glad the Gambia's flood,

Glowing like sunlight on the stream which flows,
    Hesperia, through thy land of lake and wood—
I tell thee, Percy, not one nation's breast
Bears women like our own infernal West.

But then they're mostly hasty, soon excited
    To wrath, with little reason. There's thy wife,[3]
She's just the clear dark skin, the glance uplighted
    With thoughts that always fill the soul with strife,
The gait, the form, the fervent mind benighted,
    Which might suit Italy, or else the knife
That Eastern ladies, crowned sultanas, wear—
A glittering sign to bid their lords beware!

However, I'll return again to Mary.
    There's something sweet and soothing in that word,
A dreamy charm, as if some wandering fairy
    Had breathed it, or some little spirit bird
Had warbled it unseen, for soft and airy,
    And oft divinely holy, it is heard.
I know my dark speech does not need explaining,
For, Percy, well thou knowest it hath a meaning.

Well, sir, when Mary on some pleasant even
    Has sat beside you, perhaps at Percy Hall,[4]
And in the richest, purest light of heaven
    You've seen the curls around her temples fall,
And when the coming gloom of dusk has given
    A tone of such sad loveliness to all,
Could you look on her, sir, and think that she
Must sometime be a prey to such as me?

I well remember on our marriage day,
    An hour or two after the bridal rite,
She and I somehow chanced to find our way
    Into a large and empty hall whose light,

Streaming through painted windows, shed its ray
On nothing save ourselves, the floor of stone,
And the pure fountain falling there alone.

I gazed on her Ionian face, so fair,
   In all its lines so classically straight,
Her marble forehead, with the haloing hair
   Sunnily clustering round it, whereon sate
A shade that soon might deepen into care,
   Even such dark care as has gloomed there of late,
Though then 'twas but the sadness said to lie
On the fair brows of those who early die.

I asked her if she loved me, and she said
   That she would die for me, with such a glance—
Talk of the fiery, arrowy lustre bred
   By the hot southern suns of Spain and France!
I say again, as I before have said,
   Our Western tenderness does so enhance
The ardour of our women's souls and spirits
That nought on earth such fire divine inherits.

She said she'd die for me; and now she's keeping
   Her word, far off at Alnwick, o'er the sea.
The very wind around this vessel sweeping
   Will steal unto her pillow whisperingly
And murmur o'er her form, which shall be sleeping,
   Ere long, beneath some quiet, pall-like tree.
I would she were within my reach just now;
Not long that shade should haunt her Grecian brow.

She'd feel the stream of life run strong again
   If I could only take her to my breast;
She'd feel a balm poured on her aching pain;
   Her day-long weariness would know a rest.

But then, there's the profound wide-thundering main
  Tossing between us its triumphant crest
Of snow-white foam, and then, I've pledged my faith
I'll break the father's heart by Mary's death.

A holy resolution! And it will
  Be visited upon me thirty-fold,
For human nature feels a shuddering chill
  To hear of life for bloody vengeance sold—
An animal passion when, unmoved and still
  And vulture-like, it fixes its stern hold
Deep into the very vitals of its slave,
Making his bosom but a hungry grave.

And so, my Lord, if you have ruined me,
  And ruined all the hopes I ever cherished,
I've paid you back, and that abundantly.
  You'll feel it when that flower of yours has perished:
And dark and desolate that hour shall be
  When the place where my dazzling lily flourished
Shall know no more its past significance—
Death having gathered it and borne it hence.

I'm walking on the deck, and King⁵ is leaning
  O'er the ship's rails and communing with me.
Would you could hear the bloody tales he's gleaning
  From the dark harvest of his memory!
Would you could see his eye's ferocious meaning,
  Bent gloatingly upon the surging sea!
He says that monarch of exhaustless founts
Is the best balancer of men's accounts.

He says if I'd been wise I should have taken
  My lady with me on this distant sail,
And kindly, tenderly have striven to waken
  That bliss again which had begun to fail;

And that I should defyingly have shaken
  My fist in fortune's face and made her quail—
The old, blind jade! and turned my hand like thee,
To blood and pillage on the rolling sea.[6]

And some sweet night, the hoary saint is saying,
  Some heavenly, holy tropic summer night,
When dying gales upon the deep are straying,
  As soft as if they came down with the light
The moon diffuses, while the stars decaying
Before her beam imperial, still may yield
A radiant tremor o'er that deep blue field—

Then, says the mentor, when my Mary's sleeping,
  Wrapt blissfully in dreams of love and me,
Quietly, ghost-like, to her cabin creeping,
  I should have brought her up all tenderly;
And, while the lulling waves were past us sweeping,
  Have given her to the bosom of the sea
As she still slumbered, and no sob or moan
Was wakened to tell which way the bird had flown.

It would look well, says S'death, to see her sinking,
  All in white raiment, through the placid deep,
From the pure limpid water never shrinking,
  Calmly subsiding to eternal sleep,
Dreaming of him that's drowning her, not thinking
  She's soon to be where sharks and sword-fish leap,
And if she rose again a few days hence,
Looking like death, it would but stand to sense,

To common sense: a corpse laid in the water
  Must putrefy, whosever corpse it be;
And neither Adrian's wife nor Percy's daughter
  Can be left out in nature's great decree.
He'd seen stout men who'd fallen by pirates' slaughter

A few days after float up buoyantly,
And laughed to watch the light and fleet career
They held upon the water's surface clear.

He'd seen you stand upon the *Rover's* deck
    As calm as if 'twere sea-weed floating by,
Order a weight to be tied round their neck,
    Cool as a cucumber, for, proud and high,
You'd too much sense to suffer such a speck
    To dim a moment your rejoicing sky—
Your spirit was a sun which drove away
Such slight obscurers of the light of day.*

* Here a pause is indicated in the manuscript by nine handmade stars.

Of late our ship along the coast of France
    Was gliding in the gentle gales which blow
Off from the storied hills of old Provence.
    We saw Marseilles frown on the waves below.
It's pleasant, when the sunny billows dance
    All gladsomely around the vessel's prow,
And when a town and shore before you lie,
The home of thousands neath their native sky—

It's pleasant then to think that you are hasting
    As fast as wind and flowing sail can fleet
To a black jail of rocks; and keen and wasting
    Are the strong impulses and pangs that eat
At that thought through the heart; and were they lasting
    They'd soon enfold you in your winding sheet,
But they pass off in sickness, sometimes in tears,
And then again the dim sky coldly clears.

I stood upon the deck; the vessel's rails
    I was convulsive grasping, for around
The life and gaiety of proud Marseilles
    Were poured upon its harbour. Not a sound

Rang o'er the deep, but glad as chiming bells
  It spoke of life and made my bosom bound
With a wild wish for freedom, worse than vain—
  My breast but struck the stronger 'gainst a chain.

At that dark moment something spoke my name,
  My title, rather, which ought now to die.
'Twas from a female that the soft sound came,
  She said in French, "Zamorna, will you buy?"
I turned. 'Twas like the kindling of a flame
  To utter that word 'neath an alien sky.
I saw a girl beside me, dark and tall,
Her face all shaded by her tresses' fall.

The curls as black and bright as jet descended
  From under the Provençal hat she wore;
A basket full of grapes and vine leaves blended
  With roses, all in Gallic taste she bore.
And as on her my silent gaze I bended,
  She offered me her rich corbeille once more,
Murmuring in the soft tone of sympathy,
"You shall not buy them, you shall have them free."

I took a rose-bud, dropping in its stead
  A coin of my own ruined kingdom, graced
With the wreathed impress of my own wise head,
  And then,—you know my ways. However placed,
Were it upon the scaffold flashing red
  With noble blood and forms all death-defaced,
Or were it underneath the gallows tree,
I'd kiss the lovely lips that pitied me.

My slaughtered, hunted Angrians, shall I ever,
  Your ransomer, your conquering king, return?
Your brutal taskmasters will never, never
  Rule you as I have ruled you. They will burn

The slave mark on your brows, and they will sever
  The last domestic ties and make you mourn
Wildly and hopelessly, while I am lying
Far in yon dreary isle alone—it may be, dying.

And what made me speak thus? Why, I recalled
  The times, bright East,[7] when I was king in thee,
And when thy wildest mountains, heather-palled,
  With all their iron vassalage knew me,
And my land's daughters, now with bondage galled,
  Were as the Gordon red deer—chainless, free.
And thousands of their ruby lips have known
The touch of Adrian's when he claimed his own!

Well, when I lifted up the fruit girl's head
  To give her that salute, the black curls parted,
And the revealed and flashing eye-balls shed
  A ray upon me not unknown. I started
And half indignantly I would have said,
  "This must not be"; but then so broken-hearted,
So full of dying hope was that dark eye,
I could not put its mute petition by.

And so I turned again towards the town
  And looked upon its vast and busy quay;
And meekly, obstinately the girl sat down
  Beside me on the deck, and murmuringly
She said: "Zamorna, I have borne your frown
  Often before, and now I dare not be
Delicate in my duties—Those must dwell
In gloom habitual, who would serve you well.

"I stayed in Angria, Sire, until the hour
  Was past when I could serve my master there,
Until they had dug up the cherished flower[8]
  He gave into my sleepless, deathless care,

Until they'd broken his own domestic bower,
    Shivered his shrine, scattered in the air
The relics he loved well—And, this task done,
I rose and followed where my lord was gone.

"I will be with you, Sire—you'll want me soon.
    In that lone, dreary island where you go,
You'll sicken of the melancholy tune
    The waves will play around you in their flow,
And, wandering on its shore with shipwrecks strewn,
    You'll feel its solitude, full well I know,
Go to your heart, and then a wretch like me
Might serve you still in that extremity."

She spoke; I made no answer. We were now
    Leaving the harbour of Marseilles behind.
S'death had weighed anchor, and the *Rover's* prow
    Was flashing through the wave before the wind.
The gleaming walls and towers began to grow
    Dim in the distance. Scarce the eye might find
More than the misty outline of their forms,
Shadowy as rocks obscured by coming storms.

Our captain came and swore that she should stay.
    He'd have no boats sent off to land, not he.
She might have known the ship was under weigh—
    She saw it moving through the severed sea—
And by his soul, and by the light of day,
    He'd never stir a step to pleasure me.
And Mina smiled to see her end was gained—
Fortune had favoured her, and she remained.

Now for my Mary's sake I have not given
    One smile or glance of love to that poor slave;
And I have seen her woman's feelings riven
    With pangs that made her look down on the wave

As if it were her home, her hope, her heaven,
  Because a semblance of repose it gave.
She sees I do not want her. None can tell
What torments from that chill conviction swell.

I cannot spurn her, though my wife is dying,
  Cheerless and desolate in solitude.
This moment, like a faithful dog she's lying
  Crouched at my feet, for with a sad, subdued,
Untiring constancy she's ever trying
  To gain one word, or even one look, imbued
With some slight touch of kindness. There, then, take
A brief caress for all thy labour's sake!

I did but grasp her little hand and press
  The taper fingers as a brother might,
And she looked upward in her meek distress,
  While such a glad, adoring ray of light
Shot from her large black eyes as if to bless
  A god for mercies given, and full and bright
The gathered tear ran over, then again
They bent their radiance on the solemn main.

Last night she told me all the dreary tale
  Of what has happened, Percy, to my son:
How all her watchful care could nought avail,
  How she had struggled, how her prize was won.
And the departing blood left cold and pale
  The cheek that late it glowed so brightly on,
As she revealed what floating rumour said:
That the young lord of Avon-dale was dead;

That my brave Angrians to the rescue flew,
  Urged on by Warner;[9] that the boy they found
Alive, but as their noble leader true
  A bloody bandage from his eyes unbound—

Lo, he was sightless! And a faintness grew
  Over her as she told of many a wound
In his young frame, and she fell down and prayed
That I would bear with what was still unsaid.

Ere I could speak, the impetuous words came gushing
  Forth from her lips. "It was by night," she cried,
"The tryste was on a moor, and there came rushing
  The thousand serfs to Warner's house allied.
He stood up in the midst, the red blood flushing
  His face and brow; his voice rang far and wide
As in that hour he bade them look upon
The mangled relics of their monarch's son.

"And out into the ghastly moonlight holding
  A sheet all stained with blood, he turned aside
The drapery, a gory corpse enfolding—
  A corpse, though still the blood in gentle tide
Crept through its veins. But death the face was moulding
  Rightly for that home which the earth shall hide.
O, Sire, dread was that midnight's stormy gloom
Which saw thy flower so blighted in its bloom!

"Men's hearts were toned to horror, and their feelings
  Were wound up to the highest pitch of dread;
And Warner's voice and look shot forth revealings
  Of a soul into whose wild depths was shed
A kind of inspiration. Not the sheilings
  Of Highland seers who commune with the dead
E'er gloomed in such a cloud of awe as then
Fell on that host of brave and desperate men.[10]

"In Warner's arms and on his breast reposing,
  Ernest died calmly on that awful night,
Before a thousand men his brief life closing
  Amid the wild wind and the wandering light

Of moon and stars, his death a spirit rousing,
   Through all the land which saw it, that in fight
Shall henceforth strong and terrible and dread
Burst forth and reap dark vengeance for the dead.

"Warner with knitted brow the struggle watched
   Which parted flesh from spirit; then he pressed
The little corpse whose limbs in death were stretched,
   Ardently, strongly to his noble breast,
And then his silent lifted eye beseeched
   In prayer that, though unheard, might well be guessed,
The judgment of the Highest. All was still
While thus he spoke with God on that wild hill.

"They buried Gordon on the moor that night.
   Warner with his own hands the body laid
Low in its narrow house. No funeral rite,
   No prayer, no blessing o'er the grave was said,[11]
Only, as all the hosts their lances bright
   Reversed in homage to the royal dead,
Their chief cried solemnly, 'O Lord, how long
Shall thine elected people suffer wrong!' "

How did I feel when Mina ceased her speaking—
   I, stronger than an Indian in my love
For that which now beyond the power of waking
   Sleeps in its gory grave? There's Heaven above
And Earth around me, and beneath me, shaking
   With cries of the tormented, Hell may move;
But neither from Hell nor Earth nor Righteous Heaven
Can rest or comfort to my heart be given.

Thou whom I nurtured in my bosom, child,
   Thou whom I doted on and gently cherished,
Thou to die thus, when I was far exiled!
   In gloom, in grief, in agony he perished,

Sundered from me by that storm, dread and wild,
    Which war sent over Angria. All that flourished
Fairest upon her plains died in the blast,
Leaving her lorn and barren as it past.

I've nothing but revenge to think on now,
    Nothing to lean upon; my staff is broken.
O, if exerting more than human might
    I could have burst my bonds in time to save,
I should have thought that hour more blest and bright
    Than all the triumphs I have known, which gave
My darling to my breast! My star of light,
    My first born son, snatched from a fearful grave—
Rescued from wild beasts, from the demon stranger—
"Clasped in my arms, his home in every danger!"

Oft at Fort Adrian in the nights of storm
    That used to rush all madly on the river,
I've taken protectingly his sleeping form
    To the paternal heart that beat forever
In love to him, and while all calm and warm
    My nestling boy, what cared I for the shiver
Of roof and casement, and the deepening war
Of winds that vex the impetuous Calabar?

So like his sainted mother looked he sleeping,
    The wild eyes that reflected mine being closed,
The lamps his soft and lovely features steeping
    With shaded light, the darkness that reposed
All day upon his brow, his bright dreams sweeping
    With airy wings away. Then nothing roused
That spirit of the Gordons, which, when waking,
Oft crossed his face like sullen lightning breaking.

The ringlets dark and silken, waved away
  From his young forehead, left it calm and clear;
And on his polished cheek the shadow lay
  Of lashes black as ebon. Not more fair
Helen has ever looked, and not a ray
  Of my fierce likeness mingled with the dear
And hallowed impress that so sweetly moulded
The green bud to the blossom all unfolded.

Yet he was like me, like me in his passion,
  And like me in his rapture when some sight
Of glory sent a kindling inspiration
  All through the quickened current, red and bright,
Of his high blood. He was my own creation,
  The offspring of my boyhood, the delight
Of my first fiery youth, my hope, my pride,
A mightier branch of my own kingly tide.

You would not save him, Percy! Nor will I
  Save yours from desolation. With wild pleasure
I'll now call down the doom of the Most High—
  His curse upon my head in fullest measure.
I'll fit me for a passage to the sky
  By heaving overboard my choicest treasure.
Yes, I'll leave all, take up my cross and follow—
All flesh is grass, all joys are vain and hollow!

King, dog and fiend! you cannot tell me now
  The thing I would not do to make another
Feel the same horror that bedews my brow
  With bloody sweat. Hot harried crime might smother
The choking, suffocating thoughts that grow
  Like fungi round my blighted heart and wither
Its vital greenness, deeply, deeply eating
Into my very life pulse madly beating.

Warner, I thank you! You're the only man
  I would shake hands with at this passing hour.
I thank you, for you perilled all your clan
  To save my dead child from a demon's power.
I bless you, for you nobly led the van
  To snatch from Hell my crushed, uprooted flower,
I'm bound to you forever, for your breast
Was my departed Ernest's dying rest.

Mina, come hither. Weep no more; I love you
  As a hawk loves a lark. I've cast away
Patrician ladies throned as high above you
  As that large star, serene above the ray
The glow worm flings. Let not this world's scorn move you,
  And waste not in my passion's fiery ray;
I know that you can bear a fierce caress.
My arm grows strong, nerved by my heart's distress.

You'll never fear nor tremble to draw nigh
  When I am scarce myself, with torment stinging
Into the principle of life. You'd die
  To save my bosom from a moment's wringing—
Faithful, devoted martyr! Through the eye
  Her soul its ray of fevered joy is flinging
Because I said she might the victim be
Of a chained vulture, caged amid the sea.

Beautiful creature, once so innocent,[12]
  With such a seriousness and strength of mind
Beaming upon her youthful brow and blent
  With what seemed like religion, so refined,
So firm in principle! Her soul ne'er bent
  Nor wavered midst the soft voluptuous wind
A Western palace[13] round the wild rose blew,
But shook not from it one pure drop of dew.

What is she now? Look at her as the flashing
    Of her dark Italian eye shines full on me;
Look at the little hand so proudly dashing
    The gloomy rain that will stream fitfully
From the full sphere, her cheek of roses washing
    Till even its bright bloom fades, and we may see
Traces of sorrow there, lit up the while
With that lost, fated, God-abandoned smile.

She asks for work, and now she'll labour on
    From the first murmur of the morning breeze
To the descending of the evening sun
    With careful aspect, vigilant to please.
And now and then, if she is all alone
    The tear will drop no energy can freeze,
As a remembrance comes of parted hours
Dimly discerned through years of mist and showers.

I'll go and sit beside her and recline
    My forehead on her shoulder. There all's calm.
Her faithful heart was blest as it felt mine
    Beating against it. Now amid the balm
Blown o'er the summer sea by gales divine,
    Singing as sweet as some old mournful psalm,
I'll bow resigned—a man of many woes.
The sea shall soothe me, saddening as it flows.
July 19, 1836[14]

Tormented! O tormented! Mina, love,
    Thy cheek is wet with tears—they would come forth.
I cannot one brief hour of respite prove:
    The sweetest sights and sounds that bless this earth
Only the fiend to busier madness move,
    That eats my life away. What is their worth?
Nothing! Oh Mina, love, I cannot rest!—
I could not if Heaven's glory round me prest.

And it is misery when all's so bright
   In earth and sea and sky, as they were wooing
My mind to sympathy, and in their light,
   Their evening light, I feel around me growing
Something no words can tell, an inward night
   Downward unceasingly and darkly flowing
In clouds—Yes pity me—and wildly strain
Thy master to thy breast; 'tis all in vain.

Wave thy soft ringlets round me, press my brow
   With that cool, supple hand, and point again
Unto that Western sky. I see its glow;
   I feel it so rosily upon the main
Pouring its flush; I hear the cooing flow
   Of the hushed waters lulling their deep strain,
Answering the winds, as those enkindled seas
Respond to that bright burning sunset's blaze!

I seem to have lived for nothing, wandering
   Through all my early youth 'mong fields of flowers,
Tracking the green paths where the fairest spring,
   Culling the richest bloom of dells and bowers—
When all at once the unrelenting wing
   Of some cold blast swept by with sleety showers,
Scattered the roses and buds and leaves away,
Save one or two left shrivelled by decay.

That simile's absurd; all words are weak,
   Tongue cannot utter what the victim feels
Who lies outstretched upon that burning lake
   Whose flaming eddy now beneath me reels.
All that breathes happiness seems to forsake
   His blighted thoughts; a demon hand unseals
That little well so treasured in man's breast,
Whose drop of hope so sweetens all the rest,

And out it flows and slips unseen away,
   Trickling to nothingness, and leaving gall,
Rank gall, behind—such bitter briny spray
   As might be brought up by a sulphurous squall
From the dead lake, the Sodomitish sea—
But halt, I've said enough, and yonder wave
Shall give my words an unrevealing grave.

July 19, 1836

Introduction to Canto II

WHEN Charlotte returned to Roe Head at the end of her summer vacation in 1836, the war had not been concluded. Through the autumn the tide of war changed. Branwell conducted the disintegration of the Northangerland coalition, with Zamorna's enemies falling out among themselves and dividing their own strength. Two of the once neutral states of the Verdopolitan Confederacy came to the aid of the desperate Angrians, Percy fled the country, Zamorna returned from exile and once more led his army, composed of Angrians and the new allies, to victory. On his homeward journey he was met at Calais by the news of Mary's death, and he found his feeling of triumph subdued by this news and the blight of war. While Charlotte was at Haworth for her Christmas holidays in 1836–37, she brought her poem up to date with Branwell's chronicle by adding a second canto. The greater part of this canto is taken up in Zamorna's voicing, Byron-like, his own grief at the death of his wife, though he knows it is but the execution of his own decree. The canto ends with his chant of triumph subdued to the suggestion of a funeral march.

"Zamorna's Exile"

Canto II

WELL, the day's toils are over. With success
    I've laboured since the morning hand in hand
    With those I love, and now our foe's distress
Seems gathering to its height. My stalwart band
Desperate in purpose, cool and rock-like press
Near to their aim. Before another day
We hope to smite our snared and stricken prey.

All seems in train for triumph. Calm and stern
    We see our clouded sun look out again;
Not like its summer dawn the white beams burn,
    But withering, chilly, still subdued by rain,
The rain of storms that part and still return
    In a dim shower sometimes, and momently
Cloud, as with tears, the light on land and sea.

Brief fits of weeping, they can ne'er subdue
    The hidden yet glorious sense of victory nigh!
I feel it—all whose hearts to me are true
    Feel and yet veil the impulse; still no eye
That deep and secret consciousness may view,
    Save that which would flash fierce with sympathy.
It is the avenger's latest hope, and he
Waits for its full fruition—silently!

I've borne too much to boast. Even now I know,
    While I advance to triumph, all my host
So sternly reckless to the conflict go
    Because each charm and joy of life they've lost;
Because on their invaded thresholds grow
    Grass from their children's graves; because the cost

Of their land's red redemption has been blood
From gallant hearts poured out in lavish flood.

Yet oh! there is a sure and steadfast glory
    In knowing that the scale ascends again,
And that when we with age are bent and hoary,
    And when our children's children spring to men,
As we tell o'er this dark invasion's story[1]—
    How fires and war ran wild through every glen
And crowned each blue hill-top with crimson crest;
How then at last we found victorious rest,

And did not bow to demons, though their goad
    With teeth of iron urged us to despair,
And though men called us rebels as they trode
    Upon our yoke-bowed necks, and though the air,
The pure air of our mountains, felt the load
    Of putrid plague, and corpses everywhere
Lay livid in our lonely homes, and tombs
Ceased to unclose in the rank church-yards' glooms,

For none had time to bury. If the rite
    Were half commenced, the summons of dismay,
The cry to arms, the strange, appalling sight
    Of squadrons charging, called each friend away.
And often thus, even at the dead of night,
    Corpses were left alone midst clods of clay,
And the armed mourners hurried to repel
The whirlwind onslaught of the tribes of hell.

But the bare, ravished land is swept and free;
    Out of her shattered towns, and blighted fields
The wind has driven the locusts. Gallantly
    We chased the scum before us; vengeance wields
A sword none can withstand. And as a tree
    To the bleak autumn storm its foliage yields,

So, scarce resisting, the oppressor flew
As our tornado, coming, nearer drew.

Rising at once, the peasantry hemmed round
  Arab and Scot² retreating; hearths were quenched
And homes deserted. If some hut was found
  To yield a moment's shelter to the drenched
And starved and ravenous fiends, on the cold ground
No glowing fire gleamed, and trodden bread
And scattered flour, to greet their eyes were spread.

Their corpses fell like famished wolves before us
  Along the winter roads, spotting the waste
Of drifted snow. Vindictive joy flashed o'er us,
  As the grim bolted skeletons we passed.
And were we wrong? And should remorse have tore us,
  As we beheld them in black ditches cast,
Laid under leafless hedges, pale and gaunt,
Murdered with hardships, dead with grinding want?

Should we have wept? Shades of our fathers, say!
  Spirits of our dead comrades, rise and tell!
Angels of those whose dying relics lay
  On beds of pestilence, speak where ye dwell!
Should we have wept? Some in your early day
  The plague cut down—like stricken flowers ye fell
And withered hopeless in a land of slaves,
And knew that tyrants would tread o'er your graves.³

By the last sun you saw, by the wild weeping
  That closed your earthly pilgrimage in gloom,
By the unhallowed graves, where darkly sleeping
  You lie forgetful of the sorrowing home
That wails your long departure—Vain the sweeping
  Of the sweet native breezes o'er your tomb!

Icy and mute, you never can return,
But bow from heaven and mark what I have sworn!

Oh, by your memories, martyrs, there shall be
    Bloody reprisal for your fearful fate!
My arm is strung with giant energy
    By the convulsing thought that all's too late;
New strength springs from that stinging agony
    And firmer resolutions, hotter hate.
Weep for the pang of fiends! By God! By Heaven!
I'd kill the man who wept for that, unshriven!

I am alone: it is the dead of night.
    I am not gone to rest because my mind
Is too much raised for sleep. The silent light
    Of the dim taper streams in unseen wind;
And quite as voiceless on the hearth burns bright
    The ruddy ember. Now no ear could find
A sound, however faint, to break the lull
Of which the shadowy realm of dreams is full.

So then I've time to think of each event
    That hath befallen of late to all below.
I've leisure to recall the sudden rent
    That tore my heart a few short weeks ago.
'Twas at an inn in Calais;⁴ and the faint,
    Cold sense of death brought by that deadly blow
Whitened my cheek and glazed my eyes, awhile
Darkness o'erswept the noonday's sunny smile.

In a far foreign land with strangers round,
    Reading a journal of my native West,
Rang from the black-edged funeral page the sound
    Expected and yet dreaded. There the crest,
The arms, the name were blazoned, and the ground
    Marked where the corpse should lie, and all exprest

Even to the grim procession, hearse and pall,
The grave, the monument to cover all!

I went out sick and dizzy to the street;
   The air revived me. Something inward said:
" 'Tis but thine own work finished; time is fleet,
   And early has the gloomy task been sped,
Yet still 'tis thy behest. Now firmly meet
   Its prompt fulfillment. Turn thee from the dead
And go on prospering—thy way is free,
And they are punished—crushed—that thwarted thee."

Amongst the multitude of thoughts that came
   Rolling upon me, I remembered well
My feelings some months since, before this aim
   Of death was ripe, when it began to swell
And form within my breast; and like a dream
   The keen and racking recollections fell:
How I then watched my prey and slowly wrought
My mind to union with the awful thought—

Nothing was bodied forth distinctly then—
   I was too frantic—but at this lone hour
The bitter recollection comes again
   Of many a night I spent within her bower,
Of all the musing that came o'er me when
   Gently asleep beside me lay my flower,
Blushing in blissful dreams and pressing nigher
To the dark breast then filled with fire.

Watching her there through many a sleepless night,
   I never utterly resolved to slay[5]—
I could not when all young and soft and bright,
   Trusting, adoring me in dreams she lay,
Her fair cheeks pillowed on the locks of light
   That gleamed upon her delicate array,

Veiling with gold her neck and shoulders white
And varying with their rich and silken flow
Her forehead's smooth expanse of stainless snow.

Sometimes in sleep she'd put her hand on mine
      And fold it in her slight and fairy clasp
As if my fatal thoughts she could divine,
      And, as in terror, she would faintly gasp
And nearer, closer all around me twine,
      Holding me with an amorous, jealous grasp—
And when I woke and cheered her, she would say
She had dreamt I'd cast her scornfully away.

Often at night after a long day spent
      In hearing of her father's mad designs,
In toilsomely reclaiming projects bent
      By his perverseness out of the set lines
I'd furrowed in the future, all I meant
      With deepest thought to execute, the mines
I'd laid most carefully effaced and sprung—
And all that loved me by his insult stung.[6]

Harassed by his malignancy so cold
      And unprovoked and bitter, I've come home,
And full of stricken thoughts I never told,
      Bearing upon my brow my spirit's gloom,
Entered the atmosphere of aerial gold—
      Of light and fragrance—in my lady's room,
And passing her, unable to reply
To the warm wish of her saluting eye.

'Twas strange, but Mary never seemed to dread
      Or shun me in my ireful mood. She'd steal
Silently to my side, and droop her head
      And rest it upon my knee, and gently kneel[7]

Down at my feet; and then her raised glance said:
  "Adrian, I do not fear though I can feel
Your gaze is stern and dark, but I can brook
Even ferocity in that fixed look."

Sometimes her lips as well as eyes would say:
  "If you are here, I am happy—though in wrath;
But when you keep through the long night away,
  Repose, existence, luxury I loathe;
Your presence forms the bright, the cheering ray
  That makes life glorious. Adrian, what can soothe
Your ruffled mind? Tell me, and I will try
To light the gloom of that denouncing eye."

"Trouble yourself no more with me," I said
  The last time she spoke thus. "When I took you
Unto my bosom, Mary, though your head
  Was haloed with the lustre beauty threw,
And mind and youth and glowing feeling shed,
  Yet then I swore that if your father drew
His hand from mine, I'd give him back his gift,
Of happiness and hope and fame bereft."

Percy, the demon! playing with the feeling
  Of an enthusiast's heart![8] He shall be paid
For his deceit, for his cold treacherous dealing,
  In miseries keen as those himself has made,
Wounds festered deep beyond the power of healing.
  My part in the great game is also played—
I've had his daughter, loved her, made her mine
And now the bright deposit I'll resign.

Fade, Love! Before his sigh consume away!
  Reproach him with your dying gaze, my Mary![9]
It is his fault—I love you each fresh day
  Intenselier than the last: I never weary[10]

Of gazing on that young, pale face whose ray
　Of deep, warm, anxious ardour, dashed with dreary,
Poetic melancholy, charms me more
Than all the bloom which other eyes adore!

"You love me, yet you'll kill me!" she said starting,
　While an electric thrill of passion woke
In all her veins; and, wild reproaches darting
　From her dark eye, in native heat she broke
Fully upon me, all the calm departing
　And classic grace, as if the sudden stroke
Had changed her nature, her most perfect form
Shaken, dilated, trembling in the storm.

Anger and grief and most impassioned love
　Gathered upon her cheek. Its burning blushes
One with the other, struggling, warring strove,
　And each by turns prevailed in whelming gushes.
She flashed a frantic glance to heaven above,
　She called me cruel as the fiend that crushes
Its victim after snaring it in toils
Baited with rosy flowers and golden spoils.

"Why have you chained me to you, Adrian, by
　Such days of bliss, such hours of sweet caressing,
Such looks of glory, words of melody,
　Glimpses of all on earth that's worth possessing?
And now when I must live with you, or die
　Out of your sight distracted, every blessing
Your hand withdraws, and, all my anguish scorning,
You go, and bid me hope for no returning.

"Adrian, don't leave me!" Then the gushing tears
　Smothered her utterance, so I tried my power
To soothe her terrors, and allay her fears
　And feed her passion with a sunny shower

Of my accustomed spells. As the sky clears
  After a summer storm, in one brief hour
Happy and blest she'd given again her charms,
Trembling but yet confiding, to my arms.

Did I think then she'd die, and that forever
  The grave would hide her from me? Did I deem
That after parting I should never, never
  Behold her save in some delusive dream;
That she would cross death's cold and icy river
  Alone without one hope, one cheering beam
Of bliss to come, all dark, all spectral, dreary?
Was this thy fate, my loved, my sainted Mary?

Will no voice answer, "No"? Will no tongue say
  That still she lives and longs and waits for me?
That burning still, though haply in decay
  The spark of life yet lingers quenchlessly;
And that again the bright awakening ray
  Of passion on her pale face I may see,
And waken the fervid lightning thoughts whose shine
Kindled each feature with a beam divine?

Again o'er Hawkscliffe's wide green wilderness
  The harvest moon her boundless smile will fling;
Again the savage woods will take their dress
  Of dewy leaves from the refulgent spring,
Darken in summer, and to autumn pass
  In their warm robes of foliage withering.
September's eves will close with dreary light
Of moon and holy stars foretelling night.

And shall I never wander in those shades
  Where the trees sweep the earth, o'ercharged with plumes?
Mary! among those solemn moonlight glades,
  Are all our roamings over? Will their glooms,

Parting and bending as the breezes swayed,
　　Shadow our love no more like natural tombs
Where sound breathed out of darkest hush? Each grove
Of giant oaks buried and watched that love.

Others I've met by night in field and wood:[11]
　　Many a burnside has been my rendezvous;
And anxiously, impatiently, I have stood
　　Under the sunless sky of sombre blue
While the encroaching gloaming o'er the flood
　　Crept dark and still, and gathering drops of dew
Hung on the flowers, and twilight breezes sung
Chilly and low the whispering trees among.

And some bright eyes are closed that once to me
　　Were stars of hope; and hearts that loved me well
For years have stilled their beating 'neath some tree
　　Waving above the mounds where mortals dwell
After they've put on immortality.[12]
　　But long since I have learnt the pangs to quell
Their memories brought. And now again, again
Torture is wakened by reviving pain.

It cannot be! And has she, cold and dying,
　　Been stretched alone on her forsaken bed,
A stormy midnight's voice her requiem crying
　　And hasting on the last dark hour of dread
With speed none could avert? And Mary lying
　　Conscious that death was near, her spirit led—
While her soul waved its wings prepared to soar—
Back to the days she never might see more,

The ghastly trance increasing, and above
　　Her thorny pillow bent her father's brow
In agony. A clouded glance of love
　　The lady on her sire was seen to throw,

THE BIER OF MARY PERCY

Their sad, soft beam like the subdued decline
   Of twilight parting. Could I but have nourished
Her languid, wasted strength and faded bloom,
   And taken her to my breast again, her home![14]

But that is not vouchsafed. And so at last
   I must shut out her image from my heart,
And, mingling that with other glories past,
   Look back on what I leave before I start
On a divided track. A winter's blast
   Howls o'er a desert where our journeys part.
And noon is past; the shades of eve draw nigh,
Dimly reflected from a stormy sky.

Turning amid the driving sleet and rain,
   I look along the pathway she has taken,
Now far away—a slip of emerald plain
   With lingering sun and freshened foliage shaken
By a sweet Eden breeze; and once again
   I see her like an apparition beckon
In the bright distance, ere a moment gone.
She'll ne'er return; 'tis past and I'm alone.

Victory! the plumed, the crowned, I hear her calling.
   Again my diadem, my land she flings
Redeemed before me; glorious sunlight falling
   On the vermilion banner[15] lights its wings
With the true hue of conquest.

And alone shall I be when the trumpet is sounding
   To tell to the world that my kingdom is free!
Alone while a thousand brave bosoms are bounding
   The yoke and the fetter-bolt shivered to see!

Alone in the hall where the last flash is shining
  Of embers that wane in their mid-night decay!
How shall I feel as the wild gale's repining
  Fitfully whispers and wanders away?

What will it tell me of days that will never
  Smile on the life-weary mourner again?
What will it murmur of hours that forever
  Are past like the spring-shower's glitter of rain?

Blown by the wind to the verge of the torrent,
  Cluster the last leaves that fell long ago.
Some that are scattered by chance on its current,
  Withered and light, fleet away in its flow.

Sooner shall these on the tree or the flower
  Wave in their bloom, as they waved ere they fell,
Than I shall behold the return of that hour
  Whose sorrowful parting the night-breezes tell.

Then in the silence her picture will glimmer,
  Solemn and shadowy, high in the hall,
Still, as the embers wax dimmer and dimmer,
  Stirring like life to their flicker and fall.

How shall I feel as the soft eyes revealing
  Sweetness and sorrow gaze down through the gloom?
How shall I feel when her image comes stealing
  Over me such as she was in her bloom—

Twining around me, crowding the tresses
  Curled on her white forehead into my breast,
Wooing the love that with passionate kisses
  Wildly and warmly her beauty caressed?

Then shall I know that all mutely reposing,
    Lulled in the slumbering gloom of her shrine,
With Death on her white face in shadow disclosing
    The trace of his truest and awfullest sign,

Then shall I know that her lip would not quiver
    Though with the pressure of love it met mine;
Then shall I know that no glance can dissever
    The sealed lids that cover her eyes' ghastly shine.

All will be frozen, all cold and unfeeling,
    Passion forgotten and sympathy gone;
Neither a motion nor murmur revealing
    Life in that colourless image of stone.

I shall not see it, for Mary is buried
    Far from the Calabar's war-trampled strand.
And, oh, her career to its dark close was hurried
    Many a long league from her own native land![16]

Could she have died with its woods waving round her,
    Could she have slept with their moan in her ear,
Rapt in romance, the last slumber had found her,
    Fleeting away on the tone singing near.

Oh that the sun of the West had been beaming
    Glorious and soft on the bed where she lay!
Then she had died not lamenting but dreaming,
    Borne on the haloes of sunset away!

Had she but known all the love that I bore her,
    Though I had left her in sorrow awhile,
Then when the wing of the spectre swept o'er her
    Her death-frozen features had fixed in a smile.

But she perished in exile, she perished in mourning.
  Wild was the evening that closed her decline.
She withered forever—I hope no returning,
  And tears are so fruitless I need not repine.

God gave the summons—farewell then, my Mary;
  Thou hast found haven where no tears may swell.
Hopeless and weary and joyless and dreary,
  I must forget thee—forever farewell!

CHARLOTTE BRONTË
Jan. 9, 1837

Introduction to "Mina Laury"

IN the old days of the "Young Men's Play," it had been
the custom of the Chief Genii to "resuscitate or make
alive" the heroes killed in battle, and the custom in various guises was carried over to the Angrian stories. Charlotte
enjoyed to the fullest the romantic death and spectacular
funeral of the Duchess Mary, and she made the most of
Zamorna's Byronic grief, but all of that over, she missed her
peerless heroine unbearably and must needs "resuscitate or
make her alive" again. This she did simply by substituting
in later stories temporary separation for divorce and a long
illness for death. In the post-war stories Mary is once more
the wife of Zamorna and Queen of Angria, and her husband and her father are again on their old footing of an-
tagonistic intimacy in private life, though "in a public
sense," Zamorna "had long since done with his one-time
prime minister."

The relationship between these two in the course of the
cycle is a changing conception in Charlotte's mind, involving a theme that held a strong fascination for her, one that
she never worked out to her own satisfaction: the conflict of
mutual love and hate present at the same time in the hearts
of two individuals. In the beginning of the story Douro and
Rogue had been merely conventional hero and villain, but
with Charlotte's reading of Milton's *Paradise Lost* and Byron's *Cain*—before July, 1834—Rogue had taken on the nature of Lucifer, and his relation to Douro became highly
involved and full of devious subtleties.

The outward events of their associations are easily traced.
With the creation of Angria, Northangerland became Zamorna's prime minister and contributed powerfully to the
establishment of the nation. Becoming jealous even of his
own work so far as it tended to strengthen Zamorna,

he began by devious methods to alienate from the king the affection and confidence of his subjects. When Zamorna exposed his treacheries and drew the issue, Percy joined a coalition against him headed by the Marquis of Ardrah. A few months later he effected a *coup d'état* which gave him supreme control of the forces that had gathered against Zamorna, and while he was in power, Zamorna was taken prisoner, tried by court-martial, and condemned to death. Percy, as we have seen, risked the anger of his allies, and spirited him away into exile. With Zamorna's return, Percy fled the country, but with the coming of peace and the re-establishment of the Angrian government, he was allowed to return and live his private life as he pleased, so long as he abstained from political intrigues. Zenobia, always loyal to Zamorna, remained aloof from her husband during the war, but at its close she took up again her position as Northangerland's wife. At this stage of Percy's history he is represented as a broken-down rake and hypochondriac, sensitive, irritable, and overrefined in his tastes. Zamorna in particular irritates him in his every movement and speech. Rarely do they meet without quarrelling in one manner or another. Yet Zamorna continues to visit Percy upon occasions, impelled as much by his own desire as by Mary's persuasion. The people, fearing Percy's influence, growl and threaten.

The opening scene of the present story is laid at Alnwick, Percy's house in Sneachisland—it was here that Mary had been sent when Zamorna decided to send her away. The story, left without a name by its author, has been given the tentative title "Mina Laury," following the example of Mr. Hatfield, who included one of its incidents in *The Twelve Adventurers and Other Stories*. Charlotte is now writing as Charles Townshend who, while acknowledging no family ties and no obligations to the Wellesley name, is still the brother of the great Duke of Zamorna, King of Angria.

"Mina Laury"

THE last scene in my last book concluded within the walls of Alnwick House,[1] and the first scene in my present volume opens in the same place. I have a great partiality for morning pictures. There is such a freshness about everybody and everything before the toil of the day has worn them. When you descend from your bedroom the parlour looks so clean, the fire so bright, the hearth so polished, the furnished breakfast table so tempting. All these attractions are diffused over the oak-panelled room with the glass door to which my readers have before had frequent admission. The cheerfulness within is enhanced by the dreary, wildered look of all without. The air is dimmed with snow careering through it in wild whirls. The sky is one mass of congealed tempest, heavy, wan, and icy. The trees rustle their frozen branches against each other in a blast bitter enough to flay alive the flesh that should be exposed to its sweep.[2]

But hush!—the people of the house are up. I hear a step on the stairs. Let us watch the order in which they will collect in the breakfast room. First, by himself comes an individual in a furred morning-gown of crimson damask, with his shirt-collar open and neck-cloth thrown by, his face fresh and rather rosy than otherwise, partly, perhaps, with health, but chiefly with the cold water in which he has been performing his morning's ablution, his hair fresh from the toilet, plenty of it and carefully brushed and curled, his hands clean and white and visibly as cold as icicles. He walks to the fire rubbing them. He glances towards the window meantime and whistles, as much as to say, "It's a rum morning." He then steps to a side-table, takes up newspapers of which there are dozens lying folded and fresh from the postman's bag. He throws himself into an armchair and begins to read. Meantime another step and a rustle of silks. In comes the Countess Zenobia[3] with a white gauze turban over her raven curls, and a dress of grey.

"Good-morning, Arthur," she says in her cheerful tone such as she uses when all's right with her.

"Good-morning, Zenobia," answers the Duke getting up, and they shake hands and stand together on the rug. "What a morning it is!" he continues; "How the snow drifts! If it were a little less boisterous I would make you come out and have a snow-balling match with me just to whet your appetite for breakfast."

"Aye," said the Countess, "we look like two people adapted for such child's play, don't we?" and she glanced with a smile first at the great blethering King of Angria and then at her own comely and portly figure.

"You don't mean to insinuate that we are too stout for such exercise," said his Majesty.

Zenobia laughed. "I am at any rate," said she, "and your Grace is in most superb condition. What a chest!"

"This will never do," returned the Duke, shaking his head; "wherever I go they compliment me on my enlarged dimensions. I must take some measures for reducing them within reasonable bounds. Exercise and abstinence! that's my motto."

"No, Adrian, let it be ease and plenty," said a much softer voice replying to his Grace. A third person had joined the pair and was standing a little behind, for she could not get her share of the fire, being completely shut out by the Countess with her robes, and the Duke with his morning-gown. This person seemed but a little and slight figure when compared with these two august individuals, and as the Duke drew her in between them that she might at least have a sight of the glowing hearth, she was almost lost in the contrast.

"Ease and plenty!" exclaimed his Grace. "So you would have a man-mountain for your husband at once."

"Yes, I should like to see you really very stout. I call you nothing now—quite slim—scarcely filled up."

"That's right," said Zamorna, "Mary always takes my side."

Lady Helen Percy[4] now entered and shortly after, the Earl with slow step and in silence took his place at the breakfast table. The meal proceeded in silence. Zamorna was reading. Newspaper after newspaper he opened, glanced over, threw on the floor. One of them happened to fall over Lord Northangerland's foot. It was very gently removed as if there was contamination in the contact.

"An Angrian print, I believe," murmured the Earl. "Why do they bring such things to the house?"

"They are my papers," answered his son-in-law, swallowing at the same moment more at one mouthful than would have sufficed his father for the whole repast.

"Yours! What do you read them for? To give you an appetite? If so they seem to have answered their end. Arthur, I wish you would masticate your food better."

"I have not time. I'm very hungry. I ate but one meal all yesterday."

"Humph! and now you are making up for it, I suppose. But pray put that newspaper away."

"No. I wish to learn what my loving subjects are saying about me."

"And what are they saying, pray?"

"Why, here is a respectable gentleman who announces that he fears his beloved Monarch is again under the influence of that baleful star whose ascendency had already produced such fatal results to Angria. Wishing to be witty he calls it the North[5] Star. Another insinuates that their gallant sovereign, though a Hector in war, is but a Paris in peace. He talks something about Samson and Delilah, Hercules and the distaff, and hints darkly at the evils of petticoat Government—a hit at you, Mary! A third mutters threateningly of hoary old ruffians, who worn with age and excess, sit like Bunyan's Giant Pope at the entrance of their dens, and strive by menace or promise to allure passengers within reach of their bloody talons."

"Is that me?" asked the Earl quietly.

"I've very little doubt of it," was the reply; "and there is a fourth print, *The War Despatch,* noted for the ardour of its sentiments, which growls a threat concerning the power of Angria to elect a new sovereign whenever she is offended with her old one—Zenobia, another cup of coffee, if you please."

"I suppose you are frightened," said the Earl.

"I shake in my shoes," replied the Duke, "however, there are two old sayings that somewhat cheer me: 'More noise than work'; 'Much cry and little wool,'[6] very applicable when properly considered, for I always call the Angrians 'hogs,' and who am I except the Devil that shears them?"

Breakfast had been over for about a quarter of an hour. The room was perfectly still. The Countess and Duchess were reading those papers Zamorna had dropped. Lady Helen was writing to her son's agent. The Earl was pacing the room in a despondent mood. As for the Duke, no one well knew where he was or what he was doing. He had taken himself off, however. Ere long his steps were heard descending the stair-case and then his voice in the hall giving orders, and then he re-entered the breakfast room, but no longer in morning costume. He had exchanged his crimson damask robe for a black coat and checked pantaloons. He was wrapped up in a huge blue cloak with a furred collar. A light fur cap rested on his brow. His gloves were held in his hands. In short, he was in full travelling costume.

"Where are you going?" asked the Earl, pausing in his walk.

"To Verdopolis, and from thence to Angria," was the reply.

"To Verdopolis in such weather?" exclaimed the Countess, glancing towards the wild, whitened tempest that whirled without. Lady Helen looked up from her writing.

"Absurd, my Lord Duke. You do not mean what you say."

"I do; I must go. The carriage will be at the door directly. I'm come to bid you all good-bye."

"And what is all this haste about?" returned Lady Helen, rising.

"There is no haste in the business, madam. I've been here a week. I intended to go today."

"You never said anything about your intention."

"No, I did not think of mentioning it. But they are bringing the carriage round. Good-morning, madam."

He took Lady Helen's hand and saluted her as he always does at meeting or parting. Then he passed to the Countess.

"Good-bye, Zenobia. Come to Ellrington House as soon as you can persuade our friend to accompany you."

He kissed her too. The next in succession was the Earl.

"Farewell, sir, and be d—— to you! Will you shake hands?"

"No. You always hurt me so. Good-morning. I hope you won't find your masters quite so angry as you expect them to be. But you do right not to delay attending to their mandates. I'm sorry I have been the occasion of your offending them."

"Are we to part in this way?" asked the Duke. "And won't you shake hands?"

"No!"

Zamorna coloured highly, but turned away and put on his gloves. The barouche stood at the door. The groom and the valet were waiting and the Duke, still with a coloured countenance, was proceeding to join them, when his wife came forwards.

"You have forgotten me, Adrian," she said in a very quiet tone, but her eye meantime flashing expressively. He started, for in truth he had forgotten her. He was thinking about her father.

"Good-bye then, Mary," he said, giving her a hurried kiss and embrace. She detained his hand.

"Pray how long am I to stay here?" she asked. "Why do you leave me at all? Why am I not to go with you?"

"It is such weather!" he answered. "When this storm passes over I will send for you."

"When will that be?" pursued the Duchess, following his steps as he strode into the hall.

"Soon, soon, my love, perhaps in a day or two. There now, don't be unreasonable. Of course you cannot go today."

"I can, and I will," answered the Duchess quickly. "I have had enough of Alnwick. You shall not leave me behind you."

"Go into the room, Mary. The door is open and the wind blows on you far too keenly. Don't you see how it drifts the snow in?"

"I will not go into the room. I'll step into the carriage as I am if you refuse to wait till I can prepare. Perhaps you will be humane enough to let me have a share of your cloak."

She shivered as she spoke. Her hair and her dress floated in the cold blast that blew in through the open entrance, strewing the hall with snow and dead leaves. His Grace, though he was rather stern, was not quite negligent of her, for he stood so as to shield her in some measure from the draught.

"I shall not let you go, Mary," he said, "so there is no use in being perverse."

The Duchess regarded him with that troubled anxious glance peculiar to herself.

"I wonder why you wish to leave me behind you," she said.

"Who told you that I wished to do so?" was his answer. "Look at the weather and tell me if it is fit for a delicate little woman like you to be exposed to?"

"Then," murmured the Duchess, wistfully glancing at the January storm, "you might wait till it is milder. I don't think it will do your Grace any good to be out today."

"But I must go, Mary. The Christmas recess is over, and business presses."

"Then do take me. I am sure I can bear it."

"Out of the question. You may well clasp those small, silly hands, so thin I can almost see through them, and you may well shake your curls over your face to hide its paleness from me, I suppose. What is the matter, crying? God! What the devil am I to do with her? Go to your father, Mary. He has spoilt you."

"Adrian, I cannot live at Alnwick without you," said the Queen earnestly, "it recalls too forcibly the very bitterest days of my life. I'll not be separated from you again except by violence."

She took hold of his arm with one hand while with the other she was hastily wiping away the tears from her eyes.

"Well, it will not do to keep her any longer in the hall," said the Duke, and he pushed open a side-door which led into a room that during his stay he had appropriated for his study. There was a fire in it and a sofa drawn to the hearth. There he took the Duchess and, having shut the door, re-commenced the task of persuasion, which was no very easy one, for his own false play, his alienations, and his unnumbered treacheries had filled her mind with hideous phantasms of jealousy, had weakened her nerves and made them a prey to a hundred vague apprehensions—fears that never wholly left her except when she was actually in his arms or at least in his immediate presence.

"I tell you, Mary," he said, regarding her with a smile, half expressive of fondness, half of vexation, "I tell you I will send for you in two or three days."

"And will you be at Wellesley House when I get there? You said you were going from Verdopolis to Angria."

"I am, and probably I shall be a week in Angria, not more."

"A week! And your Grace considers that but a short time? To me it will be most wearisome; however, I must submit. I know it is useless to oppose your Grace, but I could go with you, and you should never find me in the way. I am not often intrusive on your Grace."

"The horses will be frozen if they stand much longer," returned the Duke, not heeding her last remark. "Come, wipe your eyes and be a little philosopher for once. There, let me have one smile before I go. A week will be over directly. This is not like setting out for a campaign."

"Don't forget to send for me in two days," pleaded the Duchess, as Zamorna released her from his arms.

"No, no—I'll send for you tomorrow, if the weather is set-tled enough, and," half mimicking her voice, "don't be jealous of me, Mary, unless you're afraid that the superior charms of Enara and Warner and Kirkwall and Richton and Thornton will seduce me from my allegiance to a certain fair-complex-ioned, brown-eyed young woman in whom you are considerably interested. Good-bye!"

He was gone. She hurried to the window. He passed it. In three minutes the barouche swept with muffled sound round the lawn, shot down the carriage road, and was quickly lost in the thickening whirl of the snow-storm.

Late at night the Duke of Zamorna reached Wellesley House. His journey had been much delayed by the repeated change of horses which the state of the roads rendered necessary. So heavy and constant had been the fall of snow all day that in many places they were almost blocked up, and he and his valet had more than once been obliged to alight from the carriage and wade through the deep drifts far above the knee. Under such circumstances any other person would have stopped for the night at some of the numerous excellent hotels which skirt the way, but his Grace is well known to be exceedingly pig-headed, and the more obstacles are thrown in the way of any scheme he wishes to execute, the more resolute he is in pushing on to the attainment of his end. In the prosecution of this journey he had displayed a particular wilfulness. In vain, when he had alighted at some inn to allow time for a change of horse, Rosier had hinted the propriety of a longer stay. In vain had he rec-ommended some more substantial refreshment than the single glass of Madeira and the half-biscuit with which his noble master tantalized rather than satisfied the cravings of a rebellious appetite. At last, leaving him to the enjoyment of obstinacy and starvation in a large saloon of the inn which his Grace was traversing with strides that derived their alacrity partly from nipping cold and partly from impatience, Eugene himself had sought the travellers room and, while he devoured a chicken with champagne, he had solaced himself with the muttered objurgation "Let him starve and be d——."

Flinging himself from the barouche, the Duke in no mild mood passed through his lighted halls whose echoes were still prolonging the last stroke of midnight pealed from the house-bell just as the carriage drew up under the portico. Zamorna seemed not to heed the call to immediate repose which that sound conveyed, for turning as he stood on the first landing-place of the wide white marble stairs, with a bronze lamp pendant above him and a statue standing in calm contrast to his own figure, he called out, "Rosier, I wish Mr. Warner to attend me instantly. See that a message is despatched to Warner Hotel."

"To-night, does your Grace mean?" said the valet.

"Yes, sir."

Monsieur Rosier reposed his tongue in his cheek but hastened to obey.

"Hutchinson, send your deputy directly—you heard his Grace's orders—and, Hutchinson, tell the cook to send a tumbler of hot negus into my room; I want something to thaw me, and tell her to toss me up a nice hot *petit souper, a fricandeau de veau,* or an omelette, and carry my compliments to Mr. Greenwood and say I shall be happy to have the honour of his company in my salon half an hour hence, and above all things, Hutchinson," here the young gentleman lowered his tone to a more confidential key, "give Mademoiselle Harriette a hint that I am returned—very ill you may say, for I've got a cursed sore throat with being exposed to this night air. Ah, there she is! I'll tell her myself."

As the omnipotent Eugene spoke, a young lady carrying a china ewer appeared crossing the gallery which ran round this inner hall. The French garçon skipped up the stairs like a flea.

"*Ma belle!*" he exclaimed, "*permettez moi de porter cette cruche.*"

"No, monsieur, no," replied the young lady, laughing and throwing back her head which was covered with very handsome dark hair finely curled, "I will carry it—it is for the Duke."

"I must assist you," returned the gallant Rosier, "and then I shall earn a kiss for my services."

But the damsel resisted him, and stepping back showed to a better advantage a pretty foot and ankle well displayed by a short full petticoat of pink muslin and a still shorter apron of black silk. She had also a modest handkerchief of thin lace on her neck. She wore no cap, had good eyes, comely features, and a plump, round figure. A very interesting love scene was commencing in the seclusion of the gallery when a bell rang very loudly.

"God! it's the Duke," exclaimed Rosier. He instantly released his mistress, and she shot away like an arrow towards the inner chambers. Eugene followed her very cautiously— somewhat jealously perhaps. Threading her path through a labyrinth of intermediate rooms she came at last to the royal chamber, and thence a door opened direct to the royal dressing room.

His Grace was seated in an arm-chair by his mirror, an enormous one taking him in from head to foot. He looked cursedly tired and somewhat wan, but the lights and shadows of the fire were playing about him with an animating effect.

"Well, Harriet," he said, as the hand-maid entered his presence, "I wanted that water before. Put it down and pour me out a glass. What made you so long in bringing it?"

Harriet blushed as she held the refreshing draught to her royal master's parched lips. (He was too lazy to take it himself.) She was going to stammer out some excuse but meantime the Duke's eye had reverted to the door and caught the dark vivacious aspect of Rosier.

"Ah!" he said, "I see how it is. Well, Harriet, mind what you're about—no giddiness. You may go now and tell your swain to come forward on pain of having his brains converted into paste."

Eugene strutted in, humming aloud, in no sort abashed or put to the blush. When Harriet was gone the Duke proceeded to lecture him, the valet meantime coolly aiding him in the change of his travelling dress, arrangement of his hair, etc.

"Dog," began the princely master, "take care how you conduct yourself towards that girl. I'll have no improprieties in my house, none."

"If I do but follow your Grace's example I cannot be guilty of improprieties," snivelled the valet, who, being but too well-acquainted with many of his master's weaknesses, is sometimes permitted a freedom of speech few others would attempt.

"I'll make you marry her at all risks if you once engage her affections," pursued Zamorna.

"Well," replied Rosier, "if I do marry her, and if I don't like her, I can recompense myself for the sacrifice."

"Keep yourself within your allotted limits, my lad," remarked the Duke quietly.

"What does your Grace mean, matrimonial limits, or limits of the tongue?"

"Learn to discern for yourself," returned his master, enforcing the reply by a manual application that sent Monsieur to the other side of the room. He speedily gathered himself up and returned to his employment of combing out the Duke's long and soft curls of dark brown hair.

"I have a particular interest in your Harriet," remarked Zamorna benevolently. "I can't say that the other hand-maids of the house often cross my sight, but now and then I meet that nymph in a gallery or passage, and she always strikes me as being very modest and correct in her conduct."

"She was first bar-maid at Stancliffe's Hotel in Zamorna not long since," insinuated Rosier.

"I know she was, sir, I have reason to remember her in that station. She once gave me a draught of cold water when there was not another human being in the world who would have lifted a finger to do me even that kindness."

"I've heard Mademoiselle tell that story," replied Eugene. "It was when your Grace was taken prisoner of war before MacTerroglen,[7] and she told how your Grace rewarded her afterwards, when you stopped six months ago at Stancliffe's and gave her a certificate of admission to the royal household, and into the bargain—if Mademoiselle speaks truth—your Grace gave her a kiss from your own royal lips."

"I did, and be d—— to you, sir. The draught of water she once gave me and the gush of kind-hearted tears that followed it were cheaply rewarded by a kiss."

"I should have thought so," replied Rosier, "but perhaps she did not. Ladies of title sometimes pull each other's ears for your Grace's kisses, so I don't know how a simple bar-maid would receive them."

"Eugene, your nation have a penchant for suicide; go and be heroic," returned Zamorna.

"If your Grace has done with me, I will obey your wishes and immediately seek my quietus in a plate of ragout of paradise and such delicate claret as the vintages of *La Belle France* yield when they are in a good humour."

As the illustrious valet withdrew from the presence of his still more illustrious master, a different kind of personage entered by another door, a little man enveloped in a fur cloak. He put it off and, glancing round the room, his eye settled upon Zamorna, released from the cumbrous damask robe, half reclined on the mattress of a low and hard couch, his head of curls preparing to drop on the pillow, and one hand just draw-

ing up the coverlet of furs and velvet. Warner beheld him in
the act of seeking his night's repose.

"I thought your Grace wanted me on business!" exclaimed
the minister, "and I find you in bed!"

Zamorna stretched his limbs, folded his arms across his chest,
and buried his brow, cheek, and dark locks in the pillow, and
in a faint voice requested Warner to arrange that coverlet, for
he was too tired to do it. The Premier's lip struggled to suppress a smile. This was easily done for the said lip was unaccustomed to that relaxation.

"Has your Majesty dismissed Monsieur Rosier, and have you
sent for me to fulfil the duties of the office he held about your
Majesty's person?"

"There, I am comfortable," said the Duke, as the drapery
fell over him arranged to his satisfaction. "Pray, Warner, be
seated."

Warner drew close to his Grace's bedside an arm-chair and
threw himself into it.

"What," said he, "have you been doing? You look extremely
pale. Have you been raking?"

"God forgive you for the supposition! No, I have been fag-
ging myself to death for the good of Angria."

"For the good of Angria, my Lord! Aye, truly there you
come to the point! And it is, I suppose, for the good of Angria
that you go to Alnwick and spend a week in the sick room of
Lord Northangerland?"

"How dutiful of me, Howard! I hope my subjects admire
me for it."

"My lord Duke, do not jest. The feeling which has been
raised by that ill-advised step is no fit subject for levity. What
a strange mind is yours which teaches you to rush headlong
into those very errors which your enemies are always attribut-
ing to you! It is in vain that you now and then display a splendid flash of talent when the interstices, as it were, of your
political life are filled up with such horrid bungling as this."

"Be easy, Howard. What harm have I done?"

"My Lord, I will tell you. Has it not ever been the bitterest reproach in the mouth of your foes that you are a weak man, liable to be influenced and controlled? Have not Ardrah and Montmorenci[8] a thousand times affirmed that Northangerland guided, ruled, infatuated you? They have tried to bring that charge home to you, to prove it; but they could not, and you have proved it beyond dispute or contradiction."

"As how, my dear Howard?"

"My Lord, you see it—you feel it yourself. In what state was Angria last year at this time? You remember it—laid in ashes; plague and famine and slaughter struggling with each other which should sway the sceptre that disastrous war had wrested from your own hand. And I ask, my lord, who had brought Angria to this state?"

"Northangerland!" replied Zamorna promptly.

"Your Grace has spoken truly. And knowing this, was it weakness or was it wickedness which led you to the debauched traitor's couch and taught you to bend over him with the tenderness of a son to a kind father?" Warner paused for an answer but none came. He continued: "That the man is dying I have very little doubt, dying in that premature decay brought on by excesses such as would have disgraced any nature, aye, even that of an unreasoning beast. But ought you not to have let him meet death alone in that passion of anguish and desolation which is the just meed for crime, for depravity like his? What call was there for you to go and count his pulses? Can you prolong their beat? Why should you mingle your still pure breath with his last contaminated gasps? Can you purify that breath which debauchery has so sullied? Why should you commit your young hand to the touch of his clammy, nerveless fingers? Can the contact infuse vitality into his veins or vigour into his sinews? Had you not the strength of mind to stand aloof and let him who has lived the slave of vice, die the victim of disease?"

The Duke of Zamorna raised himself on his elbow. "Very bad language, this, Howard," said he, "and it won't do. I know very well what the Reformers and Constitutionalists and my own opinionated, self-complacent Angrians have been saying because I chose to spend my Christmasses at Alnwick. I knew beforehand what they would say, and, above all, I knew in particular what you would say. Now, it was not in defiance of either public or private opinion that I went. Neither was it from the working of any uncontrollable impulse. No, the whole matter was the result of mature reflection. My Angrians have certain rights over me, so have my ministers. I also have certain rights independent of them, independent of any living thing under the firmament of heaven. I claim the possession of my reason. I am neither insane nor idiotic, whatever the all-accomplished Harlaw may say to the contrary, and in two or three things I will, whilst I retain that valuable possession, judge for myself. One of these is the degree of intimacy which I choose to maintain with Lord Northangerland. In a public sense I have long done with him. The alienation cost me much, for in two or three particular points his views and mine harmonized, and neither could hope to find a substitute for the other in the whole earth beside. However, though it was like tearing up something whose roots had taken deep hold in my very heart of hearts, the separation was made, and, since it was finally completed, by what glance or look or word have I signed for a reunion? I have not done so and I cannot do so. My path I have struck out, and it sweeps far away out of sight of his. The rivers of blood Angria shed last year, and the hills of cold carnage which she piled up before the shrine of Freedom, effectually, eternally divide Northangerland's spirit from mine. But in the body we may meet; we shall meet till death interposes.

"I say, Warner, no sneers of my foes or threats from my friends, no murmurs from my subjects, shall over-rule me in this matter. Howard, you are a different man from Northangerland, but let me whisper to you this secret—you also love to control, and, if you could, you would have extended the energies of that keen haughty mind till they surrounded me and spell-bound my will and actions within a magic circle of your own creating. It will not do! It will not do! Hate North-angerland if you please, abhor him, loathe him—you have the right to do so: he has more than once treated you brutally, spoken of you grossly. If you feel so inclined, and if an opportunity should offer, you have a right to pistol him; but, sir, do not dare to impose your private feelings on me, to call upon me to avenge them. Do it yourself! In you the action would be justifiable, in me dastardly. Neither will I bend to Ardrah, or to the defiled cuckold Montmorenci. I will not at their bidding give up the best feelings of a very bad nature. I will not crush the only impulses that enable me to be endeared by my fellow-men. I will not leave the man who was once my comrade—my friend—to die in unrelieved agony, because Angria mutinies and Verdopolis sneers. My heart, my hand, my energies, belong to the public; my feelings are my own. Talk no more on the subject."

Warner did not. He sat and gazed in silence on his master, who with closed eyes and averted head seemed composing himself to slumber. At last he said aloud: "A false step, a false step. I would die on the word."

Zamorna woke from his momentary doze. "You have papers for me to sign and look over, I dare say, Howard? Give me them; I wish to dispatch arrears tonight, as it is my intention to set off for Angria. I wish to ascertain in person the state of feeling there and to turn it into its legitimate channel."

Warner produced a green bag well filled. The Duke raised himself on his couch and collecting his wearied faculties proceeded to the task. A silence of nearly an hour ensued, broken only by occasional monosyllables from the King and minister as papers were presented and returned. At length Warner locked the padlock with which the bag was secured and saying, "I recommend your Majesty to sleep," rose to reassume his cloak.

"Warner," said the Duke with an appearance of nonchalance, "where is Lord Hartford?[9] I have seen nothing of him for some time."

"Lord Hartford, my Lord? Lord Hartford is a fool and affects delicacy of the lungs. His health, forsooth, is in too precarious a state to allow of any attention to public affairs, and he has withdrawn to Hartford Hall, there to nurse his maudlin folly in retirement."

"What? The maudlin folly of being ill? You are very unsparing, Howard."

"Ill, sir! The man is as strong and sound as you are—all trash. It is the effects of his ruling passion, sir, which will pursue him to hoary age, I suppose. Lord Hartford is love-sick, my lord Duke—the super-annuated profligate!"

"Did he tell you so?"

"No, indeed, he dared not; but Lord Richton[10] insinuated as much in his gossipy way. I will cut Lord Hartford, sir. I despise him. He ought to be sent to Coventry."

"How very bitter you are, Warner! Be more moderate. Meantime, good-night!"

"I wish your Grace a very good night. Take care that you sleep soundly and derive refreshment from your slumbers."

"I will do my best," replied the Duke laughing. Warner having clasped on his cloak, withdrew. Could he have watched unseen by the couch of his master for two more hours, he would have repined at the hidden feeling that prevented the lids from closing over those dark and restless eyes. Long Zamorna lay awake. Neither youth, nor health, nor weariness could woo sleep to his pillow. He saw his lamp expire; he saw the brilliant flame of the hearth settle into ruddy embers, then fade, decay, and at last perish; he felt silent and total darkness close around him; but still the unslumbering eye wandered over images which the fiery imagination portrayed upon vacancy. Thought yielded at last, and sleep triumphed. Zamorna lay in dead repose amidst the hollow darkness of his chamber.

Lord Hartford sat by himself after his solitary dinner, with a decanter of champagne and a half filled glass before him. There was also a newspaper spread out on which his elbow leaned and his eye rested. The noble lord sat in a large dining-room, the windows of which looked upon a secluded part of his own grounds, a part pleasant enough in summer leafiness and verdure, but dreary now in the cold, white clothing of winter. Many a time had this dining-room rung with the merriment of select dinner parties chosen by the noble bachelor from his particular friends; and often had the rum physiognomies of Richton, Arundel, Castlereagh, and Thornton been reflected in the mirror-like surface of that long dark polished mahogany table at whose head Edward Hartford now sat alone. Gallant and gay, and bearing on his broad forehead the very brightest and greenest laurels Angria had gathered on the banks of the Cirhala, he had retired with all his blushing honours thick upon him from the council, the court, the salon. He had left Verdopolis in the height of the most dazzling season it had ever known and gone to haunt like a ghost his lonely halls in Angria.

Most people thought the noble General's brains had suffered some slight injury amid the hardships of the late campaign; Richton was among the number who found it impossible to account for his friend's conduct upon any other supposition.

As the dusk closed and the room grew more dismal, Hartford threw the newspaper from him, poured out a bumper of amber-coloured wine and quaffed it off to the memory of the vintage that produced it. According to books, men in general soliloquize when they are by themselves, and so did Hartford.

"What the d——," he began, "has brought our lord the King down to Angria? That drunken editor of *The War Despatch* gives a pretty account of his progress—hissed, it seems, in the streets of Zamorna, and then, like himself, instead of getting through the town as quietly as he could, bidding the postillions halt before Stancliffe's and treating them to one of his fire and gunpowder explosions! What a speech! You shall never excel.

"It's odd, but the Western Dandy knows the genius of our land. 'Take the bull by the horns': that's his motto. Hitherto his tactics have succeeded, but I think it says somewhere, either in Revelations or the Apocrypha, 'the end is not yet.' I wish he'd keep out of Angria."

Here a pause ensued, and Hartford filled it up with another goblet of the golden wine.

"Now," he proceeded, "I know I ought not to drink this Guanache. It is a kindling sort of draught, and I were better to take to toast and water; but, Lord bless me! I've got a feeling about my heart I can neither stifle nor tear away, and I would fain drown it. They talk of optical delusions—I wonder what twisting of the nerves it is that fixes before my eyes that image which neither darkness can hide nor light dissipate. Some demon is certainly making a bonfire of my inwards; the burning thrill stuck through all my veins to my heart with that last touch of the little warm, soft hand—by Heaven, nearly a year ago! and it has never left me since. It wastes, masters me. I'm not half the man I was, but I'm handsome still!"

He looked up at a lofty mirror between the two opposite windows. It reflected his dark commanding face with the prominent profile, the hard forehead, the deep expressive eye, the mass of raven hair and whisker and moustache, the stately aspect and figure, the breadth of chest and length of limb. In short, it gave back to his sight as fine a realization of soldier and patrician majesty as Angria ever produced from her ardent soil. Hartford sprung up.

"What should I give up hope for?" he said, rapidly pacing the room. "By Gad! I think I could make her love me. I never yet have told her how I adore her. I've never offered her my title and hand and my half-frenzied heart; but I will do it. Who says it is impossible? She should prefer being my wife to being his mistress. The world will laugh at me—I don't care for the world. It's inconsistent with the honour of my house— I've burnt the honour of my house and drank its ashes in Guanache. It's dastardly to meddle with another man's matters, another man who has been my friend, with whom I have fought and feasted, suffered and enjoyed. By God! it is; I know, it is, and if any man but myself had dared to entertain the same thought I'd have called him out! But Zamorna leaves her and cares no more about her—except when she can be of use to him—than I do for that silly Christmas rose on the lawn, shrivelled up by the frost. Besides, 'every man for himself.' I'll try, and, if I don't succeed, I'll try again and again. She's worth a struggle. Perhaps, meantime, Warner and Enara will send me an invitation to dine on bullets for two, or, perhaps, I may forget the rules of the drill and present fire, not from but at myself. In either case I get comfortably provided for, and that torment will be over which now frightens away my sleep by night and my senses by day."

This was rather wild talk, but his lordship's peculiar glance told that wine had not been without its effect. We will leave him striding about the room and maddening under the influence of his fiery passions. A sweet specimen of an aristocrat!

Late one fine still evening in January the moon arose over a blue summit of the Sydenham Hills and looked down on a quiet road winding from the hamlet of Rivaulx. The earth was bound in frost—hard, mute, and glittering. The forest of Hawkscliffe was as still as a tomb, and its black leafless wilds stretched away in the distance and cut off with a harsh serrated line the sky from the country. That sky was all silver blue, pierced here and there with a star like a diamond. Only the moon softened it, large, full, and golden. The by-road I have spoken of received her ascending beam on a path of perfect solitude. Spectral pines and vast old beech trees guarded the way like sentinels from Hawkscliffe. Farther on the rude track wound deep into the shades of the forest, but here it was open and the worn causeway, bleached with frost, ran under an old wall grown over with moss and wild ivy.

Over this scene the sun of winter had gone down in cloudless calm, red as fire, and kindling with its last beams the windows of a mansion on the verge of Hawkscliffe. To that mansion the road in question was the shortest cut from Rivaulx. And here a moment let us wait, wrapped, it is to be hoped, in furs, for a keener frost never congealed the Olympia.

Almost before you are aware a figure strays up the causeway at a leisurely pace, musing amid the tranquillity of evening. Doubtless that figure must be an inmate of the before-mentioned mansion, for it is an elegant and pleasing object. Approaching gradually nearer, you can observe more accurately a lady of distinguished carriage, straight and slender, something inceding and princess-like in her walk, but unconsciously so. Her ankles are so perfect, and her feet—if she tried, she could scarce tread otherwise than she does—lightly, firmly, erectly. The ermine muff, the silk pelisse, the graceful and ample hat of dark beaver, suit and set off her light youthful form. She is deeply veiled; you must guess at her features—but she passes on and a turn of the road conceals her.

Breaking up the silence, dashing in on the solitude, comes a horseman. Fire flashes from under his steed's hoofs out of the flinty road. He rides desperately. Now and then he rises in his stirrups and eagerly looks along the track as if to catch a sight of some object that has eluded him. He sees it, and the spurs are struck mercilessly into his horse's flanks. Horse and rider vanish in a whirlwind.

The lady passing through the iron gates had just entered upon the demesne of Hawkscliffe. She paused to gaze at the moon which, now full risen, looked upon her through the boughs of a superb elm. A green lawn lay between her and the house, and there its light slumbered in gold. Thundering behind her, came the sound of hoofs, and, bending low to his saddle to avoid the contact of oversweeping branches, that wild horseman we saw five minutes since rushed upon the scene. Harshly curbing the charger, he brought it almost upon its haunches close to the spot where she stood.

"Miss Laury! good-evening!" he said. The lady threw back her veil, surveyed him with one glance, and replied:

"Lord Hartford! I am glad to see you, my lord. You have ridden fast. Your horse foams. Any bad news?"

"No!"

"Then you are on your way to Adrianopolis. I suppose you will pass the night here?"

"If you ask me, I will."

"If I ask you! Yes; this is the proper half-way house between the capitals. The night is cold, let us go in."

They were now at the door. Hartford flung himself from his saddle. A servant came to lead the over-ridden steed to the stables, and he followed Miss Laury in.

It was her own drawing-room to which she led him, just such a scene as is most welcome after the contrast of a winter evening's chill; not a large room, simply furnished, with curtains and couches of green silk, a single large mirror, a Grecian lamp dependent from the centre softly burning now and mingling with the softer illumination of the fire, whose brilliant glow bore testimony to the keenness of the frost.

Hartford glanced round him. He had been in Miss Laury's drawing-room before, but never as her sole guest. He had, before the troubles broke out, more than once formed one of a high and important trio whose custom it was to make the lodge of Rivaulx their occasional rendezvous: Warner, Enara, and himself had often stood on that hearth in a ring round Miss Laury's sofa, and he recalled now her face looking up to them with its serious, soft intelligence that blent no women's frivolity with the heartfelt interest of those subjects on which they conversed. He remembered those first kindlings of the flame that now devoured his life as he watched her beauty and saw the earnest enthusiasm with which she threw her soul into topics of the highest import. She had often done for these great men what they could get no man to do for them. She had kept their secrets and executed their wishes as far as in her lay, for it had never been her part to counsel. With humble feminine devotedness she always looked up for her task to be set, and then not Warner himself could have bent his energies more resolutely to the fulfilment of that task than did Miss Laury. Had Mina's lot in life been different, she never would have interfered in such matters. She did not interfere now: she only served. Nothing like intrigue had ever stained her course in politics. She told her directors what she had done, and she asked for more to do, grateful always that they would trust her so far as to employ her, grateful too for the enthusiasm of their loyalty; in short, devoted to them heart and mind because she believed them to be devoted as unreservedly to the common master of all.

The consequence of this species of deeply confidential intercourse between the statesmen and their beautiful lieutenant had been intense and chivalric admiration on the part of Mr. Warner; strong fond attachment on that of General Enara; and on Lord Hartford's the burning brand of passion. His Lordship had always been a man of strong and ill-regulated feelings, and in his youth (if report may be credited) of somewhat dissolute habits, but he had his own ideas of honour strongly implanted in his breast, and though he would not have scrupled if the wife of one of his equals, or the daughter of one of his tenants had been in the question, yet as it was he stood beset and nonplussed.

Miss Laury belonged to the Duke of Zamorna. She was indisputably his property, as much as the Lodge of Rivaulx or the stately wood of Hawkscliffe, and in that light she considered herself. All his dealings with her had been on matters connected with the Duke, and she had ever shown an habitual, rooted, solemn devotedness to his interest which seemed to leave her hardly a thought for anything else in the world beside. She had but one idea—Zamorna! Zamorna! It had grown up with her, become a part of her nature. Absence, coldness, total neglect for long periods together went for nothing. She could no more feel alienation from him than she could from herself. She did not even repine when he forgot her any more than the religious devotee does when his Deity seems to turn away his face for a time and leave him to the ordeal of temporal afflictions. It seemed as if she could have lived on the remembrance of what he had once been to her without asking for anything more.

All this Hartford knew, and he knew, too, that she valued himself in proportion as she believed him to be loyal to his sovereign. Her friendship for him turned on this hinge: "We have been fellow-labourers and fellow-sufferers together in the same good cause." These were her own words which she had uttered one night as she took leave of her three noble colleagues just before the storm burst over Angria. Hartford had noticed the expression of her countenance as she spoke, and thought what a young and beautiful being thus appealed for sympathy with minds scarcely like her own in mould.

However, let us dwell no longer on these topics. Suffice it to say that Lord Hartford, against reason and without hope, had finally delivered himself wholly up to the guidance of his vehement passions; and it was with the resolution to make one desperate effort in the attainment of their end that he now stood before the lady of Rivaulx.

Above two hours had elapsed since Lord Hartford had entered the house. Tea was over, and in the perfect quiet of evening he and Miss Laury were left together. He sat on one side of the hearth, and she on the other—her work-table only between them, and on that her little hand rested within his reach. It was embedded in a veil of lace, the embroidering of which she had just relinquished for a moment's thought.

Lord Hartford's eye was fascinated by the white soft fingers. His own heart at the moment was in a tumult of bliss. To be so near, to be received so benignly, so kindly—he forgot himself. His own hand closed half involuntarily upon hers. Miss Laury looked at him. . . . Shocked for a moment, almost overwhelmed, she yet speedily mastered her emotions, took her hand away, resumed her work, and with head bent down, seemed endeavouring to conceal embarrassment under the appearance of occupation.

The dead silence that followed would not do, so she broke it in a very calm, self-possessed tone.

"That ring, Lord Hartford, which you were admiring just now belonged once to the Duchess of Wellington."

"And was it given you by her son?" asked the General bitterly.

"No, my lord, the Duchess herself gave it me a few days before she died. It has her maiden name 'Catherine Pakenham,' engraved within the stone."

"But," pursued Hartford, "I was not admiring the ring when I touched your hand. No; the thought struck me, if ever I marry I should like my wife's hand to be just as white and snowy and taper as that."

"I am the daughter of a common soldier, my lord, and it is said that ladies of high descent have fairer hands than peasant women."

Hartford made no reply. He rose restlessly from his seat and stood leaning against the mantle-piece.

"Miss Laury, shall I tell you which was the happiest hour of my life?"

"I will guess, my lord. Perhaps when the bill passed which made Angria an independent kingdom."

"No," replied Hartford with an expressive smile.

"Perhaps, then, when Lord Northangerland resigned the seals—for I know you and the Earl were never on good terms."

"No. I hated his lordship, but there are moments of deeper

felicity even than those which see the triumph of a fallen enemy."

"I will hope that it was at the Restoration."

"Wrong again! Why, madam, young as you are your mind is so used to the harness of politics that you can imagine no happiness or misery unconnected with them. You remind me of Warner."

"I believe I am like him," returned Miss Laury. "He often tells me so himself, but I live so much with men and statesmen I almost lose the ideas of a woman."

"Do you?" muttered Hartford with the dark sinister smile peculiar to him, "I wish you would tell the Duke so next time you see him."

Miss Laury passed over this equivocal remark and proceeded with the conversation.

"I cannot guess your riddle, my lord, so I think you must explain it."

"Then, Miss Laury, prepare to be astonished. You are so patriotic, so loyal that you will scarcely credit me when I say that the happiest hour I have ever known fell on the darkest day in the deadliest crisis of Angria's calamities."

"How, Lord Hartford?"

"Moreover, Miss Laury, it was at no bright period of your own life. It was to you an hour of the most acute agony; to me one of ecstasy."

Miss Laury turned aside her head with a disturbed air and trembled. She seemed to know to what he alluded.

"You remember the first of July, '36?" continued Hartford. She bowed.

"You remember that the evening of that day closed in a tremendous storm?"

"Yes, my lord."

"You recollect how you sat in this very room by this fireside, fearful of retiring for the night lest you should awake in another world in the morning. The country was not then as quiet as it is now. You have not forgotten the deep explosion which roared up at midnight and told you that your life and liberty hung on a thread, that the enemy had come suddenly upon Rivaulx, and that we who lay there to defend the forlorn hope were surprised and routed by a night attack. Then, madam, perhaps you recollect the warning which I brought you at one o'clock in the morning, to fly instantly, unless you chose the alternative of infamous captivity in the hands of Jordan. I found you here, sitting by a black hearth without fire, and Ernest Fitz-Arthur lay on your knee asleep. You told me you had heard the firing, and that you were waiting for some communication from me, determined not to stir without orders lest a precipitate step on your part should embarrass me. I had a carriage already in waiting for you. I put you in, and with the remains of my defeated followers escorted you as far as Zamorna. What followed after this, Miss Laury?"

Miss Laury covered her eyes with her hand. She seemed as if she could not answer.

"Well," continued Hartford, "in the midst of darkness and tempest, and while the whole city of Zamorna seemed changed into a hell peopled with fiends and inspired with madness, my lads were hewed down about you, and your carriage was stopped. I very well remember what you did—how frantically you struggled to save Fitz-Arthur, and how you looked at me when he was snatched from you. As to your own preservation —that, I need not repeat—only my arm did it. You acknowledge that, Miss Laury?"

"Hartford, I do, but why do you dwell on that terrible scene?"

"Because I am now approaching the happiest hour of my life. I took you to the house of one of my tenants whom I could depend upon, and just as morning dawned you and I sat together and alone in the little chamber of a farm-house, and you were in my arms, your head upon my shoulder, and weeping out all your anguish on a breast that longed to bleed for you."

Miss Laury agitatedly rose. She approached Hartford.

"My lord, you have been very kind to me and I feel very grateful for that kindness. Perhaps sometime I may be able to repay it. We know not how the chances of fortune may turn. The weak have aided the strong, and I will watch vigilantly for the slightest opportunity to serve you, but do not talk in this way. I scarcely know whither your words tend."

Lord Hartford paused a moment before he replied. Gazing at her with bended brows and folded arms he said:

"Miss Laury, what do you think of me?"

"That you are one of the noblest hearts in the world!" she replied unhesitatingly. She was standing just before Hartford, looking up at him, her hair in that attitude falling back from her brow, shading with exquisite curls her temples and slender neck; her small, sweet features, with that high seriousness deepening their beauty, lit up by eyes so large, so dark, so swimming, so full of pleading benignity, of an expression of alarmed regard, as if she at once feared for and pitied the sinful abstraction of a great mind. Hartford could not stand it. He could have borne female anger or terror, but the look of enthusiastic gratitude softened by compassion nearly unmanned him. He turned his head for a moment aside but then passion prevailed. Her beauty when he looked again struck through him—maddening sensation whetted to acuter power by a feeling like despair.

"You shall love me!" he exclaimed desperately; "Do I not adore you? Would I not die for you? And must I in return receive only the cold regard of friendship? I am no Platonist, Miss Laury—I am not your friend. I am, hear me, madam, your declared lover! Nay, you shall not leave me; by heaven! I am stronger than you are."

She had stepped a pace or two back, appalled by his vehemence. He thought she meant to withdraw, and, determined not to be so balked, he clasped her at once in both his arms and kissed her furiously rather than fondly. Miss Laury did not struggle.

"Hartford," said she steadying her voice, though it faltered in spite of her effort, "this must be our parting scene. I will never see you again if you do not restrain yourself."

Hartford saw that she turned pale, and he felt her tremble violently. His arms relaxed their hold. He allowed her to leave him.

She sat down on a chair opposite and hurriedly wiped her brow which was damp and marble-pale.

"Now, Miss Laury," said his lordship, "no man in the world loves you as I do. Will you accept my title and my coronet? I fling them at your feet."

"My lord, do you know whose I am?" she replied in a hollow and very suppressed tone. "Do you know with what a sound those proposals fall on my ear—how impious and blasphemous they seem to be? Do you at all conceive how utterly impossible it is that I should ever love you? The scene I have just witnessed has given a strange wrench to all my accustomed habits of thought. I thought you a true-hearted, faithful man: I find that you are a traitor."

"And do you despise me?" asked Hartford.

"No, my lord, I do not."

She paused and looked down. The colour rose rapidly into her pale face. She sobbed, not in tears, but in the over-mastering approach of an impulse born of a warm and Western heart. Again she looked up. Her eyes had changed, their aspect beaming with a wild, bright inspiration, truly, divinely Irish.

"Hartford," said she, "had I met you long since, before I left Ellibank and forgot St. Cyprian and dishonoured my father, I would have loved you. O my lord, you know not how truly! I would have married you and made it the glory of my life to cheer and brighten your hearth, but I cannot do so now—never. I saw my present master when he had scarcely attained manhood. Do you think, Hartford, I will tell you what feelings I had for him? No tongue could express them; they were so fervid, so glowing in their colour that they effaced everything else. I lost the power of properly appreciating the value of the world's opinion, of discerning the difference between right and wrong. I have never in my life contradicted Zamorna, never delayed obedience to his commands. I could not. He was something more to me than a human being. He superseded all things—all affections, all interests, all fears or hopes or principles. Unconnected with him my mind would be a blank, cold, dead, susceptible only of a sense of despair. How I should sicken if I were torn from him and thrown to you! Do not ask it; I would die first. No woman that ever loved my master could consent to leave him. There is nothing like him elsewhere. Hartford, if I were to be your wife, if Zamorna only looked at me, I should creep back like a slave to my former service. I should disgrace you as I have long since disgraced all my kindred. Think of that, my lord, and never say you love me again."

"You do not frighten me," replied Lord Hartford hardily; "I would stand that chance, aye, and every other, if I only might see at the head of my table in that old dining-room at Hartford Hall yourself as my wife and lady. I am called proud as it is, but then I would show Angria to what pitch of pride a man might attain, if I could, coming home at night, find Mina Laury waiting to receive me; if I could sit down and look at you with the consciousness that your exquisite beauty was all my own, that cheek, those lips, that lovely hand, might be claimed arbitrarily, and you dare not refuse me, I should then feel happy."

"Hartford, you would be more likely when you came home to find your house vacant and your hearth deserted. I know the extent of my own infatuation. I should go back to Zamorna and entreat him on my knees to let me be his slave again!"

"Madam," said Hartford frowning, "you dared not if you were my wife; I would guard you!"

"Then I should die under your guardianship. But the experiment will never be tried!"

Hartford came near, sat down by her side, and leaned over her. She did not shirk away.

"Oh!" he said, "I am happy. There was a time when I dared not have come so near you. One summer evening two years ago I was walking in the twilight amongst those trees on the lawn, and at a turn I saw you sitting at the root of one of them by yourself.

"You were looking up at a star which was twinkling above the Sydenhams. You were in white; your hands were folded on your knee, and your hair was resting in still, shining curls on your neck. I stood and watched. The thought struck me: if that image sat now in my own woods, if she were something in which I had an interest, if I could go and press my lips to her brow and expect a smile in answer to the caress, if I could take her in my arms and turn her thoughts from that sky with its single star, and from the distant country to which it points (for it hung in the west and I know you were thinking about Senegambia), if I could attract those thoughts and centre them all in myself, how like heaven would the world become to me. I heard a window open, and Zamorna's voice called through the silence, 'Mina!'. The next moment I had the pleasure of seeing you standing on the lawn, close under the very casement where the Duke sat leaning out, and you were allowing his hand to stray through your hair, and his lips ——."

"Lord Hartford!" exclaimed Miss Laury, colouring to the eyes, "this is more than I can bear, I have not been angry yet. I thought it folly to rage at you, because you said you loved me, but what you have just said is like touching a nerve; it overpowers all reason; it is like a stinging taunt which I am under no obligation to endure from you. Every one knows what I am, but where is the woman in Africa who would have acted more wisely than I did if under the same circumstances she had been subject to the same temptations?"

"That is," returned Hartford, whose eye was now glittering with a desperate, reckless expression, "where is the woman in Africa who would have said no to young Douro when amongst the romantic hills of Ellibank he has pressed his suit on some fine moonlight summer night, and the girl and boy have found themselves alone in a green dell, with here and there a tree to be their shade, far above the stars for their sentinels, and around, the night for their wide curtain."

The wild bounding throb of Miss Laury's heart was visible through her satin bodice—it was even audible as for a moment Hartford ceased his scoffing to note its effect. He was still close by her, and she did not move from him. She did not speak. The pallid lamp-light shewed her lips white, her cheek bloodless.

He continued unrelentingly and bitterly: "In after times, doubtless, the woods of Hawkscliffe have witnessed many a tender scene, when the King of Angria has retired from the turmoil of business and the teasing of matrimony to love and leisure with his gentle mistress."

"Now, Hartford, we must part," interrupted Miss Laury, "I see what your opinion of me is, and it is very just, but not one which I willingly hear expressed. You have cut me to the heart. Good-bye. I shall try to avoid seeing you for the future."

She rose. Hartford did not attempt to detain her. She went out. As she closed the door, he heard the bursting convulsive gush of feelings which his taunts had wrought up to agony.

Her absence left a blank. Suddenly a wish to recall, to soothe, to propitiate her rose in his mind. He strode to the door and opened it. There was a little hall or rather a wide passage without in which one large lamp was quietly burning. Nothing appeared there, nor on the staircase of low broad steps in which it terminated. She seemed to have vanished.

Lord Hartford's hat and horseman's cloak lay on the side

slab. There remained no further attraction for him at the Lodge of Rivaulx. The delirious dream of rapture which had intoxicated his sense broke up and disappeared. His passionate, stern nature maddened under disappointment. He strode out into the black and frozen night burning in flames no ice could quench. He ordered and mounted his steed, and, dashing his spurs with harsh cruelty up to the rowels into the flanks of the noble war-horse which had borne him victoriously through the carnage of Westwood and Leyden, he dashed in furious gallop down the road to Rivaulx.

The frost continued unbroken, and the snow lay cold and cheerless all over Angria. It was a dreary morning; large flakes were fluttering slowly down from the sky, thickening every moment. The trees around a stately hall lying up among its grounds at some distance from the road-side shuddered in the cutting wind that at intervals howled through them.

We are now on a broad and public road. A great town lies on our left hand, with a deep river sweeping under the arches of a bridge. This is Zamorna and that house is Hartford Hall.

The wind increased, the sky darkened, and the bleached whirl of snow-storm began to fill the air.

Dashing at a rapid rate through the tempest, an open travelling carriage swept up the road. Four splendid greys and two mounted postillions gave the equipage an air of aristocratic style. It contained two gentlemen, one a man of between thirty and forty having about him a good deal of the air of a nobleman, shawled up to the eyes and buttoned up in at least three surtouts, with a water-proof white beaver hat, an immense mackintosh cape, and beaver gloves. His countenance bore a half rueful, half jesting expression. He seemed endeavouring to bear all things as smoothly as he could, but still the cold east wind and driving snow evidently put his philosophy very much to the test. The other traveller was a young high-featured gentleman, with a pale face and accurately arched dark eye-brows. His person was carefully done up in a vast roquelaure of furs. A fur travelling cap decorated his head which, however, nature had much more effectively protected by a profusion of dark chestnut ringlets now streaming long and thick in the wind. He presented to the said wind a case of bared teeth firmly set together, and exposed in a desperate grin. They seemed daring the snow-flakes to a comparison of whiteness.

"Oh," groaned the elder traveller, "I wish your Grace would be ruled by reason. What could possess you to insist on prosecuting the journey in such weather as this?"

"Stuff, Richton, an old campaigner like you ought to make objections to no weather. It's d—— cold though. I think all Greenland's coming down upon us; but you're not going to faint, are you Richton? What are you staring at so? Do you see the D——?"

"I think I do," replied Lord Richton, "and really if your Grace will look two yards before you, you will be of the same opinion."

The carriage was now turning that angle of the park-wall where a lodge on each side, overhung by some magnificent trees, formed the supporters to the stately iron gates opening upon the broad carriage-road which wound up through the park.

The gates were open, and just outside, on the causeway of the high-road, stood a tall, well-dressed man in a blue coat with military pantaloons of grey having a broad stripe of scarlet down the sides.

His distinguished air, his handsome dark face, and his composed attitude, for he stood perfectly still with one hand on his side, gave a singular effect to the circumstance of his being without a hat. Had it been a summer day one would not so much have wondered at it, though even in the warmest weather it is not usual to see gentlemen parading the public roads uncovered. Now, as the keen wind rushed down upon him

through the boughs of the lofty trees arching the park portal
and as the snow-flakes settled thick upon the short raven curls
of his hair, he looked strange indeed.

Abruptly stepping forward, he seized the first leader of
the chariot by the head and backed it fiercely. The postillions
were about to whip on, consigning the hatless and energetic
gentleman to that fate which is sought by the worshippers of
Juggernaut, when Lord Richton called out to them for God's
sake to stop the horses!

"I think they are stopped with a vengeance," said his young
companion, then, leaning forward with a most verjuice expression on his pale face, he said,

"Give that gentleman half a minute to get out of the way
and then drive on forward like the d——."

"My lord Duke," interposed Richton, "do you see who it is?
Permit me to solicit a few minutes forbearance. Lord Hartford
must be ill. I will alight and speak to him."

Before Richton could fulfil his purpose, the individual had
let go his hold and stood by the side of the chariot. Stretching
out his clenched hand with a menacing gesture, he addressed
Zamorna thus: "I've no hat to take off in your Majesty's presence, so you must excuse my rustic breeding. I saw the royal
carriage at a distance and so I came out to meet it something
in a hurry. I'm just in time, God be thanked! Will your Grace
get out and speak to me? By the Lord! I'll not leave this spot
alive without audience."

"Your lordship is cursedly drunk," replied the Duke, keeping
his teeth as close shut as a vise. "Ask for an audience when
you're sober. Drive on, postillions."

"At the peril of your lives!" cried Hartford, as he drew out
a brace of pistols, cocked them, and presented one at each
postillion.

"Rosier, my pistols!" shouted Zamorna to his valet, who sat
behind, and he threw himself at once from the chariot and
stood facing Lord Hartford on the high-road.

"It is your Grace that is intoxicated," retorted the nobleman, "and I'll tell you with what—with the wine of Cyprus or Cythera. Your Majesty is far too amorous; you had better keep a harem!"

"Come, sir!" said Zamorna in lofty scorn. "This won't do. I see you are mad. Postillions, seize him, and you, Rosier, go up to the hall and fetch five or six of his own domestics. Tell them to bring a strait-waistcoat, if they have such a thing."

"Your Grace would like to throw me into a dungeon," said Hartford, "but this is a free country, and we will have no Western despotism. Be so good as to hear me, my lord Duke, or I will shoot myself."

"Small loss!" said Zamorna lifting his lip with a sour sneer.

"Do not aggravate his insanity," whispered Richton. "Allow me to manage him, my lord Duke. You had better return to the carriage, and I will accompany Hartford home." Then, turning to Hartford: "Take my arm, Edward, and let us return to the house together. You do not seem well this morning."

"None of your snivel," replied the gallant nobleman. "I'll have satisfaction, I'm resolved on it. His Grace has injured me deeply."

"A good move," replied Zamorna. "Then take your pistols, sir, and come along. Rosier, take the carriage back to town. Call at Dr. Cooper's and ask him to ride over to Hartford Hall. D——n you, sir, what are you staring at? Do as I bid you."

"He is staring at the propriety of the monarch of a kingdom fighting a duel with a madman," replied Richton. "If your Grace will allow me to go I will return with a detachment of police and put both the sovereign and the subject under safe ward!"

"Have done with that trash!" said Zamorna angrily. "Come on, you will be wanted for a second."

"Well," said Richton, "I don't wish to disoblige either your

Grace or my friend Hartford, but it's an absurd and frantic piece of business. I beseech you to consider a moment. Hartford, reflect; what are you about to do?"

"To get a vengeance for a thousand wrongs and sufferings," was the reply. "His Grace has dashed my happiness for life."

Richton shook his head. "I must stop this work," he muttered to himself. "What Demon is influencing Edward Hartford—and Zamorna too, for I never saw such a fiendish glitter as that in his eyes just now—strange madness!"

The noble Earl buttoned his surtout still closer and then followed the two other gentlemen who were already on their way to the house. The carriage, meantime, drove off according to orders in the direction of Zamorna.

Lord Hartford was not mad, though his conduct might seem to betoken such a state of mind. He was only desperate. The disappointment of the previous night had wrought him up to a pitch of rage and recklessness whose results, as we have just seen them, were of such a nature as to convince Lord Richton that the doubts he had long harboured of his friend's sanity were correct.

So long as his passion for Miss Laury had remained unavowed and consequently unrejected, he had cherished a dreamy kind of hope that there existed some chance of success. When wandering through his woods alone he had fed on reveries of some future day when she might fill his halls with the bliss of her presence and the light of her beauty. All day her image haunted him. It seemed to speak to and look upon him with that mild friendly aspect he had ever seen her wear, and then as imagination prevailed, it brought vividly back that hour when in a moment almost of despair her feminine weakness had thrown itself utterly on him for support, and he had been permitted to hold her in his arms and take her to his heart. He remembered how she looked when, torn from danger and tumult, rescued from hideous captivity, he carried her up the humble staircase of a farmhouse, all pale and shuddering, with her long black curls spread dishevelled on his shoulder and her soft cheek resting there as confidingly as if he had indeed been her husband.

From her trusting gentleness in those moments he drew blissful omens how—alas! utterly belied. No web of self-delusion could now be woven; the truth was too stern, and besides he had taunted her, hurt her feelings, and alienated forever her grateful friendship.

Having thus entered more particularly into the state of his feelings let me proceed with my narrative.

The apartment into which Lord Hartford shewed his illustrious guest was that very dining-room where I first represented him sitting alone and maddening under the double influence of passion and wine. His manner now was more composed, and he demeaned himself even with lofty courtesy towards his sovereign. There was a particular chair in that room which Zamorna had always been accustomed to occupy when in happier days he had not unfrequently formed one of the splendid dinner-parties given at Hartford Hall. The General asked him to assume that seat now, but he declined, acknowledging the courtesy only by a slight inclination of the head, and planted himself just before the hearth, his elbow leaning on the mantle-piece and his eyes looking down. In that position the eye-lids and long fringes partly concealed the sweet expression of vindictiveness lurking beneath; but still, aided by the sour curl and pout of the lip, the passionate dishevelment of the hair and flushing of the brow, there was enough seen to stamp his countenance with a character of unpleasantness more easily conceived than described.

Lord Hartford influenced by his usual habits would not sit whilst his monarch stood, so he retired with Richton to the deeply embayed recess of a window. That worthy and prudent personage, bent upon settling this matter without coming to the absurd extreme now contemplated, began to reason with his friend on the subject.

"Hartford," he said, speaking soft and low, so that Zamorna could not overhear him, "let me entreat you to consider well what you are about to do. I know that the scene which we have just witnessed is not the primary cause of the dispute between you and his Grace there, which is now about to terminate so fatally. I know that circumstances previously existed which gave birth to bitter feelings on both sides. I wish, Hartford, you would reconsider the steps you have taken—all is in vain: the lady in question can never be yours."

"I know that, sir, and that is what makes me frantic. I have no motive left for living, and if Zamorna wants my blood, let him have it."

"You may kill him," suggested Richton, "and what will be the consequence then?"

"Trust me," returned Hartford, "I'll not hurt him much, though he deserves it—the double-dyed infernal Western profligate! But the fact is he hates me far more than I hate him. Look at his face now reflected in the mirror. God! he longs to see the last drop of blood I have in my heart."

"Hush! he will hear you," said Richton. "He certainly does not look very amiable, but recollect you are the offender."

"I know that," replied Hartford gloomily, "but it is not out of spite to him that I wish to get his mistress, and how often in the half year does he see her or think about her—grasping dog! Another king when he was tired of his mistress would give her up—but he—I think I'll shoot him straight through the head; I would if his death would only win me Miss Laury."

That name, though spoken very low, caught Zamorna's ear, and he at once comprehended the nature of the conversation. It is not often that he has occasion to be jealous, and as it is rare so also it is a remarkably curious and pretty sight to see him under the influence of that passion. It smoked in every fibre of his frame and boiled in every vein. Blush after blush deepened the hue of his cheek; as one faded, another of darker crimson followed. (This variation of colour resulting from

strong emotion has been his wonted peculiarity from childhood.) His whiskers twined and writhed, and even the very
curls seemed to stir on his brow.

Turning to Hartford, he spoke:

"What drivelling folly have you got into your head, sir, to
dare to look at anything which belongs to me. Frantic idiot!
to dream that I should allow a coarse Angrian squire to possess
anything that had ever been mine! As if I knew how to relinquish! God d——n your grossness! Richton, you have my
pistols? Bring them here directly. I will neither wait for doc-
tors nor anybody else to settle this business—"

"My lord Duke," began Richton—

"No interference, sir!" exclaimed his Grace. "Bring the
pistols!"

The Earl was not going to stand this arbitrary work.

"I wash my hands of this bloody affair," he said sternly,
placing the pistols on the table, and in silence he left the room.

The demon of Zamorna's nature was now completely roused.
Growling out his words in a deep and hoarse tone almost like
the smothered roar of a lion, he savagely told Hartford to
measure out his ground in this room, for he would not delay
the business a moment. Hartford did so without remonstrance
or reply.

"Take your station!" thundered the barbarian.

"I have done so," replied his lordship, "and my pistol is
ready."

"Then fire!"

The deadly explosion succeeded the flash and the cloud of
smoke.

While the room still shook to the sound, almost before the
flash had exploded and the smoke burst after it, the door
slowly opened and Lord Richton reappeared wearing upon his
face a far more fixed and stern solemnity than I ever saw
there before.

"Who is hurt?" he asked.

There was but one erect figure visible through the vapour, and the thought thrilled through him: "The other may be a corpse."

Lord Hartford lay across the doorway still and pale.

"My poor friend!" said Lord Richton and, kneeling on one knee, he propped against the other the wounded nobleman from whose lips a moan of agony escaped as the Earl moved him.

"Thank God he is not quite dead!" was Richton's involuntary exclamation, for though a man accustomed to scenes of carnage or gory battle-plains, and though of enduring nerves and cool resolution, he felt a pang at this spectacle of fierce manslaughter amid scenes of domestic peace. The renowned and gallant soldier who had escaped hostile weapons and returned unharmed from fields of terrific strife lay, as it seemed, dying under his own roof.

Blood began to drop on to Richton's hand, and a large crimson stain appeared on the ruffles of his shirt. The same ominous dye darkened Lord Hartford's lips and oozed through them when he made vain efforts to speak. He had been wounded in the region of the lungs.

A thundering knock and a loud ring at the door-bell now broke up the appalling silence which had fallen.

It was Dr. Cooper.[11] He speedily entered, followed by a surgeon with instruments, etc. Richton silently resigned his friend to their hands and turned for the first time to the other actor in this horrid scene.

The Duke of Zamorna was standing by a window coolly buttoning his surtout over the pistols which he had placed in his breast.

"Is your Majesty hurt?" asked Richton.

"No, sir. May I trouble you to hand me my gloves?"

They lay on a side-board near the Earl. He politely complied with the request, handing over at the same time a large shawl or scarf of crimson silk which the Duke had taken from his neck. In this he proceeded to envelope his throat and a considerable portion of his face leaving little more visible than the forehead, eyes, and high Roman nose. Then drawing on his gloves, he turned to Dr. Cooper.

"Of what nature is the wound, sir? Is there any likelihood of Lord Hartford's recovery?"

"A possibility exists that he may recover, my lord Duke, but the wound is a severe one. The lungs have only just escaped."

The Duke drew near the couch on which his General had been raised, looked at the wound then under the operation of the surgeon's probing knife, and transferred his glance from the bloody breast to the pallid face of the sufferer. Hartford, who had borne the extraction of the bullet without a groan, and whose clenched teeth and rigid brow seemed defying pain to do its worst, smiled faintly when he saw his monarch's eye bent upon him with searching keenness. In spite of the surgeon's prohibition he attempted to speak.

"Zamorna," he said, "I have got your hate, but you shall not blight me with your contempt. This is but a little matter. Why did you not inflict more upon me that I might bear it without flinching? You called me a coarse Angrian squire ten minutes since. Angrians are men as well as Westerns."

"Brutes, rather," replied Zamorna, "faithful, gallant, noble brutes." He left the room, for his carriage had now returned and waited at the door. Before Lord Richton followed him he stopped a moment to take leave of his friend.

"Well," murmured Hartford as he feebly returned the pressure of the Earl's hand, "Zamorna has finished me, but I bear him no ill-will. My love for his mistress was involuntary. I am not sorry for it now. I adore her to the last. Flower, if I die, give Mina Laury this token of my truth." He drew the gold ring from his little finger and gave it into Richton's hand. "Good God!" he muttered, turning away, "I would have endured Hell's tortures to win her love. My feelings are not changed; they are just the same: passion for her, bitter self-reproach for my treachery to her master. But he has paid himself in blood, the purest coin to a Western. Farewell, Richton."

They parted without another word on either side. Richton joined the Duke, sprung to his place in the carriage, and off it swept like the wind.

Miss Laury was sitting after breakfast in a small library. Her desk lay before her and two large ruled quartos filled with items and figures which she seemed to be comparing. Behind her chair stood a tall, well-made, soldierly young man with light hair. His dress was plain and gentlemanly; the epaulette on one shoulder alone indicated an official capacity. He watched with fixed look of attention the movements of the small finger which ascended in rapid calculation the long columns of accounts. It was strange to see the absorption of mind expressed in Miss Laury's face, the gravity of her smooth white brow shaded with drooping curls, the scarcely perceptible and unsmiling movement of her lips, though those lips in their rosy sweetness seemed formed only for smiles. Edward Percy at his ledger could not have appeared more completely wrapt in the mysteries of practice and fractions. An hour or more lapsed in this employment, the room, meantime, continuing in profound silence broken only by an occasional observation addressed by Miss Laury to the gentleman behind her concerning the legitimacy of some item or the absence of some stray farthing wanted to complete the accuracy of the sum total. In this balancing of the books she displayed a most business-like sharpness and strictness. The slightest fault was detected and remarked on in few words but with a quick searching glance. However, the accountant had evidently been accustomed to her surveillance, for on the whole his books were a specimen of arithmetical correctness.

"Very well," said Miss Laury, as she closed the volumes.

"Your accounts do you credit, Mr. O'Neill. You may tell his Grace that all is quite right. Your memoranda tally with my own exactly."

Mr. O'Neill bowed. "Thank you, madam. This will bear me out against Lord Hartford. His lordship lectured me severely last time he came to inspect Fort Adrian."

"What about?" asked Miss Laury turning aside her face to hide the deepening of colour which overspread it at the mention of Lord Hartford's name.

"I can hardly tell you, madam, but his lordship was in a savage temper. Nothing would please him. He found fault with everything and everybody. I thought he scarcely appeared himself, and that has been the opinion of many lately."

Miss Laury gently shook her head. "You should not say so, Ryan," she replied in a soft tone of reproof. "Lord Hartford has a great many things to think about, and he is naturally rather stern. You ought to bear with his tempers."

"Necessity has no law, madam," replied Mr. O'Neill with a smile, "and I must bear with them, but his lordship is not a popular man in the army. He orders the lash so unsparingly. We like the Earl of Arundel ten times better."

"Ah," said Miss Laury smiling, "you and I are Westerns, Mr. O'Neill—Irish—and we favour our countrymen. But Hartford is a gallant commander. His men can always trust him. Do not let us be partial."

Mr. O'Neill bowed in deference to her opinion, but smiled at the same time, as if he doubted its justice. Taking up his books, he seemed about to leave the room. Before he did so, however, he turned and said: "The Duke wished me to inform you, madam, that he would probably be here about four or five o'clock in the afternoon."

"To-day?" asked Miss Laury in an accent of surprise.

"Yes, madam."

She mused a moment, then said quickly, "Very well, sir."

Mr. O'Neill now took his leave with another low and respectful obeisance. Miss Laury returned it with a slight abstracted bow. Her thoughts were all caught up and hurried away by that last communication. For a long time after the door had closed she sat with her head on her hand, lost in a tumultuous flush of ideas—anticipations awakened by that simple sentence, "The Duke will be here to-day."

The striking of a timepiece roused her. She remembered that twenty tasks awaited her direction. Always active, always employed, it was not her custom to waste many hours in dreaming. She rose, closed her desk, and left the quiet library for busier scenes.

Four o'clock came, and Miss Laury's foot was heard on the stair case descending from her chamber. She crossed the large light passage—such an apparition of feminine elegance and beauty! She had dressed herself splendidly. The robe of black satin became at once her slender form, which it enveloped in full and shining folds, and her bright blooming complexion, which is set off by the contrast of colour. Glittering through her curls, there was a band of fine diamonds, and drops of the same pure gems trembled from her small, delicate ears. These ornaments, so regal in their nature, had been the gift of royalty, and were worn now chiefly for the associations of soft and happy moments which their gleam might be supposed to convey.

She entered her drawing-room and stood by the window. From thence appeared one glimpse of the high-road visible through the thickening shades of Rivaulx. Even that was now almost concealed by the frozen mist in which the approach of twilight was wrapped. All was very quiet both in the house and in the wood. A carriage drew near. She heard the sound. She saw it shoot through the fog; but it was not Zamorna. No; the driving was neither the driving of Jehu the son of Nimshi, nor that of Jehu's postillions. She had not gazed a minute before her experienced eye discerned that there was something wrong with the horses. The harness had got entangled or they were frightened. The coachman had lost command over them: they were plunging violently.

She rang the bell. A servant entered. She ordered immediate assistance to be despatched to that carriage on the road. Two grooms presently hurried down the drive to execute her command, but before they could reach the spot, one of the horses, in its gambols, had slipped on the icy road and fallen. The others grew more unmanageable, and presently the carriage lay overturned on the roadside. One of Miss Laury's messengers came back. She threw up the window that she might communicate with him more readily.

"Any accident?" she asked. "Anybody hurt?"

"I hope not much, madam."

"Who is in the carriage?"

"Only one lady, and she seems to have fainted. She looked very white when I opened the door. What is to be done, madam?"

Miss Laury, with Irish frankness, answered directly, "Bring them all into the house. Let the horses be taken into the stables. And the servants—how many are there?"

"Three, madam, two postillions and a footman. It seems quite a gentleman's turn-out, very plain, but quite slap-up— beautiful horses."

"Do you know the liveries?"

"Can't say, madam. Postillions grey and white; footman in plain clothes. Horses frightened at a drove of Sydenham oxen, they say: very spirited nags."

"Well, you have my orders: bring the lady in directly, and make the others comfortable."

"Yes, madam."

The groom touched his hat and departed. Miss Laury shut her window. It was very cold. Not many minutes elapsed before the lady in the arms of her own servants was slowly brought up the lawn and ushered into the drawing-room.

"Lay her on the sofa," said Miss Laury.

She was obeyed. The lady's travelling cloak was carefully removed, and a thin figure became apparent in a dark silk dress. The cushions of down scarcely sank under the pressure, it was so light.

Her swoon was now passing off. The genial warmth of the fire which shone full on her revived her. Opening her eyes, she looked up at Miss Laury's face who was bending close over her and wetting her lips with some cordial. Recognizing a stranger, she shyly turned her glance aside and asked for her servants.

"They are in the house, madam, and perfectly safe. But you cannot pursue your journey at present; the carriage is much broken."

The lady lay silent. She looked keenly round the room and seeing the perfect elegance of its arrangement, the cheerful and tranquil glow of its hearth-light, she appeared to grow more composed. Turning a little on the cushions which supported her, and by no means looking at Miss Laury, but straight the other way, she said, "To whom am I indebted for this kindness? Where am I?"

"In a hospitable country, madam. The Angrians never turn their backs on strangers."

"I know I am in Angria," she said quickly, "but where? What is the name of the house? Who are you?"

Miss Laury coloured slightly. It seemed as if there was some undefined reluctance to give her real name that she knew was widely celebrated—too widely. Most likely the lady would turn from her in contempt if she heard it, and Miss Laury felt she could not bear that.

"I am only the housekeeper," she said. "This is a shooting-lodge belonging to a great Angrian proprietor."

"Who?" asked the lady, who was not to be put off by in-direct answers.

Again Miss Laury hesitated. For her life she could not have said "His Grace the Duke of Zamorna." She replied hastily, "A gentleman of Western extraction, a distant branch of the great Pakenhams, so at least the family records say, but they have been long naturalized in the East."

"I never heard of them," replied the lady. "Pakenham! that is not an Angrian name?"

"Perhaps, madam, you are not particularly acquainted with this part of the country?"

"I know Hawkscliffe," said the lady, "and your house is on the very borders, within the royal liberties, is it not?"

"Yes, madam, it stood there before the Great Duke bought up the forest-manor, and his Majesty allowed my master to retain this lodge and the privilege of sporting in the chase."

"Well, and you are Mr. Pakenham's housekeeper?"

"Yes, madam."

The lady surveyed Miss Laury with another furtive side-glance of her large majestic eyes. Those eyes lingered upon diamond ear-rings, the bandeau of brilliants that flashed from between the clusters of raven curls, then passed over the sweet face, the exquisite figure of the young housekeeper, and finally were reverted to the wall with an expression that spoke vol-umes.

Miss Laury could have torn the dazzling pendants from her ears. She was bitterly stung. "Everybody knows me," she said to herself. " 'Mistress,' I suppose, is branded on my brow."

In her turn she gazed on her guest. The lady was but a young creature, though so high and commanding in her de-meanour. She had very small and feminine features, handsome eyes, a neck of delicate curve, and fair, long, graceful little snowy aristocratic hands, and sandalled feet to match. It would have been difficult to tell her rank by her dress. None of those dazzling witnesses appeared which had betrayed Miss Laury.

Any gentleman's wife might have worn the gown of dark-blue silk, the tinted gloves of Parisian kid, and the fairy sandals of black satin in which she was attired.

"May I have a room to myself?" she asked, again turning her eyes with something like a smile toward Miss Laury.

"Certainly, madam, I wish to make you comfortable. Can you walk upstairs?"

"Oh, yes!"

She rose from the couch, and, leaning on Miss Laury's offered arm in a way that showed she had been used to that sort of support, they both glided from the room. Having seen her fair but somewhat haughty guest carefully laid on a stately crimson bed in a quiet and spacious chamber, having seen her head sink (with all its curls) onto the pillow of down, her large shy eyes close under their smooth eyelids, and her little slender hands fold on her breast in an attitude of perfect repose, Miss Laury prepared to leave her.

"Come back a moment," she said. She was obeyed—there was something in the tone of her voice which exacted obedience. "I don't know who you are," she said, "but I am very much obliged to you for your kindness. If my manners are displeasing, forgive me, I mean no incivility. I suppose you will wish to known my name: it is Mrs. Irving. My husband is a minister in the northern kirk; I come from Sneachiesland. Now you may go!"

Miss Laury did go. Mrs. Irving had testified incredulity respecting her story, and now she reciprocated that incredulity. Both ladies were lost in their own mystification.

Five o'clock now struck. It was nearly dark. A servant with a taper was lighting up the chandeliers in the large dining-room, where a table spread for dinner received the kindling lamplight upon a starry service of silver. It was likewise magnificently flashed back from a splendid sideboard, all arranged in readiness to receive the great, the expected guest.

Tolerably punctual in keeping an appointment when he

means to keep it at all, Zamorna entered the house as the fairy-like voice of a musical clock in the passage struck out its symphony to the pendulum. The opening of the front door, a bitter rush of the night-wind, and then the sudden close and the step advancing forwards were the signals of his arrival.

Miss Laury was in the dining-room looking round and giving the last touch to all things. She just met her master as he entered. His cold lip pressed to her forehead and his colder hand clasping hers brought the sensation which it was her custom of weeks and months to wait for, and to consider, when attained, as the ample recompense for all delay, all toil, all suffering.

"I am frozen, Mina," said he. "I came on horseback for the last four miles, and the night is like Canada."

Chafing his icy hand to animation between her own warm, supple palms, she answered by the speechless but expressive look of joy, satisfaction, idolatry, which filled and overflowed her eyes.

"What can I do for you, my lord?" were her first words as he stood by the fire rubbing his hands cheerily over the blaze. He laughed.

"Put your arms round my neck, Mina, and kiss my cheek as warm and blooming as your own."

If Mina Laury had been Mina Wellesley she would have done so, and it gave her a pang to resist the impulse that urged her to take him at his word, but she put it by and only diffidently drew near the armchair into which he had now thrown himself and began to smooth and separate the curls which were matted on his temples. She noticed as the first smile of salutation subsided a gloom succeeded on her master's brow, which, however he spoke or laughed, afterwards, remained a settled characteristic of his countenance.

"What visitors are in the house?" he asked; "I saw the groom rubbing down four black horses before the stables as I came in. They are not of the Hawkscliffe stud, I think?"

"No, my lord. A carriage was overturned at the lawn gates about an hour since, and, as the lady who was in it was taken out insensible, I ordered her to be brought up here and her servants accommodated for the night."

"And do you know who the lady is?" continued his Grace; "The horses are good—first rate."

"She says her name is Mrs. Irving, and that she is the wife of a Presbyterian minister in the north, but—"

"You hardly believe her?" interrupted the Duke.

"No," returned Miss Laury, "I must say I took her for a lady of rank. She has something highly aristocratic about her manners and aspect, and she appeared to know a good deal about Angria."

"What is she like?" asked Zamorna. "Young or old, handsome or ugly?"

"She is young, slender, not so tall as I am, and, I should say, rather elegant than handsome, very pale, cold in her demeanour. She has a small mouth and chin, and a fair neck."

"Humph! a trifle like Lady Stuartville," replied his Majesty. "I should not wonder if it is the Countess, but I'll know. Perhaps you did not say to whom the house belonged, Mina?"

"I said," replied Mina, smiling, "that the owner of the house was a great Angrian proprietor, a lineal descendant of the Western Pakenhams, and that I was his housekeeper."

"Very good! She would not believe you. You look like an Angrian country gentleman's Dolly! Give me your hand, my girl. You are not as old as I am."

"Yes, my lord Duke, I was born on the same day, an hour after your Grace."

"So I have heard, but it must be a mistake. You don't look twenty, and I am twenty-five. My beautiful Western—what eyes! Look at me, Mina, straight, and don't blush."

Mina tried to look but she could not do it without blushing. She coloured to the temples.

"Pshaw!" said his Grace, pushing her away. "Pretending to

be modest! My acquaintance of ten years cannot meet my eye unshrinkingly. Have you lost that ring I once gave you, Mina?"

"What ring, my lord? You have given me many."

"That which I said had the essence of your whole heart and mind engraven in the stone as a motto."

"FIDELITY?" asked Miss Laury, and she held out her hand with a graven emerald on the forefinger.

"Right!" was the reply; "Is it your motto still?" And with one of his hungry, jealous glances, he seemed trying to read her conscience. Miss Laury at once saw the late transactions were not a secret confined between herself and Lord Hartford. She saw His Grace was unhinged and strongly inclined to be savage. She stood and watched him with a sad fearful gaze.

"Well," she said, turning away after a long pause, "if your Grace is angry with me I've very little to care about in this world."

The entrance of servants with the dinner prevented Zamorna's answer. As he took his place at the head of the table, he said to the man who stood behind him: "Give Mr. Pakenham's compliments to Mrs. Irving and say that he will be happy to see her at his table if she will honour him so far as to be present there."

The footman vanished. He returned in five minutes.

"Mrs. Irving is too much tired to avail herself of Mr. Pakenham's kind invitation at present, but she will be happy to join him at tea."

"Very well," said Zamorna, then looking round, "where is Miss Laury?"

Mina was in the act of gliding from the room, but she stopped mechanically at his call.

"Am I to dine alone?" he asked.

"Does your Grace wish me to attend you?"

He answered by rising and leading her to her seat. He then resumed his own and dinner commenced. It was not till after the cloth was withdrawn and the servants had retired that the

Duke, whilst he sipped his single glass of champagne, recommenced the conversation he had before so unpleasantly entered upon.

"Come here, my girl," he said, drawing a chair close to his side.

Mina never delayed, never hesitated, through bashfulness or any other feeling, to comply with his orders.

"Now," he continued, leaning his head towards hers and placing his hand on her shoulder, "are you happy, Mina? Do you want anything?"

"Nothing, my lord."

She spoke truly; all that was capable of yielding her happiness on this side of Eternity was at that moment within her reach. The room was full of calm. The lamps burnt as if they were listening. The fire sent up no flickering flame, but diffused a broad, still, glowing light over all the spacious saloon. Zamorna touched her. His form and features filled her eye, his voice her ear, his presence her whole heart. She was soothed to perfect happiness.

"My Fidelity!" pursued that musical voice. "If thou hast any favour to ask, now is the time. I'm all concession, as sweet as honey, as yielding as a lady's glove. Come, Esther, what is thy petition? And thy request, even to the half of my kingdom, it shall be granted!"

"Nothing," again murmured Miss Laury. "Oh, my lord, nothing. What can I want?"

"Nothing," he repeated. "What! No reward for ten years of faith and love and devotion; no reward for the companionship in six months exile; no recompense to the little hand that has so often smoothed my pillow in sickness, to the sweet lips that have many a time in cool and dewy health been pressed to a brow of fever, none to the dark Milesian eyes that once grew dim with watching through endless nights by my couch of delirium? Need I speak of the sweetness and fortitude that cheered sufferings known only to thee and me, Mina? Of the devotion that gave me bread when thou wert dying with hunger—and that scarcely more than a year since? For all this, and much more, must there be no reward?"

"I have had it," said Miss Laury. "I have it now."

"But," continued the Duke, "what if I have devised something worthy of your acceptance? Look up now and listen to me."

She did look up, but she speedily looked down again. Her master's eye was insupportable. It burnt absolutely with infernal fire. "What is he going to say?" murmured Miss Laury to herself. She trembled.

"I say, love," pursued the individual, drawing her a little closer to him, "I will give you as a reward a husband, don't start now!—and that husband shall be a nobleman, and that nobleman is called Lord Hartford! Now, madam, stand up and let me look at you!"

He opened his arms, and Miss Laury sprang erect like a loosened bow.

"Your Grace is anticipated," she said. "That offer has been made me before. Lord Hartford did it himself three days ago."

"And what did you say, madam? Speak the truth now: subterfuge won't avail you."

"What did I say, Zamorna? I don't know; it little signifies; you have rewarded me, my lord Duke! But I cannot bear this—I feel sick."

With a deep, short sob, she turned white and fell close by the Duke, her head against his foot.

This was the first time in her life that Mina Laury had fainted, but strong health availed nothing against the deadly struggle which convulsed every feeling of her nature when she heard her master's announcement. She believed him to be perfectly sincere. She thought he was tired of her and she could not stand it.

I suppose Zamorna's first feeling when she fell was horror, and his next, I am tolerably certain, was intense gratification.

ARTHUR AUGUSTUS ADRIAN WELLESLEY
DUKE OF ZAMORNA

People say I am not in earnest when I abuse him, or else I would here insert half a page of deserved vituperation, deserved and heartfelt. As it is I will merely relate his conduct without note or comment.

He took a wax taper from the table and held it over Miss Laury. Here could be no dissimulation. She was white as marble and still as stone. In truth then, she did intensely love him with a devotion that left no room in her thoughts for one shadow of an alien image. Do not think, reader, that Zamorna meant to be so generous as to bestow Miss Laury on Lord Hartford. No; trust him! He was but testing in his usual way the attachment which a thousand proofs daily given ought long ago to have convinced him was undying.

While he yet gazed she began to recover. Her eyelids stirred, and then slowly dawned from beneath, the large black orbs that scarcely met his before they filled to overflowing with sorrow. Not a gleam of anger! Not a whisper of reproach! Her lips and eyes spoke together no other language than the simple words, "I cannot leave you!"

She rose feebly and with effort. The Duke stretched out his hand to assist her. He held to her lips the scarcely tasted wineglass.

"Mina," he said, "are you collected enough to hear me?"

"Yes, my lord."

"Then listen. I would much sooner give half—aye, the whole of my estates to Lord Hartford, than yourself! What I said just now was only to try you."

Miss Laury raised her eyes, sighed like one awaking from some hideous dream, but she could not speak.

"Would I," continued the Duke, "would I resign the possession of my first love to any hands but my own? I would far rather see her in her coffin; and I would lay you there as still, as white, and much more lifeless than you were stretched just now at my feet before I would, for threat, for entreaty, for purchase, give to another a glance of your eye or a smile from your lip. I know you adore me now, Mina, for you could not feign that agitation, and therefore I will tell you what proof I gave yesterday of my regard for you: Hartford mentioned your name in my presence, and I revenged the profanation by a shot which sent him to his bed little better than a corpse."

Miss Laury shuddered, but so dark and profound are the mysteries of human nature ever allying vice with virtue, that I fear this bloody proof of her master's love brought to her heart more rapture than horror. She said not a word, for now Zamorna's arms were again folded round her, and again he was soothing her to tranquillity by endearments and caresses that far away removed all thought of the world, all past pangs of shame, all cold doubts, all weariness, all heart-sickness resulting from hope long deferred. He had told her that she was his first love, and now she felt tempted to believe that she was likewise his only love. Strong-minded beyond her sex, active, energetic, and accomplished in all other points of view, here she was as weak as a child. She lost her identity; her very life was swallowed up in that of another.

There came a knock at the door. Zamorna rose and opened it. His valet stood without.

"Might I speak with your Grace in the ante-room?" asked Monsieur Rosier in somewhat of a hurried tone. The Duke followed him out.

"What do you want with me, sir? Anything the matter?"

"Ahem!" began Eugene, whose countenance expressed much more embarrassment than is the usual characteristic of his dark, sharp physiognomy. "Ahem! my lord Duke, rather a curious spot of work, a complete conjuror's trick if your Grace will allow me to say so."

"What do you mean, sir?"

"*Sacré!* I hardly know. I must confess I felt a trifle stupefied when I saw it."

"Saw what? Speak plainly, Rosier!"

"How your Grace is to act I can't imagine," replied the

valet, "though indeed I have seen your Majesty double won-
derfully well when the case appeared to me extremely embar-
rassing, but this I really thought extra—I could not have
dreamt!"

"Speak to the point, Rosier, or—" Zamorna lifted his hand.

"Mort de ma vie!" exclaimed Eugene, "I will tell your Grace
all I know. I was walking carelessly through the passage about
ten minutes since when I heard a step on the stairs, a light
step as if of a very small foot. I turned, and there was a lady
coming down. My lord, she was a lady!"

"Well, sir, did you know her?"

"I think if my eyes were not bewitched I did. I stood in
the shade screened by a pillar and she passed very near without
observing me. I saw her distinctly, and may I be d——d this
very moment if it was not—"

"Who, sir?"

"The Duchess!"

There was a pause which was closed by a clear and remarkable prolonged whistle from the Duke. He put both his
hands into his pockets and took a leisurely turn through the
room.

"You are sure, Eugene?" he asked. "I know you dare not
tell me a lie in such a matter because you have a laudable and
natural regard to your proper carcass! Aye, it's true enough,
I'll be sworn. Mrs. Irving, the wife of a minister in the North!
A satirical hit at my royal self. By G—d! pale fair neck, little
mouth and chin! Very good! I wish that same little mouth
and chin were about a hundred miles off. What can have
brought her? Anxiety about her invaluable husband—could
not bear any longer without him—obliged to set off to see
what he was doing. It's as well that turnspit Rosier told me,
however. If she had entered the room unexpectedly about five
minutes since—God! I should have had no resource but to tie
her hand and foot. It would have killed her! What the d——l
shall I do? Must not be angry; she can't do with that sort of

thing just now. Talk softly, reprove her gently, swear black and white to my having no connection with Mr. Pakenham's housekeeper."

Ceasing his soliloquy, the Duke turned again to his valet.

"What room did Her Grace go into?"

"The drawing-room, my lord, she is in there now."

"Well, say nothing about it, Rosier—on pain of sudden death! Do you hear, sir?"

Rosier laid his hand on his heart, and Zamorna left the room to commence operations.

Softly unclosing the drawing-room door, he perceived a lady by the hearth. Her back was towards him, but there could be no mistake. The whole turn of form, the style of dress, the curled auburn head: all were attributes but of one person—of his own unique, haughty, jealous little Duchess. He closed the door as noiselessly as he had opened it and stole forwards. Her attention was absorbed in something, a book she had picked up. As he stood unobserved behind her he could see that her eye rested on the fly-leaf, where was written in his own hand:

> Holy St. Cyprian! thy waters stray
>   With still and solemn tone:
> And fast my bright hours pass away
> And somewhat throws a shadow grey,
> Even as twilight closes day,
>   Upon thy waters lone.
>
> Farewell! If I might come again,
>   Young as I was and free,
> And feel once more in every vein
> The fire of that first passion reign
> Which sorrow could not quench nor pain,
>   I'd soon return to thee;
> But while thy billows seek the main
>   That never more may be!

This was dated "Mornington, 1829."

The Duchess felt a hand press her shoulder and she looked up. The force of attraction had its usual results and she clung to what she saw.

"Adrian! Adrian!" was all her lips could utter.

"Mary! Mary!" replied the Duke, allowing her to hang about him: "Pretty doings! What brought you here? Are you running away, eloping in my absence?"

"Adrian, why did you leave me? You said you would come back in a week, and it's eight days since. I could not bear any longer. I have never slept nor rested since you left me. Do come home!"

"So you actually have set off in search of a husband," said Zamorna, laughing heartily, "and been overturned and obliged to take shelter in Pakenham's shooting-box!"

"Why are you here, Adrian?" inquired the Duchess who was far too much in earnest to join in his laugh. "Who is Pakenham? And who is that person who calls herself his housekeeper? And why do you let anybody live so near Hawkscliffe without ever telling me?"

"I forgot to tell you," said his Grace. "I've other things to think about when those bright hazel eyes are looking up to me! As to Pakenham, to tell you the truth he's a sort of left-hand cousin of your own, being natural son to the old Admiral, my uncle, in the South, and his housekeeper is his sister. Voilà tout. Kiss me now."

The Duchess did kiss him, but it was with a heavy sigh; the cloud of jealous anxiety hung on her brow undissipated.

"Adrian, my heart aches still. Why have you been staying so long in Angria? O, you don't care for me! You have never thought how miserable I have been longing for your return, Adrian!" She stopped and cried.

"Mary, recollect yourself!" said His Grace. "I cannot be always at your feet. You were not so weak when we were first married. You let me leave you often then without any jealous remonstrance."

"I did not know you so well at that time," said Mary, "and if my mind is weakened, all its strength has gone away in tears and terrors for you. I am neither so handsome nor so cheerful as I once was, but you ought to forgive my decay because you have caused it."

"Low spirits," returned Zamorna, "looking on the dark side of matters! God bless me, the wicked is caught in his own net. I wish I could add 'yet shall I withal escape.' Mary, never again reproach yourself with loss of beauty till I give the hint first. Believe me now; in that and every other respect you are just what I wish you to be. You cannot fade any more than marble can—at least not in my eyes. And as for your devotion and tenderness, though I chide its excess sometimes, because it wastes and bleaches you almost to a shadow, yet it forms the very finest chain that binds me to you. Now cheer up! To-night you shall go to Hawkscliffe; it is only five miles off. I cannot accompany you because I have some important business to transact with Pakenham which must not be deferred. To-morrow, I will be at the castle before dawn. The carriage shall be ready. I will put you in, myself beside you; off we go straight to Verdopolis, and there for the next three months I will tire you of my company, morning, noon, and night! Now what can I promise more? If you choose to be jealous of Henri Fernando, Baron of Etrei; or John, Duke of Fidena; or the fair Earl of Richton, who, as God is my witness, has been the only companion of my present peregrinations, why, I can't help it. I must then take to soda-water and despair, or have myself petrified and carved into an Apollo for your dressing-room. Lord! I get not credit with my virtue!"

By dint of lies and laughter the individual at last succeeded in getting all things settled to his mind.

The Duchess went to Hawkscliffe that night; and, keeping his promise for once, he accompanied her to Verdopolis next morning.

Lord Hartford still lies between life and death. His passion is neither weakened by pain, piqued by rejection, nor cooled by absence. On the iron nerves of the man are graved an impression which nothing can efface. Warner curses him; Richton deplores.

For a long space of time, good-bye, reader! I have done my best to please you; and though I know that through feebleness, dullness, and iteration my work terminates rather in failure than triumph, yet you are sure to forgive, for I have done my best.

Haworth 1838   C. Brontë.   Jan 17th

Introduction to "Caroline Vernon"

CHARLOTTE continued her Angrian stories into her twenty-fourth year, 1839, ten years after the writing of "The Twelve Adventurers." Apparently, her last long manuscript of the series was "Caroline Vernon," now in the Widener Collection at Harvard. It is here printed in an abbreviated form—a few variants of scenes and some references contributing to the Angrian story as a whole rather than developing this particular plot, being omitted. If it is not the best of Charlotte Brontë's early efforts, it still holds the interest of the casual reader, and it has much to repay the closer attention of the student.

Its critical significance lies in its bearing on Charlotte's best-known novel. One cannot read very far before he recognizes in the plot a variation of the Jane Clairmont story, and in the heroine and her mother the prototypes of Rochester's ward, Adèle, and the opera dancer, Céline Varens, in *Jane Eyre*.

Like "Zamorna's Exile," "Caroline Vernon" has its roots deep in previous stories and cannot be understood except in terms of them. Louisa Vernon's earliest name, Louisa Dance, or Danci, dates from the "Young Men's Play" in which she was probably represented by a doll dressed as a ballet dancer. She made her first appearance in the written accounts of the play as the Marchioness of Wellesley, sister-in-law to the Duke of Wellington, and aunt by marriage to the Marquis of Douro. She says of herself that she was "born Allen," and that as a ballet dancer and opera star she enjoyed many lovers and several husbands; among them was Lord Vernon, whose name she retained as one of her various designations to the end of the story. Her daughter

Caroline, though bearing the name of Vernon, is in fact the daughter of Northangerland.

One of the few men to escape Louisa's snares, once she had fixed her attention upon them, was her nephew-in-law, young Arthur Wellesley. Toward her he always adopted a gay, half-contemptuous air of teasing, as toward a peevish, spoiled child. His attitude upon occasions drove her into fits of rage, when she could have murdered him with her own hands. She joined with avidity in all the plots against him and was the most exultant of his tormentors when he lay a wounded prisoner of war. Her anger at Percy for sending him out of her reach knew no bounds.

Upon Zamorna's restoration Percy fled the country, leaving Louisa Vernon, of whom he had already tired, to be taken into custody by Zamorna's orders. She was kept in retirement under the Duke's eye, forgotten by Percy, long after the war was over. Her small daughter, called Caroline Vernon, remained with her, the ward of Zamorna, who supervised her education and gave her a careless sort of affection—he was always tender to children who crossed his path. In an untitled story in the Wrenn Library, dated June 29, 1837, there is a scene which might have been written as an introduction to the present novel. The time is the latter part of the Angrian war, on the eve of Zamorna's final triumph. Louisa Vernon, arrested by the Duke's orders and sent to Fort Adrian, has contrived to have herself brought to his military headquarters, hoping to work her charms upon him to the extent of gaining her freedom. The scene opens with the Duke of Zamorna addressing his friend and closest military adviser, General Henri Fernando di Enara, commonly known as "The Tiger."

"Well, Henri, . . . you see matters are drawing to a crisis; our jewel must be removed. Don't you think her whim is satisfied by this time?"

"Certainly not, my Lord Duke; her sole motive for insisting upon being brought to Evesham was to obtain an interview with your Grace; you have not complied with her request yet, I believe?"

"Why no, but then she is such a little viper, and I can't be put out of the way by humouring her caprice."

"Well, I am not going to press the matter further than your Grace likes, but she'll starve herself to death if she's balked."

"Has she fallen desperately in love with me, Henri?"

"I fear I cannot flatter your Grace's vanity by answering in the affirmative."

"There's the puzzle," continued his Grace, the light of such a smile rising in his eyes as I never saw or imagined before in my life, "if she were dying for love of me, now I should know how to manage her, but really one is not prepared to meet such an unnatural crisis as the present."

General Fernando di Enara blew his nose. "Your Grace is an infernal fop," said he plainly.

The man with the conspicuous proboscis [Zamorna] threw back his head . . . and laughed. "I like a love-tryste, Henri, you know," said he, "but as for a hate-tryste, Lord! I don't understand it."

The conversation wanders for a time, then Enara returns to the matter in hand.

"However, let us settle this piece of business. Is that bird to fly back to Fort Adrian without seeing you or not?"

"Let her see me. . . . Go and fetch her, Enara."

"I'll send her; your Grace will not want a third person."

As he waits the Duke of Zamorna falls into a fit of affectionate musing concerning his wife, which is interrupted by the appearance of Caroline Vernon.

Dusk drew softly on. A faint and golden reflection of the window fell in moonlight on the floor. It fell likewise on something else—a childish figure clad in white, a creature with dark hair and Italian eyes, standing like a little spirit in the chamber. . . . The apparition saw Zamorna, paused and gazed on him with wondering solicitude. "Who is it?" she said in a tone awe had subdued to the softest whisper.

His Grace, who had watched her with interest, answered only by the word, "Caroline!"

"He knows me!" exclaimed the child. "I must have got to the right room. It is the Duke."

"Right!" said his Grace. "Come here, child."

The little girl needed no second invitation. In trembling excitement she sprang into the tall officer's arms. Her nature was seen at once; her whole constitutional turn of feeling revealed itself. She cried and shook in answer to some soothing endearment, clasped him in her childish embrace.

"Why Caroline," said he, "it is a pity you and I never made acquaintance before. Why do you cling to me so, child? I should think that you never heard much good of me."

"No, Mamma hates you, but then I don't believe Papa does, and ever since I can remember I have heard stories about you, and Papa was your Prime-minister. . . . Did you like Papa? Say you did. I never heard anybody in my life who liked Papa except some ladies."

"Ladies liked him best," replied the Duke smiling, "he never kept his word with men."

"Didn't he?" answered Caroline doubtfully. Then looking up with recovered liveliness into Zamorna's face, she went on, "Mamma told me you were a monster and a wicked man, but you have a pretty face. How large your eyes are! They are like mine. Yes, yes, just the same colour!" And she clapped her hands with joy at this discovery.

Zamorna seated the lively little thing on his knee. Gratified with this notice, she kissed his cheek as confidingly as if she had known him for years. The brightening moonlight clearly revealed her features. That eye now bent upon them could distinctly trace, even in their imperfect symmetry and foreign wildness, a resemblance which stirred sensations in his heart he would have died rather than have yielded to, sensations he had long thought rooted out. . . . "Do you know where your father is, Caroline?" he asked.

Fitful as April in her moods, she shook her head mournfully. "No. I never saw the place, but it is an Island far in the sea, a very hot country, and Papa's house is in a solitary wood. I wish I might go there. I should so like to see Papa again. Would not you?"

Zamorna bit his lip and pressed her gently to him. "Your father and I have never agreed. We should quarrel very fiercely in a week's time."

They discussed her father's wayward temper for a few minutes.

"I don't like to be contradicted. When I am a woman, I'll do everything in my own way."

"You will make much such a woman as your half-sister Mary, I fancy. Child, I could almost imagine it was her little hand that clasped mine so."

"That's your wife? Am I like your wife? When I'm old enough I'll marry you. I will, and I often tell Mamma so just to put her in a passion. Are you ever angry with Mary?"

"Ask herself, Caroline, when you see her."

The Duke's remarks, made to himself rather than to his listener, are soon over her head.

Before her doubts could be solved, the door opened and gave admission to Caroline Vernon's mother. This singular little woman, magnificently dressed, . . . paused at the threshold. "It is dark," she said, "I dare not come in."

"Why, Madam?" asked her royal jailor as coolly as if he and she had been acquaintances of a century.

She uttered a slight exclamation at his voice, "Oh, God, I feel frightened!"

"Eh!" cried Caroline delightedly, "there's going to be a scene!"

"You feel frightened, Madam?" replied the Duke. "In that case you may go back to your chamber; I wish to place no restraint on your inclinations."

"No," said she faintly, "my courage will revive soon. Meantime my conference with your Grace must be without witnesses. Caroline, go and ask Elise to put you to bed." . . . Lady Louisa with her own hand closed the door. She then glided forward again and stood so that her whole face and person received the radiance of a full and unclouded moon.

Zamorna could not help smiling. The little Siren had dressed herself in what she knew suited her best, robes of pure white that looked spiritual in that cold and silent beam. . . . Zamorna looked, and, though acquainted with all the depth of her craft, he could not steel his heart from an impulse of pity. "Lady Vernon," said he, "come here and tell me what you want."

"Nothing," said she, approaching, however, almost close to his side. "What should Louisa want when all she cares for now is divided from her by seas of a thousand miles?" . . .

"Humph," said the Duke, . . . "so you came here merely to assure me that you were quite satisfied, stood in need of nothing."

"I didn't," said she, piqued exceedingly by his indifferent tone, "I didn't; I've been cruelly used, and I'll tell the world so."

"In what respect, Madam?"

"In every respect. That brute, that Enara in whose hands you placed me on purpose that I might be maltreated, he has made my life not worth preserving."

"Indeed?" was the concise reply.

"Yes indeed, I've had to scream out, so as to alarm the whole house, and his savage ferocity has thrown me into fits more than once. . . . It is true, I tell you," cried the lady, clenching her little hands. "Do you doubt me? Yes, you are on his side, you instigated him. I have no protector now my Alexander is taken away. O Percy, why did you leave me behind? What have I suffered since we parted!"

"You may follow him, Madam; you are at liberty this very evening. . . . Yes, positively, you shall go. I'll ring for your maid and order her to prepare." He stretched his hand to the bell.

With a start of unfeigned alarm, Lady Louisa snatched it away.

"Surely, my Lord, surely you are not serious. I'm—I can't bear so long a voyage, and the climate would not agree with me. It's scorching hot, they say." . . . She looked up at him with a wild, imploring gaze of terror. "My Lord, you won't be so cruel. You are young and handsome, and if I have been spiteful sometimes, I am only a woman, you will forgive me?"

"This prison's no such bad place then after all, Louisa, nor the jailor so very brutal?" said his Grace, playing with her arts.

"No, no. Just be kind to me, and you don't know how faithful and attached I can show myself."

"Aye, but you hate me," continued the Duke.

"Indeed I don't. I only said so. The fact is I think you are very, very handsome." Lady Vernon spoke for the moment with the fervor of truth. She felt that his Grace, as he proudly smiled at her, the moonlight half revealing his splendid features and his curls half shading them, was indeed marvellously handsome. . . . She hated him still; she would have been glad to see him stretched a corpse at her feet, but yet there was an enchanting interest in this moonlight conference. . . .

Louisa, seated by the Duke on a sofa, began indulging in romantic raptures beyond the patience of his whim.

"Fudge!" interrupted his Grace with such a supreme and abrupt accent of disdain, that she started, half alarmed and wholly piqued at his bluntness.

"What," she asked, "do you say I'm telling a lie?"

"To be sure I do, a flat lie."

"I'll scream," said her ladyship, "I will; you shan't insult me so with impunity. . . . I *must* scream," she paused and looked at Zamorna to see what effect her words would produce. He seemed to have paid no attention to them. She started to her feet and uttered a frightful cry. It was such a one as from its shrill, prolonged wildness could not but strike horror into all who heard it. Before Zamorna could stop her, another and yet another followed, louder, more urgently agonized. He was infuriated. He seized both her hands with a grasp like a vise. "By G—d, Madam," he said, "squeak again, and I will give you cause for the outcry, as sure as you are a living woman." . . . The hysterical and fiendish scream rattled in her throat, but she dared not, she swallowed it. She stood white and mute in Zamorna's gripe.

Steps now approached. The door opened suddenly, and lights and people entered. His Grace was nearly sick with mortification. "A delightful predicament," he muttered, "I wish I were shot." He dropped Louisa from his arms and turned to the intruders. There were three. . . . With a bitter curse, His Grace turned his back on them all. "The worst card I ever played in my life," he said, "never was so caught, and never was so innocent."

The intruders were Rosier, the Duke's valet, Lord Richton, and General Enara. The last, in particular, enjoyed the scene, for he had once been the victim of just such a trick from the temperamental prisoner.

Thus relieved from their presence, he [the Duke] turned, his cheek still flushed, his eyes still flashing, to Lady Vernon. . . . "Tomorrow you leave Evesham peremptorily. You shall go back, properly attended and guarded, to Fort Adrian, and there you shall stay till I return—or—die."

She protested so hysterically that she could not live in the dark, lonely fortress, that he was won to amused pity.

"So we're friends; give me a kiss." Louisa leant forward. He was sitting; she was standing by him. She put his curls from his brow and kissed him as tenderly as if she loved him. She did love him at that moment, though a quarter of an hour before she had hated him.

"You may write to Percy as often as you like," continued his Grace in a comforting tone, "and you may amuse yourself by

walking on the terrace at Fort Adrian and looking at the pictures and busts in my room. You may even rummage my cabinet if you will, and my books. There are the keys. If you've a
fancy for a sail, Ryan O'Neill will row you and Caroline out in
the barge. . . . Keep in a good temper and let politics alone,
and you'll be a clever little shrew enough. Good-night."

"Don't go yet," said Lady Vernon, "I begin to like you." But
his Grace was already gone, and in less than five minutes, she
was storming at him in as frantic a paroxysm of resentment as
had ever before irritated her ungoverned mind.

Such is the background of Caroline Vernon's childhood;
and the opening scene of the present novel, of which she
is the heroine, follows close upon Percy's receipt of an un-
pleasant reminder that his half-forgotten younger daughter
is approaching womanhood. Percy is now pictured as a
broken-down rake paying in disease and shattered nerves
for his earlier dissipations. Between him and his son-in-law
there exists the old-time mutual fascination which draws
them together, though they disagree on every subject and
quarrel bitterly as often as they meet.

The Byron-Clairmont suggestion in the story, evident at
a glance, is not wholly deliberate, for both the situation
and the characters were created independently of such a
plot. Charlotte's characters had long existed, and their existence suggested the adaptation of this additional incident
from the life of Byron, in whose image Zamorna had been
developed through almost ten years of continuous writing.
Caroline Vernon was not created as Jane Clairmont, as
earlier stories prove, but such was the similarity that when
the identification came, Charlotte had but to add a few
years to her age and touch her up a bit to make her a
realistic Clairmont, with her dark beauty, her good nature
and cleverness, and her ambitions to be at any cost a heroine of romance.

But "Caroline Vernon" is more than a clever adaptation.

The merest suggestion was all that Charlotte's genius needed or would tolerate. The story of Jane Clairmont's pursuit of Byron in its stark reality was not one that would have appealed to either the moral outward Charlotte nor the *un*-moral inner Charlotte, for it had no softening excuse such as youth, ignorance, or strong emotional temptation. Jane had never spoken to Byron until she sought him out and bluntly offered herself to him; and she was twenty-two years old when she did this. Caroline is still a child, betrayed through her natural affections by one who owed her protection even from her own folly; and to her story Charlotte adds a bit of mild suspense, though she tries to make its final outcome appear the inevitable effect of a given situation upon two given natures. Caroline did not start out to commit a sin; she merely gave way to a wilful impulse, and the sin committed itself. Cleverly enough, Charlotte, while depicting clearly her heroine's looseness of character, nevertheless contrives to win some sympathy for her.

"Caroline Vernon"

WELL, reader, you have not yet heard what business it was that brought Northangerland all that long way from Ellrington House to Hawkscliffe Hall; but you shall, if you'll suppose it to be morning, and step with the Earl out of this little parlour where the Duchess is at work, sitting by a window surrounded with roses.*

As soon as ever Zamorna had had his breakfast, he had set off, and the Earl was now following him. Fortunately, he met him on the steps at the front door, leaning against the pillar and enjoying the morning sunshine and the prospects of the wild park but half reclaimed from the forest, for one moment before starting on a day long campaign in the fields.

"Where are you going, Arthur?" asked the Earl.

"To that wood beyond the river."

"What to do there?"

"To see some young trees transplanted."

"Will there be an earthquake if you defer that important matter till I have spoken a word with you on a trivial business of my own?"

"Perhaps not. What have you to say?"

Northangerland did not immediately answer. He paused, either from a reluctance to commence or a wish to ascertain that all was quiet and safe around, and that no intruder was nigh. The Hall behind was empty; the grounds in front were still dewy and solitary; he and his son-in-law stood by themselves, there was no listener.

"Well, why don't you begin?" repeated Zamorna, who was

---

* The manuscript was apparently much longer in the original, and begins with a few pages not particularly relevant to the story, "Caroline Vernon." These pages are therefore omitted.

whistling carelessly and evincing no inclination to attach special importance to the coming communication.

When our own minds are intensely occupied with a subject, we are apt to imagine that those near us are able to pry into our thoughts. The side glance with which Northangerland viewed his son was strange, dubious, and distorted. At last he said in a remarkable tone, "I wish to know how my daughter Caroline is."

"She was very well when I saw her last," replied the Duke, not moving a muscle, yet looking straight before him at the waving and peaked hills which marked the unclouded horizon. There was another pause. Zamorna began to whistle again. It was more studiedly careless than before, for whereas it had first flowed occasionally into a pensive strain, it now only mimicked rattling and reckless airs broken into fragments.

"My daughter must be grown," continued Northangerland.

"Yes, healthy children always grow."

"Do you know anything about the progress of her studies? Is she well educated?"

"I took good care that she should be provided with good masters, and from their report, I should imagine that she has made very considerable proficiency for her age."

"Does she evince any talent? Musical talent she ought to inherit!"[1]

"I like her voice," answered Zamorna, "and she plays well enough, too, for a child."

Northangerland took out a pocket book. He seemed to calculate in silence for a moment and writing down the result with a silver pencil case, he returned the book to his pocket, quietly remarking, "Caroline is fifteen years old."

"Aye, her birthday was the first or second of this month, was it not?" returned Zamorna. "She told me her age the other day. I was surprised. I thought she had hardly been more than twelve or thirteen."

"She looks childish then, does she?"

"Why, no, she is well grown, and tall. But time in some cases cheats us; it seems only yesterday when she was quite a little girl."

"Time has cheated me," said the Earl. There was another pause. Zamorna descended the steps.

"Well, good morning," he said. "I'll leave you for the present." He was moving off, but the Earl followed him. "Where is my daughter?" asked he. "I wish to see her."

"O, by all means. We can ride over this afternoon. The house is not above three miles off."

"She must have a separate establishment instantly," pursued the Earl.

"She has," said Zamorna, "that is, in connection with her mother."

"I shall either have Selden House or Eden Hall fixed up for her," continued his Lordship without heeding this remark.

He and his son-in-law were now pacing slowly through the grounds, side by side. Zamorna fell a little into the rear; his straw hat was drawn over his eyes, and it was not easy to tell with what kind of a glance he regarded his father-in-law.

"Who is to go with her and take care of her?" he asked after a few minutes silence. "Do you mean to retire into the North or South yourself, and take up your abode at Eden Hall or Selden House?"

"Perhaps I may."

"Indeed! and will Zenobia² adopt her and allow the girl to live under the same roof without the penalty of a daily chastisement?"

"Don't know. If they can't agree, Caroline must marry. But I think you once told me she was not pretty."

"Did I? Well, tastes differ. But the girl is a mere child. She may improve. In the meanwhile to talk of marrying her is rather good. I admire the idea. If she were my daughter, sir, she should not marry these ten years. But the whole scheme sounds exceedingly raw, just like one of your fantastic expensive whims about establishments. You know nothing of management, nor of the value of money. You never did."

"She must be established, she must have her own servants and carriage and allowance," repeated the Earl.

"Fudge!" said the Duke impatiently.

"I have spoken to Steaton, and matters are in train," continued his father-in-law in a deliberate tone.

"Unbusiness-like, senseless ostentation!" was the reply. "Have you calculated the expense, sir?"

"No. I've only calculated the fitness of things."

"Pshaw!"

Both gentlemen pursued their path in silence. Northangerland's face looked severe but extremely obstinate. Zamorna could compose his features but not his eye: it was restless and glittering.

"Well," said he after the lapse of some minutes, "do as you like. Caroline is your daughter, not mine; but you go to work strangely, that is, according to my notions as to how a young, susceptible girl ought to be managed."

"I thought you said she was a mere child."

"I said, or I meant to say, I considered her as such. She may think herself almost a woman. But take your own way, give her this separate establishment, give her money and servants and equipages, and see what will be the upshot."

Northangerland spoke not. His son-in-law continued, "It would be only like you, like your unaccountable frantic folly, to surround her with French society, or Italian, if you could get it. If the circle in which you lavished your own early youth were now in existence, I verily believe you'd allow Caroline to move as a queen in its centre."

"Could my little daughter be the queen of such a circle?" asked Northangerland. "You said she had no beauty and you speak as if her talents were only ordinary."

"There," replied his son, "that question confirms what I say. Sir," he continued, stopping and looking full at Northangerland, and speaking with marked emphasis, "if your fear is that Caroline will not have sufficient beauty to attract licentiousness and imagination enough to understand approaches, to meet them and kindle at them, and a mind and passions strong enough to carry her a long way in the career of dissipation, if she once enters it, set yourself at rest, for she is or will be fit for all this and more."

"You may as well drop that assumed tone," said Northangerland squinting direfully at his comrade. "You must be aware that I know your Royal Grace and cannot for a moment be deluded into the supposition that you are a saint or even a repentant sinner."

"I am not affecting either saintship or repentance," replied the Duke, "and I'm well aware that you know me. But I happen to have taken some pains with the education of Miss Vernon. She has grown up an interesting, clever girl, and I shall be sorry to hear of her turning out not better than she should be, to find that I have been rearing and training a mistress for some blackguard Frenchman. And this or something worse would certainly be the results of your plans. I have studied her character; it is one that ought not to be exposed to dazzling temptation. She is at once careless and imaginative, her feelings are mixed with her passions. Both are warm, and she never reflects. Guidance like yours is not what such a girl ought to have. She could ask you for nothing you would not grant. Indulgence would foster all her defects. When she found that winning smiles and gentle words passed current for reason and judgment, she would speedily purchase her whole will with that cheap coin, and that will would be as wild as the wildest bird, as fantastic and perverse as if the caprice and perverseness of her whole sex were concentrated in her single little head and heart."

"Caroline has lived in a very retired way, hitherto, has she not?" asked Northangerland, not at all heeding the Duke's sermonizing.

"Not at all too retired for her age," was the reply. "A girl with lively spirits and good health needs no company until it is time for her to be married."

"But my daughter will be a little rustic," said the Earl, "a milkmaid. She will want manners when I wish to introduce her to the world."

"Introduce her to the world!" repeated Zamorna impatiently. "What confounded folly! and I know in your mind you are attaching as much importance to the idea of bringing out this half-grown school-girl, providing her with an establishment and all that sort of humbug, as if it were an important political manoeuvre on the issue of which the existence of half a nation depends."

"Oh!" replied the Earl with a kind of dry, brisk laugh. "I assure you, you quite underrate my ideas on the subject. As to your political manoeuvres, I care nothing at all about them, but if my Caroline should turn out a fine woman, handsome, and clever, she will give me pleasure. I shall once more have a motive for assembling a circle about me to see her mistress and directress of it."

An impatient "Pshaw!" was Zamorna's sole answer to this.

"I expect she will have a taste for splendour," continued the Earl, "and she must have the means to gratify it."

"Pray, what income do you intend to allow her?" asked his son.

"Ten thousand per annum to begin with."

Zamorna whistled and put his hands in his pockets. After a pause, he said, "I shall not reason with you on this subject. You're just a natural born fool, incapable of understanding reason. I'll just let you go your own way, without raising a hand either to aid or oppose you. You shall take your little girl just as she is, strip her of her frock and sash and put on a gown and jewels; take away her childish playthings and give her a carriage and establishment; place her in the midst of one of your unexceptional Ellrington House and Eden Hall coteries

and see what will be the upshot. God d—n! I can hardly be
calm about it. Well enough do I know what she is now: a
pretty, intelligent, innocent girl. And well enough can I guess
what she will be some few years hence: a beautiful, dissipated,
dissolute woman, one of your sirens, your Donna Julias, your
Signora Cecillias. Faugh! Good morning, sir. We dine at three,
and after dinner we'll take a ride over to see Miss Vernon." His
Grace jumped over a field wall, and as he whisked away very
fast, he was soon out of sight.

Punctually at three o'clock dinner was served in a large an-
tique dining room at Hawkscliffe, whose walls, rich in carved
oak and old pictures, received a warm but dim glow from the
bow window screened with amber curtains. While one footman
removed the silver covers from two dishes, another opened the
folding door to admit a tall middle-aged gentleman with a very
sweet young lady resting on his arm and another gentleman
walking after. They seated themselves, and when they were
seated, there was as much an air about the table as if it had
been surrounded by a large party instead of this select trio. The
gentlemen as it happened were both very tall. They were both,
too, dressed in black, for the young man had put off the plaid
jacket and checked trousers which it was his pleasure to sport
in in the morning, and had substituted in their stead the costume of a well dressed clergyman. As for the young lady, very
fair neck and arms well displayed by a silk dress made low, and
with short sleeves, were sufficient of themselves to throw an air
of style and elegance over the party. Beside that, her hair was
beautiful and profusely curled, and her mien and features were
exceedingly aristocratic and exclusive.

Very little talk passed during the dinner. The younger gentleman ate uncommonly well; the elderly one trifled a considerable time with a certain mess in a small silver tureen, which he

did not eat. The young lady drank wine with her husband when he asked and made no bones of some three or four glasses of champagne. The Duke of Zamorna looked as grave as a judge. There was an air about him, not of unhappiness, but as if the cares of a very large family rested on his shoulders. The Duchess was quiet. She kept glancing at her helpmate from under her eyelids.

When the cloth was taken away and the servants had left the room, she asked him if he was well. A superfluous question, one would think, to look at his delicate Grace's damask complexion and athletic form and to listen to his sounding steady voice. Had he been in a good humour, he would have answered her question by some laughing banter about her over-anxiety. As it was, he simply said he was well. She then inquired if he wished the children to come down. He said no, he would hardly have time to attend to them that afternoon. He was going out directly.

Going out! What for? There was nothing to call him out.

Yes, he had a little business to transact.

The Duchess was nettled, but she swallowed her vexation and looked calm upon it.

"Very well," said she, "Your Grace will be back to tea, I presume."

"Can't promise, indeed, Mary."

"Then I had better not expect you until I see you."

"Just so: I'll return as soon as I can."

"Very well," said she, assuming as complacent an air as she possibly could, for her tact told her this was not a time for the display of wife-like petulance and irritation. What would amuse his Grace in one mood would annoy him in another, so she sat a few minutes longer, made one or two cheerful remarks on the weather and the growth of some young trees his Grace had lately planted near the window, and then quietly left the table.

She was rewarded for this attention to the Duke's humours

by his rising to open the door for her. He picked up her handkerchief, too, which she had dropped, and returned it to her.
He favoured her with a peculiar look and smile which as good
as said he thought she was looking very handsome that afternoon. Mrs. Wellesley considered that glance sufficient compen-
sation for a momentary chagrin. Therefore, she went into her
drawing room and, sitting down to the piano, soothed away the
remains of irritation with sundry soft songs and solemn psalm
tunes which, better than gayer music, suited her own fine
melancholy voice.

She did not know where Northangerland and Zamorna were
going, nor what it was that occupied their minds, or she would
not have sung at all. Most probably could she have divined the
keen interest which each took in little Caroline Vernon she
would have sat down and cried. It is well for us that we cannot read the hearts of our nearest friends, and it is an old saying, "Where ignorance is bliss 'tis folly to be wise," and if it
makes us happy to believe that those we love unreservedly give
us in return affections measured by another, why should the
veil be withdrawn and a triumphant rival be revealed to us?

The Duchess of Zamorna knew that such a person as Miss
Vernon existed, but she had never seen her, and as to Zamorna,
the two ideas of Caroline and the Duke never entered her head
at the same time.

While Mrs. Wellesley sang to herself, "Has sorrow thy young
days shaded," and while the sound of her piano came through
closed doors with faint, sweet effect, Mr. Wellesley, Junr., and
Mr. Percy, Senior, sat staring opposite to each other like two
bulls. They didn't seem to have a word to say, not a single
word. But Mr. Wellesley manifested a disposition to have a
good deal of wine, much more than was customary with him,
and Mr. Percy seemed to be mixing and swallowing a number
of little tumblers of brandy and water.

At last Mr. Wellesley asked Mr. Percy whether he wanted to
stir his stumps that afternoon or not. Mr. Percy said he felt very

well where he was, but, however, as the thing must be done some day, he thought they had better jog. Mr. Wellesley intimated that it was not his intention to make any further objections and that, therefore, Mr. Percy should have his way, but he further insinuated that way was the direct road to Hell, and that he wished with all his heart Mr. Percy had already reached the end of his journey, only it was a pity a poor foolish little thing like Caroline Vernon should be forced to trot off with him.

"You, I suppose," said Mr. Percy dryly, "would have taken her to Heaven. Now, I have an odd sort of a crotchety notion that the girl will be safer in Hell with me than in Heaven with you, friend Arthur."

"You consider my plan of education defective, I suppose," said his Grace, with the air of a school master.

"Rather," was the reply.

"You're drinking too much brandy and water," pursued the royal mentor.

"And you have had quite enough champagne," responded his friend.

"Then we'd better both be moving," suggested the Duke, and he rose, rung the bell, and ordered horses. Neither of them were quite steady when they mounted their saddles and, unattended by servants, started from the front door at a mad gallop, as if they were chasing wild fire.

People are not always in the same mood of mind, and thus, though Northangerland and Zamorna had been on the point of quarrelling in the morning, they were wondrous friends this afternoon—quite jovial. The little disagreement between them as to the mode of conducting Miss Caroline's future education was allowed to rest, and indeed Miss Caroline herself seemed quite forgotten. Her name was never mentioned as they rode on through sombre Hawkscliffe.

Talking fast and high and sometimes laughing loud—I don't mean to say that Northangerland laughed loud, but Zamorna did very frequently—for a little while it was Ellrington and Douro resuscitated.³ Whether champagne and brandy had any hand in bringing about that change, I can't pretend to decide. However, they were only gay; their wits were all about them, but they were sparkling.

We little know what fortune the next breath of wind may blow us, what strange visitor the next moment may bring to our door. So Lady Louisa Vernon may be thinking just now, as she sits by her fireside, in this very secluded house whose casements are darkened by the boughs of large trees. It is seven o'clock, and the cloudy evening is closing in somewhat comfortless and chill, more like October than July. Her ladyship, consequently, has the vapours; in fact she has had them all day. She imagines herself very ill, though what her ailments are, she can't distinctly say, so she sits upstairs in her dressing room, with her head inclined on a pillow, and some drops and a smelling bottle close at hand. Did she but know what step was now near her door—at her threshold, she would hasten to change her dress and comb her hair, for in that untidy deshabille, with that pouting look and those dishevelled tresses, her ladyship looks haggard.

"I must go to bed, Elise, I can't bear to sit up any longer," said she to her French maid, who is sewing at a window recess near.

"But your ladyship will have your gown tried on first?" answered the girl. "It is nearly finished."

"Oh no! Nonsense! What is the use of making gowns for me? Who will see me when I wear them? My God! such barbarous usage as I receive! That man has no heart."

"Ah, Madame!" interjected Elise, "he has a heart, don't doubt it. *Attendre un peu.* Monsieur loves you *jusqu'à folie.*"

"Do you think so, Elise?"

"I do. He looks at you so fondly."

"He never looks at me at all, I look at him."

"But when your back is turned, Madame, then he measures you with his eye."

"Aye, scornfully."

"Non, avec tendresse, avec ivresse."

"Then why doesn't he speak? I'm sure I have told him often enough that I am very fond of him, that I adore him, though he is so old and proud, tyrannical and cruel."

"C'est trop modeste," replied Elise very sagely.

Apparently this remark struck her ladyship in a ludicrous point of view. She burst into a laugh, "I can't quite swallow that, either," said she. "You are almost an idiot, Elise. I dare say you think he loves you, too." . . .

"Pas comme ceux de mon preux Percy," sighed the faithful ladyship, and she continued in her own tongue, "Percy had so much soul, such a fine taste. . . . He gave me trinkets. His first present was a brooch like a heart set with diamonds. In return, he asked for a lock of his love Allen's hair. My name was Allen then, Elise. I sent him such a long streaming tress. He knew how to receive the gift like a gentleman. He had it plaited into a watch guard, and the next night I acted at the Fidena theatre. When I came onto the stage, there he was in the box just opposite, with the black braid across his breast. Ah, Elise, talk of handsome men! He was irresistible in those days. Stronger and stouter than he is now. Such a chest he showed! And he used to wear a green Newmarket coat and a white beaver. Well, anything became him. But you can't think, Elise, how all the gentlemen admired me when I was a girl—what crowds used to come to the theatre to see me act, and how many used to cheer me. But he never did. He only looked. Ah, just as if he worshipped me! And when I used to clasp my hands and raise my eyes just so, and shake back my hair in this way, which I often did in singing solemn things, he seemed as if he could hardly hold from coming on the stage and falling

at my feet. And I enjoyed that. The other actresses did envy me so! There was a woman called Morton, whom I always hated so much I could have run a spit through her, or stuck her full of needles any day. And she and I once quarrelled about him. It was in the green room; she was dressing for a character. She took one of her slippers and flung it at me. I got all my fingers into her hair, and I twisted them round and round and pulled and dragged till she was almost in fits of pain. I never heard anybody scream so. The manager tried to get me off, but he couldn't, nor could anybody else. At last he said, 'Call Mr. Percy, he's in the saloon.' Alexander came, but he had had a good deal of wine, and Price, the manager, couldn't rightly make him comprehend what he wanted him for. He was in a swearing passionate humour, and he threatened to shoot Price for attempting to humbug him, as he said. He took out his pistols and cocked them. The green room was crowded with actors and actresses and dressers. Everybody was so terrified they appealed to me to go and pacify him. I was so proud to show my influence before them all. I knew that, drunk as he was, I could turn him around my little finger, so at last I left Morton with her head almost bald, and her hair torn out by the handfuls. I went to the drover.[4] I believe he would have shot Price, if I had not stopped him. But I soon changed his mood. You can't think, Elise, what power I had over him. I told him I was frightened of his pistols and began to cry. He laughed at me first and, when I cried, he put them away. Lord George, poor man, was standing by watching. I did use to like to coquette between Vernon and Percy. Ah, what fun I had in those days! But it's all gone now—nothing but this dismal house and that garden with its high wall like a convent and those great dark trees always groaning and rustling. Whatever have I done to be punished so?" Her ladyship began to sob.

"Monseigneur will change all this," suggested Elise.

"No, no! That's worst of all," returned her ladyship. "He does not know how to change—such an impenetrable iron man, so austere and sarcastic! I can't tell how it is—I always feel glad when he comes, I always wish for the day to come round when he will visit us again, and every time I hope he will be kinder and less stately and laconic and abrupt, and yet when he does come, I'm so tormented with mortification and disappointment: it's all nonsense looking into his handsome face. His eyes won't kindle any more than if they were of glass. It's quite in vain that I go and stand by him and speak low. He won't bend to listen to me though I am so much less than him. Sometimes when he bids me good-bye I press his hand tenderly! Sometimes, I am very cold and distant. It makes no difference, he does not seem to notice the change. Sometimes I try to provoke him, for if he would only be exceedingly savage, I might fall into great terror and faint, and then, perhaps, he would pity me afterwards. But he won't be provoked. He smiles as if he were amused at my anger, and that smile of his is so—I don't know what—vexing, maddening. It makes him look so handsome, and yet it tears one's heart with passion. I could draw my nails down his face till I scratched it bare of flesh. I could give him some arsenic in a glass of wine. O, I wish something would happen that I could get a better hold of him! I wish he would fall desperately sick in this house or shoot himself by accident so it would take down his pride! If he were so weak he could do nothing for himself, then, if I did everything for him, he would be thankful. Perhaps, he would begin to take a pleasure in having me with him and I could sing his kind of songs and seem to be very gentle. He'd love me, I'm sure he would. If he didn't, and if he refused to let me wait on him, I'd come out at night to his room and choke him while he was asleep, smother him with the pillow, as Mr. Ambler used to smother me when he had the part of Othello and I that of Desdemona. I wonder if I dared do such a thing." Her ladyship paused a minute as if to meditate on the moral problem she had thus proposed for her own solution.

Ere long, she proceeded, "I should like to know how he be-
haves towards people that he does love—if indeed, he ever
loved anybody. His wife now, does he always keep her at a
distance? And they say he has a mistress or two. I've heard all
sorts of queer stories about him. It's very odd, perhaps he likes
only blonds. But no, Miss Gordon was as dark as me, and eight
years ago, what a talk there was in the North about him and
her! He was a mere school boy to be sure. I remember hearing
Vernon and O'Connor bantering Mr. Gordon about it, and
they joked him for being cut out by a beardless lad. Gordon
did not like the joke. He was an ill-tempered man, that. Elise,
you're making my gown too long; you know I always like
rather short skirts. Morton used to wear long ones, because, as
I often told her, she'd ugly, thick ankles. My ankles were a
straw-breadth less in circumference than Julia Corelli's, who
was the finest figurante at the Verdopolitan Opera. How vexed
Corelli was that night that we measured, and my ankle was
found to be slimmer than hers! Then neither she nor any of the
other dancers could put on my shoe—and it's a fact, Elise, a
colonel in the army stole a little black satin slipper of mine and
wore it a whole week in his cap as a trophy. Poor man! Percy
challenged him. They had a dreadful duel across a table. He
was shot dead. They called him Markham, Sidney Markham.
He was an Angrian."

"*Madame, c'est finie,*" said Elise, holding up the gown which
she had just completed.

"O, well, put it away. I can't try it on. I don't feel equal to
the fatigue. My head is so bad, and I have such a faintness and
such a fidgetty restlessness! What's that noise?"

A distant sound of music in a room below was heard, a piano
well touched.

"Dear, dear! There's Caroline strumming over that vile instrument again. I really cannot bear it, and so it doesn't signify. That girl quite distracts me with the racket she keeps up."

Here her ladyship rose very nimbly and, going to the top of the stairs, which was just outside her room, called out with much power of lungs, "Caroline! Caroline!"

No answer except a brilliant bravura run down the keys of the piano. "Caroline!" was reiterated. "Give up playing this instant. You know how ill I have been all day, and yet you will act in this way."

A remarkably merry jig responded to her ladyship's objurgations, and a voice was heard far off saying, "It will do you good, Mamma."

"You are very insolent," cried the fair invalid, leaning over the bannisters. "Your impertinence is beyond bearing. You will suffer for it one day, you little forward piece! Do as I bid you."

"So I will, directly," replied the voice. "I have only to play *Jim Crow!* and then—" and *Jim Crow* was played with due spirit and sprightliness.

Her ladyship cried once again with a volume of voice that filled the whole house, "Do you know I'm your mother, madame? You seem to think you are grown out of my control; you have given yourself fine impudent airs of late. It's high time your behaviour was looked to, I think. Do you hear me?"

While *Jim Crow* was yet jigging his round, while Lady Vernon, bent above the bannisters, was still shaking the little passage with her voice, the wire of the door bell vibrated. There was a loud ring and thereafter a pealing, aristocratic knock. *Jim Crow* and Lady Louise were silenced simultaneously.

Her ladyship effected a precipitate retreat to her dressing-room. It seemed also as if Miss Caroline were making herself scarce, for there was a slight rustle and run heard below, as if someone were retiring to hidden regions.

I need not say who stood outside. Of course, it was Messrs. Percy and Wellesley. In due time the door was opened to them by a man servant, and they walked straight into the drawing room.

There was no one to receive them in that apartment, but it

was evident somebody had lately been there. An open piano and a sheet of music with a grinning, capering nigger lithographed on the title page, a capital good fire, and an easy chair drawn to it, all gave direct evidence to that effect.

His Grace the Duke of Zamorna looked wearily around. Nothing alive met his eye. He drew off his gloves and, as he folded them one in the other, he walked to the hearth. Mr. Percy was already bent over a little work table near the easy chair. Pushed out of sight, under a drapery of half-finished embroidery, there was a book. Percy drew it out. It was a novel and by no means a religious one, either. While Northangerland was turning over leaves, Zamorna rang the bell. "Where is Lady Vernon?" he asked of the servant who answered it.

"Her ladyship will be down stairs directly. I have told her your Grace is here."

"And where is Miss Caroline?"

"She's in the passage;" the servant answered, half smiling and, looking behind him, "she's rather bashful, I think, because there's company with your Grace."

"Tell Miss Vernon I wish to see her, will you, Cooper?" replied the Duke.

The footman withdrew. Presently the door opened very slowly. Northangerland started and walked quickly to the window, where he stood gazing intently into the garden. Meantime, he heard Zamorna say, "How do you do?" in his deep, low voice, most thrilling when it is subdued.

Somebody answered, "Very well, thank you," in an accent indicating girlish *mauvaise honte* mixed with pleasure. There was then a pause. Northangerland turned round. It was getting dusk, but day light enough remained to show him distinctly what sort of a person it was that had entered the room and was now standing by the fireplace, looking as if she did not exactly know whether to sit down or to remain on her feet. He saw a girl of fifteen, exceedingly well grown and well made for her age, not thin or delicate, but on the contrary, very

healthy and very plump. Her face was smiling. She had fine
black eyelashes and very handsome eyes. Her hair was almost
black; it curled as nature let it though it was now long and
thick enough to be trained according to the established rules of
art.

This young lady's dress by no means accorded with her years
and stature. The short sleeved frock, worked trousers, and
streaming sash would better have suited the age of nine or ten
than that of fifteen. I have intimated that she was somewhat
bashful, and so she was, for she would neither look Zamorna
nor Northangerland in the face. The fire and the rugs were the
objects of her fixed contemplation. Yet it was evident that it
was only the bashfulness of a raw school girl unused to society.
The dimpled cheek and arched, animated eye indicated a constitutional vivacity which a very little encouragement would
soon foster into a sprightly play enough. Perhaps it was a
thing rather to be repressed than fostered.

"Won't you sit down?" said Zamorna, placing a seat near
her. She sat down. "Is your mamma very well?" he continued.

"I don't know; she's never been down today, and so I haven't
seen her."

"Indeed! You should have gone upstairs and asked her how
she did."

"I did ask Elise, and she said Madame had the megrim."

Zamorna smiled and Northangerland smiled too. "What have
you been doing, then, all day?" continued the Duke.

"Why, I've been drawing and sewing. I couldn't practise because Ma said it made her head ache."

"What is *Jim Crow* doing on the piano, then?" asked Zamorna.

Miss Vernon giggled, "I only jigged him over once," she replied, "and Ma did fly. She never liked *Jim Crow.*"

Her guardian shook his head. "And have you never walked
out this fine day?" he continued.

"I was riding on my pony most of the morning."

"Oh, you were? Then how did the French and Italian studies get on, in that case?"

"I forgot them," said Miss Caroline.

"Well," pursued the Duke, "look at this gentleman and tell me if you know him." She raised her eyes from the carpet and turned them furtively on Percy. Frolic and shyness were the mixed expression of her face as she did so. "No," was her first answer.

"Look again," said the Duke, and he stirred the fire to elicit a brighter glow over the now darkening apartment.

"I do," exclaimed Caroline, as the flames flashed over North-angerland's pallid features and marble brow. "It's Papa!" she said rising, and without agitation or violent excitement, she stepped across the rug towards him. He kissed her. The first minute she only held his hand, then she put her arms around his neck and would not leave him for a little while, though he seemed oppressed and would have gently put her away.

"You remember something of me, then," said the Earl at last, loosening her arms.

"Yes, Papa, I do."

She did not immediately sit down, but walked two or three times across the room, her colour heightened and her respiration hurried.

"Would you like to see Lady Vernon tonight?" asked Zamorna of his father-in-law.

"Not tonight. I'd prefer being excused."

But who was to prevent it? Rustle and sweep—a silk gown traversed the passage—in she came. "Percy! Percy! Percy!" was her thrice repeated exclamation. "My own Percy, take me again! Oh, you shall hear all, you shall. But I'm safe now. You'll take care of me. I've been true to you, however."

"God bless me! I shall be choked," exclaimed the Earl, as the little woman vehemently kissed and embraced him. "Never can stand this," he continued. "Louise, just be quiet, will you?"

"But you don't know what I've suffered," cried her Ladyship, "nor what I've had to contend against! He has used me so ill, and all because I couldn't forget you."

"What, the Duke, there?" asked Percy.

"Yes. Save me from him. Take me away with you. I cannot exist if I remain in his power any longer."

"Ma, what a fool you are!" interposed Caroline very angrily.

"Does he make love to you?" said the Earl.

"He persecutes me; he acts in a shameful, unmanly, brutal manner."

"You've lost your senses, Ma," said Miss Vernon.

"Percy, you love me, I'm sure you do," continued her Ladyship. "O, protect me! I'll tell you more when we've got away from this dreadful place."

"She'll tell you lies," exclaimed Caroline in burning indignation. "She's just got up a scene, Papa, to make you think she's treated cruelly, and nobody ever says a word against her."

"My own child is prejudiced and made to scorn me," sobbed the little actress. "Every source of happiness I have in the world is poisoned, and all from his revenge because—"

"Have done, Mamma," said Caroline promptly. "If you are not quiet I shall take you up stairs."

"You hear how she talks," cried her Ladyship. "My own daughter, my darling Caroline, ruined, miserably ruined!"

"Papa, Mamma's not fit to be out of her room, is she?" again interrupted Miss Vernon. "Let me take her in my arms and carry her up stairs. I can do it easily."

"I'll tell you all!" almost screamed her Ladyship, "I'll lay bare the whole vile scheme! Your father shall know you, Miss, what you are, and what he is. I never mentioned the subject before, but I've noticed, and I've laid it all up and nobody shall hinder me from proclaiming your baseness aloud."

"Good heavens! This won't do," said Caroline, blushing as red as fire. "Be silent, Mother. I hardly know what you mean, but you seem to be possessed. Not another word now. Go to bed—do. Come, I'll help you to your room."

"Don't fawn; don't coax," cried the infuriated little woman. "It's too late. I've made up my mind. Percy, your daughter is a bold impudent minx; as young as she is, she's a ——"

She could not finish the sentence. Caroline fairly capsized her mother, and took her in her arms and carried her out of the room. She was heard in the passage calling Elise and firmly ordering her to undress her lady and put her to bed. She locked the door of her bedroom and then she came down stairs with the key in her hand. She did not seem to be aware that she had done anything at all extraordinary, but she looked very much distressed and excited.

"Papa, don't believe Mamma," were her first words as she returned to the drawing room. "She talks such mad stuff when she's in a passion, and sometimes she seems as if she hated me. I can't tell why, I've never been insolent to her. I only make a face sometimes." Miss Vernon lost command over herself and burst into tears.

His Grace of Zamorna, who had been all this time a perfectly silent spectator of the whole strange scene, rose and left the room.

Miss Vernon sobbed more bitterly when he was gone.

"Come here, Caroline," said Northangerland. He placed his daughter on a seat near his side and petted her curled hair soothingly. She gave up crying very soon and said smiling she did not care a fig about it now, only Mamma was so queer and vexatious.

"Never mind her, Caroline," said the Earl. "Always come to me when she is cross. I can't do with your spirit being broken by such termagant whims. You shall leave her and come and live with me."

"I wonder what in the world Mamma would do quite by herself," said Caroline. "She would fret away to nothing. But to speak truth, Papa, I really don't mind her scolding, I'm so used to it. It does not break my spirit at all, only she set off on a new track just now. I did not suspect it, she never talked in that way before."

"What did she mean, Caroline?"

"I can't tell. I've almost forgot what she did say, now, Papa, but it put me into a regular passion."

"It was something about the Duke of Zamorna," said Northangerland quickly.

Caroline's excitement returned. "She's lost her senses," she said. "Such wild, mad trash!"

"What mad trash?" asked Percy. "I heard nothing but half-sentences which amazed me, I confess, but certainly didn't inform me."

"Nor me either," replied Miss Vernon, "only I had an idea that she was going to tell some tremendous lie. Oh, what a nature! I can't tell, Papa. I know nothing about it. Ma vexes me."

There was a little pause. Then Northangerland said, "Your mother used to be fond of you, Caroline, when you were a little child. What is the reason of this change? Do you provoke her unnecessarily?"

"I never provoke her but when she provokes me worse. She's like as if she was angry with me for growing tall; and when I want to be dressed more like a woman and to have scarfs and veils and such things, it does vex her so! Then when she's raving and calling me conceited and a huzzy, I can't help sometimes letting her hear a bit of the real truth."

"And what do you call the real truth?"

"Why, I tell her that she's jealous of me, because people will think she's old if she has such a woman as I am for a daughter."

"Who tells you you are a woman, Caroline?"

"Elise Touquet. She says I am quite old enough to have a gown and a watch and a desk and a maid to wait on me. I wish I might. I've quite grown tired of wearing frocks and sashes. And indeed, Papa, they're only fit for little girls. Enara's children came here once, and the oldest, Señora Maria, as they call her, was quite fashionable compared to me, and she's only fourteen, more than a year younger than I am. When the Duke of Zamorna gave me a pony, Mamma would hardly let me have a riding habit. She said a skirt was quite sufficient for a child. But his Grace said I should have one, and a beaver, too, and I got them. Oh, how Ma did go on! She said the Duke of Zamorna was sending me to ruin as fast as I could go, and whenever I put them on to ride out, she plays up beautifully. You shall see me wear them tomorrow, Pa, if I may ride somewhere with you. Do let me!"

Northangerland smiled. "Are you fond of Hawkscliffe?" he asked after a brief interval of silence.

"Yes, I like it well enough, only I want to travel somewhere. I should like when winter comes to go to Adrianopolis. And if I were a rich lady, I'd have parties and go to the theatre and opera every night, as Lady Castlereagh does. . . .

"I should like to be exceedingly beautiful," pursued Caroline, "and to be very tall, a great deal taller than I am, and slender— I think I am a great deal too fat—and fair. My neck is so brown. Ma says I am quite a negro. I should like to be dazzling, and to be very much admired. Who is the best looking woman in Verdopolis, Papa?"

Northangerland was considerably nonplussed. "There are so many it is difficult to say," he answered. "Your head runs very much on these things, Caroline."

"Yes, when I walk out in the woods by myself and build castles in the air, and I fancy how beautiful and rich I should like to be, and what sort of adventures I should like to happen to me, for you know, Papa, I don't want a smooth, commonplace life, but something strange and unusual."

"Do you talk in this way to the Duke of Zamorna?" asked Mr. Percy.

"In what way, Papa?"

"Do you tell him what kind of adventures you should like to

encounter and what sort of nose and eyes you should choose to have?"

"Not exactly. I sometimes say I'm sorry I'm not handsome, and that I wish a fairy would bring me a ring or a magician would appear and give me a talisman like Aladdin's lamp that I could get everything I want."

"And pray, what does his Grace say?"

"He says time and patience will do much, that plain girls with manners and sense often make passable women, and that he thinks reading Lord Byron has half turned my head."

"Do you read Lord Byron, then?"

"Yes, indeed, I do, and Lord Byron and Bonaparte and the Duke of Wellington and Lord Edward Fitzgerald are the four best men that ever lived."

"Young Lord Fitzgerald! who the D——l is he?" asked the Earl in momentary astonishment.

"A young nobleman that Moore wrote a life about," was the reply, "a regular grand Republican. He would have rebelled against a thousand tyrants, if they'd dared to trample on him. He went to America because he wouldn't be hectored over in England, and he travelled in the American forests, and at night he used to sleep on the ground like Miss Martineau!"

"Like Miss Martineau!" exclaimed the Earl, again astonished out of his propriety.

"Yes, Papa, a lady who must have been the cleverest woman that ever lived. She travelled like a man to find out the best way of governing a country. She thought a republic was best, and so do I. I wish I had been an Athenian. I would have married Alcibiades or else Alexander the Great, and I do like Alexander the Great."

"But Alexander the Great was not an Athenian, neither was he a Republican," interposed the Earl in a resigned, deliberate tone.

"No, Papa, he was a Macedonian, I know, and a King, too, but he was a right kind of king, martial, and not luxurious and indolent. He had such power over his army they never dared mutiny against him, though he made them suffer such hardships, and he was such a heroic man. Hephaestion was [not] nearly as nice as he was, though I always think he was such a tall, slender, elegant man. Alexander was little. What a pity!"

"What other favourites have you?" asked Mr. Percy.

The answer was not quite what he expected. Miss Caroline, who probably had not often an opportunity of talking so unreservedly, seemed to warm to her subject. In reply to her excellent father's question, the pent up enthusiasm of her heart came out in full tide. The reader will pardon any little inconsistencies he may observe in the young lady's declaration.

"O Papa, I like a great many people, but soldiers most of all. I do adore soldiers. I like Lord Arundel, Papa, and Lord Castlereagh and General Thornton and General Henry Fernando di Enara. I like all gallant rebels, and I like Angrians because they rebelled in a way against Verdopolitans. Mr. Warner is an insurgent, and so I like him. As to Lord Arundel, he is the finest man that can be. I saw a picture of him once on horseback. He was reining in his charger and turning round with his hand stretched out, and speaking to his regiment as he did before he charged at Leyden. He was so handsome."

"He is silly," whispered Northangerland, very faintly.

"What, Pa?"

"He is silly, my dear, a big man, but nearly idiotic, calfish, quite heavy and poor spirited. Don't mention him."

Caroline looked as blank as the wall. She was silent for a time. "Bah," said she at last, "that's disagreeable," and she curled her lip as if nauseated by the recollection of him. Arundel was clearly done for in her opinion.

"You are a soldier, aren't you, Papa?" she said erelong.

"No, not at all."

"But you are a Rebel and a Republican," continued Miss Vernon. "I know for I've read it over and over again."

"These facts I won't deny," said Northangerland.

She clasped her hands, and her eyes sparkled with delight.

"And you're a pirate and a Democrat, too," said she. "You scorn wornout constitutions and old rotten monarchies, you're a terror to those ancient, doddered kings up at Verdopolis. That crazy, ill-tempered old fellow Alexander dreads you, I know! He swears in broad Scotch whenever your name is mentioned. Do get up an insurrection, Papa, and send all those doddering constitutionalists to Jericho."

"Rather good for a young lady who has been educated under royal auspices," remarked Northangerland. "I suppose these ideas on politics have been carefully instilled into you by his Grace of Zamorna, eh, Caroline?"

"No, I've taken them all up myself, they're just my unbiassed principles."

"Good!" again said the Earl, and he could not help laughing quietly, while he added in an undertone, "I suppose it's hereditary, then. Rebellion runs in the blood."

By this time the reader will have acquired a slight idea of the state of Miss Caroline's mental development and will have perceived that it was as yet only in the chrysalis form, that in fact she was not altogether steady and consistent as her best friends might have wished. In plain terms, Mademoiselle was evidently raw, flighty, and romantic, only there was something about her, and a flashing of her eye, an earnestness, almost an impetuosity of manner, which I cannot convey in words, and which yet if seen, must have irresistibly impressed the spectator that she had something of an original and peculiar character under all her rubbish of sentiment and inconsequence. It conveyed the idea that though she told a great deal, rattled on, let out, concealed neither feeling nor opinion, neither predilection nor antipathy, it was still just possible that something might remain behind which she did not choose to tell nor even hint at.

I don't mean to say that she'd any love secret, or hate secret either, but she'd sensations somewhere that were stronger than fancy or romance. She showed it when she stepped across the rug to give her father a kiss and could not leave him for a minute. She showed it when she blushed at what her mother had said and, in desperation lest she should let out more, whisked her out of the room in a whirlwind.

All the rattle about Alexander and Alcibiades and Lord Arundel and Lord Edward Fitzgerald were, of course, humbug, and the rawest hash of ideas imaginable. Yet she could talk better sense if she liked, and often did so when she was persuading her mother to reason.

Miss Caroline had a fund of vanity about her but it was not yet excited. She really did not know that she was good-looking, but rather, on the contrary, considered herself unfortunately plain. Sometimes, indeed, she ventured to think that she had a nice foot and ankle and a very small hand, but then, alas, her form was not half slight and sylph-like enough for beauty according to her notions of beauty, which, of course, like those of all school girls, approached the farthest extreme of the thread-paper and maypole style. In fact, she was made like a model; she could not but be graceful in her movements, she was so perfect in her proportions. As to her splendid eyes, dark enough and large enough to set twenty poets raving about them, her sparkling teeth and her profuse tresses, glossy, curling, and waving—she never combed these—: as beauties, they were nothing. She had neither rosy cheeks, nor a straight Grecian nose, nor an alabaster brow, so she sorrowfully thought to herself she could never be considered a pretty girl. Besides, no one ever praised her, even hinted that she possessed a charm. Her mother was always throwing out strong insinuations to the contrary, and as to her royal guardian, he either smiled in silence when she appealed to him or uttered some brief and grave admonition to think less of physical and more of moral attractions.

It was after eleven when Caroline bade her papa good night.

His Grace the Duke did not make his appearance again that evening in the drawing-room. Miss Vernon wondered often what he was doing so long upstairs, but he did not come. The fact is, he was not upstairs, but comfortably enough seated in the dining-room, quite alone, with his hands in his pockets, a brace of candles on the table beside him unsnuffed and consequently burning rather dismally dim. It would seem that he was listening with considerable attention to the various little movements in the house, for the moment the drawing room opened, he rose, and when Caroline's "Good Night, Papa" had been softly spoken and her step had crossed the passage and tripped up the stair case, Mr. Wellesley emerged from his retreat. He went straight to the apartment Miss Vernon had just left.

"Well," said he appearing suddenly before the eyes of his father-in-law, "have you told her?"

"Not exactly," returned the Earl, "but I will tomorrow."

"You mean it still then?" continued his Grace with a look indicating thunder.

"Of course I do."

"You're a d——d noodle," was the mild reply, and therewith the door banged to and the Majesty of Angria vanished.

Tomorrow came. The young lover of rebels and regicides awoke as happy as could be. Her father, whom she had so long dreamed about, was at last come. One of her dearest wishes had been realized, and why not others in the course of time?

While Elise Touquet dressed her hair, she sat pondering over a reverie of romance, something so delicious, yet so undefined. I will not say it was love, yet neither will I affirm that love was entirely excluded therefrom. Something there was of a hero, yet a nameless and formless, a mystic being, a dread shadow that crowded upon Miss Vernon's soul, haunted her day and night when she had nothing else useful to occupy her head or her

hands. I almost think she gave him the name of Ferdinand
Alonzo Fitz Adolphus, but I don't know. The fact was, he
frequently changed, his designation being sometimes no more
than simple Charles Seymour or Edward Clifford, and at other
times soaring to the titles Harold Aurelius Rinaldo, Duke of
Montmorency di Caldacella, a very fine name, no doubt, though
whether he was to have golden or raven hair or straight or
aquiline proboscis, she had not quite decided. However, he was
to delve before him in the way of fighting to conquer the world
and build himself a city like Babylon, only it was to be a place
called the Alhambra, where Mr. Harold Aurelius was to live,
taking upon himself the title of Caliph and she, Miss Vernon,
the professor of republican principles, was to be his chief lady
and to be called the Sultana Zara Esmeralda, with at least a
hundred slaves to do her bidding. As for the garden of roses
and the halls of marble, and the diamonds and the pearls and
the rubies, it would be vanity to attempt a description of such
heavenly sights. The reader must task his imagination and try
if he can to conceive them.

In the course of that day, Miss Vernon got something better
to think of than the crudities of her own overstretched fancy.
That day was an era in her life. She was no longer to be a
child, she was to be acknowledged a woman. Farewell to captivity where she had been reared like a bird. Her father was
come to release her, and she was to be almost mistress there.
She was to have servants and wealth; and whatever delighted
her eye she was to ask for and receive. She was to enter life, to
see society, to live all the winter in a great city, Verdopolis, to
be dressed as gaily as the gayest ladies, to have jewels of her
own, to vie even with those demi-goddesses, the ladies Castlereagh and Thornton.

It was too much; she could hardly realize it. It may be supposed from her enthusiastic character that she received this
intelligence with transport, that as Northangerland unfolded
these coming glories to her view she expressed her delight and

astonishment and gratitude in terms of ecstasy, but the fact is she sat by the table with her head in her hand listening to it all with a very grave face. Pleased she was, of course, but she made no stir. It was rather too important a matter to clasp her hands about. She took it soberly. When the Earl told her she must get all in readiness to get off early tomorrow, she said, "Tomorrow, Papa?" and looked up with an excited glance.

"Yes, early in the morning."

"Does Mamma know?"

"I shall tell her."

"I hope she will not take it to heart," said Caroline. "Let us take her with us for about a week or so, Papa. It will be so dreary to leave her behind."

"She's not under my control," replied Percy.

"Well," continued Miss Vernon, "if she were not so excessively perverse and bad to manage as she is, I'm sure she might get leave to go, but she makes the Duke of Zamorna think she's out of her wits by her frantic way of going on, and he says she's not fit to let loose on society. Actually, Papa, one day when the Duke was dining with us, she started up without speaking a word, in the middle of the dinner, and flew at him with a knife. He could hardly get the knife from her, and afterward he was obliged to tell Cooper to hold her hands. And another time she brought him a glass of wine, and he had just tasted it and threw the rest at the back of the fire. He looked full at her, and Mamma began to cry and scream as if somebody was killing her. She's always contriving to get laudanum and prussic acid and such trash. She says she'll murder either him or herself and I'm afraid if she's left quite alone she'll really do some harm."

"She'll not hurt herself," replied the Earl, "and, as to Zamorna, I think he's able to mind his own affairs."

"Well," said Miss Vernon, "I must go and tell Elise to pack up," and she jumped up and danced away as if care lay lightly upon her. . . .

Miss Caroline is to leave Hawkscliffe tomorrow. She is drinking in all its beauties tonight. So you suppose, reader, but you're mistaken. If you observe her eyes, she's not gazing, she's watching. She's not contemplating the moon, she's following the motions of that person who for the last half hour has been leisurely pacing up and down that gravel walk at the bottom of the garden.

It's her guardian, and she is considering whether she shall go and join him for the last time, that is, for the last time at Hawkscliffe. She's by no means contemplating anything like [the] solemnity of an eternal separation.

This guardian of hers has a blue frock coat on, with white inexpressibles, and a stiff black stock, consequently he considerably resembles that angelic existence called a military man. You'll suppose Miss Vernon considers him handsome, because other people do. All the ladies in the world, you know, hold the Duke of Zamorna to be matchless, irresistible, but Miss Vernon doesn't think him handsome, in fact the question of his charms has never yet been mooted in her mind. The idea as to whether he is a god of perfection or a demon of defects has not crossed her intellect once. Neither has she once compared him with other men. He is himself, a kind of abstract, isolated being, quite distinct from aught beside under the sun. . . .

It seems, however, that Miss Vernon has at length conquered her timidity, for lo! as the twilight deepens, the garden and all is dim and obscure. She, with her hat on, comes stealing quietly out of the house and through the shrubs, the closed blossoms, and dewy grass, trips like a fairy to meet him. She thought she would surprise him, so she took a circuit and came behind. She touched his hand before he was aware. Cast iron, however, can't be startled, so no more was he.

"Where did you come from?" asked the guardian, gazing down from his supreme altitude upon his ward, who passed her arm through his and hung upon him according to her custom when they walked together.

"I saw you walking by yourself, and so I thought I'd come and keep you company," she replied.

"Perhaps I don't want you," said the Duke.

"Yes, you do. You're smiling, and you've put your book away as if you meant to talk to me instead of reading."

"Well, are you ready to set off tomorrow?" he asked.

"Yes, all packed."

"And the head and heart are in as complete a state of preparation as the trunk, I presume," continued his Grace.

"My heart is sore," said Caroline, "I'm sorry to go, especially this evening. I was not half so sorry in the middle of the day, while I was busy. But now—"

"You're tired and therefore low spirited. Well, you'll wake fresh in the morning and see the matter in a different light. You must mind how you behave, Caroline, when you get out into the world. I shall ask after you sometimes."

"Ask after me! You'll see me. I shall come to Victoria Square almost constantly when you're in Verdopolis."

"You will not be in Verdopolis longer than a few days."

"Where shall I be then?"

"You will be in Paris or Fidena or Breslau."

Caroline was silent.

"You will enter a new sphere," continued her guardian, "and a new circle of society, which will mostly consist of French people. Don't copy the manners of the ladies you see at Paris or Fountainbleau. They are most of them not quite what they should be. They have very poor, obtrusive manners, and will often be talking to you about love and endeavouring to make you their confidante. You should not listen to their notions on the subject, as they are all very vicious and immodest. As to men, those you see will be almost universally gross and polluted. Avoid them."

Caroline spoke not.

"In a year or two, your father will begin to talk of marrying you," continued her guardian, "and I suppose you think it will be the finest thing in the world to be married. It is not impossible that your father may propose a Frenchman for your husband. If he does, decline the honour of such a connection."

Still Miss Vernon was mute.

"Remember always," continued his Grace, "that there is one nation under heaven filthier even than the French, that is the Italian. The women of Italy should be excluded from your presence and the men should be spurned with disgust even from your thoughts."

Silence still. Caroline wondered why his Grace talked in that way. He had never been so stern and didactic before. His allusions to matrimony, etc., confounded her. It was not that the idea was altogether foreign to the young lady's mind. She had most probably studied the subject now and then in those glowing day dreams before hinted at; nor I should not undertake to say how far her speculations concerning it had extended, for she was a daring theorist. But as yet, these thoughts had all been secret and untold. Her guardian was the last person to whom she would have revealed their existence. And now it was with a sense of shame that she heard his grave counsel on the subject. What he said, too, about the French ladies and the Italian men and women made her feel very queer. She could not for the world have answered him, and yet she wished to hear more. She was soon satisfied.

"It is not at all improbable," pursued his Grace, after a brief pause, during which he and Caroline had slowly paced the long terrace walk at the bottom of the garden which skirted the stately aisle of trees; "it is not at all improbable that you may meet occasionally in society a lady of the name of Lelande and another of the name St. James,[5] and it is most likely that these ladies will show you much attention—flatter you, ask you to sing or play, invite you to their houses, introduce you to their particular circles, and offer to accompany you to public places. You must decline it all."

"Why?" asked Miss Vernon.

"Because," replied the Duke, "Madam Lelande and Lady St. James are very easy about their characters. Their ideas on the subject of morality are very loose. They would get you into their boudoirs, as the ladies of Paris call the little rooms where they sit in a morning and read gross novels and talk over their secrets with their intimate friends. You will hear of many love intrigues and of a great deal of amorous manoeuvring. You would get accustomed to imprudent conversation and perhaps, become involved in foolish adventures which would disgrace you."

Zamorna still had all the talk to himself, for Miss Vernon seemed to be too busily engaged in contemplating the white pebbles on which the moon was shining, that lay here and there on the path at her feet, to take much share in the conversation. At last she said in a rather low voice, "I never intended to make friends with any French women. I always thought that when I was a woman I would visit strictly with nice people, as Lady Thornton and Mrs. Warner and the lady who lives about two miles from here, Miss Laury. They are all very well known, are they not?"

Before the Duke answered this question, he took out a red silk handkerchief and blew his nose. He then said, "Mrs. Warner's a remarkably decent woman. Lady Thornton[6] is somewhat too gay and flashy: in other respects, I know no harm in her."

"And what is Miss Laury like?"

"She's rather tall and pale."

"But I mean what is her character? Ought I to visit with her?"

"You will be saved the trouble of deciding on that point, as she will never come in your way. She always resides in the country."

"I thought she was very fashionable," continued Miss Vernon, "for I remember when I was in Adrianopolis, I often saw pictures in the shops of her, and I thought her very nice look-ing."

The Duke was silent in his turn.

"I wonder why she lives alone," pursued Caroline, "and I wonder she has no relations. Is she rich?"

"Not very."

"Do you know her?"

"Yes."

"Does Papa?"

"No."

"Do you like her?"

"Sometimes."

"Why don't you like her always?"

"I don't always think about her."

"Do you ever go to see her?"

"Now and then."

"Does she ever give parties?"

"No."

"I believe she's rather mysterious and romantic," continued Miss Vernon.

"She's a romantic look in her eyes. I should not wonder if she had adventures."

"I dare say she has," remarked her guardian.

"I should like to have some adventures," added the young lady. "I don't want a dull, droning life."

"You may be gratified," replied the Duke. "Be in no hurry. You are young enough yet. Life is only just opening."

"But I should like something very strange and uncommon. Something that I don't at all expect."

Zamorna whistled.

"I should like to be tried, to see what I had in me," continued his ward. "O, if I were only better looking! Adventures never happen to plain people."

"No, not often."

"I am so sorry that I am not as pretty as your wife, the Duchess. If she had been like me she would never have been married to you."

"Indeed! How do you know that?"

"Because I am sure you would not have asked her. But she's so nice and fair—and I'm dark, like a mulatto, Mamma says."

"Dark, yet comely," muttered the Duke involuntarily, for he had looked down at his ward as she looked up at him, and the moonlight disclosed a clear forehead pencilled with soft, dark curls, dark and touching eyes, and a round youthful cheek, smooth in texture and a fine tint as that of some portrait hung in an Italian palace where you see the raven eyelashes and southern eyes relieving the complexion of pure colourless olive and the rosy lips smiling brighter and warmer for the absence of bloom elsewhere.

Zamorna did not tell Miss Vernon what he thought, at least not in words, but when she would have ceased to look up at him and returned to the contemplation of the scattered pebbles, he retained her face in that raised attitude by a touch of his finger under her little oval chin.

His Grace of Angria is an artist. It is probable that the sweet face, touched with soft Luna's light, struck him as a fine artistical study. No doubt it is terrible to be fixed by a tall powerful man who knits his brows and whose dark hair and whiskers and moustaches combine to shadow the eyes of a hawk and the features of a Roman statue. When such a man puts on an expression you can't understand, stops suddenly as you are walking with him alone in a dim garden, removes your hand from his arm, places his hands on your shoulders, you are justified in getting nervous and uneasy.

"I suppose I have been talking nonsense," said Miss Vernon, colouring and half frightened.

"In what way?"

"I've said something about my sister Mary that I shouldn't have said."

"How?"

"I can't tell you, but you don't like her to be spoken of, perhaps. I remember now you said once that she and I ought to
have nothing to do with each other, and you would never take
me to see her."

"Little simpleton!" remarked Zamorna.

"No," said Caroline, deprecating the scornful name with a
look, and a smile showed her transient alarm was departing,
"no, don't call me so."

"Pretty little simpleton! Will that do?" said her guardian.

"No. I'm not pretty."

Zamorna made no reply, whereat, to confess the truth, Miss
Vernon was slightly disappointed, for of late she had begun to
entertain some latent embryo idea that his Grace did not think
her quite ugly. What grounds she had for thinking so, it would
not be easy to say. It was an instinctive feeling, and one that
gave her little vain female heart too much pleasure not to be
encouraged, fostered as a secret prize. Will the reader be exceedingly shocked if I venture to conjecture that all the fore-
going lamentations about her plainness were uttered with some
half-defined interest of drawing forth a little word or two of
cheering praise?

Oh human nature! Human nature! Oh experience! In what
an obscure dim unconscious dream Miss [Vernon] was enveloped. How little did she know herself. However, time is
advancing and the hours, those "wild-eyed charioteers," as
Shelley calls them, are driving on. She will gather knowledge
by degrees. She is one of the gleaners of grapes in that vineyard where all women-kind have been plucking fruit since the
world began—in the vineyard of experience. At present,
though, she rather seems to be a kind of Ruth in a corn field,
nor does there want a Boaz to complete the picture, who also
is well disposed to scatter handfulls for the damsel's special
benefit. In other words she has a mentor who, not satisfied
with instilling into her mind the precepts of wisdom by words,

will, if not prevented by others, do his best to enforce his verbal admonitions by practical illustrations that will dissipate the mists on her vision at once and show her, and show her in light both gross and burning, the mysteries of humanity now hidden, its passions and sins and sufferings, all its passage of strange error, all its afterscenes of agonized atonement.

A skillful Preceptor is that same one, accustomed to tuition. Caroline has grown up under his care a fine and accomplished girl, unspoilt by flattery, unused to compliments, unhackneyed, untrite fashionable conventionalities, fresh, naïve and romantic, really romantic, throwing her heart and soul into her dreams, longing only for the opportunity to do what she feels she could do, and to die for somebody she loves, that is, not actually to become a subject for the undertaker, but to give up heart, soul, and sensations to one loved hero, to lose independent existence in the perfect adoption of her lover's being. This is all very fine, isn't it, reader, almost as good as the notion of Mr. Rinaldo Aurelius. Caroline has yet to discover that she is as clay in the hands of the potter, that the process of moulding is even now advancing and ere long, she will be turned in the wood a perfect, polished vessel of Grace.

Mr. Percy, Sen., had been a good while upstairs and Lady Louisa had talked him nearly dead, so at last he thought he would go down into the drawing room by way of change and ask his daughter to give him a tune on the piano.

That same drawing room was a nice little place with a clean, bright fire, no candles, and the furniture shining in a quiet glow, but, however, as there was nobody there Mr. Percy regarded the vacant sofa, the empty chair, and the mute instrument with an air of gentle discontent. He would never have thought of ringing and asking after the missing individual, but, however, as a footman happened to come with four wax candles, he did just inquire where Miss Vernon was. The footman said he really didn't know but he thought she was most likely gone to bed, as he had heard her say to Mademoiselle Touquet that she was tired of packing.

Mr. Percy stood a little while in the room. Ere long he strayed into the passage, laid his hand on a hat and wandered placidly into the garden. . . . He was just entering the terrace walk when he heard somebody speak. The voice came from the dim nook where the trees were woven into a bower and a seat was placed at their roots.

"Come, it is time for you to go in," were the words, "I must bid you good-bye."

"But won't you go in, too?" said another voice, pitched in a rather different key to that of the first speaker.

"No, I must go home."

"But you'll come again in the morning before we get off?"

"No."

"Won't you?"

"I cannot."

There was silence.

A little suppressed sound was heard like a sob.

"What's the matter, Caroline? Are you crying?"

"Oh I am so sorry to leave you. I knew when Papa told me I was to go, I should be grieved to bid you good-bye. I've been thinking about it all day. I can't help crying." The sound of her weeping filled up another pause.

"I love you so much," said the mourner, "you don't know what I think about you, or how much I've always wanted to please you, or how I've cried by myself whenever you've seemed angry with me, or what I'd give to be your little Caroline and go with you through the world. I almost wish I'd never grown a woman, for when I was a little girl you cared for me far more than you do now. You're always grave now."

"Hush and come here to me," was the reply, breathed in a deep, tender tone. "There, sit down as you did when you were a little girl. Why do you draw back?"

"I don't know, I don't want to draw back."

"But you always do, Caroline, now when I come near you, and you turn away your face from me if I kiss you, which I seldom do, because you are too old to be kissed and fondled like a child."

Another pause succeeded, during which it seemed that Miss Vernon had to struggle with some impulse of shame, for her guardian said when he resumed the conversation, "Nay, now, there is no need to distress yourself and blush so deeply, and I shall not let you leave me at present, so sit still."

"You are so stern," murmured Caroline. Her stilled sobs were heard again.

"Stern, am I? I could be less so, Caroline; if circumstances were somewhat different, I would leave you little to complain of on that score."

"What would you do?" asked Miss Vernon.

"God knows."

Caroline cried again, for unintelligible language is very alarming.

"You must go in, child," said Zamorna, "there will be a stir if you stay here much longer. Come, a last kiss."

"Oh, my lord," exclaimed Miss Vernon, and she stopped short as if she had uttered that cry to detain him and could say no more. Her grief was convulsive.

"What, Caroline?" said Zamorna, stooping his ear to her lips.

"Don't leave me so. My heart feels as if it would break."

"Why?"

"I don't know."

Long was the paroxysm of Caroline's love distress. She could not speak. She could only tremble and sob wildly, her mother's excitable temperament roused within her. Zamorna held her fast in his arms, sometimes he pressed her more closely, but for a while he was as silent as she was. "Why little darling," he said, softening his austere tone at last, "take comfort. You will

see or hear from me again soon. I rather think neither mountains nor woods nor sea form an impassable barrier between
you and me, no nor human vigilance, either. The step of separation was delayed until too late. They should have parted us
a year or two ago, if they meant the parting to be a lasting
one. Now leave me."

With one last kiss, he dismissed her from his arms. She went.
The shrubs soon hid her. The opening and closing of the front
door announced that she had gained the house.

Mr. Wellesley was left by himself on the terrace walk. He
took a cigar out of his pocket, lighted it by the aid of a lucifer
match, popped it into his mouth, and having leaned himself
up against the trunk of a large birch, looked as comfortable
and settled as possible. . . .

It will now be a natural question in the reader's mind, what
has Miss Vernon been about during the last four months. Has
she seen the world? Has she had any adventures? Is she just
the same as she was? Is there any change where she has been?
Where is she now? How does the globe stand in relation to her
and she in relation to the globe?

During the last four months, reader, Miss Vernon has been
at Paris. Her father had a crotchety, undefined notion that it
was necessary she should go there to acquire a perfect finish,
and, in fact, he was right in that notion, for Paris was the only
place to give her what he wished her to have, the tone, the
fashion.

She changed fast in the atmosphere of Paris. She saw quickly
into things that were dark to her before. She learnt life and
unlearnt much fiction. The illusions of retirement were laid
aside with a smile and she wondered at her own rawness when
she discovered the difference between the world's reality and
her own childhood's romance. She had a way of thinking to
herself and comparing what she saw with what she had imag-

ined. By dint of shrewd observation she had made discoveries concerning men and things which sometimes astounded her. She got hold of books which helped her in the pursuit of knowledge. She lost her simplicity by this means, and she grew knowing and in a sense reflective. However, she had talent enough to draw from her theories [a] safe practice, and there was something in her mind and heart or imagination which, after all, filled her with wholesome contempt for the goings on of the bright, refined world around her. People who have been brought up in retirement don't soon get hackneyed to society. They often retain a notion that they are better than those about, that they are not of their sort, and that it would be letting down to them to give the slightest glimpse of their real natures and genuine feelings to the chance associates of a ball room.

Of course, Miss Vernon did not forget that there was such a thing in the world as love. She heard a great deal of talk about that article amongst the gallant monsieurs and no less gallant madames around her. Neither did she omit to notice whether she had the power of inspiring that superlative passion.

Caroline soon learnt that she was a very attractive being and that she had that power in a very high degree. She was told that her eyes were beautiful, that her voice was sweet, that her complexion was clear and fine, that her bosom was a model. She was told all this without mystery, without reserve, and the assurance flattered her highly, and made her face burn with pleasure, and, when by degrees she ascertained that few even of the prettiest women in Paris were her equals, she began to feel a certain consciousness of power, a certain security of pleasing, more delicious and satisfactory than words can describe. . . .

Miss Vernon who was tolerably independent in her movements, because her father restrained her very little and seemed to trust with a kind of blind confidence to I know not what conservative principle in his daughter's mind—Miss Vernon, I say, often at concerts and nightly soirées met and mingled with troops of these men. She also met with a single individual who was as bad as the worst *jeunes gens*. He was not a Frenchman, however, but a countryman of her father's and a friend of his first youth. I allude to Hector Montmorency, Esqr.[7]

She had seen Mr. Montmorency first at an evening party at Sir John Denard's Hotel. . . . She noticed a man of middle age, of strong form [and] peculiar sardonic aspect standing with his arms folded, gazing hard at her. She heard him ask Sir John Denard in the French language who the de——l *cette petite jolie fille à cheveux noirs* could possibly be.

She did not hear Sir John's reply. It was whispered, but directly afterward she was aware of someone leaning over her chair back. She looked up. Mr. Montmorency's face was bending over her. "My young lady," he said, "I have been looking at you for a good while, and I wondered what on earth it could possibly be in your face that reminded me so of old times. I see how it is now, as I've learnt your name. You're Northangerland's and Louisa's child, I understand; now you're like to do them credit. I admire this, it's a bit in Augusta's[8] way. I dare say your father admires it, too. You're in a good line. Nice young men you have about you. Could you find it in your heart to leave them a minute and take my arm for a little promenade down the room?"

Mr. Montmorency offered his arm with the manner and look of a gentleman of the West. It was accepted, for, strange to say, Miss Vernon rather liked him. There was an offhand gallantry in his mien which took her fancy at once.

When the honourable Hector had got her to himself, he began to talk to her in a half free, half confidential strain. He bantered her on her numerous train of admirers, he said one or two warm words about her beauty, he tried to sound the depth of her moral principles, and, when his experienced eye and ear soon discovered that she was no French woman and no callous and hackneyed and well-skilled flirt, that his hints did

not take and his innuendoes were not understood, he changed
the conversation and began to inquire about her education,
where she had been reared and how she had got along in the
world.

Miss Vernon was as communicative as possible. She chat-
tered away with great glee about her mother and her masters,
about Angria and Hawkscliffe, but she made no reference to
her guardian. Mr. Montmorency inquired whether she was at
all acquainted with the Duke of Zamorna. She said she was a
little. Mr. Montmorency then said he supposed the Duke wrote
to her sometimes. She said no, never. Mr. Montmorency said
he wondered at that, and meantime he looked into Miss Vernon's face as narrowly as if her features had been the Lord's
Prayer written within the compass of a six pence.

There was nothing peculiar to be seen except a smooth bru-
nette complexion and dark eyes looking at the carpet. Mr.
Montmorency remarked in a careless way, "The Duke was a
sad hand at some things."

Miss Vernon asked, "In what?"

"About women," replied Montmorency, bluntly and coarsely.

After a momentary pause, she said, "Indeed!" And that was
all she did say, but she felt such a sensation of astonishment,
such an electrical, stunning surprise, that she hardly knew for
a minute where she was. It was the oddest, most novel thing
in the world for her to hear her guardian's character freely
canvassed, to hear such an opinion expressed concerning him.
What Mr. Montmorency had nonchalantly uttered was strange
to a degree. It gave a shock to her ordinary way of thinking.
It revolutionized her ideas.

She walked on through the room, but she forgot for a moment who was around her or what she was doing.

"Did you never hear that before?" asked Mr. Montmorency,
after a considerable interval, which he had spent in humming
a tune which a lady was singing to a harp.

"No."

"Did you never guess it? Has not his Grace a rakish, impudent air with him?"

"No. Quite different."

"What! He sports the Simon Pure, does he?"

"He is generally rather grave and strict."

"Did you like him?"

"No—yes—no, not much."

"That's queer. Several young ladies have liked him a great deal too well. I dare say you've seen Miss Laury now, as you live at Hawkscliffe."

"Yes."

"She is his mistress."

"Indeed?" replied Miss Vernon, after the same interregnum of appalled surprise.

"The Duchess has not a particularly easy time of it," continued Montmorency. "She's your half-sister, you know."

"Yes."

"But she knew what she had to expect before she married him, for when he was Marquis of Douro he was the most consummate blackguard in Verdopolis."

Miss Caroline in silence heard and, in spite of the dismay she felt, wished to hear more. There is a wild interest in thus suddenly seeing the light rush in on the character of one well known to our eye, but, as we discover, utterly unknown to our minds.

The young lady's feelings were not exactly painful, they were strange, new, and startling. She was getting to the bottom of an unsounded sea and lighting on rocks she had not guessed at.

Mr. Montmorency said no more in that conversation. He left Miss Vernon to muse over what he had communicated. What his exact aim was in speaking of the Duke of Zamorna, it would be difficult to say. He added no violent abuse of him, nor did he attempt to debase his character as he might easily have done. He left the subject there. Whether his words lin-

gered in the mind of his listener, I can hardly say. I believe
they did, for, though she never broached the matter to anyone
else, or again applied to him for further information, yet she
looked into magazines and into newspapers. She read every
passage and every scrap she could find that referred to Zamorna and Douro. She weighed and balanced and thought
over everything, and in a little while, though removed five
hundred miles from the individual whose character she studied,
she had learnt all that other people knew of him and saw him
in his real light, no longer as a philosopher and apostle, but
as—I need not tell my readers what; they know, or at least
can guess.

Thus did Zamorna cease to be an abstract principle in her
mind. Thus did she discover that he was a man, vicious like
other men—perhaps I should say, more than other men—with
passions that sometimes controlled him, with propensities that
were often stronger than his reason, with feelings that could
be reached by beauty, with a corruption that could be roused
by opposition. She thought of him no longer as the stoic of the
woods, the man without a fear, but as—don't let us bother
ourselves with considering what.

When Miss Vernon had been about a quarter of a year in
Paris, she seemed to grow tired of the society there. She begged
her father to let her go home, as she called it, meaning Verdopolis.

Strange to say the Earl appeared disquieted by her request;
at least, he would not listen to it. She refused to attend the
soirées or frequent the opera. She said she had had enough of
the French people. She spent evenings with her father and
played and sung to him. Northangerland grew very fond of
her, and, as she continued her entreaties to be allowed to go
home, often soliciting him with tears in her eyes, he slowly
gave way and at length yielded a hard wrung and tardy assent. . . . One evening as she kissed her father goodnight, he
said she might give what orders she pleased on the subject of

departure. A very few days after, a packet freighted with the Earl and his household was steaming across the channel.

Northangerland was puzzled and uncomfortable when he got his daughter to Verdopolis. He evidently did not like her to remain there. He never looked settled or easy. There was no present impediment to her residing at Ellrington House, but when Zenobia came home Caroline must quit. Other considerations also disturbed the calm of the Earl's soul—by him untold, by his daughter unsuspected. . . .

One evening . . . Mr. Percy said, after a long lapse of silence, "Are you not tired of Verdopolis, Caroline?"

"No," was the answer.

"I think you had better leave it," continued the Earl.

"Leave it, Papa, when the winter is just coming on?"

"Yes."

"I have not been here three weeks," said Miss Vernon.

"You will be as well in the country," replied her father.

"Parliament is going to meet, and the season is beginning," pursued she.

"Are you turned a monarchist?" asked the Earl. "Are you going to attend the debates and take an interest in the divisions?"

"No. But town will be full."

"I thought you had had enough of fashion and gaiety at Paris."

"Yes, but I want to see Verdopolis gaiety."

"Eden Cottage is ready," remarked Northangerland.

"Eden Cottage, Papa?"

"Yes, a place near Fidena."

"Do you wish to send me there, Papa?"

"Yes."

"How soon?"

"Tomorrow or the day after, if you like."

Miss Vernon's face assumed an expression which it would not be entirely correct to describe by softer epithets than dour and drumly. She said, with an emphatic, slow enunciation, "I should not like to go to Eden Cottage."

Northangerland made no remark.

"I hate the North extremely," she pursued. "I have no partiality to the Scotch."[9]

"Selden House is ready, too," said Mr. Percy.

"Selden House is more disagreeable to me still," replied his daughter.

"You had better reconcile yourself either to Eden or Rossland," suggested Mr. Percy quietly.

"I feel an invincible repugnance to both," was her reply, uttered with a self-sustained haughtiness of tone almost ludicrous from such lips.

Northangerland is long suffering. "You shall choose your own retreat," said he, "but as it is arranged that you cannot long remain in Verdopolis, it will be well to decide soon."

"I would rather remain in Ellrington House," responded Mademoiselle Vernon.

"I think I intimated that would not be convenient," answered her father.

"I would remain another month," said she.

"Caroline!" said a warning voice. Percy's light eye flickered.

"Papa, you are not kind."

No reply followed.

"Will I be banished to Fidena?" muttered the rebellious girl to herself.

Mr. Percy's visual organ began to play at cross purposes. He did not like to be withstood in this way.

"You may as well kill me as to send me to live by myself at the end of the world, where I know nobody except Denard and Old Gray Badger."

"It is optional whether you go to Fidena," returned Percy. "I said you might choose your station."

"Then I'll go and live at Pequena, in Angria. You have a home there, Papa."

"Out of the question," said the Earl.

"I'll go back to Hawkscliffe."

"O no, you can't have the choice of that. You are not wanted there."

"I'll live in Adrianopolis then, at Northangerland House."

"No."

"You said I might have my choice, Papa, and you contradict me in everything."

"Eden Cottage is the place," murmured Percy.

"Do, do let me stay in Verdopolis," exclaimed Miss Vernon, after a pause of swelling vexation. "Papa, do be kind and forgive me if I am cross." Starting up, she fell to the argument of kisses and also cried abundantly. None but Louisa Vernon or Louisa Vernon's daughter would have thought of kissing Northangerland in his present mood.

"Just tell me why you won't let me stay, Papa," she continued. "What have I done to offend you? I only ask for another month or another fortnight, just to see some of my friends when they come to Verdopolis."

"What friends, Caroline?"

"I mean some of the people I know well—only two or three, and I saw in the newspaper this morning that they were expected to arrive in town very soon."

"Who, Caroline?"

"Well, some of the Angrians—Mr. Warner and General Enara and Lord Castlereagh. I've seen them many times, you know, Papa, and it would be only civil to stop and call on them."

"Won't do, Caroline," returned the Earl.

"Why won't it?"

"I prefer your going to Fidena, the day after tomorrow at the farthest."

Caroline sat mute for a moment, and then she said, "So I am not to stay in Verdopolis and I am to go to Eden Cottage."

"Thou hast said it," was the reply.

"Very well," she rejoined quickly.

She sat looking into the fire for another minute, then she got up, lit her candle, said good-night, and walked upstairs to bed. As she was leaving the room, she accidentally hit her forehead a good knock against the side of the door. A lump rose in an instant. She said nothing, but walked on. When she got to her own room, the candle fell from its socket and was extinguished. She neither picked it up nor rang for another. She undressed in the dark and went to bed ditto.

As she lay alone with the night around her, she began to weep. Sobs were audible for a long time from her pillow, sobs, not of grief, but of baffled will and smothered passion. She could hardly abide to be thus thwarted, to be thus forced from Verdopolis when she would have given her ears to be allowed to stay.

The reader will ask why she had set her heart so fixedly on this point. I'll tell you plainly and make no mystery of it. The fact was she wanted to see her guardian. For weeks, almost months, she had felt an invincible inclination to behold him again by the new lights Montmorency had given her as to his character. There had also been much secret enjoyment in her mind from the idea of showing herself to him, improved as she knew she was by her late sojourn in Paris. She had been longing for the time of his arrival in town to come, and that very morning she had seen it announced in the newspaper that orders had been given to prepare Wellesley House for the immediate reception of his Grace, the Duke of Zamorna and suite, and that the noble Duke was expected in Verdopolis before the end of the week.

After reading this, Miss Caroline had spent a whole morning in walking in the garden behind Ellrington House, . . . picturing the particulars of her first interview with Mr. Wellesley, fancying what he would say, whether he would look as if he thought her pretty, whether he would ask her to come to see him at Wellesley House, if she should be introduced to the Duchess, how the Duchess would treat her, what she would be like, how she would be dressed, et cetera, et ceterorum.

All this was now put a stop to, cut off, crushed in the bud, and Miss Caroline was thereupon in a horrid bad temper, choked almost with obstinacy and rage and mortification. It seemed to her impossible that she could endure the disappointment. To be torn away from a scene where there was so much of pleasure and exiled into comparative dark, blank solitude was frightful. How could she live? After long musing in midnight silence, she said, "I'll find a way to alter matters," and then she turned on her pillow and went to sleep.

Two or three days elapsed. Miss Vernon, it seemed, had not succeeded in finding a way to alter matters, for, on the second day, she was obliged to leave Ellrington House, and she took her departure in tearless taciturnity, bidding no one goodbye except her father, and with him she just shook hands, offered him no kiss.

The Earl did not half like her look and manner, not that he was afraid of anything tragic, but she seemed neither fretful nor desponding. She had the air of one who had laid a plan and hoped to compass her ends. Yet she scrupled not to evince continued and haughty displeasure toward his lordship, and her anger was expressed with all her mother's temerity and acrimony, with something, too, of her mother's whimsicality, but with none of her fickleness.

She seemed quite unconscious of any absurdity in her indignation, though it produced much the same effect as if a squirrel had thought proper to treat a Newfoundland dog with lofty hauteur. Northangerland smiled when her back was turned. Still he perceived that there was character in all this, and he felt far from comfortable. However, he had written to Sir John Denard desiring him to watch her during her stay at

Eden Cottage, and he knew Sir John dared not be a careless sentinel.

The very morning after Miss Vernon's departure Zenobia, Countess of Northangerland, arrived at Ellrington House, and in the course of the day, a cortège of carriages conveyed the Duke and Duchess of Zamorna, their children and household, to the residence in Victoria Square. Mr. Percy had made the coast clear only just in time.

One day when the Duke of Zamorna was dressing to go and dine in state at Waterloo Palace with some much more respectable company than he was accustomed to associate with, his young man, M. Rosier, said, as he helped him on with his Sunday coat, "Has your Grace ever noticed that letter on the mantlepiece?"

"What letter? Now where did it come from?"

"It's one I found on your Grace's library table the day we arrived in town. That's nearly a week ago, and as it seemed to be from a lady, I brought it up here, intending to mention it to your Grace, and somehow it slipped down between the toilette and the wall, and I forgot it until this morning, when I found it again."

"You're a blockhead. Give me the letter."

It was handed to him. He turned it over and examined the superscription and seal. It was a prettily folded satin paper production, nicely addressed and sealed with the impression of a cameo. His Grace cracked the pretty classic head, unfolded the document, and read:

My Dear Duke:

  I am obliged to write to you because I have no other way of letting you know how uncomfortable everything is. I don't know whether you will expect to find me in Verdopolis, or whether you've ever thought about it, but I'm not there, or at least, I shall not be there tomorrow, for Papa has settled that I am to go to Eden Cottage, near Fidena, and live there all my life, I suppose. I call this very unreasonable, because I have no fondness for the place and do not wish ever to see it. I know none of the people there, except an old plain person called Denard, whom I exceedingly dislike. I have tried all ways to change Papa's mind, but he has refused me so often, that I think it would show want of proper spirit to beg any longer. I intend, therefore, not to submit, but to do what I cannot help doing, though I shall let Papa see that I consider him very unkind and that I shall be very, very sorry to treat him in such a way.

He was quite different in Paris and seemed as if he had too much sense to contradict people and force them to do things they have a particular objection to. Will you please be so kind as to call on Papa, and recommend him to think better of it and let me come back to Verdopolis? It would, perhaps, be as well to say that very likely I shall do something desperate if I am kept long at Eden Cottage. I know I cannot bear it, for my whole heart is in Verdopolis. I had formed so many plans which are now all broken up.

I wanted to see your Grace. I left France because I was tired of being in a country where I was sure you would not come and I disliked the thought of the sea between your Grace and myself. I did not tell Papa that this was the reason I wished to remain in Verdopolis, because I was afraid he would think me silly, as he does not know the regard I have for your Grace.

I am in a hurry to finish this letter, as I wish to send it to Wellesley House without Papa knowing, and then you will find it there when you come. Your Grace will excuse faults, because I have never been much accustomed to writing letters, though I am nearly sixteen years old. I know I have written in much too childish a way. However, I cannot help it, and if your Grace will believe me, I talk and behave much more like a woman than I did before I went to Paris and I can say what I wish to say much better in speaking than I can in a letter. This letter, for instance, is all contrary to what I had in mind. I had not meant to tell your Grace that I cared at all about you. I had intended to write in a reserved and dignified way, that you might think I was changed, which I am, I assure you, for I have by no means the same opinion of you that I once had. Now that I recollect myself, it was not from pure friendship that I wished to see you, but chiefly from the [?doubt] I had reason to respect your Grace so much as formerly. You must have a great deal to cover in your character, which is not a good sign.

> I am, my dear Duke,
> Your obedient servant,
> CAROLINE VERNON.

P.S. I hope you will be so kind as to write to me. I shall count the hours and the minutes till I get an answer. If you write directly, it will reach me the day after tomorrow. Do write. My heart aches, I am so sorry and so grieved. I had thought so much about seeing you, but perhaps you don't care much about me and have forgotten how I cried the evening before I left Hawkscliffe. Not that this signifies, or is of the least consequence. I hope I can be comfortable, whoever forgets me, and of course you have a great many calls on your thoughts, being a sort of king, which is a great pity. I hate kings. It would conduce to your glory, if you would turn Angria into a commonwealth and make yourself protector. Republican principles are very popular in France. You are not popular there. I heard you very much spoken against. I never defended you, I don't know why. I seemed as if I disliked to let people know that I was acquainted with you. Believe me,

Yours respectively, C. V.

Zamorna, having completed the perusal of this profound and original document, smiled and thought a minute, smiled again, popped the epistle into the little drawer of a cabinet which he locked, pulled down his brief black silk waistcoat, adjusted his stock, settled himself into his dress coat, ran his fingers three times through his hair, took his hat and new light lavender kid gloves, turned a minute to a mirror, backed and erected his head, took a survey of his whole longitude from top to toe, walked down stairs, entered a carriage that was waiting for him, sat back with folded arms, and was whirled away to Waterloo Palace. He dined very heartily with a select gentlemen's party, consisting of his Grace, the Duke of Wellington, the Duke of Fidena, the right honourable Earl of Richton, the right honourable Lord St. Clair, General Grenville, and Sir R. Weaver Pelham.

During the repast he was much too fully occupied in eating to have time to commit himself much by any marked indecorum of behaviour, and even when the cloth was withdrawn and the wine placed on the table, he comported himself pretty well for sometime, seeming thoughtful and quiet.

After a while he began to sip his glass of champagne and crack his walnuts with an air of easy impudence much more consistent with his usual habits. Ere long he was heard to laugh to himself at some steady constitutional conversation going on between General Grenville and Lord St. Clair. He likewise leaned back in his chair, stretched his limbs far under the table and yawned. His noble father remarked to him aside, that if he were sleepy, he knew the way upstairs to bed, and that most of his guests there present would consider his room fully an equivalent for his company.

He sat still, however, and before the party was summoned to coffee in the drawing room, he had proceeded to the indecent length of winking at Lord Richton across the table. When the move was made from the dining room, instead of following the rest upstairs, he walked down the hall; took his hat; opened the door, wishing to see if it were a fine night; having ascertained that it was, turned out into the street without carriage or servant; and walked home with his hands in his breeches pocket. . . .

He had got home in good time about eleven o'clock, as sober as a water cask, let himself in by the garden gate at the back of Wellesley House, and was ascending the private staircase, in a most sneaking manner, as if he were afraid of somebody hearing him, and wanted to slink to his own door unobserved, when, hark! a door opened in a little hall behind him.

It was her Grace the Duchess of Zamorna's dressing room door. Mr. Wellesley had in vain entered from the garden like a thief and trodden across the hall like a large tom-cat and stepped on his toes like a magnified dancing master as he ascended the softly carpeted stairs. Some persons' ears are not to be deceived, and in the quiet hour of the night when people are sitting alone, they can hear the dropping of a pin indoors or the stirring of a leaf without.

"Adrian!" said one below, and Mr. Wellesley was obliged to stop midway up the steps.

"Well, Mary?" he replied without turning round or commencing a descent.

"Where are you going?"

"Upstairs, I rather think. Don't I seem to be on that track?"

"Why did you make so little noise in coming in?"

"Do you wish me to thunder at the door like a battering ram, or come in like a troop of horse?"

"Now that's nonsense, Adrian; I suppose that the fact is you're not well, and now just come down and let me look at you."

"Heaven preserve us, there's no use resisting! Here I am." He descended and followed the Duchess from the hall to the room to which she retreated.

"Am I all here, do you think?" he continued, presenting himself before her. "Quite as large as life?"

"Yes, Adrian, but—"

"But what? I presume there's a leg or an arm wanting, or my nose is gone, or my teeth have taken out a furlough, or the hair of my head changed colour, eh? Examine well, and see that your worse half is no worse than it was."

"There's quite enough of you, such as you are," said she. "But what's the matter with you? Are you sure you've been to Waterloo Palace?"

"Where do you think I've been? Just let us hear. Keeping some assignation, I suppose. If I had, I would not have come home so soon, you may be pretty certain of that."

"Then you have been only to Waterloo Palace?"

"I rather think so, I don't remember calling anywhere else."

"And who was there? Why did you come home by yourself without the carriage? Did the rest leave when you did?"

"I've got a headache, Mary." This was a lie, told to [awake] her sympathy and elude further cross examination.

"Have you, Adrian? Where?"

"I think I said I had a headache. Of course it would not be in my great toe."

"And was that the reason you came away so soon?"

"Not exactly, I remembered I had a love letter to write." This was pretty near the truth. The Duchess, however, believed the lie, disregarded the truth. The matter was so artfully managed, that jest was given for earnest and earnest for jest.

"Does your head ache very much?" continued the Duchess.

"Deucedly."

"Rest it on this cushion."

"Had I not better go to bed, Mary?"

"Yes, and perhaps it is well to send for Sir Richard Warner. You may have taken cold."

"Oh not tonight, we'll see tomorrow morning."

"Your eyes don't look heavy, Adrian."

"But they feel so, just like bullets."

"What kind of pain is it?"

"A shocking bad one."

"Adrian, you are laughing. I saw you turn your head and smile."

His Grace smiled without turning his head. That smile confessed that his headache was a sham. The Duchess caught its meaning quickly. She caught also an expression in his face which indicated that he had changed his mood since he came in and that he was not so anxious to get away from her as he had been.

She had been standing before him and she now took his hand. Mary looked prettier than any of her rivals ever did. She had finer features and finer skin, more eloquent eyes. No hand more soft or delicate had ever closed on the Duke's than that which was detaining him now. He forgot her superiority often, and preferred charms which were dim to hers. Still she retained the power of awakening him at intervals to a new consideration of her price, and his Grace would every now and then discover with surprise that he had a treasure always in his arms that he loved better, a great deal better, than the far-sought gems he dived among rocks so often to bring up.

"Come! all's right," said his Grace sitting down, and he mentally added, "I shall have no time to write a letter tonight. It's perhaps as well let alone."

Dismissing Caroline Vernon with this thought, he allowed himself to be pleased by her elder and fairer sister Mary.

The Duchess appeared to make no great bustle or exertion

in effecting this, nor did she use the least art or [*agacerie*], as the French call it, which indeed she full well knew, with the subject she had to manage, would have instantly defeated its own end. She simply took a seat near the arm chair into which his Grace had thrown himself, inclined herself a little toward him, and in a low, agreeable voice, began to talk on miscellaneous subjects of a household and family nature. She had something to say about her children, and some advice to ask. She had also to inquire into his Grace's opinion on one or two political points, and to communicate her own notions respecting divers matters under discussion, [notions] she never thought of imparting to any living ear, except that of her honourable spouse, for in anything like gossip or chit-chat, the Duchess of Zamorna is ordinarily the most reserved person imaginable.

To all this the Duke harkened almost in silence, resting his elbow on the chair and his head on his hand, looking sometimes at the fire and sometimes at his wife. He seemed to take her talk as though it were a kind of pleasant air on a flute, and when she expressed herself with a certain pleasant, grave, naïve simplicity, which is a peculiar [characteristic] of her familiar conversation, which she seldom uses, but can command at will, he did not smile, but gave her a glance which somehow said that those little original touches were his delight. The fact was she could, if she liked, have spoken with much more depth and sense. She could have rounded her periods like a blue, if she had had a mind, and discussed topics worthy of a member of parliament, but this suited better. Art was at the bottom of the thing; after all, it answered.

His Grace set some store on her, as she sat telling him everything that came into her mind in a way that proved that he was the only person in whom she reposed this confidence, now and then, but very seldom, raising her eyes to his; and then her warm heart mastered her prudence, and a glow of extreme ardour confessed that he was so dear to her that she could not long feign indifference, or even tranquillity, while thus alone with him close at her side.

Mr. Wellesley could not help loving his Mary at such a moment, and telling her so, too, and I dare say swearing with deep oaths, that he had never loved any other half so well, nor ever seen a face that pleased his eye so much, nor heard a voice that filled his ear with such sweetness. That night she certainly recalled a wanderer. How long it will be before the wish to stray returns again is another thing. Probably circumstances will decide this question. We shall see, if we wait patiently.

Sixteen years ago, Louisa Vernon gave the name of Eden to her romantic cottage at Fidena, not, one would suppose, from any resemblance the place bears to the palmy shades of the Asiatic Paradise, but rather because she there spent her happiest days in the early society of her lover, Mr. Percy. I believe that was the scene where she moved as queen in the midst of a certain set, and enjoyed that homage and adulation whose recollections she to this day dwells on with fondness and whose absence she pines over with regret.

Caroline, as may be supposed, cherished other feelings towards the place than her mother would have done, other than she herself might very probably have entertained, had the circumstances attending her arrival there been somewhat different. Had the young lady, for instance, made it her resting place, in the course of a bridal tour, had she come to spend her honey-moon amid that amphitheatre of the Highlands toward which the cottage looked, she might have deigned to associate some high or soft sensations with the sight of those dim mountains, only the portals, as it were, to a far wilder region beyond, especially when in an evening 'they crowned their blue brows with the wandering star.' But Miss Caroline had arrived on no bridal tour. She had brought no inexpressibly heroic looking personage as her comrade *de voyage,* and also her comrade *de vie.* She came a lonely exile, a persecuted and banished being, according to her own notions, and this was her Siberia and not her Eden.

Prejudiced thus, she would not for a moment relax in her detestation of the villa and the neighbourhood. Her heaven for that season, she had decided, was to be Verdopolis. There were her hopes of pleasure, there were all the human beings on earth in whom she felt any interest. There were those she wished to live for, to dress for, to smile for.

When she put on a becoming frock here, what was the good of it? Were those great staring mountains any judges of dress? When she looked pretty, who prized her? When she came down of an evening to her sitting room, who was there to laugh with her, to be merry with her? Nothing but arm chairs and ottomans and a cottage piano. No hope here of happy arrivals, of pleasant *rencontres.* Then she thought if she were but at that moment passing through the folding doors of a saloon at Ellrington House, perhaps just opposite to her, by the marble fireplace, there would be somebody standing that she would like to see, perhaps nobody else in the room.

She had imagined such an interview. She had fancied a certain delightful excitement and surprise connected with the event. The gentleman would not know her at first, she would be so changed from what she was five months ago. She would not be dressed like a child now, nor had she the air and *tournure* of a child. She would advance with much state. He would, perhaps, move to her slightly. She would give him a glance, just to be quite certain who it was. It would, of course, be him, and no mistake, and he would have on a blue frock coat and white irreproachables and would be very much bewhiskered and becurled as he used to be. Also his nose would be in no wise diminished or impaired. It would exhibit the same aspect of a tower looking towards [Damascus] that it had always done. After a silent inspection of two or three minutes, he would begin to see daylight, and then came the recognition.

There was a curious uncertainty about this scene in Miss Caroline's imagination. She did not know exactly what his Grace would do, nor how he would look. Perhaps he would only say, "What, Miss Vernon, is it you?" and then shake hands. That, the young lady thought, would be sufficient, if there was anybody else there; but if not, if she found his Grace in the saloon alone, such a cool acknowledgment of acquaintanceship would never do. He must call her his little Caroline, and must bestow at least one kiss. Of course there was no harm in such a thing. Wasn't she his ward?

And then there came the outline of an idea of standing on the rug, talking to him, looking up sometimes to answer his questions about Paris, and being sensible how little she was near him. She hoped nobody would come into the room, for she remembered very well how much more freely her guardian used to talk to her when she took a walk with him alone than when there were other persons by. So far Caroline would get in her reverie, and then something would occur to arouse her, perhaps the tinkling fall of a cinder from the grate. To speak emphatically, it was then dickey with all her dreams. She awoke and found herself at Fidena, and knew that Verdopolis and Ellrington House were three hundred miles off, and that she might wear [out] her heart with wishes, but could neither return to them nor attain the hope of pleasures they held forth. At that crisis, Miss Vernon would sit down and cry, and when a cambric handkerchief had been thoroughly wet, she would cheer up again at the remembrance of the letter she had left at Wellesley House and commence another reverie on the effect that profound lucubration was likely to produce.

Though day after day elapsed and no answer was returned and no messenger came riding in breathless haste bearing a recall from banishment, she still refused to relinquish this last consolation. She could not believe that the Duke of Zamorna

284 Legends of Angria

would forget her so utterly as to neglect all notice of her request. But three weeks elapsed and it was scarcely possible to hope any longer. Her father had not written her, for he was displeased with her. Her guardian had not written her, for her sister's charms had succeeded in administering a soft opiate to his memory, which, for the time, lulled to sleep all recollections of any other female, freed and deadened every faithless wish to roam.

Then did Miss Caroline begin to perceive that she was despised and cast off, even as she herself hid away a dress that she was tired of or a scarf that had become frayed and faded. In deep meditation, in the watches of the night, she discerned at first by glimpses and at last clearly that she was not of that importance to the Earl of Northangerland and the Duke of Zamorna which she had vainly supposed herself to be. "I really think," she said to herself doubtfully, "that because I am not Papa's proper daughter, but only his natural daughter, and Mamma was never married to him, he does not care much about me. I suppose he is proud of Mary Henrietta because she married so highly and is considered so beautiful and elegant; and the Duke of Zamorna just considers me as a child whom he once took a little trouble with in providing her with masters and getting her to play a tune on the piano and to draw in French chalk and to speak with a great Parisian accent and to read some hard, dry, stupid, intricate Italian poetry, and now that I am off his hands he makes no more account of me than of one of those rickety little Flowers, whom he sometimes used to take on his knee a few minutes to please Lord Richton. Now this will never do. I can't bear to be considered in this light. But how do I wish him to regard me? What terms shall I like to be on with him? Really, I hardly know. Let me see. I suppose there is no harm in thinking about it at night, to one's self, when one can't sleep but is forced to lie awake in bed, looking into the dark, and listening to the clock strike hour after hour." And having thus satisfied herself with the reflection that silence could have no listener and solitude no watcher, she turned her cheek on her pillow, and shrouding her eyes even from the dim outline of a large window, which alone relieved the midnight gloom of her chamber, she would proceed [then] with her "I do not believe I like the Duke of Zamorna very much. I can't exactly tell why. He is not a good man, it seems from what Montmorency said; and he is not a particularly kind or cheerful man. When I think of it, there were scores of men at Paris who were a hundred times more merry and witty and complimentary than ever he was. Young Vaudeville and Troupeau said more civil things to me in half an hour than ever he did in all his life. But still I like him so much, even when he is behaving in his shameful way. I think of him constantly. I thought of him all the time [I] was in France. I can't help it, I wonder whether—"

She paused in her mental soliloquy, raised her head and looked forth into her chamber. All was dark and quiet. She turned again to her pillow. The question which she had thrust away returned, urging itself on her mind, "I wonder whether I love him? O, I do!" cried Caroline starting up in fitful excitement, "I do, and my heart will break! I'm very wicked," she thought, shrinking again under the clothes. "Not so very," suggested a consolatory reflection, "I only love him in this way, I should like always to be with him and always to be doing something that would please him. I wish he had no wife, not because I want to be married to him, for that is absurd, but because, if he were a bachelor, he would have fewer to think about and then there would be room for me. Mr. Montmorency seemed to talk as if my sister Mary was to be pitied. Stuff! I can't imagine that. He must have loved my sister exceedingly when they were first married, at any rate, and even now she lives with him and sees him and talks to him. I should like a taste of her unhappiness, if she would be Caroline Vernon for a month and let me be Duchess of Zamorna. If there was such a thing as magic, and if his Grace could tell how much I care for him and could know how I am lying awake just now and wishing to see him, I wonder what he would think. Perhaps he would laugh at me and say I was a fool. O why didn't he answer my letter? What makes Papa so cruel? How dark it is! I wish it was morning; the clock is striking only one. I can't go to sleep; I'm so hot and restless. I could bear now to see a spirit come to my bedside and ask me what I wanted. Wicked or not wicked, I would tell all and beg it to give me the power to make the Duke of Zamorna like me better than he ever liked anybody in the world before. And I would ask it to unmarry him and change the Duchess into Miss Percy again, and he should forget her, and she should not be so pretty as she is. And I believe—yes; in spite of fate, he should love me and be married to me. Now then, I'm going mad—but that's the truth of it!"

Such was Miss Vernon's midnight soliloquy, and such was the promising frame of mind into which she had worked herself by the time she had been a month at Fidena. Neglect did not subdue her spirit, it did not weaken her passions. It stung the first into such desperate action that she began to scorn prudence and would dare anything, reproach, disgrace, disaster, to gain what she longed for, and it worked the latter into such a torment that she could not rest day nor night. She could not eat; she could not sleep. She grew thin. She began to contemplate all sorts of strange, wild schemes—assume a disguise. She would make her way back to Verdopolis. She would go to Wellesley House and stand at the door and watch for the Duke of Zamorna to come out. She would go to him hungry, cold, and weary, and ask for something. Perhaps he would discover who she was, and then, surely, he would at least pity her. It would not be like him to turn coldly away from his little Caroline whom he had kissed so kindly when they had last parted on that melancholy night at Hawkscliffe.

Having once got the notion of this into her head, Miss Vernon was sufficiently romantic, wilful and infatuated to have attempted to put it into execution, in fact she had resolved to do so. She had gone so far as to bribe the maid by a present of her watch, a splendid trinket set with diamonds, to procure her a suit of boy's clothes from a tailor at Fidena. That watch might have been worth two hundred guineas: the value of the clothes was, at the utmost, six pounds. This was just a slight hereditary touch of lavish folly. With the attire thus dearly purchased, she had determined to array herself on a certain day, slip out of the house unobserved, walk to Fidena—four miles—take the coach there, and to make an easy transit to Verdopolis.

Such was the stage of mellow maturity at which her wise projects had arrived, when about ten o'clock one morning a servant came into her breakfast room and laid down on the table beside her coffee cup, a letter, the first one she had received since her arrival at Eden Cottage.

She took it up, looked at the seal, the direction, the postmark. The seal was only a wafer stamp, the direction a scarcely legible scrawl, the postmark, Freetown. Here was mystery. Miss Vernon was at fault. She could not divine who the letter came from. She looked at it long. She could not bear to break the seal; and while there was doubt there was hope. Certainty might crush that hope so rudely! At last she summoned courage, broke it, opened the missive, and read:

My Dear Little Caroline,

Business has called me for a few days to Wood House. Freetown is a hundred miles nearer to Fidena than Verdopolis, and the circumstance of a close proximity has reminded me of a certain letter left some weeks ago on the library table at Wellesley House. I have not that letter now at hand, for, as I recollect, I locked it up in the drawer in my dressing room, intending to answer it speedily. But the tide changed, and all remembrance of the letter was swept away as it receded. Now, however, that same fickle tide is flowing back again and bringing the lost scroll with it. No great injury has been done by this neglect on my part, because I could not fulfill the end for which your letter was written.

You wished me to act as intercessor with your father, and persuade him, if possible, to change his mind as to your place of residence, for, it seems, Eden Cottage is not to your taste. On this point I have no influence with him. Your father and I never converse about you, Caroline: it would not do at all.

It was very well to consult him now and then about your lessons and your masters when you were a little girl—we do not disagree much on those subjects—but since you have begun to think yourself a woman, your father and your guardian (he and I) have started on a different tack in our notions concerning you. You know your father's plan: you must have had sufficient experience of it at Paris and now at Fidena. You don't know much about mine, and in fact it is as yet in a very unfinished state, scarcely fully comprehended by its originator. I rather think, however, your own mind has anticipated something of its outline. There were moments now and then at Hawkscliffe when I could perceive that my ward would have been a constituent of her guardian's in case the two schemes had been put to the decision of a vote, and her late letter bears evidence that the preference has not quite faded away.

I must not omit to notice a saucy line or two concerning my character, indicating that you have either been hearing or reading some foolish nonsense on that head. Caroline, find no fault with it till experience gives you reason to do so. Foolish little girl, what have you to complain of? Not much, I think. And you wish to see your guardian again, do you? You would like another walk with him in the garden at Hawkscliffe? You wish to know if I have forgotten you? Partly. I remember something of a rather round face with a dimpled, childish little chin and something of a head very much embarrassed by its unreasonable quantity of black curls seldom arranged in anything like Christian order. But that is all. The picture grows very dim. I suppose when I see you again there will be a little change. You tell me you are grown more of a woman. Very likely. I wish you good-bye. If you are still unhappy at Eden Cottage, write and tell me so. Yours etc.

ZAMORNA.

People in a state of great excitement sometimes take sudden resolves and execute them successfully on the spur of the moment, which in their calmer and more sane moments, they would neither have the phrenzy to [contrive] nor the courage and promptitude to put in practice; as somnambulists are said in sleep to cross broken bridges and walk on the leads of houses in safety, when [if] awake, the consciousness of all the horrors round them, would occasion an instant and inevitable destruction.

Miss Vernon, having read this letter, folded it up and committed it to the bosom of her frock. She then, without standing more than half a minute to deliberate, left the room; walked quickly and quietly upstairs, took out a plain straw bonnet and a large shawl, put them on; changed her thin satin slippers for a pair of walking shoes; unlocked a small drawer in her bureau; took therefrom a few sovereigns, slipped them into a little velvet bag, drew on her gloves, walked down stairs—very lightly, very nimbly, crossed the hall, opened the front door, shut it quietly after her, passed up a plantation out to a wicket gate, entered the high road, set her face toward Fidena with an intrepid, cheerful, and unagitated air, kept the crown of the causeway, and, in about an hour, was at the door of the general coach office, asking what time a coach would start for Freetown.

The answer was that there were conveyances in that direction almost every hour of the day, and that the Verdopolis mail was just going out. She took her place, paid her fare, entered the vehicle, and before anyone at Eden Cottage was aware of her absence, was already a good stage on the road to Wood House Cliffe.

Here was something more than the devil to pay: a voluntary elopement without a companion—alone, entirely of her own free will, on the deliberation of a single moment. That letter had so crowded her brain with thoughts, with hopes, with recollections and anticipations, and so fired her heart with an unconquerable desire to reach and see the absent writer, that she could not have lived through another day of passive captivity.

There was nothing for it but flight. The bird saw its cage open, beheld a free sky, remembered its own remote isle and grove and nest, heard in spirit a voice call it to come, felt its pinion nerved with impatient energy, launched into air and was gone. Miss Vernon did not reflect, did not repent, did not hear.

Through the whole day and night her journey lasted. . . . Some would have trembled from the novelty of their situation.

Some would have quailed under the reproaches of prudence. Some would have sickened at the dread of a cold or displeased reception at their journey's end. None of these feelings daunted Caroline a whit. She had only one thought, one wish, one object—to leave Fidena, to reach Freetown. That done, Hell was escaped and Heaven attained. She could not see the blind folly of her undertaking. She had no sense of the erroneous nature of the step. Her will urged it. Her will was her predominant quality, and must be obeyed.

Mrs. Warner, a quiet, nice little woman as everybody knows, had just retired from the dinner table to her own drawing room, about six o'clock one wintry evening. It was nearly dark, very still. The first snow had begun to fall that afternoon, and the quiet walks about Wood House Cliffe, seen from the long, low windows, were all white and wildered. Mrs. Warner was without a companion. She had left her husband and her husband's prodigious guest in the dining room, seated, each with a glass before him and decanters and fruit on the table. She walked to the window, looked out a minute, saw that all was cold and cheerless, then came to the fireside, her silk dress rustling as she moved over the soft carpet, sank into a *bergère* (as the French call it) and sat alone and calm, her earrings only glittering and trembling, her even brow relieved with smooth braided hair, [in] the very best of serene good temper.

Mrs. Warner did not ring for candles: she expected her footman would bring them soon, and it was her custom to let him choose his own time for doing his work. An easier mistress never existed than she is. A tap was heard at the door.

"Come in," said the lady, turning around. She thought the candles were come. She was mistaken. Hartley, her footman, indeed appeared with his silk stockings and shoulder knots, but he bore no shining emblems of the seven churches which are in Asia.

The least thing out of the ordinary routine is a subject of gentle wonderment to Mrs. Warner, so she said, "What is the matter, Hartley?"

"Nothing, Madame, only a post chaise has just driven up to the door."

"Well, what for?"

"Some one has arrived, Madame."

"Who is it, Hartley?"

"Indeed, Madame, I don't know."

"Have you shown them into the dining room?"

"No."

"Where, then?"

"The young person is in the hall, Madame."

"Is it someone wanting Mr. Warner, do you think?"

"No, Madame; it is a young lady who asked if the Duke of Zamorna were here."

Mrs. Warner opened her eyes a trifle wider, "Indeed, Hartley, what must we do?"

"Why, I thought you had better see her first, Madame. You might recognize her. I should think from her air she is a person of rank."

"Well, but Hartley, I have no business with it. His Grace might be displeased. It may be the Duchess or some of those other ladies."

What Mrs. Warner meant by the term other ladies, I leave it to herself to explain. However, she looked vastly puzzled and put out.

"What had we best do?" she inquired, again appealing to Hartley for advice.

"I really think, Madame, I had better show her up here. You can speak to her yourself and inform his Grace of her arrival afterward."

"Well, Hartley, do as you please. I hope it's not the Duchess, that's all. If she's angry about anything, it will be very awkward. But she would not come in a post chaise, that's one comfort."

Hartley retired. . . . Steps were heard upon the staircase. Hartley threw open the panelled folding-door of the drawing room, ushered in the visitor, and closed it, first, however, depositing four thick and tall tapers of wax upon the table.

Mrs. Warner rose from her arm chair, her heart fluttering a little, and her nice face—a modest countenance—exhibiting a trivial discomposure. The first glance at the stranger almost confirmed her worst fears. She saw a figure bearing a singular resemblance to the Duchess of Zamorna in air, size, and general outline: a bonnet shaded her face and a large shawl partially concealed her shape.

"I suppose you are Mrs. Warner," said a subdued voice, and the stranger came slowly forward.

"I am," said the lady, quite reassured by the rather bashful tone in which those few words were spoken, and then, as a rather bashful silence followed, she continued in her kind way, "Can I do anything for you? Will you sit down?"

The young person took the seat which was offered her. It was opposite Mrs. Warner, and the brilliant wax lights shone full on her face. [Her feeling] of apprehension was instantly dissipated. Here was nothing of the delicate, fair, and pensive aspect characteristic of Mary Henrietta. Instead of the light shading of pale brown hair, there was a profusion of dark tresses crowded under the bonnet. Instead of that thoughtful, poetic, hazel eye, gazing rather than glancing, there was a full black orb, charged with fire, fitful, quick, and restless. For the rest, the face had little bloom, but was youthful and interesting.

"You will be surprised to see me here," said the stranger, after a pause, "but I am come to see the Duke of Zamorna." This was said quite frankly. Mrs. Warner was again relieved. She hoped that there was nothing wrong, as the young lady seemed so little embarrassed in her announcement.

"You are acquainted with his Grace, are you?" she inquired.

"O yes," was the answer. . . . "I have known him for a great many years. But you will wonder who I am, Mrs. Warner. My name is Caroline Vernon. I came by the coach to Freetown this afternoon. I was travelling all night."

"Miss Vernon!" exclaimed Mrs. Warner. "What! the Earl of Northangerland's daughter? O, I am sorry, I did not know you! You are quite welcome here. You should have sent up your name. I am afraid Hartley was cold and distant to you."

"No, not at all. Besides, that does not signify. I have got here at last. I hope the Duke of Zamorna is not gone away."

"No, he is in the dining room."

"May I go to him directly? Do let me, Mrs. Warner."

Mrs. Warner, however, perceiving that she had nothing to fear from the hauteur of the stranger and experiencing, likewise, an inclination to exert a sort of motherly kindness or sisterly protection to so young and artless a girl, thought proper to check this extreme impatience.

"No," said she, "you shall go upstairs first, and arrange your dress. You look harassed with travelling all night."

Caroline glanced at a mirror over the mantlepiece. She saw that her hair was dishevelled, her face pale, and her dress disarranged.

"You are right, Mrs. Warner. I will do as you wish me. May I have the help of your maid for five minutes?" A ready assent was given to this request. Mrs. Warner herself showed Miss Vernon to an apartment upstairs, and placed at her command every requisite for enabling her to appear in somewhat more creditable style.

She then returned to her drawing room, sat down again in her arm chair, put her little round foot upon the footstool, and with her finger upon her lip began to reflect more at leisure upon this new occurrence. Not very quick in apprehension, she now began to perceive for the first time that there was something very odd in such a very young girl as Miss Vernon coming alone unattended in a hired conveyance to a strange house to ask after the Duke of Zamorna. What could be the reason of it? Had she run away unknown to her present protector? It looked like it. But what would the Duke say when he knew?

She wished Howard would come in. She would speak to him about it. But she did not like to go into the dining room and call him out. . . .

The necessity of pursuing this puzzling train of reflections was precluded by Miss Vernon coming down. She entered the room as cheerfully and easily as if Mrs. Warner had been her old friend and she an invited guest at a house perfectly familiar.

"Am I dressed now?" were her first words, as she walked up to her hostess. Mrs. Warner could only answer in the affirmative. Indeed, there was nothing of the traveller's negligence now remaining in the gray silk dress, the smooth curled hair, the delicate silk stockings and slippers. Besides, now that the shawl and bonnet were removed, a certain trim turn of form was visible, which gave a peculiarly distinguished air to the young stranger. A neck and shoulders elegantly designed, arms round, white and taper, fine muscles, and small feet imparted something classic, picturesque, and highly patrician to her whole mien and aspect. In fact, Caroline looked extremely ladylike; and it was well she had that quality, for her stature and the proportions of her size were on too limited a scale to admit of more superb and imposing charms.

She sat down. "Now I do want to see the Duke," said she smiling at Mrs. Warner.

"He will be here presently," was the answer. "He never is very long at table after dinner."

"Don't tell him who I am when he comes in," continued Caroline. "Let us see if he will know me. I don't think he will."

"Then he does not at all expect you?" asked the hostess.

"O no! It was quite a thought of my own, coming here. I
told nobody. You must know, Mrs. Warner, Papa objected to
my staying in Verdopolis this season, because, I suppose, he
thought I had had enough gaiety in Paris where he and I
spent the autumn and part of the summer. . . . He sent me up
beyond Fidena, to Eden Cottage. You've heard of the place,
I dare say, a dismal, solitary house, at the foot of the Highlands. I have lived there about a month, and you know how
stormy and wet it has been all the time. Well, I got utterly
tired at last, for I was determined not to care anything about
the misty hills, though they looked strange enough sometimes.
Yesterday morning I thought I'd make a bold push for a
change. Directly after breakfast, I set off for Fidena, with only
my bonnet and shawl on, as if I were going to walk the
grounds. When I got there, I took a coach, and here I am."

Caroline laughed. Mrs. Warner laughed, too. The non-
chalant, off hand way in which this story had been told her
completely removed any little traces of suspicion that might
have been lurking in her usually credulous mind. . . .

As she sat on the sofa near the fire, leaning her head against
the wall so that the shade of a protecting mantlepiece almost
concealed her, she did not tell Mrs. Warner that while she was
talking so lightly to her, her ear was on the stretch to catch an
approaching footstep, her heart fluttering at every sound, her
whole mind in a state of fluttering and throbbing excitement,
longing, dreading for the door to open, eagerly anticipating
the expected event, yet fearfully shrinking from it with a con-
tradictory mixture of feelings.

The time approached, a faint sound of folding doors unclosing was heard below. The grand staircase ascending to the
drawing room was again trodden, and the sound of voices
again echoed through the lobby and hall.

"They are here," said Mrs. Warner.

"Now don't tell who I am," returned Miss Vernon, shrinking closer into her dim corner.

"I will introduce you as my niece, as Lucy Grenville," was the reply, and the young matron seemed beginning to enter into the spirit of the young maid's *espièglerie*. . . .

A half smothered laugh, excited, no doubt, by Mrs. Warner's simplicity, was heard from the obscure sofa-corner. The Duke of Zamorna, whose back had been to the mantlepiece, and whose elbow had been supported by the projecting slab thereof, quickly turned. So did Mr. Warner. Both gentlemen saw a figure seated and reclining back, the face half hid by the shade and half by a slim and snowy hand raised as if to screen the eyes from the flickering, blazing firelight. The first notion that struck his Majesty of Angria was the striking similarity of that gray silk dress, that pretty form, and tiny slender foot to something that ought to be a hundred miles off at Wellesley House. In fact, a vivid though vague recollection of his own Duchess was suggested to his mind by what he saw.

In the surprise and conviction of the moment he thought himself privileged to advance a good step nearer, and was about to stoop down to remove the screening hand and make himself certain of the unknown's identity, when the sudden and confused recoil, the half uttered interjection of alarm, with which his advances were received, compelled him to pause. At the same time Mrs. Warner said hurriedly, "My niece, Lucy Grenville."

Mr. Warner looked at his wife in astonishment. He knew she was not speaking the truth. She looked at him imploringly. The Duke of Zamorna laughed.

"I had almost made an awkward mistake," said he. "Upon my word, I took Miss Lucy Grenville for some one I had a right to come within a yard of without being reproved for impertinence. If the young lady had sat still half a minute longer, I believe I should have inflicted a kiss. Now I look better, though, I don't know, there's considerable difference, as much as between a dark dahlia and a lily."

His Grace paused, stood with his head turned fixedly

towards Miss Grenville; scrutinized her features with royal bluntness; threw a transfixing glance at Mrs. Warner; abruptly veered around, turning his back on both, in a movement of much more singularity than politeness; erelong dropped into a chair and, crossing one leg over the other, turned to Mr. Warner and asked him if he saw daylight.

Mr. Warner did not answer, for he was busily engaged in perusing a newspaper. The Duke then inclined his head toward Mrs. Warner, and leaning half across her worktable, inquired in a tone of anxious interest whether she thought this would wash.

Mrs. Warner was too much puzzled to make a reply, but the young lady laughed again fitfully and almost hysterically, as if there was some internal struggle between tears and laughter. Again she was honoured with a sharp, hasty survey from the king of Angria, to which succeeded a considerable interval of silence, broken at length by his Majesty remarking that he should like some coffee. Hartley was summoned, and his Majesty was gratified.

He took about six cups, observing when he had finished that he had much better have taken as many eight penn'orths of brandy and water, and that if he had thought of it before, he would have asked for it.

Mrs. Warner offered to ring the bell and order a case-bottle and a tumbler then, but the Duke answered that he thought, on the whole, he had better go to bed, as it was about half past eight o'clock, a healthy, primitive hour, to which he should like to stick. He took his candle, nodded to Mr. Warner, shook hands with Mrs. Warner, and without looking at the niece, said in a measured slow manner as he walked out of the room, "Good night, Miss Lucy Grenville."

How Miss Vernon passed the night which succeeded this interview, the reader may amuse himself by conjecture. I cannot tell him. . . .

The next morning she woke late, for she had not fallen asleep before the dawn began to break. When she came down, she found the Duke and Mr. Warner were gone out to take a survey of the disputed Cliffe cottages, two superannuated old hovels, fit for habitation for neither man nor beast. They had taken with them a stone mason and an architect, also a brace of guns, two brace of pointers, and a game keeper. The probability, therefore, was that they would not be back before nightfall.

When Miss Vernon heard that, her heart was so bitter she could have laid her head on her hand and fairly cried like a child. If the Duke had recognized her, and she believed he had, what contemptuous negligence or cold displeasure his conduct evinced. However, on second thought, she scorned to cry. She'd bear it all. At the worst, she could take the coach again and return to that dungeon at Fidena.

And what could Zamorna have to be displeased at? He did not know that she had wished her sister dead and herself his wife. He did not know the restless, devouring feeling she had when she thought of him. Who could guess that she loved that powerful, austere Zamorna, when, as she flattered herself, neither look, nor word, nor gesture had ever betrayed that frantic dream? Could he be aware of it when she had not fully learned it herself, till she was parted from him by mountain, valley, and wave? Impossible when he was so cold, so regardless! She would crush the feeling and never tell that it had existed. She did not want him to love her in return. No, no, that would be wicked. She only wanted him to be kind, to think well of her, to like to have her with him, nothing more, unless, indeed, the Duchess of Zamorna should happen to die, and then—but she would drop this foolery, master it entirely, pretend to be in excellent spirits; if the Duke should really find her out, effect to treat the whole transaction as a joke, a sort of eccentric adventure, undertaken for the fun of the thing.

Miss Vernon kept her resolution. She dressed her face in
smiles and spent the whole day merrily and socially with Mrs.
Warner. If hours passed slowly to her, she still, in spite of herself, kept looking at the window, listening to every movement
in the hall.

As evening and darkness drew on, she waxed restless and impatient. When it was time to dress, she arranged her hair ornaments with a care she could hardly account for herself.

Let us now suppose it to be eight o'clock, the absentees returned an hour since, and they are now in the drawing room.
But Caroline is not with them. For some cause or other she has
preferred retiring to this large library in another wing of the
house. She is sitting moping by the hearth like Cinderella. She
has rung for no candles; the large fire alone gives a red lustre
and casts quivering shadows upon the books, the ceiling, the
carpet. Caroline is so still that a little mouse mistaking her, no
doubt, for an image, is gliding unstartled over the rug and
around her feet. On a sudden, the creature takes alarm, makes
a dart, and vanishes under the brass fender. Has it heard a
noise? There is nothing stirring. Yes; something moves somewhere in this wing, which was before so perfectly still.

While Miss Vernon listened, yet doubtful whether she had
really heard or only fancied the remote sound of a step, the
door of her retreat was actually opened, and a second person
entered its precincts. The Duke of Zamorna came straying list-
lessly in, as if he had found his way there by chance.

Miss Vernon looked up, recognized the tall figure and over-
bearing build, and felt that now at last the crisis was come.
Her feelings were instantly wound to their highest pitch, but
the first word brought them down to a more ordinary tone.

"Well, Miss Grenville, good evening!"

Caroline, quivering in every nerve, rose from her seat, answered, "Good evening, my Lord Duke."

"Sit down," said he, "and allow me to take a chair near you."

She sat down. She felt very queer when Zamorna drew a chair near hers and coolly installed himself beside her.

Mr. Wellesley was attired in evening dress with something more of brilliancy than has been usual with him of late. He wore a star on his left breast and diamonds on his fingers. His complexion was coloured with exercise, and his hair curled round his forehead with a gloss and profusion highly characteristic of the most consummate coxcomb going.

"You and I," continued His Sublimity, "seem disposed to form a separate party of ourselves to-night, I think, Miss Lucy. We have levanted from the drawing room and taken up our quarters elsewhere. I hope, by the bye, my presence is no restraint. You don't feel shy and strange with me, do you?"

"I don't feel strange," answered Miss Vernon, "but rather shy, just at the first, I presume."

"Well, use and better acquaintance will wear that off. In the meantime, if you have no objection, I will stir the fire, and we shall see each other better."

His Grace stooped, took the poker, woke up the red and glowing mass, and elicited a broad blaze which flashed full on his companion's face and figure. He looked first with a smile, but gradually with a most earnest expression. He turned away and was silent. Caroline waited, anxious, trembling, with difficulty holding in the feelings which swelled her breast.

Again the Duke looked at her, and drew a little nearer.

"He is not angry," thought Miss Vernon. "When will he speak and call me Caroline?"

She looked up at him. He smiled. She approached still seeking his eyes for a welcome. Her hand was near his. He took it and pressed it a little. "Are you angry?" asked Miss Vernon in a low, sweet voice. She looked beautiful, her eyes bright and glowing, her cheek flushed, and her dark hair resting lightly upon it like a cloud.

Expectant, impatient, she still approached the silent Duke till

her face almost touched his. This passive stoicism on his part
could not last long. It must bring a reaction. It did. Before she
could catch the lightning change in face and eye, the rush of
hot blood to the cheek, she found herself in his arms. He
strained her to his heart a moment, kissed her forehead, and
instantly released her.

"I thought I would not do that," said Zamorna, rising and
walking through the room. "But where's the use of resolution?
A man's not exactly a statue."

Three turns through the apartment restored him to his self-
command. He came back to the hearth.

"Caroline! Caroline!" said he shaking his head, as he bent
over her. "How is this? What am I to say about it?"

"You really know me, do you?" answered Miss Vernon,
evading her guardian's words.

"I think I do," said he, "but what brought you from Fidena?
Have you run away?"

"Yes," was the reply.

"And where are you running to?"

"Nowhere," said Caroline. "I have got as far as I wished to
go. Didn't you tell me in your letter that if I was still unhappy
at Eden Cottage, I was to write and tell you so? I thought I
had better come."

"But I am not going to stay at Wood House Cliffe, Caroline.
I must leave tomorrow."

"And will you leave me behind you?"

"God bless me!" ejaculated Mr. Wellesley, raising himself
from his stooping attitude and starting back as if a wasp had
stung his lip. He stood a yard off, looking at Miss Vernon, with
his whole face fixed by the same expression that had flashed
over it before. "Where must I take you, Caroline?" he asked.

"Anywhere."

"But I am to return to Verdopolis, to Wellesley House. It
would not do to take you there: you would hardly meet with
a welcome."

"The Duchess would not be glad to see me, I suppose," said Miss Vernon.

"No, she would not," answered the Duke, with a kind of brief laugh.

"And why should she not?" inquired the young lady. "I am her sister. Papa is as much my father as he is hers. But I believe she would be jealous of anybody liking your Grace besides herself."

"Aye, and of my Grace liking anybody, too, and Caroline—"

This was a hint which Miss Vernon could not [fail to] understand. These words and the pointed emphasis with which they were uttered broke down the guard of her simplicity and discomfited her self-possession. They told her that Zamorna had ceased to regard her as a child. They intimated that he looked upon her with different eyes to what he had done, and considered her attachment to him as liable to another interpretation than the mere fondness of a ward for her guardian. Her secret seemed to be discovered. She was struck with an agony of shame. Her face burned, her eyes fell, she dared look at Zamorna no more.

And now the genuine character of Arthur Augustus Adrian Wellesley began to work. In this crisis Lord Douro stood true to his old name and nature. Zamorna did not deny by one noble and moral act the character he had earned by a hundred infamous ones. Hitherto, we have seen him rather as restraining his passions than yielding to them. He has stood before us rather as a mentor than a misleader. But he was going to lay down the last garment of light and be himself entirely.

In Miss Vernon's present mood, burning and trembling with confusion, remorse, apprehension, he might by a single word have persuaded her to go back to Eden Cottage. She did not know that he reciprocated her wild frantic attachment. He might have buried that secret, have treated her with an austere gentleness he well knew how to assume, and crushed in time the poison flower of passion, whose fruit, if it reached maturity, would be crime and anguish.

Such a line of conduct might be trodden by the noble and faithful Fidena. It lies in his ordinary path of life. He seldom sacrifices another human being's life and home on the altar of his own vices. But the selfish Zamorna cannot emulate such a deed. He has too little of the moral Great-Heart in his nature. It is his creed that all things bright and fair live for him; by him, they are to be gathered and worn as the flowers of his laurel crown. The green leaves are victory in battle, they never fade. The roses are conquests in love; they decay and drop off. Fresh ones blow round him, are plucked and woven with the withered stems of their predecessors. Such a wreath he deems a glory about his temples. He may, in the end, find it rather like the sticky fillet which pressed Calacha's brows, steeped in blue venom.

The Duke reseated himself at Miss Vernon's side. "Caroline," said he, desiring by that word to attract her attention, which was wandering wide in the paroxysm of shame that overwhelmed her. He knew how to give a tone and accent to that single sound which should produce ample effect. It expressed a kind of pity. There was something protecting and sheltering about it, as if he were calling her home. She turned. The acute pang which tortured her heart and tightened her breath dissolved into sorrow. A gush of tears relieved her.

"Now then," said Zamorna, when he had allowed her to weep awhile in silence, "the shower is over, smile at me again, my little dove. What was the reason of that distress? Do you think I don't care for you, Caroline?"

"You despise me. You know I am a fool."

"Do I?" said he quietly, then after a pause, went on, "I like to look at your dark eyes and pretty face. Yes," he said, "it is exquisitely pretty, and those soft features and dusky curls are beyond the imitation of a pencil. You blush because I praise you. Did you never guess before that I took a pleasure in watching you, in holding your little hand, and in playing with your simplicity which has sported many a time, Caroline, on the brink of an abyss you never thought of?"

Miss Vernon was speechless. She darkly saw, or rather felt, the end to which all this tended, but all was fever and delirium round her.

The Duke spoke again in a single blunt and almost coarse sentence, compressing what remained to be said, "If I were a bearded Turk, Caroline, I would take you to my harem." His deep voice as he uttered this, his high featured face, and dark, large eye burning bright with a spark from the depths of Gehenna, struck Caroline Vernon with a thrill of nameless dread. Here he was, the man Montmorency had described to her. All at once she knew him. Her guardian was gone, something terrible sat in his place.

The fire in the grate was sunk down without a blaze. The silent, lonely library, so far away from the inhabited part of the house, was gathering a deeper shade in all its gothic recesses. She grew faint with dread. She dared not stir from a vague fear of being arrested by the powerful arm flung over the back of her chair. At last through the long and profound silence a low whisper stole from her lips, "May I go away?"

No answer. She attempted to rise. This movement produced the effect she had feared; the arm closed round her. Miss Vernon could not resist its strength. A piteous upward look was her only appeal. He, Satan's eldest son, smiled at the mute prayer.

"She trembles with terror," said he, speaking to himself. "Her face has turned as pale as marble within the last minute or two. How did I alarm her? Caroline, do you know me? You look as if your mind wandered."

"You are Zamorna," replied Caroline, "but let me go."

"Not for a diadem, not for a Krooman's head, not for every inch of Joliba waters."

"Oh, what must I do?" exclaimed Miss Vernon.

"*Crede Zamorna!*"[10] was the answer. "Trust me, Caroline, you shall never want a refuge. I said I could not take you to Wellesley House, but I can take you elsewhere. I have a little retreat, my fairy, somewhere near the heart of my own kingdom, Angria, sheltered by Ingleside and hidden in a wood. It is a plain old house outside, but it has rooms within as splendid as any saloon in Victoria Square. You shall live there. Nobody will ever reach it to disturb you. It lies on the verge of moors, there are only a few scattered cottages and a little church for many miles round. It is not known to be my property. I call it my treasure house, and what I deposit there has always hitherto been safe—at least," he added in a lower tone, "from human vigilance and living force. There are some things that even I cannot defy. I thought so that summer afternoon when I came to Scar House; I found a King and Conqueror had been before me. To him I was no rival, but a trampled slave."[11]

The gloom of Zamorna's look as he uttered these words told a tale of what was passing in his heart. What vision had risen before him which suggested such a sentence at such a moment, it matters little to know. However dark it might have been, it did not linger long. He smiled as Caroline looked at him with mixed wonder and fear. His face changed to an expression of tenderness more dangerous than the fiery excitement which had startled her before. He caressed her fondly, and lifted with his fingers the heavy curls which were lying on her neck.

Caroline began to feel a new impression. She no longer wished to leave him; she clung to his side; infatuation was stealing over her. The thought of separation and a return to Eden was dreadful. The man beside her was her guardian again, but he was also Montmorency's Duke of Zamorna. She feared, she loved. Passion tempted, conscience warned her. But in a mind like Miss Vernon's, conscience was feeble. Opposed to passion its whispers grew faint and were at last silenced, and when Zamorna kissed her and said in a voice of fatal sweetness which has instilled venom into many a heart, "Will you go with me tomorrow, Caroline?" she looked up in his face with a kind of wild devoted enthusiasm and answered, "Yes."

The Duke of Zamorna left Wood House Cliffe on Friday, the next morning, and was precisely seven days in performing the distance between that place and Verdopolis. At least, seven days had elapsed between his departure from Warner's and his arrival at Wellesley House. It was a cold day when he came, and that might possibly be the reason he looked pale and stern as he got out of his carriage, mounted the kingly steps of his mansion, and entered under its roof.

He was necessitated to meet his wife after so long a separation; and it was a sight to see their interview. He took little pains to look at her kindly. His manner was sour and impatient, and the Duchess, after the first look, solicited no further embrace. She receded even from the frozen kiss he offered her, dropped his hand, and, after searching his face and reading the meaning of that pallid, harassed aspect, told him, not by words but by a bitter smile, that he did not deceive her, turned away with a quivering lip, with all the indignation, the burning pride, the heartstruck anguish stamped on her face that those beautiful features could express. She left him and went to her room, which she did not leave for many a day afterwards.

The Duke of Zamorna seemed to have returned in a business mood. He had a smile for no one. When Lord Richton called to pay his respects, the Duke glanced at the card which he sent up, threw it on the table, and growled like a tiger, "Not at home."

He received only his ministers. He discussed only matters of state. When their business was done he dismissed them. No hour of relaxation followed the hour of labour. He was as scowling at the end of the council as he was at the beginning. Enara was with him one night and in his blunt way had just been telling him a piece of his mind and intimating that he was sure all that blackening and sulking was not for nothing, and that he had as certainly been in some hideous mess as he now wore a head. The answer to this was a recommendation to Enara to go to Hell. Henri was tasting a glass of spirits and water, preparatory to making a reply, when a third person walked into the apartment and advancing up to him said, "I'll thank you to leave the room, sir."

The Colonel of the Bloodhounds looked up, fierce at this address, but having discovered from whom it proceeded, he merely replied, "Very well, my lord, but, with your leave, I'll empty this tumbler of brandy and water first. Here's to the King's health and better temper!"

He drained the glass, set it down, and marched away.

The new comer, judging from his look, seemed likely to give the Duke of Zamorna his match in the matter of temper. One remarkable thing about his appearance was, that though in the presence of a crowned king, he wore a hat upon his head which he never lifted a hand to remove. The face under the hat was like a sheet, it was so white; and like a hanged malefactor's, it was so livid. He could not be said to frown, as his features were quiet, but his eyes were petrifying. It had that in its light iris which passed show.

This gentleman took his station, facing the Duke of Zamorna; and when Lord Enara had left the room, he said in a voice such as people use when they are coming instantly to the point and will not soften their demand a jot, "Tell me what you have done with her!"

The Duke's conscience, a vessel of a thousand tons burthen, brought up a cargo of blood to his face. His nostrils opened, his head was as high and his chest as full and his attitude, standing by the table, as bold, as if from the ramparts of Gazemba he was watching Arundel's horsemen scouring the wilderness.

"What do you mean?" he asked.

"Where is Caroline Vernon?" asked the same voice of fury.

"I have not got her."

"And you have never had her, I suppose. And will you dare tell me that lie?"

"I have never had her."

"She is not in your hands now?"

"She is not."

"By G—d, I know differently, sir, I know you lie."

"You know nothing about it."

"Give her up, Zamorna."

"I cannot give up what I have not got."

"Say that again."

"I do."

"Repeat it."

"I will."

"Take that, miscreant."

Lord Northangerland snatched something from his breast. It was a pistol. He did not draw the trigger, but he dashed the butt end viciously at his son-in-law's mouth. In an instant his lips were crimson with gore. If his teeth had not been fastened into their sockets like soldered iron, he would have been forced to spit them out with the blood with which his mouth filled and ran over.

He said nothing at all to this compliment, but only leaned his head over the fire and spat into the ashes and then wiped his mouth with a white handkerchief, which in five minutes was one red stain. I suppose this moderation resulted from the deep conviction that the punishment he got was only a millionth part of what he deserved.

"Where is she?" resumed the excited Percy.

"I'll never tell you."

"Will you keep her from me?"

"I'll do my best."

"Will you dare to visit her?"

"As often as I can snatch a moment from the world to give to her."

"You say that to my face?"

"I'll say it to the D——l's face."

A little pause intervened in which Northangerland surveyed the Duke, and the Duke went on wiping his bloody mouth.

"I came here to know where you have taken that girl," resumed Percy. "I mean to be satisfied, I mean to have her back. You shall not keep her. The last thing I had in the world is not to be yielded to you, you brutal, insatiable villain."

"Am I worse than you, Percy?"

"Do you taunt me? Are you worse? I never was a callous brute."

"And who says I am a brute? Does Caroline? Does Mary?"

"How dare you join those names together? How dare you utter them in the same breath, as if both my daughters were your purchased slaves? You coarse voluptuary, filthier than that filthy Jordan."

"I am glad that it is you who give me this character, and not Miss Vernon or her sister."

"Arthur Wellesley, you had better not unite those two names again. If you do, neither of them shall ever see you more, except dead."

"Will you shoot me?"

"I will."

Another pause followed, which Percy again broke.

"In what part of Angria have you put Caroline Vernon? for I know you took her to Angria."

"I placed her where she is safe and happy. I should say no more if my hands were thrust into that fire, and you had better leave the matter where it is, for you cannot undo what is done."

Northangerland's wild blue eyes dilated into wilder hatred

and fury. He said, raising his hand and striking the table, "I wish there was a hell for your sake.[12] I wish—" The sentence broke off and was resumed, as if his agitation shortened his breath. "I wish you might now be withered, hand and foot, and struck into a paralytic heap—" Again it broke. "What are you? You have pressed this hand and said you cared for me. You have listened to all I had to tell you, what I am, how I have lived, and what I have suffered. You have assumed enthusiasm, blushed about like a woman, and wearied me out with your boyish ardour. I have let you have Mary, and you know what a curse you have been to her, disquieting her life with your constant treacheries and your alternations of frost and fire. I have let you go on with little interference, though I have wished you dead many a time, when I have seen her pale, harassed look, knowing how different she was before she knew you and was subjected to all your monstrous tyrannies and tantalizations, your desertions that broke her spirit, and new returns that kept her lingering on with just a shadow of hope to look to."

"Gross exaggeration!" exclaimed Zamorna with vehemence. "When did I ever tyrannize over Mary? Ask herself, ask her at this moment, when she is as much exasperated against me as she ever was in her life. Tell her to leave me. She will not speak to me or look at me, but see what her answer would be to that."

"Will you be silent and hear me out?" returned Percy. "I have not finished the details of your friendship. That Hebrew impostor, Nathan, tells David, the man after God's own heart, a certain parable of a ewe lamb and applies it to his [?] deeds. You have learnt the chapter by heart, I think, and fructified by it. I gave you everything but Caroline. You know my feelings for her. You know how I reckoned on her as my last and only comfort, and what have you done? She is destroyed. She can never hold her head up again. She is nothing to me, but she shall not be left on your hands."

"You cannot take her from me, and if you could, how would you prevent her return? She would either die or come back to me now. And remember, sir, if I had been a Percy instead of a Wellesley, I should not have carried her away and given her a home to hide her from scorn, and shelter her from insult. I should have left her forsaken at Fidena to die there delirious in an inn as Harriet O'Connor[13] died."

"I have my last word to give you now," said Percy. "You shall be brought into the courts of law for this very deed. I care nothing for exposure. I will hire Hector Montmorency to be my counsel. I will furnish him with ample evidence of all the atrocities of your character, which, handled as he will handle it, will make the flesh quiver on your bones with agony. I will hire half the press and fill the newspapers with libels on your court which will transform all your fools of followers into jealous enemies. I will not stick at a lie. Montmorency shall indite the paragraphs in order that they shall be pungent enough. He will not scruple at involving a few dozen of court ladies in the ruin that is to be hurled on you. He shall be directed to spare none. Your cabinet shall be a herd of horned cattle. The public mind shall be poisoned against you. A glorious triumph shall be given your political enemies. Before you die you shall curse the day that you robbed me of my daughter."

So spake Northangerland. His son-in-law answered with a smile, "The ship is worthless that will not live through a storm."

"Storm!" rejoined the Earl. "This is no storm, but fire in the hold, a lighted candle hurled into your magazine! See if it will fall like a raindrop."

The Duke was still unquelled. He answered as he turned and walked slowly through the room, "In return, there is no such thing as annihilation. Blow me up and I shall live again."

"You need not talk this bombast to me," said Percy. "Keep it to meet Montmorency with when he makes you the target of his shafts. Keep it to answer Warner and Thornton and Castlereagh when their challenges come pouring on you like chain-shot."

His Grace pursued his walk and said in an undertone,

"Moored in the rifted rock,
Proof to the tempest's shock,
The firmer he roots him, the harder it blows."

Introduction to "Farewell to Angria"

WE have already seen in the Introduction how Charlotte submitted samples of her writing to Southey and Wordsworth, and received replies from both warning her against her tendency to romanticism. But even without these kindly admonitions she would in the course of time have sensed the artificiality of her Angrian creations, notwithstanding the vividness of her own realization of them.

In keeping with a self-denying ordinance against her dream world, Charlotte in 1839, as has been noted, took a formal farewell of the land in which her spirit had dwelt so long, a farewell written in such lyrical measures as to rank it with the final pages of *Villette*. But as a dividing line in her literary career, this farewell need not be taken too seriously. Her landscapes had long been tending toward an English and even a Yorkshire realism, and Charlotte could no more dismiss her familiar characters from her mind than she could separate her soul from her body: her new task was to naturalize her Angrians into Englishmen, a process which proved as interesting as their creation. Percy must henceforth conduct his life under the canons of probability and the English law. Arthur Wellesley, Duke of Zamorna, was reincarnated as Arthur Ripley West, the son of old General West, a handsome, clever scamp, whose personality and natural gifts obtained for him the privilege of sinning on a grander scale than his contemporaries. Between Percy and young West existed the old-time corrupting intimacy of Rogue and Douro. Marian Hume, unchanged save in name—she is now called Marian Fairburne—falls a victim to Arthur West's fascination and dies to make way for Miss Percy. It is the old story and the old friends subjected to the restraints of a realistic setting. There were times when Charlotte cast these restraints aside for a moment of old-time freedom in her Angrian world; yet gradually and surely the fusion went on, though at very uneven rates, through *The Professor, Jane Eyre,* and *Shirley* until the imaginary and actual reached a perfect blending in *Villette.*

Charlotte's farewell to Angria, an undated and untitled fragment in the Bonnell Collection, was printed in the *Brontë Society Publications* for 1924, and is here reprinted by permission of the Brontë Society and Mr. C. W. Hatfield, who prepared the text for publication.

"Farewell to Angria"

I HAVE now written a great many books and for a long time have dwelt on the same characters and scenes and subjects. I have shown my landscapes in every variety of shade and light which morning, noon, and evening—the rising, the meridian and the setting sun can bestow upon them. Sometimes I have filled the air with the whitened tempest of winter: snow has embossed the dark arms of the beech and oak and filled with drifts the parks of the lowlands or the mountain-pass of wilder districts. Again, the same mansion with its woods, the same moor with its glens, has been softly coloured with the tints of moonlight in summer, and in the warmest June night the trees have clustered their full-plumed heads over glades flushed with flowers. So it is with persons. My readers have been habituated to one set of features, which they have seen now in profile, now in full face, now in outline, and again in finished painting,—varied but by the thought or feeling or temper or age; lit with love, flushed with passion, shaded with grief, kindled with ecstasy; in meditation and mirth, in sorrow and scorn and rapture; with the round outline of childhood, the beauty and fulness of youth, the strength of manhood, and the furrows of thoughtful decline;—but we must change, for the eye is tired of the picture so oft recurring and now so familiar.

Yet do not urge me too fast, reader: it is not easy to dismiss from my imagination the images which have filled it so long; they were my friends and my intimate acquaintances, and I could with little labour describe to you the faces, the voices, the actions, of those who peopled my thoughts by day, and not seldom stole strangely even into my dreams by night. When I depart from these I feel almost as if I stood on the threshold of a home and were bidding farewell to its inmates. When I

[? try] to conjure up new inmates I feel as if I had got into a distant country where every face was unknown and the character of all the population an enigma which it would take much study to comprehend and much talent to expound. Still, I long to quit for awhile that burning clime where we have sojourned too long—its skies flame—the glow of sunset is always upon it—the mind would cease from excitement and turn now to a cooler region where the dawn breaks grey and sober, and the coming day for a time at least is subdued by clouds.

Notes

The Geography of Verdopolis and Angria

THE original of this map, now in the possession of Mr. Thomas J. Wise, was drawn by Branwell Brontë as a frontispiece to his "History of the Young Men," written in 1831. It antedates the formation of the kingdom of Angria, and is given here because no map of Angria itself has been found among the extant Brontë *juvenilia*.

With the return of the Duke of Wellington from his triumphs in Europe there set in to Africa such a stream of immigration that the population soon became too great for one man to govern, so it was decided by the fathers of the nation that the newly conquered country should be divided among the four *conquistadores* best able to hold and control it. They, of course, were the four favorite soldiers of the Chief Genii. Only Charlotte's *protégé* retained his original name. Branwell's had been rechristened Sneaky, later Sneachi, and his kingdom was known as Sneachisland. Emily's and Anne's soldiers had changed their names to Parry and Ross; their countries were Parrysland and Rossland. Charlotte's country was Wellingtonsland or Senegambia. Two islands to the southwest of the mainland were given to Monkey and Stumps. These six kingdoms, each independent in its internal affairs, constituted the Glass Town, or Verdopolitan, Confederacy, with its capital, Glass Town, or Verdopolis, "at the mouth of the Niger and thirty miles from the open Atlantic." The capitals of the separate kingdoms were called Wellington's Glass Town, Parry's Glass Town, Ross' Glass Town, and Sneachi's Glass Town. Stumpsland and Monkisland had no large cities.

in celebration of the African Olympic Games, which reveals their origin.

6. Named in honor of Frederick Guelph, Duke of York, one of the original Twelves who was killed in the Conquest.

7. The Second Twelves were a set of wooden soldiers that followed the original Twelves who founded Glass Town. The sequence is set forth by Branwell in "The History of the Young Men," 1831.

8. That this person, S'death, in the early days of the story had some connection with Branwell in his character of Chief Genius is proved by a passage from "The Pirate" (Branwell, Feb. 8, 1833). Percy, or Rogue, having clapped a pistol to the wretch's head, blowing his skull to pieces and scattering his brains around the cabin, had the body heaved overboard, crying, "I have done with thee, thou wretch!" When the body touched the water "a bright flash of fire darted from it. It changed into a vast genius . . . and seizing hold of a huge cloud in his hand, he vaulted into it crying, 'And I've done with thee, thou fool!' and he disappeared among the passing vapour. . . . He that [this] eve was that hideous old man was the Chief Genius Branni."

9. The details of these struggles were recorded two years before by Branwell in "The History of the Young Men."

10. Sai-too-too, son of Cashna.

11. Coomassie (Commaissee, Branwell spells it), the capital of Ashantee.

12. It was here that Frederick Guelph, Duke of York, was slain.

13. Lord Charles and Captain Tree, it should be remembered, were literary enemies. Neither ever missed a chance of striking at the other. It is an amusing slip on Charlotte's part that "The Green Dwarf" here ascribed to Lord Charles

Albert Florian Wellesley was listed on the title-page of "The Foundling" among the works of Captain Tree.

"Zamorna's Exile"

Canto I

1. Though Angria was in the heart of tropical Africa, and Charlotte at times realized vividly its "burning skies" and "scorching suns," she often projected into it the inclement weather of Haworth. Indeed, in the later years of its existence, Angria was very closely identified with the West Riding of Yorkshire.

2. In the Verdopolitan Confederacy, the kingdom of Wellingtonsland, lying farthest to the west, or Senegambia, as it was also called, represented Ireland. Much stress was laid on the charm of its women, represented by the Duchess of Zamorna and Mina Laury.

3. Percy's first wife, the mother of the Duchess of Zamorna, was Mary Wharton, a woman of exceptional beauty, intelligence, and virtue, who died young. Eighteen years after her death, Percy married Zenobia Ellrington.

4. Her father's ancestral home.

5. King is another name for S'death.

6. At one stage of his career, Percy was a pirate. His ship was *The Rover* and his chief lieutenant old Robert S'death. The story of his piratical activities was told by Branwell in a long narrative called "The Pirate," begun January 30 and finished February 8, 1833.

7. Just as Wellingtonsland was designated as the "West," so Angria was spoken of as the "East."

8. Edward Ernest Gordon Wellesley. The story of his capture is told in a later narrative, "Mina Laury."

9. Warner Howard Warner was the head of a great An-

grian clan. From the beginning of the new nation, he was Zamorna's Home Secretary, often critical, captious, and sarcastic, but always a faithful and devoted servant of his king, who repaid him but poorly for his services.

10. Warner was credited by his clan with the gift of second sight. A story by Charlotte, called "High Life in Verdopolis" (March, 1834), showed him in a trance, when one of his kinsmen muttered, "He sees more than we do, the second sight is upon him."

11. This passage is reminiscent of Charles Wolfe's "The Burial of Sir John Moore." Compare:

> We buried him darkly at the dead of the night
>   The sods with our bayonets turning;
> By the struggling moon-beam's misty light
>   And the lantern dimly burning.

> .   .   .   .   .

> Few and short were the prayers we said
>   And we spoke not a word of sorrow;
> But steadfastly we gazed on the face of the dead
>   And bitterly we thought of the morrow.

In a fragment from Charlotte's teaching days at Roe Head, there occurs a passage which proves that she had been much moved by this poem: "Hohenlinden! Childe Harold! Flodden Field! The Burial of Moore! Why cannot the blood rouse the heart, the heart wake the head, the head prompt the hand to do things like these?"

12. There is in the Bonnell Collection in the Brontë Museum at Haworth a fragment of verse in which Mina Laury tells the story of her seduction.

> That eye, when he by chance had found me
>   At the threshold of the door alone,
> Watching the wide expanse around me
>   Of park and wood beneath the moon—

He spoke, and at his princely bidding
  I sat down humbly at his feet;
He asked me, and, no danger dreaming,
  I sang a ballad wild and sweet.

Wild, sweet, and full of Western fire!
  I know not how the words flowed forth,
But I felt the night my heart inspire,
  And the glory of the moonlit earth;

And I felt, though I dared not look and see,
  Who stood half-bending over me.
And there was a vague, strange sense of wrong
  That he stood so near and gazed so long;
And I would not that any beside had seen
  His eagle eye and his smiling mien,
And I felt a kind of troubled joy
  That the shade was so deep in that solemn sky,
That the close veil of ivy clustered near
  Had shut out the moonbeams broad and clear;
And yet there was terror in that delight
  And a burning dread of the lonely night.
I would have given life to be away
  And out in the pure and sunny day!

13. The wickedness of the Western Court was a tradition in the Angrian cycle—"A bad set were the Western Aristocracy—terribly bad."

14. Here Charlotte had evidently intended to close her poem when another thought came to her mind which she developed in the six stanzas that follow.

"Zamorna's Exile"

Canto II

1. The history of the war was written by Branwell in wearisome detail as to numbers and movements of troops,

but not until Charlotte incorporated his incidents into her stories did they assume interest and significance.

2. In the small geography which the Brontë children used—*A Grammar of General Geography,* by the Rev. J. Goldsmith—there is the statement that Abyssinia is inhabited chiefly by degenerate Arabs. Abyssinia was one of the important allies against Zamorna. His chief enemy within the Verdopolitan Confederacy, beside Percy, was Arthur Edward, Marquis of Ardrah, Prince of Parrysland, which in the minds of the young Brontës stood for Scotland, just as Wellingtonsland stood for Ireland.

3. This is another line that was suggested by "The Burial of Sir John Moore." Compare:

> We thought as we hollowed his narrow grave
> And smoothed down his lonely pillow,
> That the foe and the stranger would tread o'er his head,
> And we far away on the billow.

4. Zamorna was then on his way back to Angria, following the quarrel among his enemies which broke up the alliance against him and opened the way for his return.

5. In "Passing Events," a manuscript dated April 21–29, 1836, one of the few of considerable length that Charlotte wrote at Roe Head, there is an incident depicting Zamorna's first attempt to cast Mary off. He had left her, with her three children, in the palace at Verdopolis, while he himself remained for weeks at Adrianopolis, sending her no message of any kind. She was on the verge of illness from suspense, when Zamorna's Secretary of State, Warner, came for some important papers in her keeping. In spite of Warner's protest, she accompanied him in disguise back to Adrianopolis and by a trick gained admittance to her husband.

The king's anger at Warner when he discovered his wife's identity approached madness:

"How dare you do what you have done?" he asked. "How dare you bring my wife here when you knew I'd rather have an evil spirit given to my arms this night? . . . You must have been conscious, sir, that I had wrought up my resolution with toil and trouble, that I had decided to let her die if her father cut loose—and decided with agony. . . . What possessed you to ruin it all and set me the whole torturing task over again? . . . You knew how I loved Percy and what it is costing me to send him to the D——l. Look at his daughter! I'm to stand her beauty, am I?"

His greeting of Mary was fiercely affectionate:

The Duke, gazing at her pale and sweet loveliness till he felt there was nothing in the world he loved half so well, . . . threw himself beside her and soon made her tremble as much from the ardour of his caresses as she had done with dread of his wrath. "I'll seize the few hours of happiness that you have thrown in my way, Mary," said he as she clung to him and called him her adored, glorious Adrian, "but these kisses and tears of thine, and this intoxicating beauty shall not change my resolution. I will rend you, my lovely rose, entirely from me. I'll plant you in your father's garden again. I must do it; he compels me."

"I don't care," said the Duchess. . . . "Tonight I may stay with you many hours. But if you *do* divorce me, Zamorna, will you never, never take me back to you?" . . .

The Duke looked at her in silence, he could not cut off hope. "The event has not taken place yet, Mary, and there lingers a possibility that it may be averted. . . . Should you be transplanted to Alnwick, do not live hopeless. . . . You may on some moonlight night hear Adrian's whistle under your window. . . . Then step out on the parapet, and I'll lift you in my arms from thence to the terrace, and from that time forever, Mary, though Angria shall have no Queen and Percy shall have no daughter, Zamorna shall not be a widower, though the world shall call him so."

6. One of Zamorna's earliest complaints against Percy—a complaint voiced before the Angrian Parliament—was that Percy slandered and insulted his most efficient and faithful ministers and tried to poison him, Zamorna, against them, by insinuating that they ruled him.

7. Mary's most marked characteristic was her tact in pleasing her husband and her ability to soothe him when he was irritated:

He took up a book which lay on the window seat and began to read. . . . Her tact, so nice as to be infallible, informed her that the pet was carried far enough. She sat down then by Zamorna's side, leant over and looked at the book—it was poetry, a volume of Byron. Her attention likewise was arrested and she continued to read, turning the page with her slender fingers after looking into the Duke's face at the conclusion of each leaf to see if he was ready to proceed. She was so quiet—her hair so softly fanned his cheek as she leaned her head towards him, the contact of her gentle hand, now and then touching his, of her smooth and silken dress was so endearing, that it quickly appeased the incipient ire her whim of perverseness had raised, and when in about half an hour she ventured to close the obnoxious volume and take it from his hand, the action met with no resistance, nothing but a shake of the head, half-reproving, half-indulgent.

8. In a story dated July 21, 1838, Charlotte analyzes at length Zamorna's early affection for Percy. If any other person than Arthur Wellesley, she says,

had turned on him these glances of feeling—clashing, ardent, enthusiastic—which sometimes glowed in the Marquis's dark eyes when they rested on the Rebellious Democrat [Percy]—if, I say, Rogue had discovered anything like attachment to his person in any other man or boy, . . . the first moment of such a discovery would have been marked by a testimony of his intense and eternal hate.

9. Percy was with his daughter when she died. The death scene is described by Branwell.

10. Compare a fragment from a passage written June 28, 1835:

He [Zamorna] drew aside the crimson curtain and let the evening sun shine upon her. He walked softly to and fro in the saloon, and every time he passed her couch, turned on her his ardent gaze. That man has now loved Mary Percy longer than he's ever loved any woman before, and, I dare say, her face by this time has become to him a familiar and household face. It may be told by the way in which his eye seeks the delicate and pallid features and rests on their lines that he finds settled pleasure in the contemplation; in all moods, at all times he likes them. Her temper is changeful; she is not continued sunshine; she weeps sometimes and frets, and teases him not infrequently with womanly jealousies. I don't think another woman lives on earth in whom he could bear these changes for a moment; from her, they almost please him; he finds an amusement in playing with her fears, piquing or soothing them as caprice directs.

11. A full list of Zamorna's amours would be a long one; the most celebrated were those with Helen Victorina, the mother of Edward Ernest Gordon; Mina Laury; Rosamund Wellesley, his cousin; and Caroline Vernon.

12. In one of Charlotte's last Angrian stories, there is a description of "a church, with a low tower and a little church-yard, scattered over with low head stones and many turf-mounds," among them one raised tomb bearing the single word "Resurgam." This was the grave of Zamorna's cousin, Rosamund Wellesley, "a woman much talked of five years ago."

She died at a house somewhere between here and Ingleside, where she had lived for some months under a feigned name. . . . She gave nature a lift, helped herself out of a world when she was quite tired of it . . . because she was ashamed of having loved his Majesty not wisely but too well. . . . She was very beautiful, . . . very tall and graceful, with light hair and fine blue eyes, . . . clever, I dare say, and sensitive. The Duke undertook to be her guardian and tutor. He exercised his office in a manner peculiar to himself, guarded her with a vengeance, tutored her until she could construe the art of love at any rate.

13. Here Charlotte is speaking for herself, rather than the Duke of Zamorna. Over and over in the diary-like fragments from her Roe Head period she speaks of the vivid reality of the scenes which rose before her mind when she thought of Angria.

14. In a story dated June 29, 1837, Zamorna is asked by a child who is sitting on his knee, resting her head against his shoulder, where his wife lives. He answers: "She has no home until I come back. Her home is just where you are at this moment; she would be happy in no other."

15. The flag of Angria was a rising sun on a crimson field; its motto, "Arise!"

16. Adrianopolis, the capital of Angria, was on the Calabar. Mary's native country was Wellingtonsland. She died at Alnwick in the north, far from the two places most familiar and dear to her.

"Mina Laury"

1. Alnwick House, one of Percy's seats in the north. It was here that Mary was sent following the break between her husband and her father, and it was here that she was said in earlier stories to have died.

2. See "Zamorna's Exile," Canto I, note 1.

3. Zenobia Ellrington, wife of Percy, was loyal always to Zamorna and during the great war had "remained aloof"

from her traitorous husband. Now, like Mary, she is back in her usual place, the separation and its occasion apparently forgotten.

4. Percy's mother.

5. Percy, since the founding of Angria, has been commonly known by his latest title, Earl of Northangerland.

6. Charlotte's story "High Life in Verdopolis" (March 20, 1834) carried on its title-page the motto: "Much cry and little wool, practically illustrated, as St. Nicholas said when he was shearing the hog."

7. MacTerroglen was commander of the allied armies against Zamorna in the great war. It was near the city of Zamorna that the Angrians were defeated and the king taken prisoner, and it was in Zamorna itself that he was tried by a court-martial of his enemies and sentenced to death.

Stancliffe's Hotel was famous in the annals of Angria.

8. Arthur, Prince of Parrysland, better known as the Marquis of Ardrah. As Admiral of the Navy of the Verdopolitan Union, he initiated encroachments upon Angria which, continued under his administration as Prime Minister of the Confederation, precipitated the great war. Montmorency was an ally of Ardrah and a familiar of Percy in his lowest crimes and dissipation.

9. One of Angria's proudest and most powerful noblemen, formerly a member of Zamorna's cabinet and one of his ranking generals in the recent war.

10. A pseudonym for Branwell. Richton first appears in the cycle as plain John Flower, M.P. Then he becomes "Baron Flower, Viscount Richton," high in the Angrian government, one of its half-dozen most important men.

11. This is the same Sir Astley Cooper that Branwell chose as one of the chief men of his island at the inauguration of the "Play of the Islanders" on a November night in 1827. See Mrs. Gaskell, Chapter V.

"Caroline Vernon"

1. Percy was a sublime musician. Charlotte frequently refers to his gift; Branwell writes long effusions in praise of it. In this, as in many other particulars, he is identified with Branwell's conception of himself.

2. Zenobia Ellrington was Percy's second wife, a brilliant and beautiful woman of strong uncontrolled temper. Obviously, she would not have welcomed Louisa Vernon's daughter.

3. Between Rogue or Percy, Lord Ellrington, the middle-aged rake, and young Arthur Wellesley, Marquis of Douro, there had existed a deep friendship, which was responsible, in part, for the corruption of Douro's naturally noble nature. See "Zamorna's Exile," Canto II, note 8.

4. At one stage of Percy's checkered career he had been the leader of a group of cattle drovers and had built up a large fortune by this trade. In this aspect he was probably drawn from a local Yorkshire character.

5. Mesdames Lelande and St. James were notoriously immoral women who had large places in Percy's life. In one of the last stories of Angria that Charlotte wrote, Zenobia, Percy's wife, spoke of Lelande as "the dirty little French demi-rep that she is."

6. Mrs. Warner, the wife of Warner Howard Warner, Zamorna's Home Secretary, before her marriage was Ellen Grenville, the daughter of one of Africa's richest manufacturers, and the ward and pupil of Zenobia Ellrington. The story of her marriage to Warner is told in a novel of 1834 called "High Life in Verdopolis."

Lady Thornton was originally Julia Wellesley, the favorite cousin of Zamorna who, as related in "The Foundling," married her for political purposes to Edward Sydney. Sydney in the course of time rebelled against Zamorna's domination, and in revenge Zamorna ordered his cousin, who had long since lost all love for her husband, to get a divorce. She obeyed, and, after a period of freedom, married General Wilson Thornton, the prototype of Mr. Yorke of *Shirley*.

7. Hector Montmorency was one of the lowest characters of the cycle, a familiar of Percy and, after the war, a proscribed refugee in the French capital.

8. Augusta di Segovia, Percy's first mistress, under whose able tutorage his dark nature was trained for his career of crime.

9. As Wellingtonsland represented Ireland, so Parrysland and Sneachisland, spoken of as "the North," represented Scotland. Fidena was in Sneachisland.

10. A paraphrase of the motto of Byron's coat-of-arms, "*Crede Byron.*"

11. This reference is to the death of Zamorna's cousin Rosamund Wellesley. See "Zamorna's Exile," Canto II, note 12.

12. Percy was an avowed atheist who did not believe in either Heaven or Hell. Now he wishes there were a Hell to punish Zamorna for the betrayal of Caroline.

13. O'Connor was one of Percy's boon companions in his most degraded day. His wife, Harriet, eloped with Percy, who later abandoned her to die of shame and want. The story was a familiar one in Angria, and even found its way into a ballad:

> Beneath Fidena's Minster
>   A stranger made her grave;
> She had longed in death to slumber
>   Where trees might o'er her wave.
>
> An exile from her country,
>   She died on mountain ground;
> The flower of Senegambia
>   A northern tomb has found.

Why did he cease to cherish
  His Harriet when she fell?
Why did he let her perish
  Who had loved him all too well?

She called on Alexander
  As she sickened, as she died;
When fever made her wander,
  For him alone she cried.

But Percy would not listen,
  Would not hear when Harriet wailed.
Where Europe's ice-bergs glisten,
  Far, far away he sailed.